By Darcy Archer

Cross My Heart

Published by Dreamspinner Press
www.dreamspinnerpress.com

CROSS MY HEART

DARCY ARCHER

REAMSPINNER PRESS

Published by

DREAMSPINNER PRESS

8219 Woodville Hwy #1245
Woodville, FL 32362 USA
www.dreamspinnerpress.com

Cross My Heart
© 2024 Darcy Archer

Cover Art
© 2024 L.C. Chase
http://www.lcchase.com
Cover content is for illustrative purposes only and any person depicted on the cover is a model.

Trade Paperback ISBN: 978-1-64108-751-3
Digital ISBN: 978-1-64108-750-6
Trade Paperback published May 2024
v. 1.0

Dedicated to all the PFLAG families who keep saving lives and helping LGBTQ+ kids build a better, braver world.

Chapter One

TYLER FANTANA slammed into the dirt, and a meteor hit his chest with scalding force. His heart had stopped beating. Sixty-nine thousand fans shouting, the smell of sweat and grass. Blinding lights, all the cameras.

Groggy, Tyler blinked and shook his head slowly, trying to situate himself.

He flinched. This had happened before, he felt certain. Why did he feel so disoriented?

Right. NFL game at the top of the season, the pinnacle of his career with the San Diego Swells. A pile of guys on top of him.

Suddenly he was back on the ground, blood in his mouth, skull echoing with the impact of the tackle that had brought him down, an entire linebacker landing on his sternum and the sudden crushing pain in his chest as he hit the thirty-yard line sideways and knew in his bones that he'd never get up again in this life.

Team gone. Light gone. Not breathing. Just that jagged, grinding agony like a fist squeezing him into paste.

I already did this. Oh God, please, I already did this.

The world had winked out, only fading back into focus as he woke up in the back of an ambulance, his heart pounding erratically as he gasped for breath and grabbed at the EMTs.

"Tyler?"

Dr. Reynolds's question yanked him back to the present. The older woman's voice was firm, professional, and had a no-nonsense edge to it. "Talk to me. Slow breaths. What happened just then?"

He tried to take deep, slow gulps of oxygen. Counted heartbeats. Visualized. All that holistic new age crap. His stupid, screwed-up heart wouldn't slow down. Where was he? He couldn't get enough breath to answer her. Why couldn't he talk? His eyes stung, and he blinked rapidly. "Bad."

Dr. Reynolds's office smelled of lemony antiseptic. It was autumn. November. Tuesday? This was another checkup with his cardiologist.

His sister had driven him. He still wasn't allowed behind the wheel. *Right.* Was Nadia here?

"Stay with me now." Reynolds stood back, giving him space. "Are you all right? Can you describe the pain? Look at me." She leaned back and ran a penlight over his pupils, frowning at something. "Your heart rate was— Does that happen often?"

"Maybe." He shook his head, then nodded. Did she want the truth or the lie? "I don't know."

"I was taking your vitals," Dr. Reynolds said briskly. "Use your three-three-three and breathe for me. Take a moment. Three objects. Three sounds. Three body parts."

Tyler nodded and tried to focus. He found the objects as he inhaled slowly and shifted his eyes around the bright room, consciously counting each one: *Clock. Pen. Shoe.* This was so embarrassing.

"I'm going to remove this, if that's okay." She leaned in to unwrap the blood pressure cuff from his thick bicep with practiced efficiency.

Velcro rip. Hum of the AC. Paper rustling under him. He held the breath inside himself, and his galloping heart slowed to a trot.

As the cuff loosened, she unthreaded it and stepped back again, presumably to give him space. She glanced over his chart, and her brow furrowed in obvious disapproval.

His muscle mass was way off, whittled down by two months of sitting on his butt.

As she paused to make a note, he made his body parts move: *open hand, lick lips, blink eyes.* He let the breath out. "Better."

"Excellent. You see?" Reynolds checked his eyes, waiting until he nodded to continue. She pressed a chilly stethoscope between his pecs and looked at the ceiling, listening for something inside him before she spoke. "Just a panic attack, yes? That's common. Nasty but normal."

"It felt like—" He shook his head, wiped his wet mouth. "How do I tell the difference?"

"You ask someone qualified." Dr. Reynolds crossed her arms. "But anecdotally, cardiac arrest feels like crushing and panic attacks sharper stabs. With arrest, the pain spreads outward from the chest, but the pain of a panic attack stays in one spot. Neither one is pleasant." Her stethoscope shifted to his back, and the slight pressure made him flinch like an idiot. "Try to distinguish between the *memory* of pain and your current level of discomfort. It's not easy."

"No." Tyler took a few more deep breaths and let the air out slowly. "These were short and sharp. Memory, I guess." He pressed a hand to his side. "Jesus."

"Talk to yourself. Listen to yourself." She pressed her lips together, regarding him as though through glass. "Blood pressure is still higher than I'd like," she noted. "And you've lost almost four pounds of muscle since our last visit. Potassium levels far lower than they should be. Iron too. Your recovery seems to have plateaued."

"Sorry, Doc." Tyler sat awkwardly, perched on the exam table, cringing as the paper liner crinkled beneath him.

"This isn't blame." She shook her head. "Your heart has been pushed past breaking, Mr. Fantana. Commotio cordis can cause severe trauma to the valve and surrounding tissues. It needs to heal. Just a time-out is all. A reasonable recovery window. You're better, but not better enough."

He nodded and waited for further scolding.

"The heart is a powerful muscle. You had significant bruising and other injuries besides. It's barely been two months. One moment." Dr. Reynolds picked up the phone and pressed a button. "Can you have Ms. Fantana come back to exam room five?"

Great. Now Nadia was going to get scolded too.

"Tyler, your sister needs to be aware. Team effort, right? Hang on. I'll be right back."

With a smiling nod, Reynolds left him sitting there feeling like a jerk. The door closed behind her with a hiss and clunk. The memory of his primetime collapse still swirled around him, almost visible, tangible around him, the exam room like a double exposure he could touch and taste. He stared at the speckled linoleum floor.

A tap on the door. "Hey, big bro. Everything okay?"

He turned to look and raised his voice so she'd hear. "Panic attack. Stupid."

Nadia poked her head in. "Okay if I come in?"

"Doctor's orders." Tyler shrugged. "I think she wants to do more scolding than one dummy can handle, so you get some too."

"Stop worrying, Ty," she said, reaching out to place a hand on his knee, stilling the judder. "It's just a checkup."

"I guess." Tyler sighed, running a hand through his shaggy hair. He couldn't help but feel vulnerable, stripped of his armor. He'd been an MVP his whole life, and now… *this*. "I think she went to pull the labs."

Tyler sat hunched, foot tapping an anxious beat. With each passing second, his eyes darted between the ticking clock and the closed door to the hall. The sterile peach walls and vague watercolor prints did nothing to soothe his nerves. Beside him, Nadia fidgeted with the strap of her purse, watching him less like a little sister and more like an anxious mom.

As they waited, Nadia tried to distract him with a silly story about Mr. Poops, a lazy marmalade cat that had wandered into her garage last year and decided her home was his, but Tyler's mind was back on a stadium field a thousand miles away with his teammates.

Grass. Mud. Tackle. Agony. A stadium full of strangers and millions of screens across the country, all roaring for blood.

"Thank you," Dr. Reynolds said to someone, then stepped back inside, flicking through a sheaf of pages. "Mr. Fantana?"

"Guilty." Tyler straightened, shooting his sister a tense smile.

"Sorry about that. I asked your sister to join us because we all want the same thing."

"Absolutely." Nadia squinted, brave-facing it.

"You aren't getting better." Reynolds crossed her arms over her white coat and squinted at him kindly. "Trouble is, you know everything that I'm going to say to you. They punched you in the heart. You're still a world-class athlete inside there, but your body and your mind need to heal."

"I understand, ma'am." He nodded, but the thought of doing anything more than what he was already managing seemed impossible. Hell, he had a worthless degree in sports medicine, and he still couldn't get his ass in gear.

She wasn't done. "I've told you before: you need to eat healthier, exercise more, and for heaven's sake, do something about your stress levels. The memories will prey upon you if you don't process them."

Tyler swallowed hard, feeling the weight of her words press down on him. How could he make her understand the nightmares and the panic attacks? It sounded stupid and melodramatic to him, and he saw them up close and personal every day of his life since the accident.

Nadia watched him take the scolding, her eyes full of awful pity.

"I've been trying, Dr. Reynolds," he protested weakly. "But it's not easy. Not when I'm… like this." He looked down at his boxer briefs, his grayish skin, his infamous muscle mass now tasked with hauling him from the bed to the couch and back. He felt like a wrecked car on cinder blocks.

"Mr. Fantana, this isn't the end, just a change. Six months ago, you were one of the fittest athletes in the world, but you are not twenty anymore. Or even thirty," she admitted. Her fierce scrutiny made him feel raw and scalded. "Your heart may have taken a hit, but it's not irreparable. You need to take responsibility for your own well-being."

"Responsibility? You think I don't—" Tyler began, anger bubbling up inside him before he caught himself, clamping down. He couldn't afford to let his rage get the best of him. Not now, when everything was so precarious.

"We can get you whatever you need, Mr. Fantana." Dr. Reynolds didn't look away. "Give yourself time."

"Time." He gave an ugly laugh as her words sent him spiraling back into that mud and pain and the game that had stopped his entire career stone-cold.

"I say the same thing, Doc." Nadia squeezed his hand, reminding him where he was. "But he's so much better than he was. Every day, he's better."

"Tyler," Dr. Reynolds said, her tone cautious, "we both want the same thing: for you to heal. But I can only do so much. The rest is up to you." She tapped his chart and raised her brows. "Your muscle tone, your blood pressure, even your oxygen levels are still way beyond normal levels for an average man your age, and the whole country knows that you are much more than average."

He bobbed his head but couldn't look her in the eye. "Yes, ma'am." He did know better.

"Your diet is critical. Lay off the starches and dairy fat. Start incorporating lean proteins and fresh produce. No soda, no snacking. Stretch!" She raised both hands in exasperation. "Again, you know all this. And you must, and I mean *today* if at all possible, start exercising regularly. Even just walking twenty minutes a day will make a big difference. Looking good is not enough. Get yourself moving again. Blood flow. You still have your drive, your competitive oomph."

He tried to focus on Dr. Reynolds's words as she scolded him, shamed him, but he wanted to *run*.

"All right," he muttered, his voice barely audible. "If it kills me, I'll try harder." Tyler clenched his fists, his clammy legs sticking to the paper under him.

"Not harder. *Smarter*," she emphasized, tapping a pen against her clipboard. "No killing. And light exercise. *All* of you. Not just your body, but your mind too. Therapy. To talk through this process. You need both to heal."

"He will. He is," Nadia said.

"Uh, yeah," he replied, rubbing the back of his neck, feeling the heaviness of stagnation and regret like a lead weight in his chest. He'd never seen a therapist in his life. "Therapy and exercise. Got it."

"Good." Dr. Reynolds gave him a stern look, her eyes drilling into him. "You need to take this seriously, Tyler. Your life depends on it."

"Understood." He swallowed hard, feeling her words more than he heard them. It wasn't like he didn't understand the severity of his situation. But it was harder than he'd anticipated to come to terms with the fact that his body, which had once been a well-oiled tackle machine, had betrayed him so completely. And now he needed to confront that reality, to face the fact that he couldn't outrun his own mortality.

"Okay," he said finally, meeting her gaze. Even the *suggestion* of therapy was a hard pill to swallow. "I'll do it. I'll take responsibility for my health."

Nadia nodded. "We got this, Ty."

"Excellent," Reynolds repeated as she looked back up. "We have faith in you, Tyler. And I know you can do this."

"Thank you," he whispered, his voice thick with misery.

"Good," she replied, giving him a curt nod. "Your team doctors will receive my report by Thursday. The Swells care a lot about you."

He didn't answer that. The team docs were nice enough, but he knew who paid their bills and why. He was already past his prime, and plenty knew it. The coaches had more complaints each year. The owners ragged him about his endorsements and his rowdy rep. The San Diego Swells cared about his cost and his stats. Keeping him healthy was money to them. Boris Jarlson wanted to squeeze as many seasons out of him as possible before tossing him on the heap.

Dr. Reynolds looked him over again, making him feel like a rump roast. "I know you can get back to top form, Tyler. You can play again, *win* again. But you need to put in the hard work. If you'll—excuse the expression—tackle this problem before it flanks you. Just take the steps. You'll get where you're going."

Tyler nodded, still avoiding her eyes. The weight of stagnation and regret settled upon his shoulders like a heavy cloak, threatening to smother him.

Dr. Reynolds opened the door and patted him on the back as he stepped through it. Nadia lingered behind to mutter something with the doctor. He didn't even have the energy to feel angry or sad, but maybe feeling stubborn would be enough.

He stepped back into the hall, and the door closed behind him. Knowing they had another long drive back to Cinnamar, he swung by the bathroom to pee and splash his face.

The real work was just beginning. He was staring down a long road to recovery, but maybe he was finally ready to tackle it head-on, fueled by the same determination and grit that had once propelled him to football stardom.

Back in the waiting room, he stood shifting his weight, anxious to escape.

Finally Nadia emerged, looking anxious, linking her arm through his in wordless support. With his sister's help, perhaps he could regain control.

"You good?" she whispered, her gentle touch a balm against the harsh reality of his prognosis.

The lingering scent of disinfectant filled Tyler's nostrils as he pushed through the glass door of Dr. Reynolds's building, the warm sunlight outside a stark contrast to the sterile environment behind him. He squinted against the brightness.

"That was fun, huh? Good ol' Dr. Reynolds," Nadia called out softly, her deep-set brown eyes searching his face with concern. She leaned against their car, arms crossed over her chest. "You look like you just went ten rounds with a grizzly."

Tyler snorted, despite the turmoil brewing inside him. His sister always had a way of lightening even the darkest moments without getting maudlin. "More like two rounds with a cardiologist who doesn't believe in sugarcoating."

"You can take it," she replied, a smirk tugging at the corner of her mouth, though her eyes remained worried. "She's tough, but she knows her stuff. Come on, let's get you home."

Nadia held the passenger door open for him, waiting until he eased himself into the seat before shutting it gently. She kept up a steady stream of chatter during the drive, clearly trying to distract him from spiraling into despair. He was grateful for her snarky optimism, even if he couldn't muster a response.

Instead Tyler stared out the passenger side window, watching the familiar scenery pass by without really seeing it: long stretches of late wildflowers over the valley slope. Cinnamar was about fifty miles northeast of Reynolds's office in San Diego, so the drive both ways ate up a lot of his sister's time. IT work was flexible, but she had her own life.

His mind kept drifting back to that fateful third quarter, the crowd's exhilaration, the lightning pumping through his veins, the satisfying smack of helmets, pads, and hard muscle colliding as he dodged tackles, in the zone.

Until suddenly, a blindside hit took his legs out from under him. Then muddy grass, staring at people's shins. He remembered the referee's whistles shrilly blaring as he clutched his chest, his vision spotting, fading, failing. Then waking up in the ambulance, an oxygen mask strapped to his face.

"Heart attack," he heard the EMT say, a hand touching his head gently. "Tyler Fantana, dude. Would you believe? We need to get him to the hospital stat before he codes."

Just like that, at the peak of his career, his whole life yanked from under him. Now here he was, trapped in his hometown, lying awake every night in his childhood bedroom, adrift and unsure how to climb back to the fancy life he'd wanted way back when.

Tyler snorted awake and realized he'd dozed off in the rocking car.

"Feel better?" Nadia glanced over at him, her expression sympathetic.

"Maybe." A late fall rain had covered the low hills with California poppies, asters, and purple lupine that would die fast once December hit. He shrugged.

She turned to consider him. "It's not a race, huh? You can do this. I know you can."

"Exercise. Therapy," Tyler muttered, staring out the window at the sloped landscape. He could feel the weight of his sister's vigilance, knew she was searching for any signs of weakness or self-pity.

Nadia glanced at the rearview before responding. "She's putting you on notice. This has as much to do with your mental state as your heart. And she wanted me as a witness. It's going to be okay."

"Therapy? I know I got to take responsibility for my health, Nadia. But it's… hard. My whole life I've been this invincible meathead, and now—"

"Hey," she cut him off gently, reaching over to place a comforting hand on his bulky forearm. "You're not a meathead. And you don't have to be invincible, Ty. You just have to be the best version of yourself that you can be right now—bum heart and all. You've faced worse than therapy."

"Thanks," he said, his voice barely audible over the hum of the car engine. He turned to look at her in a moment of raw vulnerability. "I just… I don't want to disappoint anyone, you know?"

"Wow. Okay… Tyler Fantana, NFL superstar, America's Tightest End, reduced to seeking validation from his little sister?" Nadia teased, though her voice was warm with old affection. "Who would've thought?"

"Hey, now," Tyler huffed, trying to muster a playful glare but ultimately failing. "Don't go getting a big head about it. Last thing I need is an even more insufferable sibling."

"Too late," she laughed, reaching over to ruffle his hair affectionately. "But seriously, Ty, you can't ever disappoint me. Or anyone who truly cares about you. We just want you to be happy and healthy, okay?"

"Okay," he agreed, his throat tight with emotion. He tried to smile, but it felt false.

As they drove through their small hometown, familiar streets and businesses whizzing past them, Tyler felt the first glimmers of determination blooming within him. The road to recovery might suck, but with Nadia by his side, he knew he had a fighting chance. And maybe, just maybe, he could find a little happiness in the process. Though the doctor's words still stung, Tyler felt a faint flicker of stubborn hope.

"Promise me something." Nadia took the exit that led to their childhood home. "Promise me you'll do whatever it takes to get better. No excuses, no half-assing it. No ditching me. Just… promise me you'll try."

"I promise," he whispered, meaning it for once. It was time to take control of his life again, to face his demons head-on and reclaim the future that had been snatched away from him on the thirty-yard line. "Full-ass only."

"Good," she said, her lips curving into a small, proud smile. "Now let's get you home and start planning your Super Bowl comeback."

"Easy for you to say," he muttered, crossing his arms over his broad chest.

The car turned on the block and then bumped onto the drive as Nadia slowed to a stop and glanced his way again.

"Stop. I'm fine. Reynolds is still a tightass, though," Tyler grumbled as he climbed out and slammed the car door with a huff. "Like I'm not trying hard enough. The panic attack rattled me, is all." He headed toward the porch. Nadia had renovated the place twice since their mom passed.

"Uhh. Yeah." Nadia caught up with him, keys jangling. "She's just worried. We all are. You've been through a lot, and it's time to get back on track. Baby steps."

"Mom always said I was a big baby. Like, the biggest ever in this town, twenty-two inches or something and eleven-plus pounds. A mutant." He grinned, but she didn't.

"Ty, listen," Nadia said, her voice gentle yet firm as she unlocked the door. "You need to take this seriously. Therapy and exercise will help you get better, on all fronts."

"Fine," he conceded. "But what if it's not enough? What if that's the last game I play? The last yardage. My legacy for all time. Eating mud on the thirty."

"Glory ain't everything, you know." Nadia knocked their shoulders together, giving him a small smile. "Mom wanted us to love our lives. That's all."

Tyler sighed, running a hand through his messy hair as he thought about their mom, gone almost nine years now. It felt like forever since he'd last truly loved his life.

A high-pitched meow as Mr. Poops trotted up and headbutted Nadia's leg. "See? Poops agrees." She scooped up the fat feline and draped him across her shoulder. "Hello. Yes, I know.... Hey, mister." Poops kept pushing his face against her ear and hair.

"All right," Tyler said, determination in his voice. "I'll do it. I'll go to therapy, I'll exercise, and I'll work on getting better—for myself, for Mom, and for the people who matter."

"Good," Nadia replied, squeezing his knee before unlocking the door and pushing inside. "I'm proud of you, Ty. You're stronger than you give yourself credit for. And I don't mean your biceps or your butt."

"Thanks, sis," he murmured, a small smile playing on his lips. Deep down, he knew she was right—he could face all this crap and come out stronger on the other side.

He left her checking the mail.

Tyler pushed open the door to his childhood bedroom, the creaking hinge a familiar sound that turned him thirteen again. The walls needed repainting, still hidden under faded posters of his favorite football players and bands, smothering him in memories of his early gridiron glory. *Big fish, small pond.* Old banners from childhood championships and postcards from people he didn't remember. He ran his fingers along the dusty trophies lining the shelves, reminders of a time when he was unstoppable on the field, when football was the only way he could save his life and his family.

Nadia wouldn't take his money, but at least he'd paid off the mortgage on this house. The rest of his savings was more than enough to tide him over if they killed his contract.

"Wow," Nadia said, leaning against the doorframe, cradling the cat again. "Hello, time capsule. Now I know why you've been keeping me out."

"Yeah," Tyler murmured, his hazel eyes lingering on a photo of their mother. "Feels like a lifetime ago. I've been tossing stuff, but then I lost interest." Tyler had been about twelve when their dad had finally pissed off. From that moment, his poor mom had put everything into keeping the house note paid and keeping them safe.

"Get some rest," Nadia advised softly. "We can talk more tomorrow." She left, closing the door behind her.

Alone with his thoughts, Tyler sat down on the edge of his twin bed, the springs groaning beneath his beefy frame. His glamorous NFL career now felt like a mirage.

Guilt gnawed at him as he remembered every well-wisher, every teammate, every fan he'd let down. He clenched his fists as he laid back, the frustration building inside him like a bonfire. But beneath it all, he still felt that dim glimmer of hope—the chance to rebuild himself, maybe even find happiness again.

"Mom only wanted us to care about stuff," he whispered to himself. "I've got to try, for her sake."

But sleep eluded him as he lay in the dark, his mind racing with thoughts of his past and the uncertain future that awaited him. Restless and agitated, he finally threw off the covers and padded to the window. The night sky beckoned, stars sparkling like distant promises.

"Maybe some fresh air," he muttered. He slipped quietly out the back door and into the cool night. He knew staying with Nadia was only enabling his inertia.

Baby steps for the biggest baby.

The soft grass whispered beneath his feet as he walked, the familiar scents of the small backyard calming him: mowed grass, his mom's beloved gardenias, the tangled passionflowers covering the back fence. He gazed up at the stars, feeling small but maybe connected to something bigger than himself.

"All right, universe," Tyler whispered, his breath visible in the chilly air. "I'm going to take control of this healing crap. I'll work out, I'll eat organic broccoli, I'll even get counseling—whatever it takes to get back to the stuff I know how to do better than anyone."

His decision made, determination surged through him like an electric current. He knew the road ahead would suck, but with Nadia's support and their mother's memory just out of sight, he was ready to get in the game.

"Here's to getting better," Tyler murmured, raising his gaze to the heavens once more before turning back toward the house, a newfound sense of purpose propelling him forward.

A couple minutes later, the dim glow of Tyler's laptop lit his rough knuckles as he sat at the kitchen table, surrounded by the quiet darkness of the house. He could hear the faint ticking of an old clock on the wall, a gentle reminder that time was still moving forward, even when he felt stuck in place.

Even without having a panic attack, he used Dr. Reynolds's three-three-three trick to anchor himself where he was. Raising his eyes, he saw three things: juice, flowers, cat. He heard three things: the hum of the fridge, the hall clock, Poops purring on the sill. He moved three things: opened the laptop, patted his chest, sat down.

"All right," he whispered to himself, inhaling deeply. "Let's do this."

His oversized fingers skittered across the keyboard as he tapped out an email to a local therapist he'd found through a quick search. His hands always seemed clumsy using any kind of technology. The weight of admitting he needed help was heavy, but with each word he typed, he felt a little bit lighter.

Hi, Dr. Bailey, Tyler wrote, swallowing his pride. *My name is Tyler Fantana, and I'm interested in scheduling an appointment to discuss my current issues. I don't know if you follow football, but I've experienced a major health setback at the start of the season, and I'm not coping so great with the necessary adjustments.*

He hesitated for a moment before adding, *I want to get better, but to be honest, I don't know how to do that without some professional help.*

Before he could start messing or second-guessing, he clicked to send the email on its way. First step toward regaining some balance. His stupid heart pounded in his chest, a mixture of anxiety and hope swirling within him. He allowed himself a slight smile, proud of taking the initiative to confront his depression head-on.

Next, Tyler turned his attention to finding a place where he could begin his physical rehabilitation. He browsed through various gym websites, but he quickly realized that he couldn't just walk into any random workout studio without drawing all the wrong kinds of attention. The locals would get weird, and once the word got loose, the paparazzi would be relentless.

"Damn," he muttered under his breath. "Going out in public will just make things worse."

A small head butted his leg. Mr. Poops obviously thought a human in the kitchen meant mealtime and mandatory massage.

Tyler bent to scritch the purring cat's ears and give him one long stroke to smooth his back and up his extravagant tail. "No way, Poops. I feed you now, I'm toast come morning." Mr. Poops had been a feisty stray that just kept being cute until Nadia gave up and offered him room and board in exchange for being loud and adorable.

Though skeptical at first, Tyler had become a big fan. Poops spent a lot of nights curled up on the foot of his bed, for which he was deeply grateful. Some nights, just having another heartbeat close made all the difference.

Lost in thought, Tyler chewed on his lip as he tried to come up with a solution. He knew how badly he needed to regain his strength, but the thought of being hounded by photographers, their cameras capturing his every hiccup and falter, was unbearable.

"Maybe there's a private gym somewhere," he mused, fingers tapping restlessly on the table. "Or a trainer who can come to the house." Mr. Poops hopped into his lap, stalked in a circle, then settled down to nap while Tyler googled and growled at the screen.

Money was no problem, but privacy was something else entirely. He continued his search for someplace close enough to use often, growing more frustrated by the minute as he scrolled through endless listings that wouldn't suit his odd situation.

"Come on, there has to be something," Tyler whispered to himself, determination refusing to let him give up. As he browsed, he absentmindedly stroked the dozing cat.

To be fair, he'd started his physical rehab and occupational therapy in San Diego five weeks ago, until the team's primary PT had leaked a story and pictures of his big naked butt to TMZ for fifty grand. The pictures didn't bug him all that much, but the "insider" gossip made him sound like a grouchy basket case with a sex addiction. The team had clamped down swiftly, but the press proceeded to lose their minds with theories and predictions based on nothing.

The Swells owners had apologized and groveled, but Tyler wasn't having it. He'd put his foot down: no more NFL leeches, no more leaks, no more Mr. Nice Patient. Apart from cardiac oversight from Reynolds, he'd do his recovering in Cinnamar. With that much egg on their face, the Swells didn't have much choice.

Trouble was, organizing discreet treatment and physical rehab out here in Never-Heard-of-It, California, was almost impossible.

As the first hint of dawn filtered through the curtains, Tyler's eyes remained glued to his laptop, his fingers clattering on the keyboard to suss out a solution. He rubbed his weary eyes, but he refused to give up.

The soft creak of the kitchen door caught his attention, and Nadia shuffled in wearing her favorite fuzzy socks and yawning behind a hand. The cat hopped down to greet her with a hopeful yowl. Nadia's gaze fell on Tyler, and she made a grim face.

"Tyler, tell me you have *not* been up all night flipping out," she said, her voice tinged with worry. "You should have woken me."

"Couldn't rest, stay still," he admitted, running a hand through his unkempt hair. "I been trying to figure out this workout situation. Sounds dumb, but I'm not just some guy when I go to a gym, so I need a PT clinic or a club where there's no cameras allowed."

"Oh. Oh shit. Yeah. I didn't even consider—" Nadia leaned against the counter, studying him for a moment before completing the thought. "You know, there might be another option," she said, her words slow and thoughtful. "What if you went back to our old high school and asked if you could use their gym and track after hours? It'd be private, and if paparazzi hassle the kids, the sheriff will throw 'em in jail."

"Hey. Hey!" A wide grin spread across Tyler's face. He closed the laptop, pushed it aside, and stood up from the table, his eyes wide. "Nadia, you're a genius!" He swept her up in a bear hug that lifted her off her feet and shook her until she giggled.

"Hey, easy there, mister!" she laughed, playfully swatting at his arm. "I'm just trying to help."

"So you did," he assured her, setting her down gently. "This may be exactly what I need. Thank you." For the first time in months, he felt right about something. Confident. Baby steps.

"Hey, no problem." Nadia smiled wide. Mr. Poops made a plaintive, pitiful sound at her shins. "Now, how about some breakfast, huh? You look like you could use some fuel."

"Deal," Tyler agreed. "As a reward for your brilliant idea, I'm making you a huge spread. Flapjacks, eggs, bacon, the works!" Even that felt like a step. Getting off his ass. Participating in the world.

Nadia laughed. "You don't have to do that."

"I want to," Tyler insisted, already gathering necessaries from the fridge, pantry, and cabinets. "It's the least I can do. And I'll even clean up when we're done!"

"Wow, and next thing pigs fly," Nadia teased, her laughter filling the kitchen. "I need to feed Mr. Poops."

As Tyler bumped around the kitchen, he couldn't help but feel grateful for his sister's unwavering support. Her offhanded suggestion had given him something to strive for, a concrete goal that could help him take back control of his life.

"How about this?" Nadia broke through Tyler's thoughts by rattling the canister of cat food like a maraca. "Maybe you should stop by the school this morning and see if it's possible. No time like the present, right?"

"Right." Tyler nodded, flipping pancakes with a casual dexterity that surprised even him. For the first time in a long while, he felt motivated. "I will. Right after breakfast."

"Mom would be really happy to see you being so brave, getting back up," Nadia said gently, as if reading his mind. "She only wanted you to be happy, Ty. However you make that happen."

"First, though," he added with a grin, "I got to get my ass back to high school."

Chapter Two

JOSH AYRES strode into the Hamilton High Athletics office, glancing at his watch.

Ten minutes was plenty of time to check the weight room and swing by Carver's office. He tossed his bag on the chair and slapped his abs before wading back into the hall.

"Morning, Coach," said Elise from behind her desk. She wiggled and winked. "Looking buff."

"Feeling tough." He shrugged and smiled.

This back-forth fake flirting was a morning ritual they had started back when Elise Tattersall began lifting weights in earnest after her divorce. She'd lost sixty pounds, joined the athletic department here, and started teaching yoga to seniors at the local community center.

Josh turned back to her. "All good?"

Elise seemed to be sizing him up, which made him feel awkward. "You should come do some hot yoga once a week. My ladies would sure appreciate those shorts in downward dog. Well, not the shorts, but you know…. A little healthy inspiration never hurt nobody."

"Oh, uh, thanks, Elise." Josh reddened slightly, wishing his clothes were a bit looser. High school Josh would've pissed his pants and melted into the floor from hot shame. "I'm really a running and weights guy."

She nodded. "Well, one of these days."

He slapped her desk but didn't linger. After grabbing a protein shake from the office fridge, Josh poked his head into the empty gym and headed out to the hallway to start his morning patrol.

He tugged on the trusty whistle around his neck and shook his head. Elise didn't mean any harm. The whole staff knew he was gay. She treated Josh more like a kid brother, but even so, any compliments always sat weird with him.

His fitness was hard-won, not genetic accident.

Four years of roaming these halls as a kid, overwhelmed and adrift, pining after unattainable jocks, had kicked his ass harder than the most ruthless trainer. Discipline, nutrition, and a healthy dose of hormones had done him no harm. As his late uncle used to say, "We all become the thing we desire."

Thank God.

He glanced at his reflection in the trophy case. One thing about coaching and teaching at his alma mater: not a day went by without some reminder of how much he'd changed in the past twelve years. He tucked his polo into the shorts, smoothed the front, and double-checked his zipper.

He waved hello to Mrs. Grappo as she affixed a glittered Fri-YAY! sign to her door. Down the hall, Otis the janitor whistled tunelessly while mopping up a purple puddle, spilled juice or punch.

"Morning, Coach Ayres!" called out a student in a group of high schoolers, who all waved and grinned. Josh flashed them a smile and a nod, never taking for granted the respect he'd earned in this tight-knit community.

As one of the "cool" teachers at Hamilton High, Josh took his unofficial role as mentor and confidant seriously. He kept a sharp eye out for struggling students who needed a helping hand or a stern glare.

Wednesdays were easy. He wasn't teaching a history elective this year and he didn't have a gym class till late morning, so he usually grabbed a bagel in the cafeteria before teaching, but today he needed to see if Principal Carver had approved the bus budget for their spring season. Hauling kids around rural California cost money.

"Hey, Mr. Ayres," stammered a lanky freshman clutching his schedule. "I'm lost again. Can you help me find Mr. Chan's room?"

The boy's hunched posture and nervous energy telegraphed plenty. Josh remembered wanting to melt into the linoleum.

"No sweat, Kevin. I'm headed that way myself," Josh replied with a mellow shrug.

As they crossed the atrium, Josh couldn't help but flash back to his own puberty lost in these halls. High school Joshua wouldn't have recognized his physique or his confidence, but that awkward adolescence was the root of everything he'd become. Back then he'd been an uptight misfit who eyed and envied the hunky athletes from the sidelines. He felt ashamed of it now.

"Here you go, Kev." Josh gestured to the classroom door. "Just remember, this hallway loops around like a square. Third door on the left. You'll get the hang of it soon, promise."

"Thanks, Coach. You're the best." Kevin swallowed nervously and dropped his eyes. With a grateful nod, he hurried into the classroom just as the bell rang.

Josh watched him take his seat.

"Josh, my man!" came a booming voice from behind him. He turned to see Principal Carver approaching. "Thanks for helping Kevin. His parents just moved here, and he's still a bit off-kilter. You've got a real gift, you know that?"

"Thank you, sir," Josh replied with heartfelt gratitude. "It's an honor to be able to help these kids. They deserve our best. I wanted to ask about the buses."

Carver gave him a thumbs-up and Josh grinned in gratitude.

After high school, a determination to improve himself had led Josh to commit to health and fitness. He'd promised himself to help the kids who struggled the way he had. Now as a teacher and coach, Josh strove to make school a welcoming place for all types of students.

Sure, he got lonely sometimes, even panicky. In general, being single and gay in a small town sucked. Still, even if he never met that special someone who "got" him, he could make a difference. He had nothing to gripe about.

Instead he focused on taking the steps every day, away from his past and closer to the person he dreamed of becoming: a protector, a mentor, and a friend to people who didn't always know how to ask.

Josh entered the gymnasium, the scent of freshly polished wood and the echo of bouncing basketballs filling the air. He loved this space; it was a sanctuary for so many students, a Pause button on the pressures of high school life—a place they could focus. As he surveyed the room, his eyes fell on a group of athletes gathered around a scrawny sophomore struggling with a set of dumbbells.

"Hey, knock it off," Josh barked, his voice firm yet compassionate. The athletes scattered like startled birds, leaving the freshman trembling in their wake. "You all right, Sanjay?" he asked. The boy's cheeks were flushed with embarrassment.

"Y-yeah," he stammered, wiping sweat from his brow. "Th-thanks, Coach."

"Remember, we're all here to help each other grow." Josh clapped him on the back. "No one should ever feel intimidated or unwelcome in this gym."

"Yes, sir." Sanjay nodded.

"Good man," Josh said, smiling warmly. "Now, let's find you a more appropriate weight and work on your form."

As he guided the boy through a series of exercises, he tuned out the teenage gossip around him. His focus was on helping young athletes build confidence and strength, regardless of what anyone else might think or say. After all, it wasn't his job to entertain idle chatter; it was his job to challenge bullies, protect the vulnerable, and help every student realize that a healthy body was something they all deserved.

Josh smiled. "Remember, you get where you're going one step at a time."

Just before lunchtime, Josh was on his way back to the athletics office when a loud commotion down the hall turned his head: students laughing and shouting in a clump near the main office. He frowned at the raised voices and what looked like teenaged animals jostling and crowding closer around someone. *Please don't let them be hassling a kid.*

But then, as he got about twenty yards away, a familiar figure stopped him cold. Josh's heart skipped and shunted him right back to horny teen anguish, his one hopeless schoolboy crush that had driven him nuts for longer than he liked to admit.

Tyler.

Towering over the students. Moving with the same feral intensity. Drop-dead handsome as ever. Tyler Fantana—NFL bad boy, America's Tightest End, the cockiest heartthrob that ever graduated from Hamilton High—strode toward Principal Carver's office, his legendary build commanding attention at this distance. Captain Fantastic.

After all these years, he came back.

As Tyler vanished behind the office door, scalding memories of high school flooded back to Josh, along with the intense yearning that had obsessed him from sophomore year on. He thought he'd outgrown that sweet pang, but his racing heart proved that was a lie.

He'd pined the way only a hormonal fourteen-fifteen-sixteen-year-old boy can pine. He'd cried and sulked. He'd studied football obsessively. He'd made emo playlists. He'd drawn elaborate pictures and doodled Tyler's name in his margins. He'd written passionate letters full of football-themed fantasies. He'd scanned every room he entered for that perfectly tousled dark hair, jacked body, and sly hazel eyes. He'd ridden his bike past Tyler's house so many times that even now he knew the way and could draw several routes from memory.

Without even realizing it, Tyler had ended up symbolizing a whole bunch of things to Josh during the hell of puberty. No human could live up to those expectations.

He gulped, feeling embarrassed by his visceral reaction. He'd let it go. It'd been a crazy crush. He'd been a horny idiot.

Fantasy. Insanity.

Shaking off the swoony nostalgia, Josh went to the office bathroom and splashed his pinked face with cold water. *Grow up, Ayres.* In hindsight, Nadia must have suspected back in high school, but she'd never broached the subject.

He hadn't laid eyes on Tyler in more than a decade, and somehow nothing had changed. Josh was hardly that awkward, gawking stalker anymore, but surely Tyler's celebrity had only widened the impossible gap between them.

Or had it? Josh's new, improved body might not be ready for pro ball, but nobody could say he wasn't built solid. That thought alone startled him.

Tyler Fantana was back in town, only now Josh wasn't invisible anymore. Gone was the skinny dweeb lusting after the homecoming king from the bleachers. Josh had grown up. Collegiate swimming and regular rock climbing had transformed that anxious kid inside and out.

After he'd gotten a grip, he made his way back to the weight room, where he found a group of students working out during their lunch break.

"Hey, Coach, did you hear?" one of the boys blurted out between bench press reps. Josh had coached his brother but only knew his last name was Rawls. "Tyler Fantana's here at school!"

"Really?" a freckled boy exclaimed, momentarily abandoning his squat. "Like, *the* Tyler Fantana? From the Swells?"

A girl named Debbie slapped the freckled kid's arm. "Duh. He went here, like, a hundred years ago. Did you get a selfie?"

"His hair grew, I think," the Rawls boy said from the bench. "I don't know. He was fire, yo. Rich and ripped."

"Duh. My sister said he used to date Carl Nassib *and* Megan Thee Stallion." Debbie shrugged with perfect adolescent logic. The students probably knew more about Tyler than Josh did. "I mean, not at the same time." She laughed, and the others laughed along at her gossipy tone. "But still…."

"Guys, focus," Josh chided gently. Nowadays Tyler slept around plenty, guys and girls both if you trusted the tabloids, but nothing serious far as he could tell. That reveal hadn't hurt Josh's fantasy life any. The world had changed a lot in fifteen years. "This is your time to work on yourselves, not stalk the alumni. Don't get weird."

"Come on, Coach Ayres," Debbie piped up. "It's not every day an effing NFL superstar comes to Nowheresville."

Josh sighed, understanding their excitement but wanting to keep the kids from doing anything foolish or dangerous. He leaned against a nearby weight rack, crossing his arms as he addressed the group. "I get that it's exciting, but Tyler's been through it this year. He deserves his privacy just like anyone else. If he's visiting school, it's probably for a good reason. Be cool. Give the guy some space."

There was a grumble of reluctant agreement, and the students returned to their exercises, albeit with slightly deflated enthusiasm.

As Josh observed them, his mind wandered back to Tyler, wondering what had brought him back to their hometown. He knew about the heart attack, of course. The whole world had watched it happen in real time. The hit, the fall, and the rush to the hospital. Just last month, ESPN had spent a week theorizing that Tyler planned to retire.

Was this trip home just a visit, or something more permanent? Josh found himself imagining a chance to reconnect with the guy who'd occupied so much of his teenage daydreams. *Talk about ancient history….*

Nah. They'd been strangers. Tyler had never even noticed him and certainly wouldn't recognize him after all this time. Josh barely recognized himself.

"All right, gang," Josh called out as the lunch break came to an end. "Great work today. Remember to respect each other and everyone else on campus—even famous football players."

"Got it, Coach," they chorused, and he watched them file out of the weight room, their Fantana chatter fading into the hallway.

Josh allowed himself a tiny smile, hoping that maybe, just maybe, he might get the chance to see Tyler again. Even just to say hi. And this time he wouldn't be the skinny, awkward nerd he'd been in high school. Who knew—he might be someone Tyler would actually notice.

After lunch, Josh tried to act nonchalant as he meandered through the school's corridors toward the principal's office. The mob had dispersed, but the kids still seemed keyed up and chatty about their infamous visitor. A lot of texting and gossip seemed to be happening in Tyler's wake.

Tyler Fantana had always had that effect on crowds. Josh hesitated against the wall a moment, second-guessing this dumb impulse.

The memories of his teenage fantasies came surging back: stolen glances in the halls, Tyler goofing around with his buddies, muscle straining beneath his jersey, his big laugh, teasing smile, and that insane rush the few times their eyes happened to meet by accident.

"Get a grip, Joshua," he muttered under his breath, shaking his head to clear away the lingering images. "Be cool."

The door to the college counselor's office opened ahead, and Myra Waxman stepped out to sniff the air, no doubt lured out by the hubbub.

As subtly as possible, Josh angled to the other side of the hall, out of her grab radius.

Myra didn't usually get handsy in front of the students, but she clutched at him at the most awkward moments under the camouflage of motherly affection. *No, thanks.* Unlike Elise and her friendly flirting, Myra could get aggressive and seemed a little too serious for comfort, mothering him about the oddest things. Groping and scolding seemed to be her only modes with him. Probably, she just kept herself too lonely for her own good.

As he turned the corner, he spotted Principal Carver's door slightly ajar. He could hear faint voices from within, and his pulse quickened. With every step closer, he felt the pressure of his own advice to the students in the weight room earlier: respect Tyler's privacy. Yet here he was, teetering on the edge of hypocrisy.

Am I really going to do this? Josh felt queasy and emboldened. *It's hardly fair to barge in and slobber over him. I just finished lecturing the kids about space and courtesy.*

He flexed his shoulders and back, mustering the strength and confidence he'd worked so hard for over the years.

He has no idea who I am. He hesitated in front of the door, biting his lip as he weighed his pitiful options. Torn between satisfying his own urges and respecting the person who had unwittingly inspired him to transform himself into the man he was today.

A long shot, but even the chance of a glimpse of Tyler or a quick hello made *trying* seem important. Both thrilling and terrifying, the idea that they could meet again as equals.

"Coach Ayres!" Carver's voice called from inside, tugging Josh out of his dilemma. "Come on in. I was just talking to someone about you."

Josh took a breath, a small smile playing at the corners of his mouth, as though he was walking to the end of a high diving board. He hesitated another moment before pressing the door open and plunging in.

"Hey, Principal Carver." Josh stepped into the office, doing his best to keep his voice level. Tyler was gone. He couldn't help the surge of irritation, however irrational. "Word has it we had a famous visitor today."

"Indeed. Tyler Fantana!" the principal gushed, his eyes lighting up. "Can you believe it? Crazy. Our very own hometown hero, right in that very seat."

It was still warm. "Yeah. Some of the students were talking about it. What brings him back?"

"Recovery from that heart thing. You know. Terrible." Carver frowned and glanced out at the quad. "But get this—he came to ask you a favor. Well, us."

Josh sat up. "What favor?" His hands tightened on the arms of the chair.

"Working out. Well, if you'd feel okay if he used our gym for his rehab. Can you imagine? I told him he's more than welcome. An alum? A big-deal alum?"

"Obviously." Josh nodded. His heart pounded at the thought of Tyler working out in his gym. With him. "That's cool. Terrific, actually."

"I thought so. Sorry I didn't ask you beforehand." Carver looked sheepish. "You don't have an AP history class this year. I just figured it wouldn't be a problem."

"An NFL celebrity in and out of this place? Get serious." Josh waved away the apology. Then he'd see Tyler more than once, maybe hang out some. "No problem at all."

"Fantastic! I told him to swing by your office to discuss it."

"You mean now? Then I should—"

"Indeed." Carver rose. "Let me know if anything comes up."

Josh was confident that plenty would come up, but he was barely listening. As he left the office, his mind raced with possibilities… and doubts.

Would Tyler even remember him? Did Josh want to be remembered as the nerdy kid two years below him who'd mooned around the bleachers? First thing: he needed to get a grip. He'd been dreaming about Tyler for all this time, but if he wasn't careful, Tyler would see him as another pushy stalker who wanted something.

As much as he tried to quell it, the nagging impatience refused to dissipate. He'd been waiting a long time, expecting never. But if Tyler wanted to use the gym facilities while he recuperated, it would create plenty of opportunities for them to cross paths.

Only time would tell, but Josh headed back to the athletic department, hopeful about this unexpected second chance.

The afternoon hallways seemed quiet. He swung by the cafeteria to wolf down a wrap and then picked up a package at the front desk.

After, Josh navigated the halls back to his office more slowly than strictly necessary, heart galloping but prudence holding the reins. He could picture Tyler there, all grown up and more handsome than he remembered—his powerful shoulders, that wicked smile—maybe needing a rubdown or some expert advice on his recuperation from a friendly coach willing to put in the hours.

Cool it.

When Josh reached the athletics office, however, it looked exactly as he'd left it: empty, except for the usual papers and abandoned gear the kids left behind them. The realization that Tyler had come and gone without crossing paths with him hit harder than it should've. Josh's shoulders fell.

Back at his desk, he sank into the worn chair and took a steadying breath. He regarded the framed photo of his college swim team. He'd come a long way since his time at Hamilton. A smile tugged at the corner of his lips.

Eyes, prize, he told himself firmly. So what if he missed Tyler on his first visit?

Afternoon sun sliced through the blinds, casting slats of buttery light across the memos and mail he needed to sort.

"Get it together, Ayres," he muttered to himself, trying to smooth his springy hair down. The familiar knot of doubt tightened in his chest, an old terror that still crept up on him when the going got messy.

His own pathetic crush aside, Tyler being here offered more than just selfish wish fulfillment. A real-life NFL superstar around the school. A hometown hero? Living proof that kids should work hard and commit to excellence if they wanted to do jack with their lives.

Who knows? he mused, still daydreaming. *Maybe this time around, things will turn out different.*

A yelp of adolescent laughter from the hall yanked Josh out of his reverie. He still had a job to do and students waiting on him. With a final glance around his office, he stood and went to the door.

"Here's hoping," he whispered, stepping back into the teenaged tangle between fifth and sixth periods, squaring his shoulders to face the afternoon with a tickle of anticipation. Already he could see the usual suspects clowning around by the double doors.

"Hey, Coach Ayres!" a voice called out from behind him, jolting him back to the here and now. A group of young players clustered outside the gym entrance, their faces flushed with excitement, probably wanting to use the weights during a free period. "You won't believe it! We saw Tyler Fantana!"

"Really?" Josh feigned surprise. His heart might have been off-kilter, but that was no one's business, least of all his students'. He laughed. "Did you attack him with TikTok?"

"Actually, we took your advice, Coach," Debbie replied, grinning and tucking her hair behind her ear.

He nodded. "Good choice."

"And he's, like, way hotter and nicer than Gronk is, or Drake even. Which is basically impossible."

"Eww, Deb. Gross," said Mark, one of the wrestlers. "We didn't harass him, Coach. Honest."

Debbie rolled her eyes. "We played it chill, and like, instead of a million lame pics, we got to talk to him. Like, actual real talk. And he asked questions, and get this: he'll be hanging around while he's in town. Like, here!" She pointed at the polished floor.

Josh pretended Tyler's gym plan was news, but his smile was genuine. Tyler probably had no clue what he'd done for the school—for Josh—simply by asking for a favor. "See? Giving people space is a good call."

The freckled boy next to her bobbed his head at that. "So cool."

"Well, let's make him feel welcome." Josh squinted at the random bags and papers littered around the echoing room. "How about you kids try and pick up after yourselves a bit more? Even show up to practice on time. Volunteer to show a frosh around? You never know—if you get lucky, maybe Fantana will throw some pigskin your way."

"Deal!" Debbie said. The rest of the gangly athletes bounced and muttered happily, eyes shining.

As they dispersed, Josh allowed himself a cautious smile. This might not have been the reunion he'd hoped for—might not ever be—but the possibility of seeing Tyler again at a time when Josh felt comfortable in his own skin made him happy in his bones.

Better late than never, right? If and when Tyler showed up wanting to work out, Josh would be ready. And who knew? Maybe this time, they'd meet each other properly.

After all, awful high school years might make for awesome reunions.

Chapter Three

THE MORNING sun was just beginning to peek above the horizon when Tyler arrived at the Hamilton High School track. The dew lay thick on the grass, and the sky above was still a deep blue that seemed to hold secrets. He needed this time alone, away from prying eyes and the relentless attention that came with being a pro athlete—especially one recovering from a very public heart attack.

For most of Tyler's life, mornings had sucked. Now he loved them, enthusiastically. Since he'd woken up in the hospital, every damn one felt like a big, shiny wrapped present because it meant he'd woken up to another chance, another choice. *Still alive. Still fighting.* Infinite possibility, all laid out for anyone willing to wake up and claim it.

Since his Reynolds checkup, he'd gotten into a little habit of pausing to pay attention anytime he caught himself stuck in his head or replaying the past. Even though her three-three-three routine was for panic attacks and crisis mode, it had evolved into a touchstone; he tried to notice things as they appeared and to move intentionally around them rather than rushing. Stupid as it sounded, simple focus blunted all kinds of sharp edges. He'd started doing it yesterday by accident, to help him navigate the school hallways, all those people, but it worked wonders.

Inhaling deeply, he could smell the damp earth beneath him as he stepped onto the track. For some stupid reason, he felt too anxious to even bother stretching or warming up; he simply started running, almost stumbling into motion. With each stride, the rhythmic pounding of his footsteps echoed across the empty field. A cool breeze made his pitiful pace feel less embarrassing.

"Damn." As Tyler trudged around the track, he discovered just how much his body had changed since the attack. In two months, his strength and reflexes had crumbled. His breath wheezed in his ribs. The consequences of hiding out on Nadia's couch for a month, binge-watching Hallmark movies. He could feel the stiffness in his joints, the weakness and tightness that had crept across his once-powerful frame.

His sinew felt slack, and his mood soured with each leaden step around the track. He couldn't shake the worry that full recuperation would take much longer than anyone was willing to predict.

He muttered under his breath, pushing himself harder. "I'm not giving up."

Growing up broke teaches you plenty. Tyler had never expected anything from anyone. He'd fought for scraps long before the NFL rescued him and saddled him with impossible expectations and pressures. Being number eighty-six for the Swells hadn't come easy.

As a kid in this crappy town, football had been an escape from hurt and hunger, a way to channel his anger and frustration over an alcoholic father who had smacked them around and an over-gentle mother who made excuses about "God's will" right up to the minute until the cancer took her. He'd gone to college for football and only studied sports medicine so the coaches would play him in front of the scouts. His degree had only ever been a way to stay on the team. The game was everything he did and was.

In the quiet of the morning, with only the sound of his own breathing and footfalls for company, Tyler found solace in the memories of simpler problems, smaller pain. His dad abandoned them when Tyler turned twelve, leaving the family buried in debt without warning or explanation. Secretly, he'd celebrated the departure, same as Nadia, although they never admitted that to their heartbroken mom.

Keep going, asshole, he told himself, his breath coming in short, ragged gasps. *You can do this.*

More than anything, he hated feeling like a failure and a fake—all the names his dad had ever called him in anger when Tyler had been too small to fight back.

He knew that the track wouldn't stay empty for more than an hour. By seven thirty the students and faculty would begin to arrive, and this quiet bubble of infinite possibility would come to an end. But for now he reveled in the solitude and the chance to focus on himself—a luxury he hadn't known for years.

As the sky above began to lighten, Tyler couldn't help but feel a renewed sense of determination. He would face the challenges and beat them, because that's what he always did. He'd emerge stronger than ever.

"Come on," he urged, feeling the burn of exertion in his legs. *One step at a time.*

As Tyler rounded the curve of the track, the first rays of sunlight began to streak the sky. Dew glistened on the grass like scattered crystal, and the air was still crisp and cool. He focused on his breathing, in and out, in time with each stride, trying to ignore the stiffness in his legs and the lingering weakness from his heart attack. *Tree. Cloud. Man.*

Because right then, Tyler saw him.

A tall figure in the distance caught his eye, a muscular guy wearing a coach's uniform, jogging toward him onto the track with an easy confidence that seemed almost magnetic.

Damn, Tyler thought, his eyes tracing the stranger's impossible build. *Who is that?*

The man moved in perfect balance, his chiseled body, square jaw, and sandy hair gleaming dark gold in the rising light. No dumb gym body either. This guy had a build like a professional athlete—not football, but more like baseball or hockey maybe. He gave off an aura of command, authority even, that looked effortless and earned. Nothing exaggerated, nothing fake, nothing for show.

Tyler thought, quite clearly, *Now that right there is a man I'd follow into any kind of trouble.*

He blinked in genuine desire, battling the urge to close the distance between them and get a better look. Was that even possible?

Curiosity aroused, he tried to quicken his lumbering pace. His heart pounded in his chest—not just from exertion but from honest-to-God excitement. It had been so long since he'd allowed himself to feel anything like this, to want someone real, and it thrilled him as much as it scared him.

Still, he knew good looks were an awful basis for any relationship. And heaven knew he'd dated plenty of hot jerks. This was something else.

Easy there, tiger, Tyler admonished himself, struggling to catch his wheezing breath as he closed in on the handsome figure. *You're still healing.*

Still, he couldn't help but push himself harder, driven by a sense of yearning he hadn't experienced in years. As he drew closer, the tightness in his chest seemed to subside, replaced by an electric curiosity that both exhilarated and terrified him.

A sharp pain in his ribs made him falter. He couldn't do it. His pace slowed to a humping trudge. Heart pounding, a stitch in his side, he eased up again. He'd pushed too hard, and he'd pay the price later. His racing heart struggled in his chest, and he fought to keep his breath deep and even to calm himself. He knew better. *Pay attention.*

In the end, the man closed the gap for him, coming up on his right flank, first as a steady pounding of the track, and then breaths, and then a presence.

As the man lapped him, he slowed down a moment and turned to nod at Tyler with a gentle smile that made Tyler's heart stutter. Graceful and confident as an ancient warrior, the kind of hero kids try to impersonate on playgrounds. *Perfection.* The sudden rush of attraction took him by surprise.

Tyler smiled back as he passed and then dropped his eyes. That guy was familiar. Who was he?

And so beautiful. Like, catch-your-breath, stop-your-heart gorgeous. Perfect balanced strength. For a moment Tyler felt humiliated by his own hulking physique and crappy form. His body was a tank designed for rough combat.

The sun had begun to cast long shadows over the dew-silvered grass. Running like this felt good, right. He was weak, but not as weak as he'd feared. The gorgeous guy almost felt like a sign.

This was a good thing he was doing. *Thank you, Dr. Reynolds.*

When Tyler looked up again, his silent companion had moved ahead steadily with aggressive focus. He couldn't help but be drawn to this guy; it was the first time he'd felt any arousal or even social interest since his heart attack. Tyler let his eyes linger with hollow longing on the muscular legs and the perfect V of his back, bisected by a stripe of healthy sweat.

He felt certain he recognized the guy. But from where? A player on another pro team? An actor or a model? How could anyone with that physique end up out in the middle of Nowhere, California, at this time of year? He knew that jaw, that nose, that face.

And then it hit him.

"Josh?" Tyler said out loud, with a rush of recognition that made him smile to himself. "Josh... umm. Ames? Aaron?" Just barely, he recalled the gangly boy from Nadia's high school class, so shy he stuttered. "Ayres. Joshua Ayres." Skinny as a fence post with hand-me-down clothes and huge damp eyes. Cute for sure, but so nervous.

"Damn." A soft chuckle as Tyler watched grown-up Josh's glorious butt pulling away from him. "Josh Ayres."

He'd been one of the nerdy football groupies that hung around practices and came to away games no matter how far. They hadn't known each other at all, for all the dumb adolescent reasons.

Early on, Tyler's buddies had pegged Josh as a "homo" lurking at the back of the bleachers because of his intense eyes. Even before that, Tyler had noticed Josh's hopeful stare and steered clear of him to protect them both.

Tyler didn't even know if Josh *was* gay, but as a junior, the last thing he'd needed was rumors dogging him when college scouts visited. Nowadays, who cared? But back then, Tyler had known the only way he'd ever make the NFL was inside a rock-solid closet with multiple locks.

Nadia had known Josh a bit, if memory served. From… drama or math? Something foofy like that. Tyler couldn't recall. Some terrifying subject cooler and smarter than Tyler was, for sure. Like Josh. One of the nerds who did their homework and used the library for more than whacking off between classes. "Holy shit."

Nowadays libraries and smarts made Tyler's heart go pitty-pat… and the way Josh looked in those shorts would most likely keep him up at night for the foreseeable future. *Jesus crickets. Little Josh, all buffed up and ready for thirst traps.*

He sure had blossomed. Tyler hoped he hadn't been too gross or rude to him, back in the day.

Being in Nadia's class meant Josh Ayres had to be two years younger, at least. Somewhere around thirty, maybe? Tyler tried to recall specific moments or a single conversation they'd shared back then, but all he could summon were hazy impressions of laughter and distant jeering, the ugly edges of teenage social hierarchies that made him feel like a closeted homophobic dick after the fact.

They'd probably never spoken a single word. *Dumbass.*

Tyler's breath hitched slightly as he envisioned the younger, weaker Josh 1.0, a knobbly teen with smudgy glasses clutching books to his chest and hunching his shoulders to make himself invisible to the predatory jerks who roamed the halls. Tyler's douchebag friends, most of them. Ugh.

Man, I should've been friendlier back then. Kinder, Tyler mused, his breath coming in short bursts as he strained to maintain his pace. Everything had seemed scarier then. He'd fought his own battles. The realization stung, sharpening his resolve to make amends, albeit years later, and gave him a renewed resolve.

He knew Nadia would smack him and say, "And that is what we call *privilege*, doofus." Tyler felt that truth in his aching bones. In high school he'd been determined to save himself and his family. Football or nothing, feelings be damned.

His gaze kept darting to Josh, and he took in the smooth lines of his sweat-slicked legs propelling him forward, the sunlight catching his dark blond hair, the line of his throat, and the teasing swell in his coach's shorts. The years had blessed Josh mightily.

The sky blazed up peach and rose as they continued running in parallel. A newfound sense of lust and curiosity stirred within him for the first time in months. A rush of heat coursed through his body, catching him off guard and making him feel alive again. Though he didn't dare admit it, even to himself, the sensation of attraction and the stirrings of arousal brought a mixture of embarrassment and pride—a reminder that his libido hadn't been busted along with his heart.

The realization sent a jolt through Tyler, awakening long-dormant feelings of desire and anticipation.

Tyler didn't even fight the smile on his face.

To think he was now a virtual invalid who could barely drag himself off the couch, and that anxious, wimpy chess-club string bean had evolved into the rugged hunk currently stirring his loins and lapping him. *Payback for the homecoming king.* Tyler felt about two feet tall and ugly.

He snuck another long glance at those perfect arms, the square jaw. "Jeez."

He couldn't help but be fascinated by the transformation that had taken place in Josh over the years, the way his once scrawny frame had grown into sculpted muscle, how his tawny skin caught the rising sun.

As they circled the track, Tyler and Josh maintained a comfortable silence, their breaths and footsteps syncing. Josh might be running about twice his speed, but having him there definitely kept Tyler motivated, which was no bad thing.

Plus, the shared quiet was a balm to Tyler's soul, allowing him to focus on the steady rhythms of his body and the easy company of someone who seemed to understand the luminous miracle of this time of day. What was the opposite of panic? Who needed three-three-three when you were suddenly seeing, hearing, moving everything right now on this track under this perfect sunrise?

After a half hour, their mutual silence became an unspoken understanding, allowing them to run together yet apart, free from the usual distractions of conversation or expectation.

Maybe that was the thing. Everyone wanted things from him, demanded favors, expected their backs scratched. Josh's encouraging smile offered the first real hint of camaraderie he'd felt in years, without the assumptions and illusions some jerk had cooked up about the "rowdy, randy NFL star."

The sun continued its slow ascent, tracing the dew in diamond light. For the first time since his heart attack, Tyler felt alive and present in his body. This simple act of running in the quiet had awakened something—a hunger for connection, for pursuit, a need to look closer, and the stupid hope that maybe here, around this track, for once he wasn't running in circles.

Life is so funny.

As they continued their parallel journey, Tyler knew that whatever lay ahead for him—healing, self-discovery, or whatever—it all began here, behind the old gym, with a familiar stranger running in tandem on the other side of the track.

Tyler's initial wariness about crossing paths with someone from his past melted away, replaced by a growing curiosity about Josh's obvious transformation.

Josh lapped him again and, without breaking stride, cast another sideways glance at Tyler, and offered that friendly nod of acknowledgment again. This silent greeting had become part of the ritual. So Josh must have recognized him, which felt more surprising and important than it probably should have, given Tyler's notoriety.

He smiled and nodded back, appreciating the tacit agreement to preserve the beauty of the predawn stillness. As their gazes met, Tyler felt a thrill of recognition and confirmation that this was indeed Josh Ayres, the timid teenager grown into a genuine grade-A stud.

As they continued their silent run and the sun crawled higher, Tyler felt his spark of hope catch flame, real eagerness now—for his recovery, for new connections, and for the chance at a future that was finally beginning to look bright again. Josh's quiet strength and unbelievable transformation proved that possibilities were… possible.

Tyler nodded to himself. A real MVP pays attention to every member of the team. How many chances and choices had he missed while he was aimed at the life he thought he wanted? How many small miracles lay hidden beneath the surface of people he hadn't noticed?

The rhythmic pounding on the track became a sort of meditation mantra, sanding the sharp edges of Tyler's thoughts. Gradually, he allowed himself to slip into a zone where he could shed the weight of expectation and escape his fame and simply exist, free from judgment or assumptions. Each step brought him closer to a sense of purpose and self-worth.

After all, if Josh could change so dramatically, couldn't he?

Tomorrow, Tyler vowed, a silent promise to the virtual stranger who had unknowingly lit a spark inside him. *I'll be back here tomorrow, and maybe something more might happen.*

On Tyler's last loop, both men gradually slowed their pace, their chests heaving with the effort. In unison, they slowed to a walk. The morning was nippy enough that steam rose from Josh's skin and his. As they paced in place, they again exchanged another friendly nod, an unspoken understanding passing between them.

This brief morning encounter had changed everything for Tyler.

Josh ambled to the gym's back door to stretch against the rail. Tyler kept his distance, unsure of how welcome he'd be any closer than this.

As Tyler made his slow trek off the field, they smiled at each other as though they shared a secret, a kinship formed and a tacit promise of… something. He hadn't felt this kind of absolute focus and calm in months. *Anticipation*—that was the word.

See you tomorrow? Tyler considered saying, rehearsing the words in his mind, but he hesitated, unsure if asking was too rude, too weird, too selfish. Instead, he simply held Josh's smiling gaze for a moment longer and let the soft silence speak for itself.

Before he could do anything dumb or embarrassing, Tyler turned and strode away from the track, his body thrumming with adrenaline and a delicious heat he hadn't felt in way too long.

With a renewed sense of purpose, Tyler walked out through the field gates to the car, his banged-up heart swelling with gratitude for the unexpected encounter.

Josh Ayres. Who would've thought?

Tomorrow, then. Without fail. He'd be back here tomorrow, and the tomorrow after. And hopefully, Josh would too.

Tyler had initially planned to run a couple times a week, to use these early mornings as a bare minimum to escape his rut and clear his mind. But now, thanks to the haunting beauty of Josh, Tyler found himself with a rock-solid reason to return every single day.

Tyler barely remembered the drive. At some point on the way home, he swung by the farmer's market to pick up eggs like a normal person would. He didn't remember opening his wallet, so he hoped he'd paid for them. He'd check tomorrow, and pay triple just in case.

By the time he was back at his sister's front door, full daylight blazed at the horizon, kissing Tyler's back as he unlocked and entered the little foyer. The familiar creak of the floorboards and the faint scent of his mother's drugstore perfume brought a comforting sense of nostalgia, grounding him in the place where he'd made himself up. For the first time in years, Tyler felt like he truly belonged somewhere.

"Tyler? Were you out this early?" Nadia called from the kitchen, her voice rising over the sizzle of bacon on the stovetop. Mr. Poops wove hopefully between her legs, bleating for his bowl. "How was your run?"

"Better than I expected," he replied, dropping his duffel bag by the door. "I met someone."

"You— You what? Really? Whore," she said, raising an eyebrow playfully as she plated the bacon and eggs. "Do tell."

"Not *meet*, meet. But I saw someone who I don't really know. I didn't know exactly." He shook his head to try and make it make sense to her. "Something happened."

She frowned and stepped toward him. "Something bad? Are you okay?"

"Something great, actually. I think." Tyler rubbed his face, still uncertain how to explain.

She gave him a weird, worried look. "Uhhh-kay. Who did you meet at this hour?"

"Josh Ayres," Tyler confessed, leaning against the kitchen counter and watching as Nadia's eyes widened in surprise and pleasure. "Remember him? Scrawny kid in high school, bookworm, lived in the library. Chess or drama a lot too, I think."

"Both, actually. Wow, that's a nice surprise." Nadia chuckled. She bent to pour kibble into the cat's bowl and scratched under Mr. Poops's chin before straightening. The cat squeaked approvingly. "Coaches football and track at the high school now. And teaches advanced history or philosophy sometimes. Something hard." She shrugged. "Nice guy."

"Yeah. He's… different now. Stronger, confident. And, well, not so scrawny anymore," Tyler said, a hint of awe coloring his tone.

"Not even a little. He grew up hot. Like porn hot. Wild."

"You've seen him, then."

"Duh! Dumbass, I live here. We've been friends forever. Mom knew him. We didn't stop existing when you moved away. Cinnamar ain't big. I've known Joshua my whole life."

"I guess, but I didn't realize you two were that tight." He knew he was acting strange but couldn't stop.

"Everybody knows everybody. But he's a really close friend." She swatted at him with the spatula. "FYI, for the record, the whole entire town is, like, obsessed with his butt."

"Mmmh?" Tyler tried to look nonchalant.

"Legs too. And his arms, actually. Big blue eyes. And Bernice at the drugstore has a real thing about his dimple."

"He has a dimple too?"

"Well, well, well…." Nadia crooked an eyebrow and an evil grin, no doubt aware of the implications. "Is the big bad jock getting worked up working out with a nice small-town boy? I think I saw that Christmas movie, doofus."

"Come on, it's not like that," Tyler protested, but his cheeks flushed hot. He couldn't help but find himself drawn to Josh, his beauty and the strange silent connection they'd shared.

"Right," Nadia teased, handing him a plate stacked with breakfast. "I'm sure your appreciation of his massive deltoids is purely platonic."

"I didn't— We didn't even talk, Nadia. How would I? I didn't even know him."

"You're an NFL player, doof. The whole town knows you. Doreen keeps a goddamn scrapbook on you that she takes to people's houses. Swear to God." She raised her right hand.

"No. I meant in school. *Me*-me. Real me. He probably doesn't even remember me from back then. Or maybe I was a dick. He probably hated my guts."

Nadia paused then, just searching his eyes a moment, as though she wanted to confess something, but after a long awkward silence, she did not.

"What?"

"Y'know?" She stole a piece of bacon off his plate and ate it as she teased him. "He does the town calendar every year as a favor, and he's not even a firefighter. But he's always July, so it's always Lycra trunks. *Child!* Hot. And smart. And nice. I mean, I know you got all them athletic supporters on speed dial in San Diego, but y'know: hamburger, steak." She mimed scales and weighed the gay hookup options for him.

"Okay, fine," Tyler admitted, rolling his eyes. "I'm not blind. He's attractive, for sure. But it was a… a *feeling* more than anything. A good one. He gave me space. I can't remember the last time someone gave me that kind of space."

"Well, good," Nadia mused, her teasing tone replaced with gentle warmth. "Wait, so you didn't talk. Were you rude? I hope you weren't rude to him. He's, like, the nicest."

"No? I don't think so. I'm not sure. Well, maybe," Tyler allowed, taking a bite of eggs. "I can't explain it. It felt right." In his heart, he knew something had shifted this morning, a first step. "Running. Sunrise. Breathing. He just… helped me being there."

"Of course he did. That's Joshua." She nodded like she understood, and maybe she did.

They tucked into breakfast, including Mr. Poops, who smacked happily at his bowl in the corner.

"Well, I'm definitely running again. It felt great. Which means I guess I'll probably see him tomorrow. He seemed like a good guy."

"He is. So promise me one thing," Nadia said, her voice suddenly serious. "Let yourself heal, Ty. Catch your breath. You deserve happiness just as much as anyone else."

Tyler looked into his sister's eyes and saw all the worries and hopes she kept to herself. He nodded, holding tight to this funny, sunny feeling he couldn't shake. He held up his index finger and dragged two lines across his chest. "Cross my heart."

Chapter Four

JOSH ARRIVED at the school in his running gear feeling almost eager. He unlocked his office door, grabbed a towel and water bottle, and then made his way down to the track before the sun had even begun its climb.

As he walked, Josh couldn't help but give in to a flutter of excitement under his ribs. For the past week, these quiet morning runs with Tyler had become the highlight of his day, even though they still hadn't *actually* spoken. He longed to break the ice and get to know Tyler a little, but caution and gut instinct held him back, reminding him of the shy, awkward teenager he used to be.

Once on the track, Josh began his warm-up routine, stretching his muscles as his eyes flicked toward the parking lot every few moments. He was delaying, waiting for Tyler's arrival, unable to shake the concern that he should have arrived by now. Finally Josh spotted Nadia's car pulling into the lot and felt a wave of relief wash over him.

As Tyler exited the car and headed toward the track, Josh noticed something amiss. Tyler's muscular mass and imposing presence were undeniable, even after a couple months out of the game, but he moved stiffly; instead of stretching properly, he seemed to be halfheartedly going through the motions, as if he was distracted or perhaps rushing through the warm-up. *Yikes.*

Josh wanted to call out to him, to nudge him to take better care of himself, but he hesitated. Would Tyler appreciate the advice or see it as an unwelcome intrusion? Who was he, after all? Some stranger that Tyler had never noticed in fifteen years.

That wimpy uncertainty held him back, and he continued stretching in silence, watching Tyler from the corner of his eye.

As Josh finished stretching and prepared to begin his run, he couldn't help but steal one more glance at Tyler. His concern for Tyler's well-being was genuine, and he wished he had the courage to offer some guidance to help his recovery. They just weren't friends like that. As best as he could remember, despite spending at least two years in high school together, they'd never spoken twenty words to each other in the course of their lives.

Ugh. Being a kid was awful.

For now, all he could do was watch and hope that a couple of friendly nods and this strange morning ritual of running in silence at sunrise might someday give him the courage to be the friend and support Tyler seemed to need so badly right now.

As they started their run, Josh felt the familiar rhythm of their feet hitting the track. The sun was just beginning to peek over the horizon, casting a soft, pale glow over the stands and the trees beyond. The air was still, and the only sounds were their steady breaths and the gentle thud of their footsteps. They had fallen into this routine almost effortlessly, and even without interacting much, Josh found comfort in Tyler's presence.

Despite their vastly different backgrounds—Josh the high school nerd turned coach and Tyler the celebrated NFL quarterback—this small hometown track had forged an unspoken bond that made these early mornings feel like a sanctuary, free of judgment or expectations.

On their third lap, several minutes into their run, Tyler suddenly twisted in pain, dramatically struggling to catch his breath. Panic flashed across his face as he clutched his side and went down hard, and Josh's heart lurched in response.

In that moment, all his reservations fell away—his concern for Tyler overrode any lingering awkwardness or fear of rejection.

"Tyler!" Josh called out, cutting across the field to rush to his side. "Are you okay? What's wrong?"

Tyler tried to straighten but winced at the effort. "Stupid heart… and cramp, I think. Thanks, Josh."

"Wow, you remember me?" Josh grinned, genuinely surprised and pleased. "I didn't think anyone would, especially not someone like you."

"Someone like me?" Tyler raised an eyebrow. "A beat-up meathead living at his sister's who struggles to get out of bed every morning?"

"You know." Josh shrugged, a teasing smile playing on his lips. "A big-shot celebrity football superstar. Captain Fantastic."

Tyler laughed, and the tension between them melted. "Well, at the moment, I'm just some dude trying to get his life back together. And running."

"Looks like home isn't always a bad idea," Josh mused. "Maybe there's something to this small-town peace-and-quiet nonsense."

Tyler shook his huge hands. "My head feels so weird. Blurry."

"Here, let me help." Josh moved closer and placed a supportive hand on Tyler's back. The guy's pupils were enormous, and he looked gray under a sheen of perspiration. "Have you been hydrating properly?"

"Probably not," Tyler admitted with a frown. He blanched like he was breathing through serious discomfort.

"I'm betting blood sugar and potassium are both low. And did you stretch enough before we started?"

"Huh-uh. Not really." Tyler's cheeks flushed with embarrassment. He pressed a fist to his side with a scowl. "I know, I know. I never really bothered with that crap before. I've never needed—" Tyler offered him a tentative smile that got him too flustered to cover.

"It's okay. We all have to learn sometime." Josh gave him a reassuring head bob. "Just take a few deep breaths and try to relax your muscles."

As Tyler followed Josh's instructions, his breathing began to slow and even out. "Thanks, man," Tyler said softly. "I really appreciate this."

"Of course," Josh replied, feeling an unfamiliar warmth spread through him. For the first time, he felt a real connection with Tyler—not the fantasy but the man, flaws and all.

"Let me check your pulse," Josh suggested. Gently, he pressed his fingertips against Tyler's wrist, feeling the strong rhythm beneath his skin. "It seems fast, but not too bad considering. Just keep breathing deeply and let's get you moving a little and some water. Your muscles are going to hurt worse if they cramp. You should be eating a banana every morning and night for the potassium. Good sugar for the run too."

"Thanks," Tyler murmured, allowing Josh to continue assessing his condition without protest. It seemed as if the trust between them was growing. Tyler's vulnerability was wrecking all Josh's noble intentions.

"All right, I'm going to try to massage out that cramp in your leg." Josh carefully placed his hands on Tyler's huge calf, which was every bit as powerful as it looked. He could feel the tight knot of muscle beneath his fingers and began to gently knead the area, hoping to release the tension.

Tyler didn't seem to mind the contact at all. He groaned in pleasure. "God. That." He glanced at Josh. "You teach too, right?"

"Yeah." Josh rolled the muscle more slowly. "History, electives and AP sometimes. But not every year."

"I love history. *Used* to love history, I guess. I was a crap student." He chuckled and groaned again, watching Josh's hands on his big calf.

"Is that helping?" Josh asked, looking up into Tyler's bright hazel eyes. Touching him like this made Josh feel almost guilty.

"Unnh. Yeah, it's starting to feel better already. Wow, man. That feel effing amazing," Tyler replied with a relieved smile and a twinkle in his eye. "You really know what you're doing."

"Coach high school a while and you see every kind of injury." Josh chuckled, trying to hide his own nerves. "But seriously, make sure you take care of yourself. Stretching and hydration are key. And a big banana." He pointed at Tyler with a comic scowl.

"That's what they all say." Tyler nodded as he straightened. Finally he reached for Josh's hand, and he stood without wincing. "Yes, Coach."

"Good. Now, why don't we try walking the track for a few minutes? Grab some water. We want to ease your muscles back into motion before you even think about running," Josh suggested, releasing Tyler's leg as he stood up.

"Sounds like a plan," Tyler agreed, taking a tentative step forward.

Josh slowed his pace deliberately. Clouds scudded over the peaceful track. By now, the crickets seemed just about done and the air was warmer, carrying the scent of fresh-mown grass. They stopped at the fountain and then ambled back. Already Tyler looked less grim.

"Really beautiful out here." Tyler blinked at the horizon. "I never noticed all this when I was younger."

"That's high school. Hormones and homework. Who has time for a sunrise?" Josh glanced over at Tyler. Their eyes met for a moment—a deeper connection than anything Josh had experienced in a long time. Did Tyler feel it too?

As they walked side by side, Josh couldn't help but notice the slight hitch in Tyler's stride. They needed to slow down. "You said you're into history? Anything in particular?"

"Renaissance, probably. No, how about Roman empire," Tyler replied, his face lighting up. "They just did so much modern stuff for the first time. Roads, coinage, junk food, plumbing."

"Public games!" Josh exclaimed, excitement filling his voice. "I've never been."

Tyler laughed and pushed him. "To ancient Rome? Obviously."

"No, Italy. I've never—" Josh looked down at the grass. "I've never gone anywhere, really."

"Highly recommend. Italy is…." Tyler fell quiet. "Sorry. That's a crappy thing to say."

"Why?"

"I've only been to Italy with the team. We shot an advertisement. I didn't really go anywhere or see anything. You know, a day in the Vatican, an hour at the Trevi Fountain. So I haven't really been there either. Not really, like, *actual* me."

"You should." Josh shrugged.

"Well, you should too."

Josh looked across the field to the gym and the school beyond. "Hardly. With the school's schedule? I barely have time to go to the grocery store."

Tyler stared at him for a quiet moment. "One of these days, then."

"Absolutely. One of these days." Josh shook his head. "I don't want you to think I don't go anywhere. Never been anywhere. I'm not a shut-in. But mostly travel means hauling teenagers around in a bus. Or quick road trips for an overnight. But I've never been farther east than the Rockies."

"I love road trips." Tyler's breathing and gait were steadier now. "Football doesn't leave me a lot of downtime during the season, but when I can? Just pack a bag and hit the road with nowhere to be."

Josh nodded, a genuine smile spreading across his face. "That's the best."

"Well, the best would be a road trip in Italy, but I don't think that's happening anytime soon." He frowned down at his body. "When I first got back into town, my sister dragged me up to this tiny little town in the mountains with the most amazing diner."

"Hearthstone! I love that place."

"That's the one." Tyler nodded. "Home-churned butter?"

"Exactly." Josh bobbed his head back. "In fact, guess who took Nadia her first time?" He pointed at his own chest.

"Aw, man." Tyler beamed back at him. "Really? Then I owe you one. Best damn waffles I've ever had."

As they continued to walk and talk, Josh could see Tyler improving. After walking two laps, his breath came smoother, his steps steadied, and his shoulders released. It felt incredible to connect with him like this. It was something he hadn't expected but couldn't deny—he felt drawn to Tyler in a way that made anything seem possible. Which seemed both ridiculous and important at the same time.

Finally they resumed their run, a little slower now. Josh's thoughts ran alongside them. Could Tyler actually be interested? In *him*? Or was he simply being friendly and appreciative? Only time would tell, but one thing was certain: Josh planned to find out.

As they continued jogging, the conversation flowed easily between them, touching on favorite hikes, old classmates, and even a few embarrassing high school memories.

With each shared laugh and knowing glance, the bond between them deepened, and Josh found himself falling more and more under Tyler's spell.

"Did you ever watch cartoons growing up?" Tyler asked, turning to face Josh as they jogged.

"You kidding?" Josh enthused. "Cartoon Network was sacred in my house. *South Park* obviously, and *Dexter's Laboratory*. The big one for me was *Powerpuff Girls*."

That last one popped out before he thought about how queer that might sound to a big buff jock, even one that dated other jocks sometimes, but Tyler's eyes and smile widened abruptly, as if some secret joy had lit up his whole body.

"No way!" Tyler smacked him. "I was obsessed with the Powerpuff Girls. Buttercup all the way. Let me tell you, I did not advertise *that* in the locker room."

"Seriously?" Josh hesitated, not sure how to respond. What did he mean? Maybe because it wasn't a "boy" cartoon? Was Tyler hinting that he knew Josh liked him? Maybe the Powerpuff Girls were Tyler's way to signal he wasn't opposed to the idea. This kind of code-cracking was the worst part of growing up gay in a small town. "You... are full of surprises."

"I am." Tyler laughed and winked. "Hands-down the funniest show on TV. I had posters, sheets, and everything. I still binge-watch them when I'm feeling crappy." Then his face darkened. "My dad made so much fun of me."

Josh frowned. "Sorry."

"Don't be. He was an asshole." Tyler shook his head and seemed to emerge from whatever dark memory had dimmed his spirits. "I turned out okay."

Josh smiled. "Indeed you did."

Their eyes caught again.

Just then, with Tyler so open and trusting, Josh wanted to confess everything: his crush, his hopes, his pleasure, his gratitude. Before he did anything stupid, he made a quick decision and punted. "Thirsty."

Tyler jerked his chin toward the empty bleachers. "Water break?" He panted slightly as they slowed to a walk in tandem.

"Please." Josh followed him to the water fountain, skin prickling from exertion and adrenaline, grateful for the chance to catch his breath and regain his composure.

Tyler stepped aside to let Josh at the fountain. As he did, he pulled off his dripping shirt and tucked it into his waistband. "So damn hot." A crisp dark treasure trail rose to his perfect navel. As Tyler wiped his mouth with the back of his hand, he shot Josh a flirtatious grin that made Josh's stomach flip.

Josh practically lunged for the water and tried to keep his eyes on the spigot, not on the span of tan muscle a few inches away.

Unintentional, right? Was Tyler feeling the same magnetic pull, or was it all just wishful thinking?

They traded places again for round two at the fountain. As they guzzled water and wiped sweat from their brows, laughter came easier.

Josh soaked up every crinkle-eyed grin Tyler offered like a desert tasting rain. Tyler didn't put his soaking shirt back on, and little by little Josh got used to seeing all of him up close and impossible.

"Thanks for putting me back together again today," Tyler said, sincerity muffling his voice. "I was in a bad way. I think I needed this. You."

"Anytime," Josh replied, struggling to keep his voice steady. "We make a good team."

"Agreed." Tyler's gaze lingered on Josh's face for a moment longer than necessary. "We really do."

"So, think you've got your legs back under you now? Let's take it again, but at a more chill pace," Josh suggested, worried about his bulge but keeping his eyes on Tyler. Lord, he smelled good. "No racing. Take it down. Less Buttercup. More Blossom."

"Deal," Tyler agreed, bumping shoulders with Josh like they were old friends.

They took off around the track again, slower this time. Josh matched Tyler's labored pace, stealing sideways glances, still tingling from their charged proximity. The safe distance between them now felt scarier than wet, bare skin and racing pulses.

As they ran, the light conversation flowed with long stretches of comfortable silence. With each footfall, Josh's heart swelled with a mixture of joy and uncertainty. He couldn't help but enjoy the easy camaraderie they'd fallen into. Even minimal acquaintance was way better than silent infatuation.

The sun climbed behind the haze of clouds, and around seven, the parking lot tide started to come in as the school geared up for another day. Josh noticed Tyler's breathing had returned to normal, and his earlier discomfort seemed to have vanished. Relief washed over him, then a pang of disappointment as he realized their run was coming to an end.

As students began to arrive for the school day, their laughter and chatter floated through the crisp morning air. Despite the growing clamor, Josh found himself lost in Tyler's warm solidity and the friendly tangle of their conversation.

Josh tried to focus on the rhythmic sound of their shoes hitting the track and the cool breeze brushing against his skin, but his thoughts kept drifting back to Tyler, his deep laughter, his wounded eyes, and the sense that a door between them had been unlocked. He wouldn't risk their fledgling friendship over something that might only exist in his imagination.

"Hey, you all right?" Tyler asked, squinting as he glanced over at Josh.

"I'm good. So good. Great, actually," Josh replied, forcing a smile.

"Just checking." Tyler patted him on the back.

Josh glanced at his watch and sighed. "About that time. Carver asked me to come by his office."

"Last lap, then. I don't want to make you tardy." Tyler knocked into him, chuckling.

"We're fine." His heart raced. His mind raced. If this was a second chance, was he blowing it? This was going to take some getting used to, being up close and personal with Tyler. But so far, the reality had only deepened the fantasy.

As they rounded the final bend of the track, Josh pushed to finish strong, and Tyler kept pace with him. Their feet stuttered to a walk at the finish line as they tried to cool down. They both panted and kept moving, their legs jerky with exhaustion. Josh bent forward for a moment, and sweat dripped onto the grass.

When he straightened, Tyler was watching him intently. "That's what I'm talking about." Tyler winked and felt his own pulse. "Nice one, Coach."

"Same," Josh began, deciding to make the attempt. "We could do some stretching. It'll help keep your muscles limber."

"Sounds good," Tyler agreed with a nod, his hazel eyes meeting Josh's for a moment.

They stepped down onto the scrubby grass of the football field. Josh ran through simple stretches, muscles releasing slowly as the school woke up on the other side of the fence.

Tyler followed each movement stiffly, frustration playing across his handsome features with every twinge and pull as they reached, twisted, and gently urged the muscles to let go. Josh ached to smooth away that pain somehow.

"You're okay, Ty," he said in a low voice. He put his hand on Tyler's huge back, feeling his ribs rise and fall. "Take a breath. You just have so much muscle mass it needs a moment to give in."

Tyler nodded, scowling, but little by little, the tension released. He grunted in pleasure. "Oh yeah. God, that's better."

The two of them mimicked each other's movements. Now long shadows fell across the track as they worked in tandem, occasionally balancing against each other like bona fide teammates.

Josh demonstrated a standing stretch by grabbing his ankle and pulling his foot toward his glutes. He extended a hand. "Quadriceps?"

Tyler just chuckled with a sheepish grin and let himself be pulled up. "They're killing me, thanks for asking."

"Let's give it a shot."

As he started the stretch, Tyler lost his balance, bumping into Josh. He caught himself on Josh's shoulder. His big fingers gripped the muscle hard, his spicy scent everywhere. Before he could second-guess the impulse, Josh covered Tyler's fumbling fingers with his own, applied a firmer pressure, and leaned his body in to increase the stretch.

"Now hamstrings." He demonstrated, bringing his own chest toward his knee, feeling the pleasant pull.

Heat rolled off Tyler's broad torso, stirring a treacherous yearning in Josh's belly, but he kept his voice as steady as he could. "Easy. Easy does it. Take it slow."

"Ugh. Jeez." Tyler grunted, trembling with effort. "C'mon, you bastard hams.... My ass and legs have always been so overdeveloped. Tree trunks."

"No kidding, Fantana. I've seen the memes." Not for nothing, Tyler's outrageous bubble butt had gone viral many times over. Even back in high school, the junk in his trunk was a part of his myth. Feeling emboldened by their banter, Josh leaned right across Tyler's back with his own torso, using his weight as firm counterbalance, the sweat sliding between them.

Tyler froze at the contact, then sank deeper into the stretch with a groan. "Oh damn... that's it! Oh my—Jesus.... Good. Ooof." Relief flooded his scratchy voice. His eyes closed, and he grunted in raw, rumbling, extended animal pleasure.

Suddenly Josh's shorts were way too small to do their job properly, but Josh stayed put and took his time helping Tyler balance himself, wallowing in the casual intimacy of the moment.

Too soon, Tyler eased out of the stretch with a satisfied sigh. When he twisted to grin at Josh, their faces only inches apart, time collapsed to single matched heartbeats. Then Josh broke the sudden tension by springing upright abruptly and pacing backward toward the gym.

Tyler looked confused. "I should probably get a move on too. I've got an appointment with my new shrink."

"Hey, don't forget to hydrate after all this, okay? Throughout the day even," Josh teased gently, trying to mask the bittersweet emotions churning in him.

"Oh yeah. And my big banana." Tyler winked.

Josh shrugged and chuckled. "I don't want to find you lying in a fetal ball in the lot tomorrow morning because you acted stupid."

"Deal." Tyler laughed, then wiped his face and his wet chest. "I think I need a shower."

Josh froze. "Uhh, sure."

"Nah. Kids are here, and that means phones, which means pics and video. Bummer. Last thing I need is nudes in the tabloids when I'm this run-down."

Josh rolled his eyes. "Tyler, you're in amazing shape. You know that, right? You have an eight-pack."

"No, you know what I mean. NFL shape." Tyler huffed a rueful laugh through his nose. "I know it up here." He tapped his head. "But in here...." He thumped a fist over his heart.

Josh nodded. He knew plenty about that.

Tyler raised his eyes longingly at the doors to the locker room. "I've got to admit… a hot shower beating on my skin sounds like heaven right now."

Don't say it. "We got a grown-up shower. You could use my office. You know, if you wanted," Josh suggested, heart drumming. He was torn between wanting Tyler wet, naked, and alone versus Tyler safely headed home to his own place. He didn't need any further temptation.

"Twist my *arm*. But you got work." Tyler's eyes twinkled with humor and something more—something that made Josh's heart hammer. "Wishful thinking. I should get home."

"Well…." Off that smile, Josh had an outrageous impulse to invite Tyler to hang out. He didn't want to waste his shot, but he didn't want to jump the gun either. Instead, he crossed his arms and used his best coach voice. "Good job today, Fantana."

"Thanks for looking out for me, Coach."

"Anytime, superstar," Josh shot back playfully, nudging Tyler's shoulder as they approached the parking lot.

"Seriously, though," Tyler continued in a lowered voice. "I appreciate it. You're… you're a good guy."

"Thanks," Josh replied, feeling the heat rise in his cheeks. "You are too."

"You don't even know, man." Tyler just kept smiling at him. The moment felt both surreal and all too real.

Before Josh could dwell on the implications of their exchange, they arrived at Tyler's car. As Tyler fumbled with his keys, Josh took a deep breath, gathering the courage for what he knew he needed to say.

"Tyler," he began, his voice dipping, "I'm glad you're doing this."

"Me too," Tyler admitted, his gaze softening. "I really dig the quiet, but it's great to talk too. To you, I mean. I didn't know if I was allowed to talk to you."

"Allowed? Of course you can. It's been a long time since I felt comfortable training *with* someone."

"Same." Tyler nodded back at him, toeing the asphalt. "It's been… well, it's been a miracle, actually."

"Good." Josh nodded, relief washing over him. Maybe, just maybe, there was a chance for something more between them. "Same. Morning runs have always been sacred for me."

"Exactly how I feel." Tyler's famous smile spread across his face. He smacked Josh's shoulder, his hand lingering a heartbeat too long. "I think this means we're officially running buddies now. With big bananas."

"Looks that way," Josh agreed gently. "But you promised to take it easy and listen to your body. No weird jock masochism?"

"Deal." Tyler nodded, his hand lingering on the car door for a moment. Then he climbed inside with some winces and groans. "Well, tomorrow morning, I guess."

"Count on it," Josh replied, then glanced at his watch. He didn't have time to rinse before he swung by Carver's office.

Tomorrow can't come fast enough.

In Hamilton High's main office, the smell of stale coffee and fresh photocopies filled the air. He hesitated in the doorway, still toweling his face.

Why would Principal Carver summon him this early?

"Hey, hot stuff!" Vicky called out, cradling the phone between her shoulder and cheek. Her eyes twinkled mischievously as she winked at him. "He'll be just a sec."

"Vick, you leave that nice boy alone." This from Otis, the school's janitor, who was wiping down the office windows.

Josh couldn't help but smile at the flirty receptionist, wondering what wild theory she'd come up with about their imaginary romance this time.

"Can't blame a girl for trying, though." Vicky knew he was gay. The flirting had become a kind of friendly game she played to lighten the mood and let him know she had his back. She'd even set him up on a blind date with her cousin the bookkeeper three years ago.

Just then Myra Waxman poked her head in and frowned at the sight of him. "If you can spare me a moment, Mr. Ayres." Why did she look so put out? "I wanted a word."

Just in time, Vicky rescued him. "Head on through." Glancing in Myra's direction, she gave a comedic grimace. Every year Myra got another bee in her bonnet and wanted everyone involved.

Otis chuckled, scratching his graying beard. "Luck," he said in a low voice, his eyes serious. Vicky flirting, Myra waiting to scold him, and now this? Something was up.

"Got a minute, Josh?" Principal Carver poked his head out of his office, his dark skin contrasting with the light blue door.

As Josh passed, Vicky offered a nervous, silent thumbs-up. Her encouragement did little to quell the rising anxiety within him. What was this meeting about?

Carver gestured to the chair across from his cluttered desk. "It's bad news. Not athletics, but I want you to hear it from me first."

Ominous. Swallowing again, he nodded and sank into the chair, his mind darting through every possible scenario.

"So...." Carver rubbed his temples wearily. "The library. The busybody brigade has gotten permission to shut it down entirely."

"What?" Josh felt the blood drain from his face. "What now?"

Carver clicked and reclicked his pen. "You warned me. I should have taken these people more seriously."

"A crusade." Josh stiffened and felt like his heart had fallen through the floor. "I knew they'd try. When Mr. Dobbins first complained about *Heartstopper*, I knew."

"Well, last night they got to *Maus* and *Beloved*. Pretty nasty." The principal wiped his face.

"Oh. Jesus." Josh scowled. He knew all too well how quickly "concerned" citizens and book-banning could snowball into something dangerous. "Revolution of the Stupids."

"The board voted on a new list of titles. Boom. But then Suarez called an executive session and threw us out of the room."

Josh rolled his eyes. "Passing the buck and caving to bullies, as usual."

Carver held up a folded piece of paper. "I just got the memo. End of term, they're closing the doors pending review."

"Phil, kids have a right to access books and information." Josh struggled to keep his indignation under control. "You got to be kidding me."

"It kills me." Carver looked utterly defeated. "We fought them hard on this, Josh. Assholes with too much time on their hands."

"Well, my degree is in history. And let me tell you, it always starts with books...." He held Carver's gaze long enough to make his meaning plain.

Carver's eyes met his in unspoken understanding. Objections to *undesirables* would come next. "Any ugliness, I need to know pronto."

"Students have a right to read." Josh was stiff with rage. "You realize the kids will flip out. *All* the kids. Especially the ones whose parents did this."

Carver frowned. "Then we all need to keep our eyes open. Any backlash from students, any attacks on faculty or staff, you come to me immediately. Intolerance has no place in education."

"But it's a school. We're a school. We've got the only library for twenty miles." Josh rubbed his eyes. The Hamilton High library had been his safe haven most of his teenage years. He'd spent hours and hours curled up in there trying to make sense of his world. He'd crammed for tests and written every paper in those kiosks. He shook his head in impotent disgust. "Idiots."

"Well, last night they axed the library budget. Meredith and Stan will work through end of term, but then... pfft." He opened his fingers like the librarians were evaporating before his eyes.

Josh nodded, his mind churning and his stomach in knots. What was Carver working up to? "It's a crusade, Phil. Next thing they'll want to shutter the whole school."

"Oh, I don't think they're that crazy." Carver sighed, folding his hands on the desk. He leaned back in his chair, clicking and reclicking his pen again. "Tyler Fantana doing okay with the facilities?"

Even hearing the name made him smile. "Oh yeah. Tyler's recovery is... slow but steady. He's... uh—" Josh froze. He didn't want his face to give anything private away, so he pivoted. "An NFL pro around the place? I got kids who never played so much as Ping-Pong volunteering around the gym, but fame makes people nuts. Makes my job a heck of a lot easier."

"Love it." Obviously Carver was circling to something else. "So he has a way with a crowd."

"Like you can't imagine." Josh shrugged. "At a minimum, litter is down, and everyone's suddenly started washing their gym clothes more often. Win-win from where I'm sitting."

Carver laughed. "Having an MVP defending literacy and diversity might make a difference. He's beloved around here. A real hometown hero."

So that was it. Carver hoped their homegrown NFL star would run library interference before the clock ran out. *Except tight ends are offense.*

"Tyler's still recovering, sir," he said gently. "I'm not sure he's ready to step into the spotlight."

"If he's feeling grateful, a few well-placed interviews, some op-eds... could keep our library open."

Josh shifted his weight, considering. He wanted to keep Tyler from getting snagged in this local mess. He'd been staying out of the limelight since he'd come home. Last thing Tyler needed was local drama. But Carver made an excellent point: a famous local who was not exactly straight, not exactly white. Tyler's support might turn the tide.

Josh's phone buzzed insistently in his pocket. "My gym class. I should get going." He ran a hand through his hair, exhaling sharply.

"I don't want to overstep," Carver began. "But the one and only Captain Fantastic might remind this town what matters. And what shouldn't."

He didn't come right out and say, *We're both minorities*, but the unspoken danger seemed palpable.

"Agree, sir." Josh had never dragged his personal life into the school, but there are no secrets in a small town. He met Carver's eyes. "I'll see where he's at, but I don't want to push."

Carver clapped Josh on the back. "I appreciate it."

Josh took a deep breath as he left Carver's office and then navigated the halls back toward the gym, his mind muddled and messy. Despite his reservations, Josh had to try.

Tyler would be there at sunup. Josh just had to figure a way to broach the subject.

A whistle pierced the air and a couple of Josh's students came bounding up to him, breaking his train of thought. A short boy named Miguel said, "Yo, Coach, for real. I thought I was late."

Josh laughed and bobbed his head. "Then I better hustle, huh?" The junior coach was already taking attendance and herding the kids toward the doors.

"We going to start class or what?" asked DeSean, balancing a football on his index finger.

Josh squared his shoulders, back in coach mode. "Sorry, gentlemen, be right there." He took a deep breath and let it out slowly.

He swung by his desk to change his sweaty shirt and then trotted out to the field. As he stepped outside, the afternoon sun momentarily blinded him.

He could do this. For the team, for his town, for himself.

Chapter Five

AFTER TWO weeks of meeting Josh each morning, Tyler had slipped into a routine that got him up while the moon still hung over the streets of Cinnamar.

Barely pausing to turn on a light, he'd shower, shave, and pull on running shorts and one of the baggy T-shirts he usually kept for off-season training camp.

Keeping quiet, he'd head to the kitchen, accompanied by Mr. Poops.

The marmalade tabby had nominated himself as Tyler's sous chef but in actuality wasn't much more than a warm, squeaky kibble addict who demanded food first and then rewarded him by rolling around on his back and watching with huge, devoted orange eyes as Tyler cooked and fed himself woefully healthy food.

Usually by the time Nadia made it to the kitchen, Tyler would be drinking a second glass of OJ with Poops purring on his lap, soaking up the affection. Tyler would chat with his sister for a bit as she ate her plate of eggs or waffles, and then head to the school track, wolfing down a big banana on the way like Josh had told him.

He'd never been a morning person, but for some reason this cheerful rhythm had put a fire under his tail. As a web designer, Nadia worked from home, so he did her errands after the run on the way home from the Hamilton track.

Just having a routine to follow and Josh's friendly face to look forward to had made a huge difference. All day long, the run kept him pleasantly sore, and he'd even started doing some minimal weight training at Hamilton in the afternoons after school got out, when the teams were at practice and he had the whole place to himself. Josh even had him stretching now, although to be honest sometimes the stretching gave him a boner because of the associations.

Best of all, he hadn't had a panic attack in six days.

When Tyler pulled out of the drive, the sky was still deep blue, and the headlights clicked on automatically. When he parked at Hamilton, Josh met him with a happy wave.

It felt like magic. Each night, he went to sleep satisfied and woke up psyched.

Today, the early morning air was foggy as Tyler and Josh ran side by side around the rubberized track. The rhythmic sound of their footsteps, accompanied by the muffled hush, wove a soothing cocoon for them.

"Hey, remember that time in high school when Nadia tried out for the cheerleading squad?" Tyler asked, his breath coming in short huffs. "She just *knew* she had it in the bag, but during her audition, she turned left instead of right and took out half the girls with her." He snickered.

Josh chuckled, shaking his head and grimacing. "Yeah. Messy! But Nadia didn't let that stop her. She just laughed and picked herself right back up. Spirit in spades, for sure."

"She's always been like that," Tyler agreed, a surge of affection warming him. "Like our mom. She never lets anything get her down for long."

As they continued their run, Tyler couldn't stop stealing glances at Josh. He'd always been attractive in a boyish way, but seeing him now—grown, fit, confident—stirred up stuff Tyler hadn't felt in… well, a long time. He felt alive, or at least as alive as you can be with a battered ego and a heart that stutters.

Still, there was more to it than just physical attraction. Tyler admired this guy so much—the way Josh carried himself, his kindness and courage with the kids, standing up for his coworkers. Nadia had mentioned something—apparently some local nutjobs were hassling the school librarian, and he had a sense that the bullying and scrutiny weighed heavily on Josh. He wished he could help somehow, return the favor.

Josh never wavered. He didn't coach by demanding things or scolding his students, but by doing the thing he expected from others. If you want kids to try, you show them what trying looks like. If you want a team to win, you play harder. If you want bullies to back down, you face them.

"Your pace has improved a lot. And your stamina, since our first run," Josh said, pulling Tyler out of his thoughts.

"Not that much."

"That much. Maybe it's your big banana." Josh did have a dimple, after all.

Tyler opened his mouth to joke but then hesitated as he searched for the real words. "I just want you to know that I really appreciate these morning runs. Coming out here every day has helped more than you can imagine."

"Good. Of course. I got you," Josh replied with a quick smile.

"Thanks."

"You've come pretty damn far in a couple weeks, Fantana. Someone might start to think you're a professional athlete." His dark blue eyes sparkled.

"Thanks to you," Tyler replied. His eyes stung, so he turned to watch the track ahead. "Couldn't have done it without you, Ayres. I mean it."

Josh chuckled and pushed ahead a bit, forcing them both to work just that little bit harder.

As they rounded another lap, Tyler bit his tongue. He was fighting hard against the growing attraction he felt for Josh, because he was afraid of what it meant—for his career, for his future, and for their time together as long as he could make that last.

In general, Tyler had always acted on impulse, jumping into situations and then figuring out the mess after. But the past week especially, he'd struggled like hell to keep his natural urges in check. For whatever dumb reason, running alongside Josh each morning made him feel like maybe, just maybe, something might work out between them.

If Josh wanted it, that is. He wasn't so sure.

Josh bumped into him, his damp arm sliding along Tyler's. "What's up?"

"You're so quiet this morning." Tyler shook his head. "Everything okay in your neck of the woods?"

"Uh, yeah. Yeah, we're good." Josh sounded stiff and looked away, focusing on the track before them.

"If something's bothering you, you can talk to me. You know that, right?" Tyler didn't want to pry, but he hoped Josh felt like he could share whatever was bugging him. "If I can help at all."

"Of course. Just... I don't know, school politics. Work crap. Nothing worth you worrying about it," Josh replied, his voice hesitant and guarded.

"Work? Like coaching? You seem pretty amazing, from what I seen," Tyler pressed, hoping to break through Josh's defenses.

"Thanks. It's just… complicated." Josh sighed, still not meeting Tyler's gaze.

"Complicated how? Maybe talking about it might help," Tyler encouraged gently. This had to be the library thing preying on him. He wanted to be there for Josh, just as Josh had been there for him.

"Maybe some other time," Josh finally said, shaking his head. "Right now, let's just focus on the run. Getting somewhere good, huh?"

"All right, but remember, I'm here for you if and when talking makes sense." Tyler couldn't help but wonder what the real trouble was. Maybe this library mess was worse than Nadia suspected. He'd do some digging today after Dr. Bailey.

Josh nodded, guarded gaze on the ground. "I appreciate it."

"For that matter, we could also just hang out and take your mind off. You know? Meet up and do something that doesn't involve running? I mean, I love this, but even meatheads can have a life off the field. Buddies. You know." Asking it out loud made Tyler feel pitiful.

"Uh, sure. That sounds… nice," Josh replied hesitantly, a hint of surprise in his tone.

"Cool." Tyler beamed and pressed the advantage. "You mentioned you like hiking, right?"

"Love it." Josh's face brightened for a moment before he quickly hid his enthusiasm behind a neutral expression.

Something was definitely eating at him. "Perfect. We could go on a hike this weekend. Palomar, maybe. Even Mesa Grande or out in the desert. Great trails around here." Tyler tried to sound casual, but his heart galloped at the thought of spending more time with Josh.

"Maybe," Josh said noncommittally, looking thoughtful. "We got games all season. My schedule at this time of year is…." He didn't finish the thought.

"Play it by ear," Tyler reassured him. He decided to change the subject, hoping to ease some of the odd tension. What kind of school politics could there be out here in the boonies?

Josh seemed to pick up on his frustration and changed the subject. "So, I been doing a little research on cardiac rehab. Nothing nuts, but in general. Interesting, as it happens. I found some exercises that might help." He shrugged. "Not that I'm an expert or anything, but if I can help."

"I appreciate you taking the time." Tyler's heart swelled with gratitude. "It means a lot."

"Duh. I just want you to get better, Tyler," Josh replied softly, finally raising his guarded eyes.

"You're the best." No matter how many walls he had to bust through, Tyler was determined to get to the bottom of Josh's weird funk.

Josh made a goofy face at him. "No, dummy. According to ESPN, *you're* the best. The Tightest End in the USA."

"Piss off." Tyler changed tack. "Actually, Dr. Reynolds mentioned that I should try a Mediterranean diet. You know, lots of vegetables, grains, whole foods… that kind of stuff."

"Seems like a good idea," Josh agreed with a nod.

"Right? And it's always more fun to cook for someone else," Tyler hinted. "Maybe we could give it a whack together sometime?"

"Well…." Josh hesitated, his expression hard to read. "I don't know about *that*. I'm actually a pretty rotten cook, to be honest."

"Hey, same," Tyler laughed, hoping to put him at ease. "But that's part of the adventure, right? We already know we're good at tandem training." He indicated the track around them.

"True," Josh said, his tone cautious and guarded. "Let me see."

"Of course." Tyler sighed. Something personal was eating away at Josh. Maybe it was more than the library deal. "Look… I know something's bugging you. I'm here if you need help. Deal?"

"Thanks," Josh murmured, offering a weak smile. "I appreciate that."

"Anytime." Tyler dropped it. Josh would open up when he felt ready.

The silence stretched between them, not unpleasant but definitely awkward. A vague, unspoken *something* hung heavy in the air over the pound of their feet hitting the track. The surrounding landscape seemed to mirror Tyler's disappointment. The silvery green colors of the early morning now appeared clammy, and the muggy air made him wish he'd just stayed under the covers.

Oppressive unspoken tension, but Tyler kept his mouth shut. Anything he said would only make things worse, obviously. He couldn't force Josh to open up, but it was hard not to feel frustrated by the distance between them. Even the isolation of the track, the two of them so removed from the school, the town, and their actual real lives, felt fake and impersonal.

Tyler had always hated television cameras for the same reason. Some loud flack barking questions stuck a piece of equipment in your face and you were supposed to chat with it like a friend, a fan. The team had sent him for media training and interview coaching, but staring into a lens always felt *so* bogus.

He loved his fans. He volunteered for charity visits and school talks. He knew how much sports and fame meant to kids struggling in a small town. He'd been one not so long ago. Nevertheless, he couldn't stand all the technical TV flimflam that was supposed to bring him closer to people trapped on their couches.

Josh was two feet away and might as well have been on the other side of the moon. Jogging in tense silence next to a man he genuinely liked—more than liked, even—and not addressing the big gay elephant in the room felt the same.

Without warning, Josh stopped running, walking to a halt. Tyler went back to him, still confused but trying to give him whatever space he needed. In the parking lot, the students had begun to show up in earnest. Tyler just waited, watching Josh's handsome, worried face.

Finally, after what felt like an eternity, Josh broke the silence. His voice wavered with the vulnerability he'd been trying so hard to hide. "There's something I've been meaning to ask... but I wasn't sure how to bring it up. But you did. Well, not exactly, but I think you'll get it."

"Hey," Tyler whispered and bobbed his head as if giving permission for anything, everything Josh wanted. "You can tell me anything, okay? I'm here for you too."

Josh swallowed hard and wiped his flushed face. "It's about Hamilton. Not just me, even. The library."

"Nadia told me a little bit."

"Banning books. Like, *diverse* books. Black, Brown, LGBT, Jewish, you name it. All the stuff you'd expect. Pretty gross. Local jerks."

"Oh. Oh jeez." Tyler nodded. He knew all about small minds in small towns. Assholes sprang up like weeds anywhere you let them. "Whatever you need. Count me in."

"We've been under a lot of pressure from the kind of people who have strong opinions and lots of time to meddle, and Principal Carver thought that if you—maybe if you could say something or do something supportive, it might help. It's just...." He trailed off, seemingly unsure of how to continue.

"Something?" Tyler's heart pounded. Protective anger washed through him, churning in his belly. "You just have to ask. Josh, I'd say anything you want. I mean it. I got a publicist who hasn't done jack in three months. Team publicist too. What kind of thing? Name it, buddy."

Josh looked up at him. "Well, something positive about books. Or tolerance. Even *diversity* at the school. Inclusion and not being stupid bigots." He shrugged, his eyes hollow and haunted. "I'm sorry. It's just so gross. I feel gross even asking, but someone is going to get hurt."

"Don't apologize," Tyler urged. "Swear to God, that's an easy one. That's personal for me anyways. I can't stand bullies."

Josh's mouth and brow tightened. "It's just I know you've been staying out of sight. Since the accident, I mean. Recuperating. I didn't want to mess with any of that. Put you in the line of fire. But it's getting ugly." He looked across the field at the school and the town beyond.

"Oh. Got it." He did. Now he understood. Josh had been protecting him, not dodging him. "Are they only after the Hamilton library?"

"Mmh. Yeah. Well, so far." Josh wiped his forehead. "Look, last thing you need is more drama. And I didn't want to impose or make you feel obligated." His eyes seemed to search Tyler's for understanding.

"Hey. Joshua. Hey. I am your friend." Tyler squeezed his shoulder. His mind raced as he flicked through favors he could use and calls he could make. "Seriously. I'm glad you told me. Are you kidding? Believe me, I've had people ask me for way, way, *way* worse. Like illegal and immoral worse. You're not imposing, and I'd be honored to help you, the library, and the school. I'd do anything for you."

Josh looked startled. "Thanks."

"Frankly, it's the least I can do, and the Swells will be ecstatic. Football grunt standing up for literacy? This is a win-win from where they're sitting. We'll nuke them. Watch. You're not alone, Josh. You say the word, I'm here for you, remember?"

"Thank you," Josh whispered, a grateful smile breaking through his anxiety. "Your support means... a lot, Tyler." His searing blue eyes were teary and unguarded.

Tyler almost kissed him then, or something just as scary or foolish. He almost gathered Josh into his arms and held him the way he wanted. Surely Josh felt this too. Instead, he smiled back at Josh, hoping this moment of vulnerability had taught him that Tyler could be trusted.

Just as Tyler was about to suggest they finish the last couple of laps, his phone buzzed in the pocket of his shorts. He fumbled for it and saw Boris Jarlson's name flash on the screen. With an apologetic glance at Josh, he reluctantly answered.

"Mr. Jarlson. I was just talking about you." He tried to keep the irritation out of his voice. He hated being pulled away from Josh right now, but Boris wrote the checks.

"Fantana! How's our MVP's recovery coming along?" Boris boomed, not even bothering with a proper greeting.

"Recuperation is going well, thanks. I found this sports medicine genius who's been kicking my ass every morning before sunrise." He pointed at Josh, who rolled his eyes but grinned at the compliment, with the dimple no less. "Back in the gym, even."

"Good, good. Only the best. Whatever you need, kid. I'm just calling to bust your balls." Boris sounded distracted. Then again, he might be calling from the golf course or one of his ex-wives' condos. He was always somewhat distracted.

Tyler held up a finger at Josh to let him know it would take a minute. "Funny enough, I was just singing your praises. Well, the Swells', but by extension, yours too. I've got a lead on some good local PR for the team." He winked at Josh.

A yelp and a stumble from the other end of the call. "Stupid thing." Boris wheezed at whatever it was as he moved around. "Here's the deal. The coaches and I were talking over you too. I'm just sharing the love. Nobody is you, huh. Tightest End in the NFL, right?"

"Right." Tyler nodded. He knew his rep as a player in the league. He wasn't as great as Gronk or Travis Kelce, but he was getting closer all the time. What Jarlson missed most was the merchandising and licensing. They'd even tried to trademark that sleazy "Tightest End" slogan until Tyler's agent threatened them. The Swells used Tyler as a beefcake poster boy every chance they got. With Tyler in his thirties now, winning games was gravy.

Boris chuckled and sighed. "All sort of plans, we got, but nobody wants to bug you. What I'm saying is, Miratto is doing fine, but he ain't you, huh? Crossed eyes and a flat ass."

"Uh, no. I guess not." He scowled. He saw Josh noticing it and wished he could explain or reassure him. He closed his eyes and tried to focus on the smell of the grass, the pleasant soreness in his legs, the warmth of Josh close beside him.

Boris got to the point. "Any chance you might be ready before end of the season?"

The abrupt question squeezed Tyler's chest like a giant calloused fist. All the pressure of returning to the NFL and walking away from Josh held him tight and shook him. Here was the real reason for this friendly call from the owner.

Tyler started to pace, just to keep his muscles moving and his mouth shut. In the background, he could see Josh's worried eyes, clearly picking up the vibe from Tyler's half of the conversation.

Boris pushed harder. "All I'm saying, the hot second you're ready, the Swells are eager to get you back out on that field. Even if it's just a couple plays in the last game, some camera time for the fans. A wave and a couple passes. Nothing strenuous, but to show you're back, all new and improved."

"Uhh, loud and clear. I'm still working with my doctors and my genius, Mr. Jarlson. I can't promise anything definite." Tyler knew full well what Boris wanted to hear. "But believe you me, I'm really putting in the hours, sir."

"Good man! Just remember, we've got your back, kid. And your front," Boris said, his voice soggy with insincerity. "Take care of yourself, but don't forget where you belong."

"Sure thing, Boris," Tyler replied, biting back the urge to snark. He hung up and shoved his phone into his pocket with more force than necessary.

Josh touched his arm. "You okay?"

Tyler nodded. "I'm thirty-three years old and he still calls me a kid. Captain Fantastic, my ass."

"Hey. Hey. We're okay. You're going to be okay. I promise. Cross my heart."

As they continued their run, Tyler couldn't shake the looming feeling of uncertainty. He knew he couldn't put his life on hold indefinitely, but the thought of leaving this, of going back, was almost unbearable. For better or worse, San Diego was dead ahead. For now, he decided to focus on the present and cherish every second he had left. He would help Josh and fight for the library while he got strong enough to do whatever the hell came next.

Tyler nodded. "Look, I know I've got to do what I've got to do with football and all, but right now, it's you and me."

Josh glanced over at him, a small smile playing on his lips. "Okay?"

"What do you say?" Tyler grinned. "Let's plan something off the track, away from our morning runs. You know, hang out."

"Really?" Josh hesitated for a moment before nodding. "Sure. I'm in. Absolutely. Though hiking might be a bit ambitious at the moment. Any ideas?"

"Actually, I was hoping you'd have some," Tyler admitted, chuckling. "It's been a minute since I spent any real time around this place."

"Well...." Josh squinted at the horizon, "We could go to Hearthstone. Or I know this little tourist trap farm stand about thirty-five or forty miles up the interstate. They got fresh peppers, weird crafts, and the best jalapeño cornbread you've *never* had. Some food trucks. If nothing else, it's great people-watching. Not anything fancy, but maybe a quick road trip?"

"Road trip!" Tyler smacked his arm. "Perfect. Maybe I can pick up a couple healthy ingredients. Is cornbread on a Mediterranean diet?"

"We'll get you hooked up." Josh looked dubious but happy.

Even if Josh didn't know it, Tyler planned to spend every second he had left in this town living his life the way he wanted. He couldn't remember the last time he'd gone out with someone because he liked them, instead of staging racy pictures for his publicist to post on Instagram.

They finished their run, and Josh walked Tyler back to his car. "How about Saturday, then?" Josh thumped his hood as Tyler climbed inside.

Tyler rolled down his window to say, "Well that, Mr. Ayres, is a date." He winked at Josh and pulled away, grinning to himself, before Josh could react.

Halfway home, he realized their road trip was exactly that: a date. He had a date with Joshua Ayres.

Chapter Six

JOSH'S HEART raced as he pulled up to Tyler's house; the familiar red brick exterior unleashed a flood of memories.

He'd biked past this place too many times to count, back when he'd been too young and horny to know how weird that looked. For two whole years, he'd swing by just on the off chance he'd see Tyler or get to know something about him. Even Nadia hadn't known about how often, and once they became friends, he'd been too ashamed to confess it.

Taking a deep breath, he climbed out of his truck and rang the doorbell.

"Josh!" Nadia greeted him warmly, her dark eyes sparkling with excitement. "Tyler's taking his sweet time getting dressed. Come on in."

"Thanks," Josh said, stepping inside. The first time he'd actually set foot in this place, Tyler had already graduated. Nadia had invited him over to cram for a physics midterm, and they ended up study buddies the next two years. "I know I haven't been around. Sorry it's been so long."

"Life, huh? You don't have to punch a clock. You're my friend."

"Thanks." Josh nodded.

"I want to thank you for what you've done for…." Nadia jerked her chin toward the bedrooms. "You saved him."

Josh shrugged. "He's been working pretty hard."

"Uh-huh." Her gaze held him for a long moment, steady and knowing, before she turned to the fridge. A high-pitched sound came from the pantry. "That's Mr. Poops."

At first Josh had no idea what she was talking about, and then he felt something weave between and around his legs. Sure enough, a plush orange tabby with a fluffy plume of a tail looked up at him with giant eyes and squeaked plaintively, like a starving orphan in an infomercial. "Mr. Poops?"

"Don't believe any of his pity-party con job. He pretends he's starving, but he's eaten his weight in kibble the past six hours." She bent and scooped up the cat, cradling him against her chest. "He tricks Tyler into double feeding him because *someone* is a big mushball. Isn't he, Poops?" The cat started purring and rubbing his face against her throat and ear. "Can I get you anything? Coffee? Breakfast?"

"Actually, I plan to drag your brother to eat up at Tia Tamale," Josh replied, feeling his cheeks warm under her scrutiny. "Or, uhh, you could come with. I mean, if you want."

"I'm good. It's all good. I love that place." Nadia's lips curved into a teasing smile. "Tyler could use someone to count on right now." She paused, her eyes twinkling. "Someone special."

"Hang on." Josh swallowed hard. "I'm just trying to help."

"Of course you are, Joshua." She patted him on the arm affectionately before turning away, leaving him to wonder how much she remembered about his feelings for her brother. "And I'm just trying to help you."

"Sorry."

Just then, Tyler appeared at the top of the stairs. His damp brown hair looked almost black, his shirt stretched by the muscle. His shoulders seemed to brush the walls of the small hallway.

"Hey, man! You ready?" Tyler asked, his hazel eyes alight with anticipation.

"Absolutely," Josh replied, glancing at Nadia and her blissed-out con-artist cat. "Let's hit the road."

"Play nice, boys," Nadia called after them as they headed out the door.

"Was Nadia giving you crap?" Tyler asked, his gaze flicking between them.

"Nothing I can't handle," Josh replied with a grin. "Now, let's go buy some produce. We've only got an hour at the farm stand, after all."

As they climbed into the truck, Josh reminded himself to keep a lid on his feelings, past and present. He knew it wouldn't be long before Tyler split back to his fancy NFL life in San Diego and everything went back to normal, but for now, he'd savor this moment, this brief window of time when everything he'd ever hoped still felt possible.

The highway stretched out before them, a scatter of clouds casting odd shadows that slipped across the blacktop. Josh gripped the wheel of his truck, stealing glances at Tyler as they drove east toward Ocotillo Heights. Anticipation made it hard to focus on the road.

"Man, it's been ages since I've been up this way," Tyler said, gazing out the window.

"Getting out of town for a bit will be good for both of us." Although he said it casually, Josh needed this day to be perfect, to find a way to bridge the gap between them without revealing too much.

"Where's this farm stand at?"

"West of Ocotillo. I think the main building was originally built for crop storage, but stalls popped up and it grew into a farmer's market. And then a whatever-the-hell emporium."

Tyler poked him and winked. "My favorite kind."

As they pulled into the bustling farmer's market, the scent of fresh produce and spices filled the air. They hopped out and walked over to the entrance table to pay their five-buck entries. Josh noticed some double takes at Tyler's famous face, but for the most part folks left them alone.

After so many years, this place had become a huge draw for anyone within a thirty-mile radius, guaranteeing a mix of farmers, old hippies, and funky artists who gathered here each weekend to buy and sell. People milled about, examining weird handmade gifts and sampling food from various stalls. Tyler's eyes widened with excitement as they wandered through the vibrant chaos.

Josh nodded at the entrance. "I hope you're hungry."

"Can we look around first?" Tyler seemed fascinated by the cheerful mishmash of it all. His grin kept getting bigger as his eyes roamed from stall to stall.

"Of course! Trust me, you won't be disappointed," Josh replied, grinning. "They got food trucks, a swap meet, and games for the kids. They even do a maze at Halloween."

"And some kind of breakfast." Tyler sounded skeptical.

"Well... more like brunch. But delicious. There's a crepe stand inside. And Westfall Orchards does a homemade fruit-yogurt thing if you want. Or you could hold out for the real deal." Josh waggled his brows, trying to make a joke of his suggestion.

Tyler looked him up and down and smiled slowly. "Yeah? That's pretty mysterious. What does that mean exactly?"

"If you can hold out and work up an appetite, I can make it worth your while."

"I like the sound of that, Ayres." Tyler didn't laugh. Actually, he leaned in closer and his voice got husky, as though he were swapping secrets, mumbling right into Josh's ear. "I'm a sucker for delayed gratification."

The hair on Josh's neck stood up at the shivery tickle, though he kept his voice level. "That so?"

But Tyler had walked on, leaving Josh stunned in his wake.

Had Tyler just been flirting with him? That had to be serious flirting, right? Or was this like their "big banana" joke? Did bros talk like that to each other outside of porn?

"This is way more than a farm stand, though. I mean, I see some produce, but it seems more like a fancy flea market."

"You got weaving. Pottery. Taxidermy. Candy. Leatherwork. Rabbits." Josh nodded at some of the stalls in their immediate vicinity, raising his hand to a couple of vendors who knew him on sight. "You never know what'll turn up."

"Music to my ears, my man." Without warning, Tyler wrapped a heavy arm around him and squeezed him in a hard side hug. "And I brought cash for both of us."

"No, no. This is on me."

Tyler rolled his eyes. "Humor me. Who are the regulars?"

"Sometimes a local barber comes to cut hair. A bunch of local farms and orchards bring produce. That family down there makes the world's best jalapeño cornbread. Nadia's favorite."

"I didn't know that."

"Then your sister has been hiding it from you out of pure selfishness for more than ten years."

"Nadia's been here?"

"Oh God. All the time. We used to come out every weekend in high school. I even worked here one Christmas, wrapping presents. Your mom loved the strawberries from that place on the right. Huge."

"Josh?" Tyler said quietly and touched his arm. "Do you think we could stay a little longer? Just to explore some more."

"Sure." Josh tried to ignore the flutter in his chest at the prospect of spending more time together. "I'm in no hurry."

Just then, a young mom browsing a macramé stall with her kids spotted Tyler Fantana, NFL superstar.

Josh watched the whole celebrity sighting experience unfold in real time: America's Tightest End in the flesh. First the realization dawned on her face, and her whole body stiffened, like a dog seeing a steak hit the floor. The minute she decided to raise a ruckus, the whole crowd would rush them and the day would be ruined.

Josh shifted to Tyler's left to block her view and to get away from the most active cluster of stalls. Tyler didn't seem to realize he'd been spotted or clock the danger. He must be used to this kind of continual hassle from strangers. Josh stared at the woman as they approached, willing her to look up and see him.

Finally she did.

She looked from Tyler to Josh and their eyes caught. He saw the urge to interrupt sweep over her face. Holding firm, he shook his head side to side, not grinning or giving her an ounce of permission. Her face fell, but to her credit, she stayed put with a rueful nod. She watched them pass, hope and disappointment warring on her face.

Tyler never noticed.

"I never had a clue this was out here," Tyler exclaimed, picking up an intricately carved wooden lizard studded with agates.

"Maybe you had other things to think about. Games to win, girls to charm."

Tyler made a face. "Yeah. Shows you what I knew."

Josh looked at him a moment before confessing, "I always admired that. Your certainty."

"How's that?"

"You always knew exactly what you wanted. Always. You went after things. You worked like hell to make your life happen. You never hesitated or wavered. Captain Fantastic."

"Oh man!" Tyler laughed at that. "Did I have you fooled."

Josh shook his head. "C'mon."

"I did nothing but waver. Every move, every choice. After my father pissed off to wherever, my mom took everything on herself. I was just a stupid jock. The least I could do was try to make something of myself. Hell, I only started playing football because they fed us breakfast, which saved money."

Josh fought to keep his emotions under control. "Oh, Tyler."

"Don't misunderstand. I'm proud of it. Big as I am? Five breakfasts a week and away games saved my mom a hundred bucks a month."

Josh hadn't known. He knew money had been tight for the Fantanas. Nadia had hinted a few things about her awful father, and their mom working so many jobs. How had he not known? Blinded by Tyler, maybe.

They browsed the farm stand, picking up three hefty cornbreads for Nadia and some ingredients for Tyler's new Mediterranean diet. Tyler even found a handsewn rat stuffed with organic catnip. "For Mr. Poops."

As they wandered and shopped, a couple of aggressive Swells fans stopped Tyler for autographs and pictures, drawing attention to them. But Josh was quick to step in again, helping Tyler escape when needed. He couldn't help but feel a measure of pride in his ability to protect Tyler from the constant attention, even if it was just for the day.

Tyler took his time browsing, dawdling and doubling back. "I can't get over all the different vendors."

"Some are local, but some drive a couple hours coming and going because they love the vibe so much. Bands play at night, and they set up a little dance floor. People do fundraisers out here, even a kids' rodeo in the spring. It's a great place."

As they continued their exploration, Josh realized that for whatever reason, Tyler was deliberately stretching their time together. Maybe he just needed some time away from home. Josh decided to seize the opportunity and make good on his original meal offer before heading back.

"Tyler, there's an amazing tamale stand near the entrance. How about we get a bite to eat before we head home?"

"Sounds good to me!" Tyler replied enthusiastically, his eyes shining with genuine happiness.

That sweet, shared spark slipped into Josh like a match touching paper and spread through him like wildfire, and he couldn't help but think that maybe, just maybe, today would be the start of something wonderful between them.

With giant cups of fresh lemonade in hand, Tyler and Josh paused their shopping escapades to regroup. The sun blazed overhead, baking their skin as the sweet tartness quenched their thirst. Tyler's stomach let out an audible growl, making him chuckle sheepishly.

"Okay, I admit it. I'm starving," he confessed, grinning at Josh. "You're officially starving me now."

"Perfect timing. Tia Tamale is calling our name," Josh replied with a smile. "Amazing Mexican food truck near the entrance. Trust me, you're going to love it."

"Lead the way," Tyler said, his hazel eyes glimmering.

They approached the bright pink food truck.

"I didn't realize how late it was." Tyler squinted at him. "Sorry. We should've gone home an hour ago."

"No, sir. We're good."

"But I feel like I'm wasting your day."

"We're not wasting anything." Josh shook his head, chuckling. "You want to hang a while longer?" His chest tightened with pleasure at Tyler's obvious enthusiasm.

"Duh," Tyler exclaimed and poked him in the ribs.

Josh squawked with laughter and squirmed away. "Jerk."

Suddenly they were spending the whole afternoon together instead of heading home as planned. A morning had turned into an entire shared day. Josh exhaled happily. "You okay?"

Tyler eyed the crowd, shifting his weight. "Just noticing people noticing me. I should duck out, maybe." So he did pay attention to it when he had to.

"Absolutely. I got this." Josh had been tracking the wary, eager look in people's eyes as they tried to angle toward Tyler. People were pressed close and getting closer. "Anything you don't eat?"

"You're funny. Try me." Tyler snorted. "I dare you. Please. I've eaten mud, my friend, and cardboard. I've eaten salty jockstraps." He squeezed Josh's shoulder and sauntered away before Josh realized what he'd said.

He meant jockstraps on the field. Right? That was a metaphor, right? Josh wiped sweat from his face, trying not to think about Tyler in a jockstrap.

While Tyler went to claim a large rock under a stand of yucca trees, Josh stepped up to the counter and ordered a real mix: venison, quail, trout, even alligator. At least the crowd had calmed down some once the hometown heartthrob removed himself from the fray.

"This is perfect." Josh returned to Tyler with a tray piled high with steaming tamales. "You better be famished. I'm counting on you, superstar."

Tyler's eyes widened in amazement, and his grin grew even wider. "Wow, you weren't kidding about this place!" he exclaimed as they dug in.

Josh started with the quail, the rich, smoky flavor dancing on his tongue. Tyler's favorites turned out to be the venison and the alligator, of all things, although that might have been because Josh only left him one quail to try.

Tyler tried to look offended. "You're not even sorry."

Josh shook his head, chewing. "Not even a little."

"This is how you do me." Tyler pressed his hands to his heart. "Have to come back, I guess."

Tyler patted his stomach. "You've got a deal, my man."

After they finished their meal, they tossed the garbage.

"Thank you for spending so much time with me today, Josh," Tyler said sincerely. "I can't remember the last time I just goofed off like this."

"Hey, no problem," Josh replied, trying to keep his voice steady. "I'm having a blast."

A pretty server from the tamale stand approached them. "Mr. Fantana, is it okay if I ask for an autograph?"

"After that meal?" Tyler didn't flinch. "Of course. Your food is phenomenal."

"My mother's. Would you tell her that yourself? She'd just die."

"Well, hopefully not that." Tyler looked up at her. "What would you like me to sign?"

She held up a paper plate and a sharpie. "This is all I could find."

"Works for me." Tyler grinned and scrawled his jagged autograph on the plate. "Now where's your amazingly talented mama?"

She quietly led them back to the food truck and then took Tyler in the side door.

Josh shook his head at them. "I'll wait here."

From inside there was a muffled squeal and then a gabble of voices. He couldn't hear what Tyler was saying, but even without words, his exuberance and affection were completely audible. It sounded like Tyler was speaking Spanish.

A couple of moments later Tyler's dark head popped out.

Josh grinned. "Well, you just made her day."

"Are you kidding? She just made mine. Those tamales were next level." He opened his arms like he wanted to hug the whole food truck. "Phenomenal. How did I not know about this place?"

"They've been here twenty-nine years. What she didn't tell you was that her mother learned to cook from her mother." Josh sighed happily. "I used to bring anyone I could drag out to Ocotillo. Nadia's been a bunch of times."

"Not with me." Tyler pretended to be offended. "Which means there is going to be hell to pay when I get home."

Josh laughed. "Be nice. I could have brought you in high school, but we weren't friends back then."

"All my fault." Tyler draped one huge arm around his neck and tugged him close in a bro hug. "See? If I'd have known you all this time, I'd be a much happier man. Goes to show what happens when you don't act right."

Just then the young server popped her head out, beaming. "Thank you, Mr. Fantana. She's so happy. She's going to frame that photo."

"Good. You tell her I can't wait to come back."

"I didn't know you spoke Spanish. You should check out the art festival in Ocotillo Heights."

"Thanks."

She tucked her hair behind her ear. "I mean…. It's not far from here. Soon as we finish lunch, I'm, uhh, headed there myself."

Uh-oh.

Tyler nodded at her, seemingly oblivious to her obvious invitation to get a bit more personal. "Maybe we will."

On impulse, Tyler and Josh decided to visit Ocotillo as she suggested, which only extended their time together. The thrill of spontaneity surged through Josh, and he couldn't help but feel as if they were circling something special.

After lunch, they climbed back into Josh's truck and drove into town to check out the festival. The small-town square was packed with local artists, crafts, and even a dance floor, with bands playing everything from Tejano to bluegrass. The atmosphere was electric, alive with people enjoying the various attractions. As they walked through the crowd, Tyler's fans got more aggressive than the people at the farm stand.

"Hey, isn't that Tyler Fantana?" someone shouted, pointing at him. Soon enough, a throng began to gather around them, clamoring for autographs and photos.

Josh's protective instincts kicked in. He steered Tyler off the main street, seeking refuge down one of the quieter side streets. Their hands bumped and brushed, but neither took hold. It was a delicate dance, but Josh was too uncertain of where they stood.

"Sorry about that," Tyler said, his voice apologetic as they strolled along the nearly deserted sidewalk.

"Hey, don't worry about it," Josh reassured him. "We're here to have fun, right?"

Tyler nodded, his hazel eyes crinkling with a smile. "You're right. Thanks, Josh."

As they continued walking, they stumbled upon a quaint used bookstore tucked away between two brick buildings. A hand-painted sign above the door read Off the Beaten Shelf. The afternoon sun blazed overhead, and escaping into the cool, quiet sanctuary of the shop seemed like the perfect way to spend their time.

"Want to browse a bit?" Josh suggested, already stepping toward the entrance.

"Definitely," Tyler agreed.

The store smelled of old paper and candle wax, a comforting scent that enfolded them as they entered. Homemade shelves lined the walls, filled with an assortment of creased paperbacks, coffee table books, and hardbound oldies.

As they perused the various sections, Josh felt a warmth in his chest watching Tyler peer at a pile of battered gothic romances with majestic bafflement, like a lion considering a bathtub. Something about juxtaposing Tyler and the comforting familiarity of books felt almost hopeful, a quiet bubble away from the festival.

"So what's your go-to?" Tyler asked, tapping the spines of the books and drifting along the shelves.

Josh laughed softly. "I used to be really into sci-fi and fantasy when I was younger. Give me epic quests and faraway planets any day. But these days if I'm teaching an elective, a lot of history and biography. Whatever ties into the topic."

Tyler nodded. "Yeah, with football I never really have time to read for fun anymore. But I kind of miss it, you know? Getting lost in a story." He paused, glancing over at Josh. "Maybe you could recommend something good for me?"

Josh felt a swell of affection for Tyler in that moment, touched that this football star who could have anything he wanted sought his input.

"Sure, let me see what I can find," Josh said. He scanned the shelves intently until his eyes landed on a familiar title: *The Three Musketeers*. It had been one of Josh's favorites in college. He plucked it from the shelf and held it out to Tyler.

"Classic but fun. Less stuffy than it looks. Great adventure. Killer villains. Swashbucklers, sword fights, seductions, slapstick… guaranteed good time."

"Slapstick and seductions. My faves." Tyler grinned, turning the book over in his hands. "Good call, Coach."

They made their purchases—the *Musketeers* for Tyler and a bio of Teddy Roosevelt for Josh. As they stepped back out into the sunlight, Josh felt closer to Tyler than ever.

Tyler and Josh climbed back into Josh's truck, the day's purchases stowed safely on the floorboard behind them.

As Josh turned the key in the ignition, he paused and looked over at Tyler. "Hey, if you're not in a rush to get back, there's a pretty cool spot not too far from here that I think you'd like. It's a bit of a hike, but I used to go there all the time as a kid."

"Please." Tyler's face lit up with interest. "Count me in."

Happy that he still seemed keen on extending their day, Josh drove them about twenty minutes south and west in the direction of the Palomar Observatory, eventually parking in a small dirt lot at the base of a hiking trail.

"It's just up this way." Josh pointed to a narrow path leading up the mountainside.

They set off, making casual conversation as they hiked. The exertion felt good after spending so much time in the truck. About halfway up, the trees thinned out and they found themselves high above the valley, with views stretching for miles. Josh's truck was a speck on the road below, dwarfed by the wide valley oaks hugging the slope.

Josh led Tyler off the main trail for another few minutes. "If you need a break, you say something."

Tyler shook his head. "Are you kidding? This is heaven." He drew up short and turned to Josh in confusion, because the winding dirt path ended abruptly at a rock face that hid something spectacular.

"Trust me." Josh grinned and beckoned him, ducking under some low branches until they emerged in a rocky clearing. "This is it," he announced, his voice barely above a whisper. "My secret spot as a kid."

This view never failed to make him feel small in the best possible way.

Tyler turned in a slow circle, taking in the incredible panoramic view of the valley, Mesa Grande in the distance with Ocotillo Heights and even their hometown nestled farther to the west. "I... this is—I don't have the words."

Josh nodded. "Right?"

Tyler let out a low whistle as he took it all in. "Not too shabby, Joshua. Pretty effing terrific."

Josh tipped his head. "Come here." They sat on the edge, legs dangling over the cliffside, shoulders just barely touching. A comfortable silence settled between them. Josh snuck a glance at Tyler, his handsome face serene as he watched the sunset smear brilliant peach and gold across the horizon. His eyes were damp. "You okay?"

Tyler wiped his eyes roughly. "I'm so much better than okay. I'm great."

Josh nodded, waiting for him to continue.

Tyler sighed. "I'm not sure I can go back," he finally said.

"Home?"

"No." Tyler kept his eyes on the orange horizon as he began to speak. "Can I tell you something?" he asked softly.

"Anything," Josh replied. Inside, his heart beat faster.

"Lately I've been thinking about making a change. Something. Hard to explain. Can't let fear run my life anymore, you know?" Tyler chuckled and glanced up at him. "I've been thinking a lot about the future, my future. Whether football is even something I want to do anymore."

Josh was too startled to respond.

Tyler let out a long exhale before continuing. "Eleven years in the league takes its toll. But it was always worth it, you know? The fame. The fans. The team." His low voice took on a raw huskiness that made Josh ache. "But now? I'm not sure my body can handle the punishment. And even if it could…." He trailed off, brows bunched with worry.

Josh listened intently, trying to give Tyler space to wrestle with the turmoil on his face. "*Should* you take the punishment."

"Exactly. Part of me would give up anything to get back out on that field again. I miss the team, the rush of it. But ever since the heart attack… I don't know. Why? It just doesn't seem as important anymore."

"Choices." Josh's cheeks warmed, but he took a deep breath before continuing. "For what it's worth, I get it. I've felt stuck here. Did I play things too safe? Never left home, never took a risk, never played to win."

"Hardly." Tyler counted off on his big fingers. "Students who love you. Cool job. No stalkers. Supportive community. Real roots. From where I'm sitting, you got the world by the tail."

Josh snorted. "You make my life sound way cooler than it feels."

"I'm scared of taking another hit, of risking my health again. I don't want to die at thirty-five," Tyler admitted. "But I'm also scared of walking away completely. Football has been my whole life since high school."

"Of course it has." Josh kept his gaze fixed on the reddening sky, heart thumping.

"I don't know how to explain it. Maybe I already wanted a change. Even before the attack. I can't remember now, but I think I did. Maybe it's time to figure out who I am without football being my whole identity."

"Wherever you end up, they'll be lucky to have you," Josh offered.

Tyler bumped his shoulder against Josh's a second, then furrowed his brow. "I just don't like going out this way, like a failure. After I blew it. On my knees eating dirt in front of the whole world. It's one thing to go out a champion—"

"But you are a champion, several times over. Anybody who gives you crap was full of crap to start with."

Tyler laughed at that. "Fair enough."

"You've got nothing left to prove. Anyone who matters knows how great you are." Josh squeezed his shoulder.

"That means a lot coming from you." Tyler finally turned to look at him fully.

Josh let himself get lost in those warm eyes. "You don't have to make any big decisions right now," he said gently. "One day at a time. Do what feels right, deep down. Trust your heart. And no matter what, I'll be right here supporting you."

Tyler gave a tiny, grateful smile. "Thanks, Josh. That really means a lot." By now, he was silhouetted by the blazing horizon, his white teeth a gleam in the shadows of his face. "Jeez. Look at that sunset."

Josh turned to look. "Yeah."

"I see why you love it up here."

Josh stared into his eyes a moment. "Mmmh." For that endless second, he fought the urge to take Tyler's hand, to confess his feelings, to say something sappy and irrevocable.

Instead he just sat thigh to thigh with America's Tightest End, hand pressed alongside his hand, and watched the sun put itself to bed. His heart swelled to bursting, and he savored every second they sat there together in his favorite place.

They stayed sitting in the quiet until the last rays disappeared below the horizon.

As the early darkness settled around them, Josh nodded slowly, taking in the beauty of the vista one last time before turning to Tyler. "We should probably start heading back before it gets too dark to find our way back down."

"Okay." Tyler nodded.

From the way he moved, Josh could tell his body was starting to ache after the wandering and the long hike. Keeping one steadying hand on Tyler's flexing back, Josh carefully maneuvered them down the trail back to his truck, hating that he couldn't protect Tyler from his pain.

"It's good." Once they were back on the road home, Tyler leaned his head against the window, eyes closed. "Thanks for wasting your whole day off with me," he murmured.

Josh's hands tightened on the steering wheel. "Wasn't a waste at all," he countered.

He drove extra slowly over the bumpy back roads, not wanting to jostle Tyler and exacerbate his discomfort. By the time they pulled up to Tyler's sister's house, he was barely keeping his eyes open.

Josh walked him to the front door, neither of them in a hurry to say goodbye. They lingered on the porch, Tyler swaying slightly as if tipsy with exhaustion, clutching an armful of his collected farm stand booty. "Bummed."

"Why bummed?"

"This was… an amazing day."

Again, Josh's heart jumped as he looked up into Tyler's intense hazel gaze. Tyler's face seemed to hold a question or an expectation, but for what? Was Josh just projecting his own fantasies onto someone who deserved better? He wanted so badly to say something, to pull Tyler into his arms, but the risk felt too real.

"Well… good night," Josh finally rasped, his voice strained.

Tyler bobbed his head and rocked back on his heels. "Night, Josh. And thanks again, for everything."

Josh managed a tight nod before forcing himself to walk away. He could feel Tyler's eyes following him until he climbed into his truck. As he turned the key and pulled away from the curb, his heart overflowed with hope, happiness, and no small amount of anxiety about what exactly he was supposed to do now.

Chapter Seven

TYLER LAUGHED out loud so abruptly he startled himself. *Three Musketeers* was way more fun than he'd expected. Classics are classics for a reason.

He leaned back against the sycamore in his sister's backyard and lowered the book to rest on his lap. He was still wearing his shorts from the run this morning.

The sun was almost overhead. Was it noon already? *Wow.* He'd come outside, ostensibly to fetch Mr. Poops and stretch a little, but then he'd just plopped down to read and plunged back into *Musketeers*, not even bothering to shower.

He sniffed his pit. *Yikes. Ripe.*

A movement across the yard caught his eye. Up on Nadia's back fence, Mr. Poops was patrolling the top of the overgrown passionflower vines, nose brushing the tendrils.

For a week, Tyler had stayed up most nights reading, and now he couldn't stop. He couldn't remember the last time a book took hold of him this way. The story felt like a key unlocking some dusty, rusted part of him. During their run he'd wanted to ask Josh questions, but then he decided that he needed to finish before he made himself sound stupid.

When Josh gave him the book last Saturday, it had felt thoughtful, but once Tyler started reading, it seemed important—as though Josh was trying to tell him something secret and pivotal.

A grin played on his lips as he ran his finger over the pages, pondering Josh's reasons.

From what he could tell, *Musketeers* was all about manliness— honor and duty, balls and brains. Obviously that meant Josh's gift was some kind of a message about football or high school, facing your fears. Tyler wasn't smart enough to make sense of it.

Seventeenth century or seventeen years old, trying to be a good guy was a mess: expectations and anger, macho posturing and trying not to think with your dick. *The merit of all things lies in their difficulty.*

Was Athos supposed to be Tyler? Or perhaps cocky Porthos? Tyler chuckled to himself. Which would make Josh into Aramis, scholarly and romantic.

I wish.

He shook his head, amused by his own musing.

Tyler reminded himself that the thing in his lap was a book and nothing more. No need to read too much into it or pick it apart. This trip home to recuperate was just a temporary time-out. Josh was just a nice guy with good taste in fiction. Nothing could happen between them anyway. Drastic career changes aside, in a couple of months, he'd be back in San Diego.

Still, flirting wasn't hurting anybody.

And yet, Tyler couldn't help but return again and again to their trip to the farmer's market. Everything they'd done, said, and seen. He'd leaned into Josh's calm strength and quiet humor and let him guide him through the stalls and the streets of Ocotillo Heights. Tyler replayed it constantly in his mind, trying to make sense of it: eating tamales and laughing at nothing, the dusty bookstore and that last wild view from the peak. He had a suspicion Josh had even subtly shielded him from the fans.

The whole day echoed inside Tyler, that patient quiet kindness Josh offered so easily. Like Tyler deserved something better than fame.

His time with Josh worked on him in ways he didn't fully understand, easing his restlessness and doubts, replacing them with a quirky, sturdy hope he'd never felt before. He knew it couldn't last, but every day felt like gratitude.

Tyler grinned and closed the book with a shushed snap, squinting out at the day as he ran his hand over the binding. How could he show Josh his gratitude? Maybe even return the favor? There had to be some way to help with the library, at least. PR was low-hanging fruit for him. But he also wanted to do something special, personal, for Josh himself, some special gesture to express the exhilaration he felt.

He'd just have to come up with something spectacular. He tucked the book under his arm and stood, twisting to crack his back. Josh deserved so much more than he knew how to give.

"Hey, bud. I think I stink." Tyler turned to Mr. Poops on the fence. "Wanna go inside?"

Poops blinked at him and flicked his enormous tail. But when Tyler picked him up and carried him into the dim and cool house, he was purring.

Tyler took a leisurely midday shower and even jerked off just to make sure things were operational. He didn't even bother to feel guilty about his fantasies about Coach Ayres.

Over the past six days, Tyler had fallen into a healthy routine: morning runs, therapy twice a week, reading his Dumas somewhere out of doors or in a café, walking the familiar streets in his hometown, light weights at the Hamilton gym, then quiet evenings with his sister and Poops.

In this tranquil space, Tyler had time to reflect on his heart attack, his stalled career, and life beyond sports. And also on the tender and tenacious connection between himself and Josh.

By degrees, Tyler caught himself opening up about his fears, failures, and secrets he'd kept tucked out of sight a long time. And Josh listened with the understanding of shared humanity, not pity.

With Josh, Tyler didn't have to be a celebrity or a football hero. He could just be himself, fragile and flawed. If anything, that made him even more confident. Josh had said it a couple of days ago: "Bones are strongest where the break mended."

At some point, almost by accident, Tyler had remembered how to heal.

The morning runs with Josh were still Tyler's favorite part of the day, the perfect sync, breathing in unison, stealing glances, talking about stuff he hadn't even told his therapist. They'd taken a couple short hikes, a couple lunches. Just being near Josh anchored him and energized him. He started to feel confident again, more like himself and less like a cardboard standee held together with masking tape.

After the past weeks, surely Josh had to feel the chemistry between them, even if neither of them wanted anything to happen. Right?

Tell that to his heart. Tyler knew he was falling for Josh, and maybe Josh felt the same way.

NFL players take risks for a living, right? He was determined to take a chance and let Josh know how he felt before reality came crashing back in. He only hoped that Josh felt something close.

THE NEXT day, Tyler pulled a little too fast into the parking lot of Dr. Reynolds's office, gripping the steering wheel with clammy hands.

So much for swashbuckling heroism.

He slowed as he navigated the lot toward the lobby doors, his stomach knotting with nerves and his hackles raised. A muscle in his jaw ticked with tension because apparently he'd been unconsciously grinding his teeth the whole way. He wiped his mouth.

The past hour had marked the first time he'd driven on the highway alone since the heart attack. No Josh grinning with him. No Nadia riding shotgun, ready to catch him if he stumbled. Just Tyler and the cold open road of I-15. A necessary step, but a stark contrast to his previous visits.

He cut the engine and grabbed his duffel bag, swallowing the stupid anxiety that rose in his throat like bile. He tugged his baseball cap lower. Hardly a disguise, but he felt like he should make an effort. He took a moment to three-three-three himself back into his body.

Keys. Bench. Door.

Engine ticking. Shush of traffic. Two girls chatting by their car.

Wipe hands. Crack neck. Open door.

He closed his eyes and let out a slow, ragged exhale.

What would Josh tell him if they were on the track at sunrise?

Take a breath. Let all the craziness out of you. You got this. Just thinking about Josh's eyes settled him a bit.

After closing and locking the car door, Tyler strode toward the entrance, slowly letting some of his nerves go. Josh's voice in his ear: "One step and then another and you can go anywhere, buddy."

He walked briskly toward the entrance, but before he could reach for the door handle, a voice stopped him in his tracks. "Tyler Fantana!"

Six feet from his cardiologist's door, a rail-thin woman with unnaturally bright red hair ambushed him from behind a trash can to jam a microphone in his face. "Cilla Miller, Channel Twenty-four Sports."

"Holy—" Tyler recoiled. His heart slammed against the inside of his ribs, each beat painful as an ax. He struggled to keep his face blank, but his vision blurred with each beat of his pulse. "Warn a guy, huh?"

He didn't recognize this chick, and after a decade, he knew the San Diego regulars. The helmet-haired redhead looked perky and carnivorous, a glossy shark with threaded eyebrows. Her camera crew scrambled around them, capturing every facet of Tyler's surprise.

"Care to comment on rumors you're getting traded away from the Swells this season?" She was flanked by a scruffy cameraman and a stocky soundman holding a mike on a boom over their heads. The men looked bored and maybe a little embarrassed by her strident style. Even the adamant artificial red of her hair felt aggressive.

"No comment, ma'am." He tried to step past or around them. No dice. She had installed carefully to block his path into Reynolds's office.

Normally he'd have simply pushed through, but now Tyler vibrated with rage and panic, his mouth dry and his shirt soaked with cold sweat. Why hadn't he brought Nadia when she insisted? He should have known the press would track him down eventually.

The reporter persisted, shoving the fat foam knob of her mic at him. "How's the comeback going? What about your heart condition?"

"Ma'am, this is me being polite." Tyler knocked the boom from overhead, and the sound guy stumbled. He started to push through the scruffy crew. "I asked you to back off."

Was she really arrogant enough to try and manhandle a 260-pound NFL tank who played offense? She might imagine she was pushy, but pushing giants around was what he did for a living.

Undeterred by the security guard approaching from the lobby and Tyler's mounting aggression, Ms. Miller jostled closer with the microphone. The capped teeth and the stiff hair made her seem like an angry doll. "Heartthrob to heart slob. Think that bum ticker will hold up? Are you willing to risk your life?"

Tyler's mouth clicked shut. Fury boiled in his veins. He tried to think like a musketeer: a little brash, a little reckless, and a little more polite than necessary. *Panache.* Big cocky Aramis grin. "I said no comment, Cindy."

She didn't like that one bit. "Cilla." Her frozen smile cracked. "I'm Cilla. Miller. KSDF. Reporting for Channel Twenty-four."

He rolled his eyes. "My apologies." He'd done it on purpose, misnamed her and shamed her so she couldn't use any of this footage to sleaze her way up the ladder. The only reason he didn't physically lift her out of his way was because the Swells didn't need any more reasons to kill his contract.

"We've heard reports—"

"Then you're all set." And with that, he rammed past them and burst through the doors into the safety of Dr. Reynolds's office. The receptionist looked up, startled. Tyler's heart pounded, adrenaline scorching his veins.

Outside, the guard had reached the camera crew, but slender Cilla Miller bulldozed past the poor guy. "Mr. Fantana?" She trailed Tyler, headed straight for the front desk, mic at the ready. "Are the Swells fixing to nix Eighty-six?"

Eighty-six was his jersey.

What Tyler needed right now was a door between him and her. He shouldn't have come alone. *Stupid.*

Cilla wouldn't stop. "Mr. Fantana?" The cameraman trailed behind her, lens looming with the boom swinging and bobbing in pursuit. "Just a few questions for San Diego's hottest, Tightest End...."

Cilla Miller had sat in her cubicle and planned that crap so she could come stick a mic in his face. *Is Fantana getting eighty-sixed?* How many junior reporters had pulled this same routine with him the past two months? He wasn't anything but a headline to them.

"Lady. We've been polite." A bald, thickset nurse in scrubs held open his hands in protest, his arms too wide and visible for her to dodge safely as he advanced at her. "We've warned you people several times already."

"Hmph." She frowned and flicked the red bob.

The security guard inched inside behind the sound guy. "That was assault."

The nurse scowled and herded the invading crew back toward the parking lot like an aging defensive lineman. "We got you on tape, lady. And I saw you strike a patient. I'll testify."

Cilla gasped. "Ridiculous. That's a lie."

"We'll press charges. I'm happy to call the police again. If you persist, I can guarantee the rest of your afternoon is a thorough cavity search."

Tyler turned away from the melee to face the desk.

"Limelight, huh?" The receptionist shot Tyler a sympathetic smile and muttered, "Exam room's open. Number five."

"Thanks," Tyler mumbled with a grateful nod. He fled down the hall into an exam room and slammed the door shut.

Tyler leaned against the closed door, allowing the coolness of the metal handle to ground him. His heart raced like he'd run wind sprints at the combine. Damn vultures would kill him if they could, just to climb whatever crappy ladder. All they cared about was the story, not the person they used to prop it up.

His big hands shook as he stripped to his shorts.

Tyler hopped onto the table, his fingers drumming an erratic rhythm on the thin paper covering. Little by little, his eyes adjusted to the bright fluorescent lights of Dr. Reynolds's office.

His old life left a lot to be desired.

Tyler took a few deep breaths to calm himself as he waited for the doc. Despite the reporter ambush, his relief and anticipation were genuine.

Though he'd dreaded this checkup, Tyler felt lighter and more energetic than he had in years. For the past month, each visit had marked real progress in his recovery, which had stagnated those first two months after the heart attack.

Even the idea of driving this far alone would've paralyzed him. Today, he felt stronger than he had in a long time, maybe since his first year with the Swells. His heart beat steady behind his ribs.

All thanks to Josh.

A knock came at the door before Dr. Reynolds entered.

"Mr. Fantana?" Dr. Reynolds closed the door, her brow furrowed in concern. "You look flushed. Everything okay?"

"Ran into a tacky reporter outside," he admitted, rubbing the back of his sore neck. "Didn't expect that kind of ambush so soon. I should've known."

She stepped closer. "My apologies. My staff should have been better prepared."

"Press. Some kid trying to make a name for herself. It's not her fault, really. They can be… impolite." He grinned. "I'm fine."

"You are." And then Dr. Reynolds seemed to really *look* at Tyler. "Aren't you. Hale and hearty." She glanced at the door. "I am sorry for the excitement out front."

"No need. It bothered your people more than it did me. Although the shock did get my heart thumping. I'm not used to that anymore. Out of practice."

"No." She raised her cold stethoscope to his chest and back to listen. As she began the examination, Tyler couldn't help but notice how different he felt compared to his last visit. "But your breathing is strong, and your heart sounds great, if slightly elevated, for obvious reasons."

"I bet."

"Your vitals are looking good, Tyler," Dr. Reynolds observed, checking off notes on her clipboard. "And if I'm not mistaken, you seem… noticeably happier. A great deal happier."

"Guess I've been making some changes," he admitted, a faint smile tugging at the corners of his lips. It was true. Ever since Josh entered his life, something inside him had shifted.

"Changes?" She raised an eyebrow. "Care to share?"

"Been working out," he said, avoiding the question's emotional implications. "Running every morning. Easy weights."

"Oh! That explains it." Her face was pinked with pleasure. "Mr. Fantana, congratulations. Truly. That's wonderful to hear. Your color has improved drastically. Blood sugar. Potassium. Iron. Magnesium. Superb."

The doctor's praise filled him with pride. Tyler smiled, thinking of his early morning runs with Josh, the trips and jokes and everything else that had turned his life around so much the past few weeks. "Some easy hikes with a friend. Even strength training a couple times a week. Nothing extreme, but still… I sort of got my blood flowing again."

"Ah. It's definitely flowing." Dr. Reynolds nodded. "You look so much more grounded than you did during our last visit."

"Feels good," Tyler agreed with a tickle of pride.

She made some notes and then glanced over his charts again. "Marvelous news on all fronts, it seems. And therapy? How have you been feeling since our last visit? Do I even need to ask?"

"Much better, actually," Tyler said. "Therapy has been good. I've been three-three-threeing like there's no *mañana*. I'm watching what I eat. I'm learning to cook, even, with a friend." He stopped himself before Josh's name came up. Last thing he needed to tell his cardiologist.

"You've clearly been taking better care of yourself."

"Couple gallons of water every day. Bananas. Kale." Tyler nodded, thinking of Josh pushing him on their runs, believing in him when Tyler didn't believe in himself. "I've had help. A friend has really been there for me through all of this."

Dr. Reynolds fixed Tyler with a knowing look. "A new relationship?"

"No, actually. An old friend from my high school." Caught off guard, Tyler had reddened. He pictured Josh's warm eyes and easy grin but blinked the thought away.

"I assume they get some credit for this remarkable turnaround?"

"Sure. Yes. Josh." He hadn't considered how he was supposed to discuss Josh with anyone else.

She raised her eyebrows with a gentle smile of interest. "Someone back home?"

"Exactly. From Hamilton. A coach who still lives there." He knew she'd assume he meant some old man who'd coached him fifteen years ago, but no harm done. "Really gifted sports medicine guy, as it happens."

"You mean your coach still works there? What a blessing." Dr. Reynolds hesitated, squinting. "But nobody else? I could've sworn you had that glow about you. Someone special."

Tyler's chest tightened, and he swallowed hard. His mind raced. He was wary of saying more than he meant to, so he froze and fibbed. "Josh has been training me, keeping me motivated. Good guy."

"Great coaches can be life-changing." Dr. Reynolds patted his knee. "And you seem so... grounded today. I'm thrilled by your progress."

Though he dodged her questions, she'd noticed plenty. "Thanks, Doc," he mumbled, still evasive. "I appreciate that."

Her voice softened, as though she sensed his reluctance. "I only ask because I care about your well-being. Helping you heal is a wonderful thing. Your coach must care a lot about you."

He felt crappy not giving Josh full credit, but he still wasn't sure what Josh wanted. Saying something out loud would make it real, and that was a risk he wasn't ready to take, not with reporters hovering in the lobby. He forced a casual laugh, shrugging his broad shoulders. "Just been focusing on my health, Doc. That's all."

"Well, whatever you're doing, keep it up. And don't worry about any reporters outside. My staff can make sure you leave without issue. If you'll wait here, I'll have someone escort you out."

"No, Doc. I'm fine now. I'm just out of practice running offense."

As she left the room, Tyler couldn't suppress a grin. He felt lighter, stronger, and more alive than he had in months, and he knew exactly whom to thank for it.

He headed down the hall and discovered Cilla and crew had been booted.

"She's toast." Standing at the reception desk, the male nurse gave him a nod. "Escorted off the property. We called her station manager for good measure. She's a nut. Mark my words, she's got a wall covered with your stats and old socks."

"Thanks, man." Tyler extended a hand to him.

The nurse shook it firmly with a big grin and ran a hand over his bald scalp. "Thank you. I'm such a big fan, Mr. Fantana."

Tyler left Dr. Reynolds's office. Did his growing fondness for Josh really show that plainly? The thought made Tyler blush. He wasn't ready to define whatever existed between them, even to himself.

He hated lying, but it also felt wrong to say something to his cardiologist before he worked up the nerve to see if Josh was interested. Whatever he felt, Josh deserved to hear it first.

Still, the doctor's intuition rang true. Josh had changed everything for Tyler. His encouragement and caring had pulled Tyler from his self-pitying haze, kicked his ass, and steered him right. With Josh, the world seemed full of opportunity, not obstacles. Tyler felt stronger, mentally and physically, than he had in years.

The more he pondered, the more Tyler warmed to the idea. The time they shared already felt so intimate. Surely Josh felt the spark between them.

Pursuing Josh was a risk, but the thought of not trying at all left him with a hollow ache in his chest. Could exploring those feelings jeopardize their friendship? Tyler hadn't been sure he was ready to risk it. But what if this was his chance at real happiness?

As Tyler headed to the car, his heart swelled with tentative hope. For the first time in ages, he felt eager to embrace whatever the future held, so long as Josh was by his side.

Tyler stepped out of the doctor's lobby and scanned the parking lot, his eyes darting from one end to the other. He couldn't shake the feeling that his life was at a critical juncture, and one wrong move could topple everything.

As he drove, Tyler replayed the doctor's exam. His improvement was undeniable, but the threat of returning to the NFL plagued him.

Just thinking about returning to the Swells stirred up a storm of conflicting emotions. The ruthless competition and media circus felt at odds with the balance Tyler had enjoyed so much lately. Part of Tyler missed the thrill and challenge of the game in his bones. Yet the heart attack had completely undermined his confidence. What if his body failed him again? What if his heart was never going to be strong enough to go back?

If his face was plastered all over the news, would it drive Josh away? Would the pressure of being in the spotlight again wreck any chance for a real relationship? Then again, Josh might not be interested in some average nobody.

"Get it together, Tyler," he muttered to himself. It was useless to dwell on the uncertainties.

One thing was clear. Tyler refused to waste another minute of the time he had with Josh. Their relationship, no matter what form it took, meant far too much. Tyler just prayed he'd find the courage to face what came next.

Tyler pulled into Nadia's driveway, his thoughts a tangled heap, and steeled himself for the inevitable questions from his sister. He was relieved to be home, but he knew Nadia would be relentless interrogating him. As he climbed out of the car, the front door swung open.

"There he is!" Nadia called out, bounding through the door. She threw her arms around Tyler in an enthusiastic hug. "One piece, no disasters."

"Whoa, hey," Tyler laughed, returning the embrace.

"You did just fine. See? You can drive. Yay!"

"I did. Everything's cool. Everything is fantastic, actually."

"Wait, I know that look." Nadia stepped back, peering closely at Tyler's face. "You okay? You've got your brooding look going on." She scrutinized him for a moment. "*Something* is up. What's going on?"

"What? No, I'm good." With a casual shrug, Tyler brushed past her toward the house. "Nothing, just a long day."

Nadia followed on his heels, undeterred. "Uh-huh. So report. How'd the checkup go? Spill."

"Fine, everything's excellent," Tyler said over his shoulder as he walked into the kitchen. He opened the fridge and filled a tall glass with water from the pitcher, avoiding Nadia's gaze.

"You're an awful liar, you know that? Like, maybe *two* out of ten for believability." Nadia crossed her arms and leaned against the counter. "Pathetic. Lie harder, at least."

Tyler's eyes shot up to meet hers. Heat rose in his cheeks. "The doc was over the moon. Muscle mass. Blood pressure. Oxygen. Mineral levels. You name it. Way better than she'd even hoped."

"Oh, Tyler, that's awesome." She squinted. "So what's eating you?"

Tyler sighed, rubbing the back of his neck. He glanced at his sister, then looked away. "It's nothing, really. Just… thinking."

"Uh-oh." Nadia tilted her head. "When is that ever a good thing?"

"It's… nothing." He took a long swing of water, feeling its chilly path down his throat and into his belly.

Nadia leaned against the counter and squeezed his wrist. "Talk to me, huh?"

"I don't think I can… explain."

"I'm not stupid." Nadia frowned and laughed.

"I don't mean that. I don't think you're the person I should be talking to first."

"Oh. Ohhhh!"

He shook his head. "Don't start."

"Wait a minute. Tyler Fantana… are you saying—?"

"Everything is complicated. I mean…." Tyler rubbed his face roughly and then tugged on his hair in frustration. "I'm not just me. I'm a contract player with the NFL, with a whole team. I got licensing deals and press calls. I'm a character in three different video games, for Christ's sake. I'm a machine." He thumped his pecs.

"Bull. You are a grown-ass man, Tyler Fantana—"

He interrupted her, "I know that—"

But she didn't let him finish. "And if you are having actual human feelings about another actual human being, then you'd best act like a grown-ass man."

"It's complicated, Nadia."

"Boo-frigging-hoo." She smacked him and cocked her head. "Tell me something simple. Huh? What in this life is easy? Nothing anybody wants."

"I don't want to hurt anybody." He crossed his arms over his chest and sighed.

"Too late, boo. Life hurts people. You got a big fancy job in a big fancy game for big fancy money that's nothing *but* hurting people. You're a pro."

Tyler wavered between embarrassment and the trust he had in his sister. He looked up into her earnest eyes and something inside him broke so the words spilled out. "I might… I think I'm falling for Josh Ayres."

Nadia squealed and pulled Tyler into a hug. "I knew it!"

"You did? I didn't. I really like him, Nadia. Like, a lot."

"He's the sweetest. I knew this would happen. You guys are perfect together, for each other. I knew it. I'm so happy for you."

"Really? You don't think it's… weird?" Tyler asked, seeking reassurance from the one person who knew him best. "I know he's your friend."

"Absolutely not. I have too many friends for that to bug me," Nadia insisted, squeezing his arm affectionately. "If anything, it's overdue."

"Easy. Hey." Tyler laughed, shaking his head. "I don't even know if he feels the same way."

"Then ask him, genius."

Tyler's phone buzzed on the counter.

Nadia grinned. "I wonder who that might be."

"Team owner. Or one of the coaches," he said. "They must've just this second gotten the doc's glowing report on my prognosis."

Her face fell.

"I still have to decide about going back to the team next season. What if a new relationship isn't a good idea?" He hadn't said anything to her about the mounting pressure from the Swells yet. She already distrusted them.

Nadia put a hand on his shoulder. "You deserve to be happy."

Tyler nodded slowly. She had a point. He picked up his phone, hesitating.

Jarlson's familiar gruff voice spoke up. "Tyler! How'd that doc appointment go? A little bird told me you're looking pretty good."

"Yep. Saw Dr. Reynolds for my checkup." Tyler grimaced. "Not quite cleared to play, but on the mend for sure."

"Fantastic, Fantana!" the owner bellowed. "Great work. Great work. The team can't wait. You just say the word."

Tyler spent the next ten minutes walking Boris through the doc's report. To be honest, he seemed more interested in getting Tyler back in front of the cameras than back on the field.

"A couple photo shoots wouldn't kill you, huh? These cereal guys are busting my balls, and all you got to do is smile and show off your tight end, my friend."

Tyler nodded, then realized Boris couldn't see him and said, "Right."

"But no pressure. Zero pressure from the team, kid. You're a fighter. We just want you at a hundred percent and bushy tailed. You let us know. You just keep doing what you're doing."

"So far so good, huh?" The stupid part was that Josh was the only thing making him better, but going back would probably kill any hopes he had with Josh.

"Trust me, kid, you've got this. We'll talk more soon." And with that, Boris ended the call, leaving Tyler with unanswered questions and a lingering sense of unease.

He stared at the phone in his hand, his jaw clenched as frustration bubbled within him. The conversation had only served to deepen his conflict about the stark contrast facing him.

Tyler set down his phone. Nadia raised her eyebrows expectantly, but he just shrugged.

After a shower and some grilled trout, Tyler sat alone on the front porch steps, watching the sunset smear the horizon. The past couple of hours had really run the gamut: his sister, Cilla Miller, Boris, even that big bald nurse at Dr. Reynolds's place trying to help.

For so long, he had kept his feelings bottled up inside, afraid to make himself vulnerable again after all his dumb hookups and fake dates for ESPN. But now, something had shifted. Being with Josh had awakened a part of Tyler he thought he'd lost.

In Josh, he might have found an honest-to-God partner… someone who could challenge him, support him, and perhaps even teach him to see the world through new eyes. Given Tyler's dodgy track record with dating and commitment, that was no small thing.

Tyler realized he didn't need absolute guarantees or assurances. He just needed to take a chance. He wanted to help Josh, make him laugh, fight dragons, save the library, and anything else that Josh was willing to accept. Plus, better to know before he did anything about the NFL. For once in his life, he needed to trust his heart no matter how battered or broken it might be. After all, who took hits better than him?

Tyler closed his eyes, enjoying the light breeze over his upturned face.

No need to rush, no dumb gestures, but he would start working toward telling Josh exactly how he felt. *Think like a musketeer, man.* A proper date maybe, someplace special, something out of the ordinary. He tried to recapture that feeling he had when he was reading: cocky and courteous, with more panache than he had any right to claim. He'd find the right moment and lay himself bare.

When he opened his eyes again, the first stars of evening had winked into view.

Tyler smiled then and bowed to the sky in thanks. He knew exactly what he needed to do.

Chapter Eight

"NOPE. WE'RE on a secret mission." Tyler sounded infuriatingly pleased with himself.

Josh shifted in the passenger seat; the velvet of his Renaissance courtier breeches kept sliding on his truck's work vinyl. He glanced at Tyler beside him, one massive hand casually guiding the wheel as the other drummed along to the radio against his dark tights. Even with half his face obscured by a black bandit's mask, Tyler's excitement was palpable.

"Come on, just tell me where we're going." Josh couldn't contain his curiosity any longer. Tyler had commandeered his truck and everything. Seeing Tyler behind that wheel felt more intimate and significant than it probably should have.

Tyler grinned, eyes fixed on the road ahead. "What's the fun in that? Don't you trust me?"

Josh laughed. "With my life and limbs. But kidnapping me before breakfast is pushing it."

Not so secretly, he was thrilled by Tyler's spontaneous road trip, made all the more tantalizing by his elaborate secrecy—not to mention being kidnapped by Mr. Tall, Dark, and Undressed.

And the glimpse of Tyler's brawny chest and powerful thighs beneath his outrageous bandit costume certainly didn't hurt. Josh worried the elaborate embroidered outfit Tyler had surprised him with was a bit much for an outing, but once Tyler had begun to manhandle him into these clothes, he surrendered to the goofiness.

Today was Sunday. Josh's doorbell had rung just after nine, and Josh had gone to the door expecting Amazon Prime or a hopeful tree trimmer hustling for work, only to find Tyler standing on the mat, grinning and bare-chested, wearing dark leggings and a bulging codpiece.

"Are those tights?" Josh laughed and opened the door wider. "Tyler. What happened?"

"I'm a bandit, and you're being abducted."

Without any further preamble or explanation, Tyler had simply pushed inside his house, stripped Josh to his boxer briefs in his front hallway, and then dressed him out of a pile of folded garments, while Josh concentrated on not getting a big stonking stiffy while standing so exposed in front of the man of his dreams.

That had taken willpower, what with Tyler's big, capable fingers fumbling with the elaborate buckles on a pair of borrowed breeches, pulling a pressed cotton shirt over his head, then tucking it in so gently that the hair on Josh's neck stood on end. Tyler had knelt to lace Josh into glossy boots that hugged his calves, then pulled his arms into an elaborate waistcoat stitched with silver. When Josh finally saw himself in the hall mirror, he gasped.

No words would come. He had lost his capacity for speech.

"Prince Charming," said Tyler, looming behind him like a lusty robber king. Then he reached up to softly brush Josh's hair off his brow. "Perfect."

"I don't look like that." Josh straight-up shivered.

Tyler gestured at the door. "Your rusty carriage awaits, my lord. Unless you trust me with your big pickup."

Josh most certainly did… and handed over his keys.

After an hour wearing breeches on the interstate as a willing prisoner, Josh had learned two absolute truths:

A) Tyler loved dressing up in extravagant costumes, and

B) Boners were impossible to conceal under velvet.

Still baffled about the actual destination, Josh satisfied himself with trying to gather clues from the signage. They had driven north on I-15 and been on the road at least an hour. "Los Angeles…? Malibu?" With a smile, Josh turned to his handsome abductor. "Dude, are you taking me to Disneyland?"

"Relax, we're almost there." Tyler took the exit for North Sunset Ave., and then Josh scanned the signs for clues. Irwindale… that rang some long-ago bell. Then something called Santa Fe Dam Recreational Area.

"Wait." Josh turned to look at a cross street. "I think they make sriracha here."

Tyler neither confirmed nor denied reports of local hot sauce production.

As they turned down a tree-lined street, Josh spied a vast parking lot with a looming archway at the opposite end. A combination of T-shirted tourists and fully costumed patrons milled about the entrance under a sign that read Renaissance Pleasure Faire.

"No way!" Josh sat up straight. He'd always wanted to attend one of these but had never had the nerve.

Tyler beamed and threw an arm around Josh's shoulders. "Welcome, good sirrah, to a world of knights, jesters, and lusty escapades."

Despite his initial apprehension, Josh couldn't suppress an excited grin. How had Tyler known? How did he *always* know? Mr. Fantana never stopped surprising and delighting him. The real Tyler was so much more wonderful than the imaginary "alpha jock" he'd pined for way back when.

Josh goggled at the sights and sounds as they strolled through the Faire gates. Minstrels plucked lutes, jugglers tossed flaming batons, and the air smelled of roasted meat and fresh-baked bread. Costumed villagers hawked their wares from makeshift wooden stalls draped with vivid silks and tapestries. The crowd was a jolly mix of hard-core costumes and average civilians wearing shorts and flip-flops.

"Milord, since you are my prisoner this day, I offer you my protection and patronage in this lawless domain," Tyler said in an exaggerated and terrible British accent. "Perhaps a flagon of ale?"

Josh laughed. "Indeed not, villain. I'll have my revenge. But first, we must away to yon field of valor, where my knights clash in contest!" He pointed to a sign for the jousting arena.

Tyler's eyes lit up. "I can but agree! Let us make haste, lest we miss the fray!"

As Tyler hurried off, Josh watched him walk away, feeling absolutely no guilt. That butt, that back, those arms were something else. If Tyler wanted to showcase his extraordinary assets under Lycra that thin, Josh for one was not willing to waste a miracle by walking in front.

And for the first time, he got a proper head-to-toe gander at Tyler's outrageous chest-baring costume.

Tyler looked every inch the storybook rogue, all bulging biceps and bunching pectorals with a dusting of crisp dark fuzz across them. At six foot five and two hundred and sixty-something pounds, Tyler stood a head taller than anyone else in the Faire. His abs flexed every time he chuckled, and the wide V of his back looked like a D&D campaign waiting to happen.

However, the real public nuisance was presented by his massive lower half.

The folks wandering the Faire might not recognize America's Tightest End behind his half mask, but everybody in striking distance was having a hard time keeping their eyes above his beltline, fore and aft. Josh could sympathize.

For whatever nefarious reason, Tyler had opted to wear darkish tights, somewhere between brown and purple and textured like hide, that showed off every intense inch of his jacked legs and backside. His gigantic thighs looked like carved tree trunks, and his meaty calves rose out of a pair of fold-top cavalier boots. And the crowning glory front and center? A literal glittering codpiece cupping his huge bulge behind a jeweled rooster picked out in red, black, green, and orange gems, its beak tipped up to nip at the perfect dark treasure trail reaching up from his waistband toward his navel.

A glittering cock? For real? He must have done that on purpose, right?

Thing was, the whole getup might look obscene in its particulars, but more than anything, he looked *perfect*. Tyler might have stepped out of a fairy tale to ravish someone.

"My lord?"

Busted. Josh raised his eyes and realized Tyler had caught him staring, but he seemed pleased, if anything. Obviously he didn't mind anyone getting an eyeful. Tyler beckoned him with a roguish grin. "Shall we?"

"Right." Josh finally got his legs moving and closed the distance separating them. "These costumes are amazing."

"I know a gal in La Jolla who hooked us up." Tyler spun in a slow circle, looking down at himself. "She designs for the opera."

Football players go to opera? As soon Josh reached his bandit king, Tyler threw an affectionate arm around his shoulders. For the past couple of weeks, Tyler had become more openly tactile, and Josh cherished those casual moments of closeness.

He wondered whether—hoped—it meant Tyler's feelings had nudged beyond mere friendship. But he dared not assume too much. For now it was enough just to share this adventure together.

Tyler looked down at his codpiece and boots. "Granted, it may not be *strictly* AP history accurate."

"Accuracy be damned. It looks sexy as hell." Josh even felt bold enough to wink.

Tyler paused at a stall selling masks and selected a bejeweled bull with curling horns, holding it to his face.

"A minotaur."

"What do you think?" Tyler asked, his voice rumbling behind the mask. "Strong like bull?"

Josh laughed. "It definitely suits your stubbornness. But I think it distracts from the rest of your, uh, package." He raised his eyebrows at Tyler's sparkly cock-a-doodle bulge. "Cock and bull?"

"Touché." Tyler grinned and set the mask back down. "Besides, I'm horny enough as it is."

Every time they paused to browse, Josh caught himself staring at Tyler striding through the crowd. The aggressive jut of his haunches and the powerful thighs demanded attention. But he seemed so much happier and calmer, just being around people without having to be anyone but himself.

Aside from vendors and actual staged shows, a few characters roamed the Faire as well, acting out small skits and interacting with kids.

Josh turned to watch an alchemist entertaining a circle of kids by performing legerdemain with his flasks and flames. "You know... AP history aside, this is what studying the past should feel like. Curiosity and connection."

"Right?" Tyler nodded at a knight arguing with a tonsured monk over a sack of loot. "I know it's not accurate, but it's like seeing a book come to life."

Interspersed with the "shoppes" and "taverns," Josh noticed a scatter of games and challenges that provided different kinds of fun for different kinds of guests, from rowdy to reticent. "I can't get over this place."

Tyler pointed out an Axe Throw, a Ring Toss, and even a Grand Battle of Wits, which pitted teams of guests against a huge puzzle with hidden prizes. Jugglers and bubble sculptors. Small stages crowded with boisterous performers dotted the whole Faire. There really was something for whoever might wander past.

As they looped back toward the jousting ground, they spotted a cloak stall that offered options in leather, silk, velvet, and even feathers. Tyler insisted he try a few on, but Josh felt funny when people began to gather and take pictures of him. He still struggled with that kind of direct attention from strangers. Tyler tried to buy him a gigantic royal cape, but Josh begged off. "It looks cool standing here, but imagine dragging it for a couple miles."

"Ah. True."

They paused to watch the end of a deadly serious archery competition between a group of small hyperfocused kids wearing crowns, glitter, and diaphanous fairy wings. An eight-year-old boy in lavender batwings won in a squeaker. His name must have been Luis, because the crowd cheered his name loudly.

As soon as they stepped back into the flow of visitors, a family with three little ones stopped to take pictures with them, possibly because they looked like performers. Tyler lifted one of the girls onto his shoulder so fast that all the kids wanted a ride.

As they walked away, Tyler leaned over to mutter, "This I miss. Just being able to walk around and be with people like a person."

Josh nodded. Maybe that was the difference. Wearing a mask for a day let Tyler relax. Josh had never seen him so playful or easy in a large group of civilians.

They continued browsing the stalls until Tyler insisted they stop to try on silly hats and then some custom chainmail. In the distance, Josh could hear the thunder of hooves. Jousting maybe? Or a race. They passed a huge maypole in full braid and a contortionist rope dancer balanced over a pond.

At the next big intersection, a roaring crowd stood gathered in a ring around a raised log that stretched over a pit padded with giant cushions.

A graceful girl standing up on the log called down to Tyler. She wore a leather jerkin and loose green trousers that laced up the side. "Give you good day, sir."

Tyler chuckled and shouted back to her in his rough bandit voice, "And you, wench."

"I am no wench but the sheriff's daughter." She moved like a gymnast, and maybe she was. She hopped up on the log and walked toward Tyler's taunting. He stood so tall and handsome above the crowd that she probably assumed he was one of the characters hired to improvise during the Faire.

"Aye. But who is your mother, wench?" Tyler squinted at her, obviously enjoying himself.

"At that you have me, sir. She were not the sheriff's wife." The crowd cackled at that. By all appearances, she really did expect Tyler to jump in and play at sword-fighting on her log, and Tyler seemed more than willing.

Tyler crossed his arms until his chest bulged and barked up at her, "Many a night have I spent in your sire's cells crying at the moon like a dog."

"Like the dog you are! A robber. A thief. Will you not fight me honorably?" The girl raised two padded swords and nodded hopefully.

"I have no honor but his—this prince you see by my side." Tyler turned to Josh. "Him will I fight. This noble man rules my land and my hand."

Her face lit up. "Well said."

"I do what? Rule?" Josh muttered to Tyler. "Hang on."

"Well met! Indeed." The girl laughed with genuine pleasure and encouraged the mob of visitors to clap with her for Tyler's speechifying. "Is it not? Well said. Well met. Hie you hither, Master Robber. And bring your shining lord."

Suddenly Tyler strode right into the clapping crowd, which parted before him like they'd rehearsed it. Feeling more than slightly ridiculous, Josh followed, keeping his eyes on Tyler's broad flexing back and butt so he wouldn't turn around.

"Consequences be damned!" The girl got the crowd to roar and curse at Tyler, and he hopped up onto the log with easy athleticism, his legs bunching with explosive power. She seemed startled by his height up close, but then slipped aside to let Josh climb to the log. "Your Grace." She bowed to Josh.

Josh nodded and mumbled, "What the hell?"

Tyler reached forward to pluck the smallest of the two padded swords from her grip. "I challenge you to a duel, my lord!" he declared. "Your life or your freedom."

Josh grabbed the longer sword. "I accept!"

The crowd cheered. Josh saw a few of the folks they had bumped into earlier: the mask vendor, the bubble sorceress, one of the joust knights mopping his brow, Luis the batwing champion on his dad's shoulders.

Against all his better judgment, Josh took one look at Tyler's twinkling eyes and jumped right into the silliness of it.

The swords felt like repurposed nerf bats. The log was broad enough that balancing was easy. All his rock climbing had done wonders for his equilibrium. And he was strong enough to hold his own, certainly, if Tyler went easy.

They faced off, swatting at each other with greater and greater force as they realized just how safe they were up here. They began to grunt, shout, and made a good show of it. Once she knew they were safe, the girl catcalled and the crowd jeered, mostly at Tyler as the burly bad guy.

Emboldened, Tyler attempted an obvious feint and sweep, over which Josh jumped pretty easily. The crowd shouted and hooted. Tyler swung down, hitting the flat of Josh's shoulder but not moving him an inch.

He wants me to win. He winked at Tyler, and Tyler winked back.

Josh bent low and then swung his sword in a wide arc that slammed into Tyler's side, knocking Tyler completely off balance.

Tyler's arms pinwheeled a moment with him balanced on the edge, body arched, which shamelessly showed off his abs, pecs, and overstuffed codpiece.

With a dramatic cry, Tyler toppled into the cushions below and gave a roar of terrible defeat.

Josh smiled and raised his arms in victory. The girl got the crowd cheering and clapping again, but then the crowd booed as treacherous Tyler reached up and tugged Josh down into the pit on top of him.

For one perfect, breathless moment, Josh lay sprawled across Tyler's broad, damp, heaving chest as Tyler's arms caught him and held him steady. Their eyes met, faces inches apart.

Josh's heart pounded. Tyler licked his lips, watching Josh's eyes on him. Slowly, so slowly Josh could feel himself stiffening again in his breeches, Tyler released his powerful grip, and they helped each other to their feet, both flushed and off balance.

The girl shook her head ruefully at Tyler. "A lusty fighter—"

"Fights hardest still." Tyler nodded and shrugged at her teasing abuse.

"Your lord is merciful." The log wench invited them up for final hurrahs and a last bow to the crowd. She gave them a friendly, knowing glance.

Tyler turned to eye Josh softly. "More than you know."

Josh tried to read his expression behind the smile and the mask.

Balanced on the log, they turned to face different sections of the crowd, bowing several times.

Tyler tipped his head to say softly to Josh, "A draw, then."

Josh nodded, pulse racing. The full-length press of Tyler's body still burned through his costume. What did it mean? He needed to know… but he suspected the day wasn't close to over.

After their impromptu duel on the log and whatever had happened between them pressed together down in the pit, Josh needed a breather.

Tyler stopped to splash his face at a water fountain. "You hungry? After all that hard combat and shopping, I'm about to starve." Then the rough accent again and the rogue's grin. "But as it seems now I am *your* prisoner, I can but beg your indulgence."

"Indulge away." Josh laughed, following Tyler to a vendor offering massive turkey legs. The scent of roast meat and spices filled the air.

Tyler snorted, handing Josh a huge, greasy drumstick and a mug of cider. "I got you pretty good."

The cider was cold and tart. "You just can't handle defeat, Fantana."

"Maybe 'tis you can't handle victory, milord." Tyler claimed his own leg and tankard from the counter, then asked the server, "Might I steal a couple sheets of that parchment?" He rolled the blank pages and tucked them in his belt.

As they walked away, Josh took an enormous bite of turkey, savoring the burst of flavor. "Wow. So good."

Tyler tore into his own turkey leg with gusto, leaving a smear of grease on his cleft chin. "Let's find a table."

"You know I went easy on you." Tyler's eyes crinkled at the corners, teasing.

Warmth flooded Josh's cheeks. "I certainly didn't go hard on you." He realized what he'd said and stopped while he was ahead.

Tyler shrugged with a roguish smirk. "Well. Hard or soft, what would I not do to protect my liege?"

They found a semisecluded picnic table under a broad oak and sat to watch the crowd drift by. Up on a stage across the way, a troupe was doing some kind of lowbrow farce with a wizard, a jester, and a dragon puppet that farted fire.

Tyler took another bite of turkey and washed it down with a swallow from his mug. "You having an okay time?"

"Okay? Tyler, that was— You're so— The best Sunday, maybe ever." Josh shook his head, trying to find the words. "I don't know. In my life. Thank you for this." He wiped his face with a paper napkin. "I don't even think I can explain. I'd never be brave enough. Or crazy enough. You always make me feel like I can do anything."

Tyler gave him a funny look then and blinked. "Uh. Likewise."

"Well, yeah. Okay, running and dumbbells. But I mean…." Josh looked down at the embroidered waistcoat. "This costume? A sword? Ye Olde Times wish fulfillment? Turkey? You in a bedazzled codpiece flexing your tight end with a thousand people clapping for us?"

"More like forty, but point taken." Tyler raised his tankard and did the accent again. "You are most welcome, sir. And as you are a clever lad, you'll have realized by now that all this abduction and Renaissancing isn't just for sweaty fights and fistfuls of greasy meat." He pulled out the paper and a pencil.

Josh didn't follow. "It isn't?"

"It's also a solution to Hamilton's busybody problem. Your library dilemma." Tyler put his half-eaten turkey leg down on a napkin and wiped his greasy hands before picking up the pencil again. "So, I was thinking the reason this place works so well is that it meets the visitors where they need to be met. It interacts with them, but each of them differently. They willingly do most of the work."

"I don't understand."

Tyler began doodling a familiar building. "The library. The reason dummies attack libraries is that books are quiet and still."

Josh squinted and chuckled. "Well, yeah."

"A building for readers seems passive to bigots who don't know better because they're too lazy to pay attention." Tyler drew a tiny mob with pitchforks. "Libraries just sit there full of books. Books are inanimate. They can't fight back. They can't vote. They can't shout assholes down. They have to take the abuse like a tackle dummy unless someone fights for them."

"Oh. Oh!" He nodded now.

"Let's just say… what if we make the library more than a single inanimate thing and make it into a Pleasure Faire?" He opened his arms to include their surroundings. "A bunch of interactive experiences for different kinds of visitors. No longer a passive target." He took another bite of turkey and wrote something down. "Bring the books to life a bit."

"That's brilliant. You're brilliant. Why didn't I think of that?"

"Well, Joshua, I think probably because you got a full-time job with kids and you've been saving my ass and putting me back together on the daily. While I, on the other hand, have got time to spare and a crappy attitude." Tyler winked and wrote something else down with another doodle.

"You mean we can raise money. Open it up so more kids use it for something other than napping and making out."

"For starters." Tyler nodded and wrote down FUNDS, circled it and drew a bunch of lines like rays of sunlight. "I mean yeah… a fundraiser, but more than just that. Remind people that the library is always doing all kinds of stuff that they forgot about. It only interacts with them if they bother to notice. Like put the 'fun' in fundraiser. We make them—" He extended his hand.

Josh reached out and squeezed his fingers. "Pay attention. Sorry."

Tyler squinted in confusion. "For what?"

"I'm super greasy."

"It's turkey. I'm already covered in it, and it's delicious." Tyler grinned and sucked Josh's grease off his fingers. He made another note, then looked across at the wizard and the dragon puppet snuggling on the stage. Behind them, the crowd applauded at something.

"Okay."

"And this Faire is just a jumping-off place." Tyler kept scribbling ideas and doodling on the page in front of him, bullet points and shapes connected by lines and even a couple small figures that looked suspiciously like medieval Powerpuff Girls. "The library events don't need to be themed like this place, but we could do some games, a lock-in night with popcorn and reading a classic aloud. Or used book adoptions."

Josh saw where he was going. "A costume contest connected to curriculum. Some adult writing classes or literacy challenges."

"Exactly. It's harder for the jerks to hit a moving target. So we *move* people. They'll do most of the work." He looked around pointedly at the crowd of folks who'd worn their own costumes to come play today.

Tyler's enthusiasm was infectious. Josh could picture the whole scheme so clearly, and the possibilities for promotion and fundraising looked endless.

"It's perfect, Tyler. Carver will get behind this whole deal. The library needs help, and the students would love it, especially if you'll be involved. Local businesses can sponsor prizes, do a book drive, some local charity awareness. Especially those doodles." He gestured at Tyler's artistic additions.

"Hey, don't knock the Powerpuffs. They kick ass in any era." Tyler grinned, playfully elbowing Josh. "Keep reminding folks their library is working hard all the time, quietly interacting with everyone. It'll be great. We got this."

Josh found himself unable to shake the nagging question: *We?* Just how long would Tyler stick around Cinnamar once his injuries healed? He couldn't figure out how to ask without seeming weird. Instead, he focused on what was right in front of them.

"And then there's the obvious thing," Tyler said, breaking Josh's train of thought. "I've been thinking about tapping the San Diego Swells to generate more buzz. They always need positive PR. Maybe some of the guys could come out for a charity game or an autograph auction."

"Really? That would be amazing!" Josh exclaimed, his heart swelling with gratitude. But Tyler's impending return to San Diego hovered somewhere close, shadowing his excitement.

"Absolutely. I mean, it's not every day you get a chance to save a library," Tyler replied, his eyes never leaving Josh's.

"And here I thought today was just tights and turkey legs." Josh bumped shoulders. "You're pretty sneaky, Master Robber."

Next to the word MOVING on his paper, Tyler doodled another hovering Powerpuff Girl to protect it with a punch. "Josh, I want to help however I can. Those book-ban biddies won't know what hit 'em."

Joy and purpose filled Josh's chest, along with a surge of affection for Tyler's passion. On impulse, he leaned against Tyler's shoulder with a contented sigh.

After a beat, Tyler draped an arm around him, casual and warm. They sat together, watching the world go by in a sea of cloaks and crowns.

Tyler had become the adventure he never thought he'd find.

Eventually they stood, and Josh noticed the lines of strain around Tyler's eyes and mouth. "You okay?"

"Just a little sore. It's been a long day." Tyler grimaced. "Back. Hips. Methinks your prisoner needs a rack in a soft dungeon."

"Let's get out of the crush, then." Josh stood, catching Tyler's hand to help him up and tug him along. "This way."

He led Tyler into the shady hedge maze, but only realized he was still holding Tyler's hand when they passed the first bend. Self-conscious, Josh let go and guided Tyler to an empty stone bench under a canopy of woven branches from two trees.

Josh looked up. "How do they do that? That must take forever."

"Braid the trees? Well, this Faire has been here fifty or sixty years, I think. It's the original, after all." Tyler closed his eyes and leaned back. His powerful thighs fell open, exposing his sparkly rooster as he relaxed against the cool stone. He sighed. "That feels so good. I pushed it hard today, huh? Plus you beat me up but good."

"After you dragged me through a mob onto a log and threw a sword at me."

"Hardly threw." Tyler smiled, though his eyes stayed closed. He crossed his arms and scrunched down a bit, as if snuggling into the stone bench. "I'm going to tell Nadia... and then you are in *trouble*."

"Uh-huh. You do that, Fantana." Josh sat back too. It did feel great to sit in the quiet. "Oh. Nice." The air was cooler now, though Tyler's thigh was warm against his.

"Thank you for kidnapping me," Josh said at last. "Today has been incredible."

"My pleasure. So fun. I like seeing you cut loose, enjoy yourself that much." Tyler smiled, dozy and close.

Away from the surge and flow of the other Faire visitors, that odd timeless quality returned, almost like their silvery morning runs or the quiet time driving. The fading afternoon seemed to waver on the edge of something lovely and hushed, just offstage.

Josh might have dozed a bit too, because he noticed the sun had fallen toward the horizon. The maze was now dim and bluish.

Josh didn't have a watch to check, but from the angle of the sun, he suspected it was late afternoon. "Ty.... We should head out soon, before it gets full dark."

"Yeah." Tyler roused and brought his legs together to stand. "Your wish is my only desire, milord. And your desire my only wish."

Outside the maze, long shadows now streaked the jousting field and paths as Josh and Tyler emerged into the main grounds again.

As dusk fell, the Renaissance Pleasure Faire began to wind down. Stalls shuttered their windows, and performers took their final bows. Everyone seemed happy and muted.

Josh and Tyler sauntered back toward the entrance, their path illuminated by arches and trees twined with pale fairy lights. Outside the main gate, the vast lot had started to empty, exposing their truck, which mercifully shortened their search.

Tyler pointed at it with a cry. "My kingdom for a pickup."

Once they reached it, Josh pressed the key ring fob and the lights flashed and the locks beeped open. Tyler hesitated for a moment before grimacing. "Do you mind if I change out of this gear?"

"'Course not."

"I'm too tired to do it inside the cab." Tyler opened the driver's door and stood behind it, his thick belt dangling from one fist. "But I don't want anyone— Can you stand guard and watch for any dick pic drones or iPhones?"

Josh nodded and faced the main gate, trying to be a gentleman. As it happened, the door mostly hid Tyler from nipples to knees.

"We need to bring back codpieces." There was rustling and some groans as he tossed something onto the seat, presumably his bedazzled rooster cup. "Still good?" Tyler asked.

"You're good. Not a soul but us for fifty yards." A couple of the streetlamps had clicked on. Josh hadn't realized how late it was.

One boot came off and then the other. Tyler's bare feet lowered carefully onto the ground. "Better. Much better."

Josh blinked. "Dude, your feet are gigantic."

"Yep. Size seventeen." Tyler's head poked around, still wearing the half mask. In one hand he held a loose T-shirt and jeans. "Last call. I'm about to get butt-ass naked right here in Los Angeles County. Full dangle. Am I clear?"

"No stalkers. No paparazzi." Josh scanned the lot and sky and saw no movement at all. "Clear for naked."

Tyler bent over and hissed at something. "Yessss. Jesus." He straightened again and adjusted something. "Oh, that's better. Whew. Oh, my nuts."

Up top, his upper chest showed through the window. On the bottom, Josh could only see his calves flex and his ginormous bare feet on the hard-packed dirt one at a time as he skinned out of the tights. Tyler leaned into the truck, and the feet stepped into blue jeans; then he reemerged looking sheepish and shy. "Thank you most heartily, my lord.

My butt was wet and my balls were about to bust. Both butt and balls express their most salty gratitude." He bowed.

Tyler seemed sore and tired after their long day together.

"Hey, why don't I drive us home?" Josh said. "You can even conk out if you want."

"Deal." Tyler's smile deepened. "Thanks, Coach. I knew there was a reason I always do what you tell me."

"Always?" Josh teased.

"Mmh." Tyler said softly. "Big bananas."

"Let me take the keys," Josh offered, concern lacing his voice. "I'm pretty sure I know the way."

Tyler looked up with a grateful smile as he held out the keys. "It's your day off, after all. You got school first thing. You sure?"

"I'm kidnapping you this time, big guy," Josh insisted, sliding behind the wheel. "Get some rest."

As they cruised south on I-15 in the dark, a huge grin spread across Josh's face, his heart full to bursting.

Twenty minutes out of Irwindale, Tyler fell asleep, first leaning back in a doze but then gradually drifting sideways until his head rested gently on Josh's shoulder. His hair smelled like cider and sunlight. The intimacy of the moment felt like home, and after the amazing day they'd shared, Josh reveled in the fantasy of Tyler as his happy other half.

Josh drove through the sparkling dark, glancing over now and then at Tyler dozing against his shoulder. His heart swelled with tenderness at how vulnerable Tyler seemed in sleep, the handsome face softened by dreaming. All his wild bravado had fallen away, leaving the real Tyler that Josh had always glimpsed beneath the swagger.

I have to say something while I have the chance.

With each mile that passed, Josh's determination to confess his true feelings solidified. Before Tyler left to rejoin his team in San Diego, Josh vowed to come clean about the crush and everything else.

Consequences be damned.

For now, though, he focused on the gleaming road ahead of them, enveloped by the comforting weight of Tyler's head on his shoulder and the simple pleasure of being rocked together in the dark.

Chapter Nine

IN THE Fantana family kitchen, Tyler fussed with the place settings again. His mother's good china, cloth napkins, candlesticks—nothing needed to be fancy, but he wanted it right.

Mr. Poops meowed and wound between Tyler's ankles, nearly tripping him again. "Hush, you menace." Tyler scooped up his marmalade overlord and cuddled him close, breathing in the familiar warmth of his fur. "What if he hates enchiladas? Or Nadia's snarky matchmaking? Or… this shirt? I still think it's too tight."

"Tyler. It's fine. He doesn't hate anything." Nadia was being very patient with him.

A sharp rap rattled the front door, and Tyler's heart leaped. He put the cat down and caught sight of his own shirt. "Aw, Poops. Now I'm covered in fuzz." He brushed his chest with his hands and then rolled the sticky lint roller across himself.

Nadia reappeared in the pantry doorway. "Calm down. You're fine. Promise." She dragged a big X over her heart with her finger and winked at him. "You look very eligible."

Tyler consciously forced his shoulders to relax. At least he knew she knew; that would be a help. If it killed him, tonight he was going to tell Josh the truth.

Defuzzed and a little calmer, he followed Mr. Poops into the living room as Nadia opened the door. Josh stood beaming on the threshold, gripping the necks of two wine bottles in one hand and handing Nadia a bouquet of sunflowers with the other.

"You shouldn't have," Nadia said, ushering him in.

Josh rolled his eyes. "Your brother is poisoning me for dinner. It's the least I can do." His gaze found Tyler's, and a slow smile bent his mouth. "And it's good to see you all scrubbed up."

Heat flushed Tyler's cheeks. "Are you calling me dirty?"

"Boys, behave." Nadia plucked the wine and flowers from Josh's grip. "I'll put these in water. Tyler, why don't you take Josh to the living room."

A squeak from below as Mr. Poops demanded his share of the conversation. Tyler obliged and scooped him up. "This is Mr. Poops. You've met him before, I think. If anyone gets poisoned, he did it."

With Mr. Poops balanced across his shoulder, Tyler showed Josh to the cozy living room, past the hallway gallery of family portraits and school photos and the dogleg den that had been his and Nadia's playroom as children when his mother was working. Josh's arm brushed Tyler's, sending a skitter of sparks across his skin.

"Looking good." In the kitchen, Josh nodded at Nadia. "You made a bunch of changes."

"Nadia made some renovations a few years back." Tyler jerked his chin at the new windows and polished terracotta floors.

"After our mom passed. Just to refresh. You know." Nadia handed Josh a knife. "Make yourself useful, Joshua. Bell peppers."

"I can only cook because Tyler keeps trying to teach me." Josh nudged Tyler's elbow, his dark blue eyes dancing. "Bossy."

"Welcome to the Fantana house of horrors," Tyler said, nudging him back.

"Pure torture." Josh's gaze softened, bright with affection.

Tyler's chest tightened. Tonight, he'd tell Josh the truth. That he was terrified of losing his best friend, but he couldn't ignore the incendiary chemistry between them. A risk, but one he needed to take. He only hoped Josh wouldn't get weird if he didn't feel the same.

Tyler chopped onions and stole glances at Josh, who hummed along to the radio as he worked. The familiarity warmed Tyler, reminded him of cooking with his family before his mom got so sick, talking and teasing each other.

"Earth to Tyler." Nadia snapped her fingers in front of his face. "You're not chopping, you're just staring. Those onions won't dice themselves."

Tyler blinked, cheeks heating. "Just thinking."

"Do tell." Nadia raised an eyebrow.

Tyler shot her a warning look, but she only laughed.

"We need to get these in the oven or I'm sending you up to Famiglia for a pizza."

Josh glanced between them, eyes curious, but he didn't pry. Tyler was grateful for his tact. He focused on dicing the onions, but his thoughts continued to drift, imagining what might come after dinner.

The onions stung his eyes, and he told himself that was the reason for the prickling behind his lids.

With the prep work done, they slid the enchiladas into the oven. "Perfect timing," Nadia said. "Dinner in twenty. You guys go set the table."

"I live to serve," Tyler said, giving her a mock salute.

In the dining room, Josh nudged him again. "Everything okay? You seem… I don't know. Worried about something."

"Nope." Tyler gulped and grinned. "A little news is all. We can talk after dinner. Everything good. Thanks for coming over."

Josh studied his face, then blinked, slow and sweet. "Okay, I'm here."

Tyler nodded, a tickle of sweat along his ribs. Tonight, everything might change.

With Nadia finishing the poblanos, they settled in the living room, the savory aroma of enchiladas wafting through the house. Tyler sank into the sofa, pulse skittering as Josh sat beside him, their thighs barely touching.

As soon as they sat, Mr. Poops padded over and leaped into Josh's lap with a plaintive yowl. "You're a big loaf of cat." Josh laughed, scratching the purring fuzzball behind his ears. "I think he's adopted me."

"He knows a sucker when he sees one," Tyler said. But the sight of Poops kneading Josh's leg, eyes closed in exquisite pleasure, stirred a rush of affection.

Nadia came in, carrying a photo album. "So, I hate when assholes do this to a guest, but we've been making her enchiladas, and the oven needs us to kill a couple minutes, so tough…."

Josh craned forward. "Your mom?"

She nodded and sat on the ottoman across from them and opened it to a picture of their mom at the beach, smiling into the camera.

"I only met her a few times, before she got—"

Tyler nodded. Their mom's cancer had been fast and taken her almost without warning. He'd just signed his second NFL contract with the Swells, and Nadia dropped out of college to nurse her. A rough time.

"We don't have many photos of her," Nadia said, watching Tyler's eyes, then Josh. "But I thought you might like to see. This is when we planted the gardenias in the backyard. She loved white flowers."

Josh gazed at the picture of the tiny dark woman who'd raised them so well, his eyes softening. "She looks so happy."

"She was," Tyler said. "The best." He peered at the photo, a familiar ache blooming in his chest. How he wished his mom could've really known Josh now, as a man. "Her family was from Caracas, but they immigrated in the sixties. She grew up in Temecula."

Nadia turned the page. "Here we are as kids. Gymnastics, I think. Yeah. And that's first communion, which may have been the only time Tyler washed his face before he moved into the locker room."

Josh cocked his head at Nadia. "I didn't remember that your mom was so tiny."

Nadia shrugged. "Venezuela."

Tyler nodded. He got his dark hair and skin from her, but his size from his horrible dad.

As she flipped, Tyler noticed that Nadia had carefully removed and cropped every single photo of their father. With good reason. He frowned at his knuckles. He really appreciated her keeping what mattered and weeding out so much of the ugliness.

"That's our tacky cousins. Then… I think that's Disneyland." Nadia kept flipping, leaning forward so that Josh and Tyler had to press shoulder-to-shoulder to see. "And Tyler winning something else, again. That looks like Easter. Oh hey, me playing beauty parlor…. Look at Tyler's hair!"

"No, don't show him that!" Tyler protested, but Josh was already chuckling at the sight of ten-year-old Tyler in baggy Spider-Man briefs with a spectacular cowlick.

"Wow." Josh's eyes crinkled at the corners, and Tyler's heart squeezed.

"I was not exactly adorable." Tyler gave Josh's arm a shove, but he was fighting a grin.

Nadia poked him. "Very adorable. Even Poops thinks you're adorable."

"You're ganging up on me again."

"That's what we do." With a sniff, Nadia closed the album and stood. "Humiliation complete. Enchiladas headed your way. Coming?"

In the dining room, Tyler served as they sat, and everyone dug into the enchiladas with groans and exclamations of appreciation. Tyler's nerves had mostly settled into a warm hum of contentment. Having Josh here, sharing this meal, felt so comfortable, so real.

"Well, this is the best dinner I've had in I don't know how long. So thank you both." Josh lifted his wine. "I'd like to raise a glass to your mom. I wish I'd known her sooner and better."

Tyler gave Josh a grateful nod. Nadia raised her glass and carefully wiped her eyes, trying not to smudge. "*Salud.*"

Nadia sat back. "I am stuffed. Shall we?"

Tyler stood and followed Josh to the living room.

They sat on the couch, their legs knocking together companionably. Tonight, Josh had worn chinos and a deep blue knit shirt, just about the color of his eyes, that made his hair seem even more gold.

Tyler looked up and caught Nadia watching him watch Josh and blushed.

"Anyone need a top-up?" Nadia held up the wine.

"Please." Tyler raised his glass. If nothing else, the alcohol was keeping his nerves at bay. He wasn't letting Josh leave before he made things plain between them.

Nadia poured. "Josh?"

"I'm good. I have to drive."

"So, uhh, Josh…." She tipped her head at him with a wicked expression. "Has America's Tightest End shown you his time capsule?"

"Nadia." Tyler pointed a warning finger. "Don't you even."

"I mean, we're talking about boy archeology." She squirmed away, laughing.

Tyler stiffened, pretending to be more defensive than he felt. "Oh no…. Don't you dare. Again with the ganging up."

"It's like, old-school Smithsonian puberty in there, fascinating and mysterious but also a little scary."

Tyler drained his glass and put it down. He needed his hands free. He stood and playfully grabbed his sister.

Josh chuckled. "I can imagine. After all, my room was probably worse. You don't even know."

"Impossible." She dodged Tyler, trying to cover her mouth, both of them laughing. "Pennants and deflated balls. Scout badges and snapshots pinned to the corkboard. Weird costumes he wore for pep rallies. Pro-wrestling posters."

"Hey! Don't judge," Tyler barked in wounded laughter. "You had posters."

"Nice ones. You had boy bands, spandex wrestlers with mullets, and worse, I swear."

Josh nodded, grinning.

"Don't encourage her." Tyler tried to cover her mouth, but she ducked and slipped away.

"Rows of these little dusty trophies for anything: under-five karate, hot-dog eating, butt-juggling. But freakiest of all—" She turned to Josh again, laughing and scurrying to keep away from Tyler. "A hidden jar of finger-scooped Vaseline that expired in 2006. I mean! And so help me, a pile of crusty magazines under that saggy, stained twin bed like an NC-17 medical experiment. That whole room is only held together by semen and pigskin." Nadia was laughing so hard that now Josh was laughing too.

"You're both horrible and I hate you." Tyler rubbed his face and let his shoulders fall, mock defeated.

Nadia shrugged. "No big deal. Masturbation is normal and healthy."

He turned to Josh. "She is lying to you now."

Nadia shook her head. "As if."

Tyler winked. "I threw out the magazines."

Josh laughed, and Tyler laughed with him, but Nadia gave them a knowing smile and herded them toward the hall. "Take all the time you need."

As requested, Tyler opened the door to his boyhood bedroom and let Josh explore for himself.

Josh took his time, handling the bits of Tyler's memories with almost conscious care. He read the invites and the clippings, brushed the little trophies and model cars. He clocked all the cheesy, beefy athletes and pretty boys that had shaped Tyler's fantasies and ambitions. His methodical scrutiny didn't seem invasive, more understanding, as though he was deciphering the code of Tyler's secret heart.

Seeing Josh browse the abandoned clutter of his whole life felt… odd and vaguely sweet, private in a good way. He had nothing to hide, certainly not from someone who had come to matter so much.

Tyler sighed. He had half a mind to confess everything right now.

Josh looked up with a kind expression. "This is a great room. It feels like you."

Tyler laughed. "Not quite. Look at all this."

Since he'd come back, Tyler hadn't had the heart to change anything in here. He didn't want to get too comfortable, and remembering this other life accurately, honestly, felt essential somehow. His shrink could probably explain. Maybe something about his mom, his life, his path. He shook his head to clear the thought.

"Don't tell your sister." Josh leaned over to whisper. "Mine was way worse."

"I refuse to believe that."

Browsing the shelf above the desk, Josh flipped open a yearbook full of signatures. "Your mom kept the past safe for you. And then your sister. So you could go out and conquer the world. I love that."

Tyler nodded, stunned by the way Josh always cut right to the point, his absolute clarity. "They did."

"Hey...." Josh picked up the copy of *The Three Musketeers* he'd bought Tyler in Ocotillo Heights. "You're reading it."

Tyler's brow furrowed in confusion. "Of course I am. Why wouldn't I?"

"No, I don't mean it like that, but...." He blinked and ran his hand over the old cover. "I mean, you started right away."

"Well it's either that or *Atlas Shrugged*. No thanks. I hated that crap the first time."

"No lie." Josh nodded and chuckled, then riffled the pages.

"I thought you knew.... I love it. I should've said something."

"About *Musketeers*?" Josh looked perplexed.

"That's where our whole library scheme came from. It's D'Artagnan's fault, actually." He poked Josh with a wicked grin.

Josh laughed and squirmed. "Do what now?"

"That guy! What a dumbass. He shows up with all these assumptions and barges into everyone else's fights. At first I thought I was Porthos. But I'm not. Or I'm not always. No one is." He shook his head, feeling like he'd said too much. "That's not the point. What I mean is, the book came alive. So really this whole library rescue scheme is your fault."

Josh handed the book back. "Where are you at?"

"D'Artagnan just beat DeWinter and met Milady. You know." He cocked one rakish eyebrow and put his hands on his hips like a swashbuckler. "The more hearts are worth the capture, the more difficult they are to be won."

Oh.

He realized what he'd said, but he just left Dumas's words right out there.

"Uhh." Josh's gaze held his for a moment, but then before either of them said anything too crazy, he dropped his eyes to the twin bed. "I'm going to take your word on the spank bank under there."

Tyler held up two fingers. "Scout's honor."

"Sorry, Fantana. There's no honor in spank banks." He grinned. "Let's get back. I don't want your sister to have to wash up."

Tyler followed Josh back to the kitchen, passing Nadia sipping wine on the couch. "We call dishes."

She raised her glass. "Music to my ears."

They ended up washing in tandem, like a four-armed octopus, rinsing, and loading the machine. Tyler's skin tingled with each accidental brush of their skin.

Then they tackled the big pots.

At one point while scouring the roasting pan, Tyler playfully splashed Josh with suds. Josh laughed and sprayed him back in retaliation, and they wrestled, wet, for control of the faucet.

They froze, dripping in each other's arms, pulses thrumming where their hands grasped slick wrists. Josh's face only came to Tyler's shoulder, and Tyler felt super aware of his groin against Josh's abs. Just like when he'd pulled Josh down onto him after their duel, Tyler panicked. For a breathless moment, neither one seemed to know what to do.

Nadia called from the living room, "For the record, you two hoodlums are cleaning up whatever mess is happening in there."

They separated sheepishly to dry off as Nadia poked her head in, cradling a sleepy Mr. Poops. "Fellas, I'm pretty wiped out. A little tipsy probably, so me and this rascal are heading to bed." She gave them a knowing look. "No puddles. Play nice."

Josh raised a soapy hand. "G'night, Nadia."

"Night, sis." Tyler bussed her cheek, certain he was blushing.

Once she was gone, the silence between them grew charged. They began tucking the leftovers into the fridge and freezer as needed. Josh grinned at something.

"What?"

Josh shook his head. "Those enchiladas are *serious*. The whole dinner. Delicious."

"Awesome. Thanks for hanging out tonight."

"Are you kidding?" Josh shrugged.

"We can do it whenever you want. Nadia loved it. I loved it."

Josh blinked at that and nodded. Mr. Poops wandered back in for a drink of water or maybe to spy for Nadia.

Tyler cleared his throat, focusing on covering the tray of enchiladas with foil. "Oh! I forgot to say before: our library lock-in's all set for next month. The librarians loved the idea of *Three Musketeers*, and Carver gave us the green light."

"Seriously?" Josh's smile was incandescent as a sunrise. "That's—wow. *Musketeers* is a perfect idea. How did you manage that?"

Tyler shrugged, heat creeping up his neck. "Just got to get approval from the school board. But it's a classic. And with Principal Carver on our side, should be simple enough."

As Tyler and Josh finished cleaning the kitchen, an easy silence fell between them, broken only by Mr. Poops's rumbling purr where he curled up on the windowsill, blinking his enormous orange eyes at them like a drowsy chaperone.

As they moved around the kitchen, Tyler savored each glance and casual touch, thrilling at the secret intimacy.

Once the kitchen was spotless, they stood there a moment, the only sound the dishwasher's muted churn. Josh leaned against the counter, smiling at Tyler in a way that made him short-circuit.

Josh asked, "All good?"

"So good." Tyler ambled back into the living area and realized that before Nadia hit the hay, she had gone for full, obvious, bachelor-pad mood lighting. Only things missing were low sax music, a bowl of condoms, and an ice bucket.

Tyler winced, torn between annoyance at his sister's meddling and gratitude she approved of Josh.

"I guess my sister turned everything down when she went to bed." He scratched the back of his neck. The low lights and plumped cushions all felt fake, like a staged seduction on a soap opera. "We could go outside. Get some air maybe? The moon should be risen by now."

Tyler appreciated Nadia's efforts, but Josh deserved something better, something real. He opened the door to the patio.

"Sure." Josh followed Tyler out the back door into the cool night. "Oh… this is lovely. I've never seen all this."

"Nadia's kept it up. My mom put this in after my dad split."

Josh nodded. "And that's the gardenia. White flowers."

"From the picture. Yeah."

They wandered the garden path, shoulders brushing. Tyler stared up at the sky as a nervous energy crackled between them.

"Is that a little tree house?" Josh was looking up at a tiny cottage and a series of small ledges nailed to a trellis that led up to it.

"I built that for Mr. Poops." Tyler frowned. "When I first got home and I could barely get out of bed. Nadia knew I needed a project, so she asked me to make something out here for that crazy cat."

"He's pretty terrific."

Tyler pointed at Josh and chuckled. "See, that's how he gets you. We never had pets growing up. My father hated animals. But about a year ago, Nadia came home from the grocery store and Mr. Poops was sitting inside the garage yowling at her like she was late for an appointment. Dumb cat."

"Not so dumb."

"Well, no. That's the thing. He wouldn't scram. He just kept being loud and cute until Nadia gave up and gave in. Now it's like he's always lived here. Sleeps in my bed most nights."

"I've always wanted a pet, but I've never had the nerve." Josh sounded sheepish at the confession.

Tyler looked at him like he was bananas. "They aren't scary."

"I think it's all the feelings. I worry too much. If something happens, what do you do?"

"You deal." Tyler turned and tapped his heart. "I mean… right?"

Josh laughed. "Yeah. Of course."

"Until you do, you're welcome to come borrow Poops anytime."

"Deal." Their eyes held again for a bunch of heartbeats.

The backyard was bright under the moon, the air balmy and soft.

After a few minutes of companionable silence, Josh turned to say, "Well… it's getting late. I should head home."

"No." Tyler didn't want him to go. He still hadn't said any of the things he needed to. "Don't go yet."

Josh looked surprised. "Oh. Okay. If you want."

"That sounded bad." *Say something, dummy. Tell him.* "I just like you being here. A lot. If you need to go, I'm not going to keep you prisoner."

Josh bumped against him. "You already abducted me once, remember?"

Tyler stepped in to stand behind Josh under the twinkling stars, close enough to feel the warmth of his body.

Josh turned as if to ask him a question. For one long moment of anticipatory silence, Tyler felt the shimmer of all his unspoken emotions hanging in the air. And then Josh reached up and touched Tyler's face wonderingly.

All his fears fell away. Tyler turned his face into Josh's palm and kissed it with passionate intensity, trying to communicate everything in him in one movement. "I can't help it."

Josh froze again but didn't take his hand away. At first his eyes looked terrified and titillated.

Unable to resist one more second, Tyler leaned in and kissed Josh, folding him in his arms and devouring him, claiming him, pouring all his longing and desire into the burning place where their mouths met.

"Unf." Josh made a happy sound at the back of his throat. After a startled heartbeat or two, Josh's arms rose and closed around Tyler. Josh tipped his head and kissed back with real hunger, growling and grinding against him.

Tyler couldn't get close enough. Bending his knees, he pressed Josh back into the tree trunk. He pulled and grabbed at Josh's flesh, grappling with all the raw strength bundled in his arms.

Josh grunted at something and stumbled a moment, but then they were braced solid and his erection pressed hard against Tyler's belly, humping against him. The pleasure was exquisite.

Tyler ground his own boner into Josh's muscle. His skin was fire, and heat crackled around them both. If he wasn't careful, he'd lose control standing in his boyhood backyard and cum in his boxer briefs. "Wait—wait. Hold up."

"Sorry. Oh." Josh raised a shaking hand to his lips. "Sorry."

"No. Not that. No, Josh. Look at me. Not sorry. For this? Please don't ever be sorry. I'm sorry. I didn't even ask. I shouldn't have jumped you like that, but you make me so crazy."

Josh blinked. "Know the feeling."

Tyler bent down and pressed a firm kiss to Josh's mouth again, savoring it. "I couldn't stop myself. Swear to God I tried, but I just couldn't keep control of it anymore."

Josh looked stunned and nodded. "Seriously?"

"Josh, I've been trying to find a way to say something. You don't even know. All these weeks going out of my mind." He raised a hand and touched Josh's beautiful face, traced the perfect line of his jaw. "But I saw you back then. High school and all. I mean, there was me, some dumb jock, and you were a genius. What chance did I have? And if I'd done anything, said anything…."

Josh squinted at that. "I don't believe you."

"I know. I'm sorry. But I was too scared. Of the guys. Of you. I couldn't be queer back then. Captain of the team. MVP. They would've been awful to both of us. I couldn't take the risk. And back then football was my only ticket out, state then pro. I had to save my family, and I had one shot."

Josh nodded, looking over Tyler's face like he was reading it. "I get it. I can't quite believe, but I understand."

"But when I saw you at the track, that first morning, I couldn't believe. Like a miracle. I can't explain." Tyler bent to kiss him again, pushing his tongue across Josh's and gripping his biceps hard. He pushed one arm behind Josh's back and pulled him closer, tighter. He'd never felt so possessive of anyone. He hitched Josh closer, almost lifting him off the ground.

A hand on his chest pushed back. Josh was holding him at bay gently, eyes lowered as if burdened by a secret of his own.

"Hey. What is it?"

Josh stepped back from him. His arms hung limp at his sides, and his eyes were shadowed by the moon. He looked pale and haunted. "Tyler…."

"Tell me."

"I've had a crush on you since, well, forever." He swallowed, licked his lips. "I've wanted you for most of my life. Since high school. Way before you were famous. I guess it's good you never knew. I have been pining for you since I was fourteen years old."

"You did? You do?" Tyler's heart roared in his ears.

"Terribly. Continually. I've wanted you for so long, and I needed to be honest before anything else happens. And after tonight, I'm not going to be able to fight the feelings anymore when I'm with you."

"Okay. That's okay. You liking me is *more* than okay."

"I don't think so. All this past month, you kept being so funny and charming. Almost like flirting."

"Because I *was* flirting. And getting nowhere, I might add." Tyler couldn't understand why Josh suddenly seemed so sad. "I feel like an idiot."

"No. I figured you guessed or knew about… everything."

Tyler shook his head. "How could I know?"

Josh laughed and wiped his eyes. "Well, as it happens… lots and lots of complete strangers pine over you all the time. But not like I do."

"I don't care about them." Tyler kissed him again, until Josh pulled back, his brow creased.

"That's not what I mean, Tyler. Before you got famous. I *fantasized*."

"I'm not mad. Why would I be mad?"

A tear slipped down Josh's face and fell. "You don't understand. I feel gross admitting it now. But I want to be honest with you. I don't—" He sighed. "The way only a horny, lonely teenager does. I *used* you. I must've biked past this house a couple hundred times, right out front. Stalking you. I mean, worse than magazines under the bed. I jerked my dick raw. It's embarrassing to admit it. Every game. Every rally." He was crying for real now.

Tyler blinked at the intensity of Josh's confession, trying to feel like he deserved all that devotion. "Hey. It's okay. You didn't hurt anything. Don't." He brushed away Josh's tears. "I've got you."

"Seems crazy now, because I know you now. Real you." Josh shook his head. "But back then, I spied on you. When our eyes met, or if you bumped against me by accident in the hall, I'd shake. I couldn't help myself."

"Josh. Don't cry." Tyler raised a hand a stroked his hair, his face. He pressed a kiss against his brow and held him close. "I'm right here. It's okay. Shhh. Hey. I've got you. C'mere."

Cradled against his chest, Josh stilled. "Unhealthy, I know. All of it. All these things I projected onto you when you were a kid yourself. And totally unfair to you. Because I knew you were unattainable. Any kind of relationship was impossible."

"It wasn't, though. I wasn't, Josh. I was just too stupid to notice. My family was broke, and as long as I could play football, I had a shot."

"But you came back. After all these years, you got hurt and came home. We spent all this time and then I got to know you, and now… I think I'm an asshole. For treating you like that for so long. I was an asshole to you all this time."

"Why? No. Hey… look at me. Because you had feelings?"

Josh lifted his damp face to look directly into Tyler's eyes. He frowned and shook his head "You're better. You're so much better than I knew. And funnier, sexier, smarter, kinder. I feel like a complete jerk."

Tyler ran a hand up his neck and into his soft hair. "Not even a little." He tenderly cupped the back of Josh's head.

"I don't want to freak you out or scare you away, but I had to tell you, and I did not have the nerve until you kissed me like that, like you meant it."

"Then I better kiss you again, sweet boy. A whole bunch of times."

Josh smiled at that, and Tyler bent down and kissed his chuckle—slow, sliding kisses until Josh stopped crying against his cheeks and Tyler cradled him like something fragile.

"Shhh. Now listen. You are...." Tyler pressed his lips to Josh's forehead. "The most wonderful person I've ever met in my life, Joshua Ayres. A blessing. And if you want to stalk me, harass me, or molest me in any way, you have my absolute permission to use me as much as you're able. Anything. I want every filthy bit of it. Your absolute worst. You hear me?" He kissed Josh's lips and squeezed him hard. "I want it bad."

"Ugh. Awful." Josh hiccupped and laugh-cried at that, wiping his smiling face. "Jeez."

He kissed the side of Josh's head. "What's the matter?"

"It's too much. I don't know where to put everything you're doing to me."

"Right here, man. You give it all to me. I can take it." Tyler flexed his arms and made a dumb face. "I wish you'd said something. All that time."

"I couldn't back then. And now, I was terrified of wrecking this... whatever has happened between us since you came back, if I screwed up," Josh confessed, voice shaking. "Impossible. I thought you'd hate me."

"Good luck with that."

Josh looked him in the eye. "Thanks for understanding."

"We're a pair, huh?" Limbs still tangled, he touched Josh's mouth, his damp lips swollen with kisses.

Josh tipped his head back. "You think?"

"And plenty possible. Your heart's beating so fast." Tyler pressed a hand there and peered at Josh a moment. "You realize that we're both so afraid of messing this up... that we almost messed this up."

Josh frowned. "This is what we get for tiptoeing around each other second-guessing everything. Pretty dumb."

"Maybe. I would say pretty." He kissed Josh. "And smart. Seems like we got where we needed to when it was time."

Josh smiled at that. "If you say so. I don't know about you, but I've been quietly going out of my gourd."

"The past couple weeks have got me rethinking everything I do, all I am." Tyler pressed a hand against Josh's heart, feeling the hungry thump of it. "Truth is, I want you more than anything, Joshua Ayres. And I'm going to work like hell to deserve anything you're willing to let me have."

Tyler kissed him again and then licked down the line of his throat, gnawing on the muscle while Josh whimpered and squirmed against him.

"Hang on, Ty. Hold up."

But Tyler sucked harder at the salty flesh, stealing the sweet sounds from Josh like a robber. He pinched Josh's stiff nipples through the shirt, and delicious sweat ran down his face and chest. Tyler groaned in pleasure as Josh started to quake, twitch, and pant.

"Whoa. Easy. Eeeasy, fella." Josh pushed back again and laughed. "You're going to make me embarrass myself more. Jesus." He reached down and adjusted the stiff ridge behind his zipper. "Gimme a sec or I'm going to lose it."

"We could take this inside."

Josh glanced at the house. "We could."

Tyler leaned back against the tree now, bracing himself against it, dying to take his dick out right here. "I mean, we'd have to keep quiet, but I'm willing if you are. Nothing crazy. We're consenting adults."

Josh shook his head. "I don't think tonight. God, I want to, but I think a little time isn't a bad idea. We've had quite a night already. We could both use some sleep."

"Josh, come on. Look what you're doing to me." Pushing back against the bark, Tyler reached down and squeezed his own straining lump of cock through the jeans.

"Same. All the more reason." Josh wiped his mouth and nodded down at their pressed erections. "It's a school night. We have an early run."

Tyler kissed his throat and bit Josh's earlobe.

Josh whimpered in pleasure and licked into his mouth, sucking at his tongue with gentle insistence.

Pulling back, Tyler pressed their cocks together through the denim. "Evil."

"Hey. You gave me permission. You just said you wanted it bad."

"Jeez. *Seriously* evil." Tyler ground into him, savoring the friction and knowing how close he was to the edge.

They kissed once more, slowly, breathing each other in, pulling closer and marking each other. By now, Tyler could feel the outer limits… if he kept going a little further, he'd fall over the cliff just like this.

Tyler tried again, flashing his most winning grin. "Okay—okay. Second offer, we'll just sleep. Just spend the night next to me. No wanky.

No hanky-panky. Just to be able hold you and sleep would be better than anything."

Josh had the nerve to laugh at him. "Uh-huh. Like that would happen."

"Argh." Tyler's heart thudded with a mix of disappointment and gratitude; he tried to ignore his hardness throbbing between them. He whispered, "Joshua. You're so cautious."

"I try to be."

Tyler smiled, staring up at the dark sky then back into the dark blue eyes. "Don't you ever do anything half-assed?"

"Nope. Full-assed only." Josh looked wicked and took two big handfuls of Tyler's glutes, spreading them and kneading them with a hard grip. "I'm a demanding bastard. I want the whole damn thing to myself for as long as you'll let me."

Tyler groaned and kissed him, tasting his tongue and pushing back into his hands. His dick flexed in his pants again, flexed hard, the crown almost cresting his waistband. A little more, just a little more pressure and he was going to—

Josh stepped back. "You think I'm naïve, Fantana? With that big knob dribbling on me? Not going to happen."

Tyler sighed, disappointed and weirdly elated too. Not many people had ever resisted a charm offensive that way. "You're in charge."

"Hardly." Josh took his hand and tugged him away from the tree, heading for the curved path. "Walk me out?"

Tyler nodded and let Josh lead him to the gate and out to the curb, feeling the ache in his dick, a heavy longing but also a funny peace. Josh had promised nothing, yet given everything.

Standing beside the truck, Josh turned to Tyler one last time. They kissed under the starlit sky, nothing raunchy but so real, so true it burned his lips. Tyler felt so full he thought his heart might melt.

Josh pulled back, eyes bright in the half light. "Tomorrow?"

"That's a start."

Josh's truck engine started, and he drove off, leaving Tyler leaning against the front door watching, his humming heart on his sleeve.

He watched until the tiny red taillights slipped out of sight, the night suddenly chilly and clear, and he knew that nothing would ever be the same again.

The stars shone down on him from above, and he didn't even need to look up to feel them.

Chapter Ten

JOSH LEARNED quickly that pro athletes play to win.

The next day, Tyler made Josh feel foolish for ever doubting his intentions. The next week even more so.

Since their backyard kiss in the gardenias, Tyler had set about courting him as though they actually had a stern chaperone and Tyler needed to prove his worth on the field of honor.

The mutual attraction was already a matter of record, so rather than jumping Josh's bones, Tyler seemed determined to savor all the small steps, continually testing and exploring what Josh liked, what he needed, what he wanted.

And vice versa. Now that the ice was broken and all bets were off, Josh learned to read Tyler's moods and messages without second-guessing himself. Josh didn't need to wonder about the myth of Tyler, so instead he indulged his genuine curiosity about the man.

They still ran every morning and worked out in the weight room a couple times a week. Only now they ate together most nights, either at his place or Tyler's. They dated each other like actual adults, blue balls and all. And Tyler sometimes came by the school to help out with busywork.

The kids and faculty knew they were friends, so Tyler's presence wasn't weird. Plus, Tyler seemed to relish being productive, having something to *do*. His recovery was visible now and more rapid every day.

Nine days after their first kiss, Josh was loading the bus for an away game in Escondido when Tyler turned up in the parking lot by the gym.

"Well, you're a sight for sore *everything*." Tyler ambled toward him.

"Hey, superstar." Their eyes and smiles held a few extra beats. They had to be cautious on school grounds, and PDAs were a no-go, obviously. And Josh knew that kids would be turning up in the next hour.

"I was worried I missed you." Tyler thumped the bus. "Escondido tonight, right?"

"Mmh." He patted his pocket to make sure he'd brought the rolls of tape and the extra ankle brace for his quarterback.

Tyler passed him two of the duffels filled with the team's pads. "I wish I could come watch."

"Same. Sorry." Josh could only imagine what the appearance of an NFL player at a scruffy high school stadium would do to the crowd.

"Nah." Tyler frowned and lowered his voice. "It should be about them. I'm just bored and horny. Missing somebody."

"Sorry." The game wouldn't finish till late, so they'd make it back to school sometime after ten. As they circled the bus, Josh ran through his mental prep list. "And sorry about dinner too. I'll make it up."

"We're good. Promise. I actually came to ask a favor."

Something in his voice made Josh pause in his prep and turn.

"If you're cool with it. I wanted to ask.... Any chance you could drive me to the cardiologist after practice tomorrow? I know it's a long way—"

Tyler had never let anyone but Nadia meet his doctors. "To Reynolds? Of course." He knew this was a bigger deal than Tyler made it seem. "Is Nadia okay?"

"Oh. Yeah. She just thought...." He looked at the ground, hands in his pockets, before continuing. "Well, actually I'd like you to know what's what. With me."

"You've got a deal. Thank you."

Tyler looked up, eyes bright. "Yeah?"

"Yeah. For real." He blinked. "That means a lot. What time?"

Tyler looked sheepish. "Late afternoon. I sort of snuck into your office to check your calendar. Elise might have verified your times."

"Then you've got yourself a chauffeur." Josh chuckled as he finished checking the first aid kit.

Tyler climbed into the bus behind him to load the two empty Gatorade drums in beside the other gear. "I don't want you thinking I'm sneaking off to meet some secret boyfriend in San Diego."

"Duh. No." Josh made a face but then realized he'd never asked the question. Everything he knew about Tyler's love life was local gossip and tabloid guff. "Have you dated a lot?"

"Of guys?" Tyler shrugged. "A few. Athletes and actors mostly, because that's what my publicist sets up. But I kept it quiet. I've never... uh—" He pressed his lips together. "Gotten serious. About anything other than football, I mean."

"Me neither."

"Mostly I hooked up with people who knew the deal. Simpler. Safer. Mainly dudes because they seem to get it more. The team owners can get exploitative about our personal lives."

"So… not homophobic."

"Less than you'd think. But more than you might notice. They don't much care. They care about the money more than who's in my bed. Nobody important gives a hoot nowadays. It's a relief." Tyler glanced through the bus windows at the parking lot. "Funny to think how much energy I used to spend keeping up appearances with models or whatever. Chicks."

Josh knelt to slide the first aid box into the rack. "But you like guys."

"Amen." Tyler grinned. "I slept with plenty of girls back when I thought I had to, but if I'm bi, it's maybe 15 percent." He held a hand out.

Josh let Tyler tug him up, and when he rose, he stood maybe an inch away. Close enough that heat sprang up between them, as well as the urge to kiss that mouth. Josh stepped back to a safer distance. "I never knew."

"You never asked." Tyler licked his lower lip. "Can you imagine if we'd gotten to know each other in high school?"

Josh smiled at that. "Yep. I sure can. I did. I imagined it a whole hell of a lot. As you are well aware, Fantana."

"So you say." A sneaky grin crept onto Tyler's face. "I got a filthy imagination myself, Coach."

"Ha-ha. Very funny."

"You should see your face." Tyler's voice got lower, huskier, so that Josh had to step closer to hear properly. "You think I don't have locker room fantasies, weight room fantasies, shower fantasies?" He groped himself. "What's your pleasure?"

Josh laughed. "Oh no. Out here like this? Not a chance." He stepped back and clomped back to the door of the bus and down to the pavement. "Thanks for the hand. Team will be here soon."

From behind him, Tyler growled, "Any time, Coach."

Someone sniffed. Josh turned to find Myra Waxman about twenty feet away, framed in the doorway that led into the athletics annex. High points of color dotted her cheeks like rouge, her disapproving frown making Josh feel a foot tall. It probably showed on his face. She hadn't even caught them flirting and he still felt guilty. "Myra. Afternoon."

"Coach Ayres." She looked over his shoulder. "Mr. Fantana."

Behind him, Tyler made some kind of sound, but Josh didn't want to turn and find out what it was or why.

Most days, Myra tended to mother him, patting and stroking him a bit too much. He also knew that she was the kind of person who was pious as a hobby, and that she fixated on people to an unhealthy degree. But at the moment her waxy lips were so tight they looked pale.

Before things got weirder, he gave Tyler a fake thumbs-up and pointed. "Car."

When they reached it, Tyler said, "Bet you anything that old bat's still watching us."

Josh frowned. "She's just lonely."

"You trust people too much." Tyler unlocked the door and climbed into the driver's seat. "Kick ass tonight, Coach."

"I'll tell you all about it in the morning. And we're good for Reynolds. I'll come get you soon as I wrap up practice."

"Thanks." Then Tyler whispered, "You can't tell, but I'm kissing you goodbye."

"I can tell just fine. And me too." He closed the car door.

By the time he walked back to the bus and the building, Myra was gone, but he had the weirdest sense she was still watching them both.

THE NEXT afternoon, Josh paced the sterile waiting room of Dr. Reynolds's office, sneakers squeaking on the polished floor. His stomach churned as the minutes crawled by. What was taking so long? His eyes darted between the parking lot outside and the exam room door.

Despite the nurse's assurances, Josh couldn't shake the feeling that Cilla Miller or some other sports flack might pull up to ambush Tyler if they didn't get moving soon.

"Relax, Mr. Ayres," the bald nurse said with a gentle smile. "Tyler's in good hands."

"Thanks," Josh muttered, forcing a tight smile of his own. He knew the man was right, but each minute ticked by more slowly, until he glimpsed a flash of movement as the exam room door creaked open.

Tyler emerged, followed by Reynolds, her looking pleased and his face pale and tight, and though he tried to plaster on a smile, it faltered at the corners.

Josh's stomach clenched as he took in Tyler's defeated expression. Something had gone wrong. Reynolds shook Tyler's hand and ducked into another exam room.

"Hey, superstar." Josh stepped closer, reaching out to touch Tyler's arm. "You good?"

"Uh, yeah. Great." Tyler bobbed his head.

"If you say so." Josh frowned.

"Promise." Tyler's tone and body language didn't match his words. "Just processing, you know?"

Josh wouldn't pry, but the urge to comfort Tyler was overwhelming. Instead, he focused on their escape plan. "Listen, I've figured out a way to get us out of here without being seen. They got a maintenance exit down the hall we can sneak out."

"Nice thinking, Batman," Tyler said, his smile genuine this time. "Right behind you."

As they made their way down the bright corridor, Josh's mind raced. What had Dr. Reynolds told Tyler? Was he in worse shape than they thought? Tyler would tell him when he was ready. For now they just needed to get out of this place without any photos.

"Almost there," he whispered, gesturing to a nondescript gray door ahead. "Cilla Miller and all the rest can kiss my behind."

Tyler nodded, his strong hand gripping Josh's shoulder in gratitude. "Thanks. For everything."

He shot Tyler a grin. "Always."

Josh popped open the maintenance exit. He checked the alley but saw no one. Heads down, he and Tyler trotted toward the safety of the parking lot.

As they approached, Josh popped the locks, then swung into the driver's seat as the passenger door opened opposite. "Ta-da! No jerks. No footage."

"Mission improbable." Tyler jumped into the truck himself and closed his door. "You're a miracle worker."

Josh drove them away from the doctor's office, checking the rearview mirror. "All clear. We're good."

"Thanks for bringing me today. After my run-in last time, I was trying to be careful. And Nadia got stuck on a conference call."

"You kidding?" Josh glanced at him. "The staff gave me all the dirt. I know your stats, your BMI, your cholesterol levels, your allergies. No more secrets, baby."

Tyler chuckled. "Well, one or two."

"That's what you think. I had Reynolds install a tracker, and now every time you sneak off for tamales without me, I'll know." He squeezed Tyler's thigh and patted it with affection. "Consider yourself warned, Captain Fantastic."

"Mmm. Tamales." Tyler closed his eyes with a smile and rested his head back on the seat.

"You hungry?"

"No." Tyler turned. "Overwhelmed, I think. My health. Nadia. The school. Team. Heart. You." He shook his head. "Everything."

"Okay." Josh kept his eyes on the road. "Are we moving too fast?"

"No! God, no. Not at all. I don't mean that. Please don't think— Oh Josh, I would never…." Tyler sighed, and for a disconcerting moment, he stared out the window. "Reynolds, uh… she gave me the all-clear. I'm healthy."

Josh turned in shock, worried he might steer them off the road. "Do what now? You what?"

"Not games right away. Not yet, at least. But my heart's strong enough now to start training again. Light stuff to start, but in a month or two I'll be ready to rejoin the team."

"Tyler, that's amazing!" Josh exclaimed, beaming. "That's phenomenal news. I'm so proud of you."

"You should get the credit." Tyler took Josh's hand and squeezed their laced fingers, then raised the knuckles to his lips to kiss them. "I wanted to tell her, Dr. Reynolds. Nothing would be possible without you." The raw tenderness in his voice hurt to hear.

"You know…." Josh squeezed back. "You know I'd do anything."

"Yeah." Tyler nodded, but his smile seemed bittersweet. "Yeah. It's pretty crazy to think I might actually play again after everything that happened."

Trying to lighten the mood, Josh said, "You know… this calls for a real celebration. How about I take you out for a nice dinner tonight? We can toast to your recovery, eat like pigs, and… whatever comes next."

"Please." Tyler reached over and squeezed Josh's hand. "I'd really love that." He exhaled. "You're right. We should go out."

"Well, Mr. Fantana… then will you allow me to squire you out for drinks, dinner, and possible debauchery?"

"In a heartbeat." Tyler laughed at that. "I am prepared to get away with pretty much anything you're willing to allow. Especially debauchery." Still, for all his sexy banter, he seemed troubled by something he wouldn't share.

Josh kept his foot on the gas and eyes on the road for home, excited to take his man out properly. Best to let Tyler find the words when the time was right.

They pulled up to the house, and Josh took his time locking the truck. By the time he reached the door, Tyler already had it open and ushered him into the empty living room.

Josh looked around. "Nadia's still on her call?"

Tyler glanced across at her office door. "Probably." He unbuckled his belt.

"Then you better get a move on."

"That's what I was thinking." Tyler smiled slowly as he pulled the belt free and popped the top button on his jeans. "I'm pretty dirty."

"So"—Josh refused to take the bait—"take a shower."

Tyler skinned out of his shirt and leaned against the arch. "What if I need help washing my back? Or my front."

"Well, God gave you giant hands for a reason. You'll manage." Josh shook his head and bent his face to the cat's exploratory sniffing. "Besides, I think Mr. Poops needs to tell me something important."

"I may be a while. I feel extra filthy." Tyler undid more buttons. Now his tighty-whities were showing, and his hand traced the top of them idly. "You want to come help?"

"Tyler, if we get wet now, we'll never make it out the door."

Tyler kicked off his jeans where he stood, revealing a whole lot of rippling muscle and bulging briefs. "I'll be good."

"Then I'll be better. Go wash." Josh blinked and looked back at the cat before he did something foolish.

Tyler groaned and left. "Evil," he said.

To his credit, Tyler was showered and changed in less than ten minutes. When he emerged, the sight of him in jeans and a burgundy button-down shirt stole Josh's breath. "Presentable?"

Josh didn't trust himself to speak, so he just nodded.

"Hey…. We could stay in. You want a shower? I still feel dirty as hell."

"Tyler." Turning before he said anything dumb, Josh led the way back outside.

Tyler jogged to catch up with him. "Just so you know... I'm wearing those briefs you liked under this." He kissed Josh's surprised face, then hopped into the passenger seat.

"Now who's evil?"

"Don't look at me. I'm nice. I'm the nice one tonight." Tyler kissed Josh's hand and put it on top of his packed zipper.

Josh let himself feel the full heft of him before snatching his hand back. "Rude."

"Maybe. But if I were being evil, we would not be wearing pants. Where are you taking me?"

Josh laughed and swatted at him. "To a kennel."

"Oh, honey... we're eating dogs?"

"No, nutjob, you *are* a dog. *We're* eating Greek." Josh pulled away from the curb. "Mediterranean diet still in effect, yes? I mean, you're healthy for now, but let's keep you that way."

Saganaki was the only Greek food in town, and Josh figured it was healthy enough for Tyler. He'd made the reservations while Tyler cleaned up.

When they arrived, the place was cuter than he'd expected. And mostly empty. Maybe four booths and twelve tables.

"Mr. Fantana! Such an honor." A squat dark man with a gigantic mustache barreled toward them. "This is my restaurant. I am the owner, Stavros. I had no idea. We're most honored, sir."

Tyler turned the charm on immediately, dazzling the owner and his two waitresses—his daughters, as it turned out. "My doctor told me I need Greek food for my heart."

"Your heart. Your heart, yes." The owner seemed hypnotized by the idea of Tyler, the glamor of an NFL player. "Yes. Greek is the healthiest. You know!"

The owner spread his arms, and Tyler did the same, smiling, accepting the bear hug enthusiastically. "Stavros, I need a favor. Can you help?"

"For you, sir, anything." The owner's black eyes were huge as saucers. "My family, we watch every game."

"My friend and I are celebrating something special, but we don't want any pictures. You know? No press." Tyler winked, as though the international paparazzi often camped out in this tiny bistro hidden in the middle of the remote California suburbs.

"Of course." The owner bowed and nodded. "Naturally. Our best booth for you, Mr. Fantana." He ushered them back to the rear of the restaurant, to a high-back booth tucked in a small nook.

Following Stavros, Tyler escorted Josh to the table, his hand on the small of Josh's back.

Before they took their seats, Tyler palmed something to the owner—folded cash, it looked like. "You take care of us, I'll make sure you get a signed picture and tell all my buddies about this place."

"Thank you, sir. Yes, sir. The best." Stavros kept bowing as he backed away. "Here are my girls with water and wine. Menus to come. Thank you, Mr. Fantana."

The two quiet daughters could have been twins, both thin and dark. One poured water and the other opened a carafe of red wine on the table with two delicate glasses. They nodded and left.

Josh squeezed his hand. "That was pretty cool. You made his month."

"I wanted you all to myself. No cameras. No eavesdroppers. And now he'll make sure it stays you and me just as long as we want."

"Yes, please. How much did you give him?"

"Five hundred. This place is pretty quiet, and I want them to take care of you."

Josh chuckled. "Well, for five hundred bucks, they'll certainly make an effort." He knew the money didn't matter to Tyler, but he had wanted to take care of tonight. "I've never seen you do that before... be Tyler Fantana, NFL superstud. No wonder the whole world wants you."

"Let me tell you, celebrity can be gross, but it has its uses. Wine, check." Tyler raised his head to peer around, scanning the room to make sure they were unobserved. "Privacy, check." He kissed Josh. "You, check."

"Food, check." Josh kissed him in retaliation. "And I get the check."

Tyler didn't like that, apparently. "Hey!"

"No arguments. This is a celebration and you're my date. So can it, buster."

"Deal." As if making up for griping, Tyler was extra affectionate, his hand often finding its way to Josh's thigh or resting on his shoulder.

Josh raised his glass of wine. "A toast."

Dutifully, Tyler raised his glass, a smile playing on his lips.

"Strength," Josh said, as a toast. "I've never met anyone stronger, and I never will."

"Well... I had a little help."

"Nice try. Drink."

"Yes, Coach." Tyler dropped his eyes to the table, mulling something over.

Just then Stavros came back with menus. Tyler told him it all looked too delicious to choose and asked him to surprise them.

The chance to really show off his food seemed to thrill the man even more. "I will. You will see. Your heart has never been stronger." He scurried back to the kitchen.

"He's right." Tyler ran a finger around the lip of his wineglass. "And you aren't going to like it, but I need to say this. You saved my life." He raised his hazel eyes, damp with suppressed emotion. "I don't think I would have made it back."

"Bull."

"I don't think I'll ever be able to show you or make you understand how lost I was."

Josh took his hand. "It's okay. We're okay."

"I could barely stand, and you got me to run." His eyes glittered. "You taught me to fly. Look at me, Josh."

Josh did, his mouth dry and his hands shaky.

Tyler's voice dropped almost to a whisper. "The thing is...." His voice hitched slightly, and he stopped short of whatever he wanted to say.

Josh didn't dare breathe for fear he'd miss it.

"It's just—" Tyler shook his head and looked down. "I'm trying to say that I'm—"

"Avgolemono!" Stavros stood in the plaster archway, holding a tray with two wide steaming bowls. He closed his mouth, as if aware he'd interrupted something, his mustache flexing like a caterpillar as he tried to decide what to do.

Tyler clapped his hands and spread his arms, welcoming the intrusion. "Beautiful, sir. You are the best."

Stavros deposited the bowls, topped up the wine, and vanished. And after that, his entrances were more inconspicuous.

But the moment was gone, and Tyler seemed unable to finish his thought.

Josh sighed, frustrated. *It's okay. We'll get where we need to.* Whatever Tyler wanted would be worth the wait.

For the next two hours, Stavros and his family brought a stream of bowls and plates to the table: Steamed eggplant. Some kind of sour chicken soup. A tray of mixed olives. Tiny meatballs in sauce. Tomato fritters. Grilled lamb. And a sweet cheese thing with peppers. Between bites of their delicious meal, they joked and flirted, tucked in their own little world.

The rest of dinner passed in a soft haze.

And then for dessert, a delicate flaky pastry with honey, butter, and ground nuts. *Baklava* was what Stavros called it. Tyler couldn't get enough of it, which delighted the owner greatly.

When they were finished, Josh asked for the check, but Stavros wouldn't hear of it. Family, he called them. "Like sons."

Stavros insisted the whole meal was on the house, and he looked hurt when Josh tried to put a couple hundred bucks on his counter.

After much back and forth, Josh gave in, and Tyler shook the man's hand and promised to bring back some of his teammates. As they left, he grabbed a business card.

Josh asked, "A card?"

"I'll have Chuck send headshots for me and a couple of the guys signed to him and praising the restaurant."

"So you're not going to bring the guys here."

"Oh, I absolutely will. You kidding? Odell, Vance, Felix, and definitely Rodrigo. They will flip over this place." He bumped against Josh. "I always keep my word."

"You do." Josh paused and looked at him head-on. "You always keep your promises. That's true."

"Ever since I was a kid. My father was such a rotten liar that I think I did it just to be a pain in his ass. The habit just stuck. So does that make me honest or just stubborn?"

Clouds scudded past the stars overhead. They'd been a long time; it had to be ten o'clock or later.

Josh unlocked the truck. "Where to now?"

"Well, I'm not about to turn into a pumpkin."

"Where do you want to go?"

Tyler bent his head and inhaled deeply. "Anywhere so long as it's with you. How do you always smell so good?"

Josh asked, "Mine?"

Tyler straightened.

Josh blinked at him innocently. "What? Yes? Any interest?" The nerves were real, but more than anything, he didn't want to let Tyler go away.

"Interest! Do you mean what I think you mean?" Tyler's voice got husky. "Are you inviting me to come home with you? Is this a trick?"

"No trick."

Without bothering to say another word, Tyler scrambled into the truck so fast Josh started laughing.

"Well, okay then."

The whole way home, Tyler touched and nuzzled him. Little by little, he undid Josh's buttons and buckle until his clothes were open to Tyler's insistent hands.

"You're going to run me off the road. Or I'm going to spray the steering wheel."

After that, Tyler contented himself by holding Josh's balls in one big hand, his thick wrist grazing Josh's raging boner with maddening gentleness for the entire drive. "Serves you right."

At the front door, Tyler took the keys out of his hand, unlocked Josh's door, and pushed him over the threshold, forcing him backward into the parlor.

Josh's open pants kept slipping down his thighs, and his unbuttoned shirt flapped around him. Mostly he kept having to pull things up and across his skin so he didn't end up naked before he stopped moving.

Tyler rubbed his smooth cheek against Josh's. "I can't believe you invited me home."

"Not like I didn't want to before."

"I think about this a whole lot, you know. You don't *even* know. Weeks. At this point, the jerking off I'm doing is mostly for your safety and my sanity."

Josh laughed. "Well, you don't seem too tired." He pressed his hand against Tyler's thudding heart. "And we know that's healthy now."

"Wait a minute." Tyler's eyes flared. "Hold on a second. Josh? My heart? Have you been waiting this whole time to make sure my blood pressure can handle…?"

"No." Josh winced. "Maybe." He held up his hands. "What if something happened? I didn't want to hurt you or risk anything."

Tyler growled and tugged at his belt. "Are you telling me I've been taking icy showers for three weeks and jerking myself raw every night because you had concerns about my cardiac safety?"

Josh grinned apologetically. "Umm."

"You are the craziest…." He kissed Josh's neck and kicked out of his jeans. "Sexiest…." "Stubbornest son of a biscuit I ever knew in my life." He went to his knees and licked across Josh's hip at the waistband of his briefs.

"It hasn't exactly been a treat for me either, big guy. Two to tango." Josh glanced down at the lump of his cock in front of Tyler's face.

Tyler grinned and sat back on his heels, looking up at him. "Unbelievable." He kissed Josh's stomach.

"But be honest. You can get a little out of control, which is great, mind you." Josh stepped close, pressing himself into Tyler's face. "I never want you to have to hold back with me." He dragged his cotton-covered erection along Tyler's jawline.

Tyler shivered and groaned. "Help."

"What's the matter, big guy?" Josh leaned down to kiss him and bit his lip gently, then sucked on it.

"Unf. Joshua. Come here. Come down here. Come be with me." Tyler scudded backward until he met the couch and then tugged Josh onto the full, hot length of his body. "Oh my God. Joshua." Opening his mouth, he pulled Josh down to claim a kiss, wrapping him in those massive arms that squeezed the breath out of him.

Josh shifted upward, his hard dick drilling into Tyler's abs, and licked his throat with languid appetite.

"You're going to make me cum like that."

"Licking your neck? Noted."

"Weak spot." Tyler laughed. "Don't judge."

"Won't judge. Won't budge." He licked Tyler again, starting at one stiff nipple and then right up the length of his throat to suck on his lobe. "You taste so good. I'm going to need time to learn every inch."

"Anything." Tyler was panting now and had made a definite wet spot on his stretched briefs. His breath came fast and short. "Oh. Oh, Josh…."

Again, Josh lowered himself and licked, this time starting at his small navel while Tyler jerked and cursed, along the ridged abdominal muscles, across the chest and then up to the other lobe to suck and nurse at it.

Tyler shuddered. "Oh! Oh no. I can't—"

"You can. You're so strong for me. Look how strong you are. You can take anything. You told me so. You asked for the worst."

Josh indulged every worshipful fantasy he'd ever dreamed in the darkest stretches of tenth grade, slobbering and sucking on Tyler with frantic appetite while the poor guy bucked and shuddered against Josh's mouth. Under his reverent ministrations, Tyler twitched and quaked in ecstasy, clutching at his shoulders and cradling his head. The wet spot on his briefs leaked through onto Josh's belly.

The next time he crawled down Tyler's body, he tugged the briefs free, exposing the full thickness of him. It was so perfect his mouth literally got wet. "Jesus, Tyler." He dragged his mouth up the broad shaft, across the chiseled landscape of flexing muscle, until he was kissing Tyler hard and hungry. He kissed Tyler without pulling back, as if trying to find whatever he kept hidden and holy.

Tyler shook then, a raw barking scream building and building until he wrapped his legs around Josh's back and squeezed them together. His heart hammered against Josh's, healed and helpless. Tyler arched and tightened his limbs around Josh hard enough to bruise.

Tyler's shaft spat between them, and Josh felt himself coming unraveled at the same time, groaning his own perfect pleasure into Tyler's mouth as they finally spilled together.

In the dim light, the world narrowed to the space where Josh and Tyler clung together, their breaths mingling in the still air. Josh marveled at the weight of Tyler's muscular arm draped over his back, the past few hours resonating through every inch of his body. All those dormant feelings had paled beside the reality, the real Tyler with him like this.

Gradually they caught their breath, and Tyler gathered him closer, tucked Josh's head under his chin, and kissed it possessively. "I love your couch."

But the odd tension Tyler had carried out of Dr. Reynolds's office still hung in the air like a promise or a threat.

"Ty," Josh murmured, tracing lazy circles on Tyler's chest as he nuzzled closer. "What was bothering you before?"

"Reality, I think. Time." Tyler shifted against him, hazel eyes meeting his with unwavering intensity. "We'll make it work. I promise. I will." His cocky grin put in a cautious appearance. "It's going to suck sometimes, the pressure, but I will do every single thing in my power for you."

Josh nodded, but uncertainty gnawed at the edges of his happiness. "What pressure?" He searched Tyler's face. "You mean reporters or whatever."

"Long distance." Tyler's voice was playful as he stroked Josh possessively. "It can be brutal. I'll come back as often as I can. Training and traveling eat up a lot of my life. But there's an upside. My reputation helps. My fans too. The team. They don't take crap from anyone. But I'm gone a lot. Part of the gig."

The prospect of a life lived under the microscope of celebrity unsettled Josh, and the idea of being away from Tyler so much sounded awful. He crossed his arms over his chest and scooted back against the arm of the couch so he could see Tyler's eyes.

Now Josh understood. The good news Reynolds had given him meant their time was running out, as of today. Their fairy-tale detour from the hard knocks of real life was ending. Now that Tyler's heart was better, he'd have to leave. "Right."

"We're okay. I promise. You watch. You've healed me so much I'm going to do great." He chuckled. "Boris should pay you a bonus to come be my trainer."

"I don't think so."

"I do. This is going to sound weird, but I feel like myself, like I can see myself for the first time in I don't know how long. Thanks to you."

"You're giving me too much credit. I'm nobody special."

Tyler took his hand and squeezed and kissed their joined knuckles. "See, that's where you're wrong, Mr. Ayres. In a way, we just met. Like, actually, for-real met as real three-dimensional human beings. That's such a gift. So I want us to have time to get to know each other. I'll make all the time you want."

"Same."

"And hey, maybe… maybe one day you'll want to leave this place and come join me. Wherever. San Diego or anyplace else, really. There's so much out there I wish I could show you. I mean, someplace that isn't as backwards."

That was the deal. Cinnamar would always be a place Tyler had left so he could succeed. Now that they were an item, he hoped Josh would work up the nerve to do the same, eventually.

Tyler whispered, "Maybe someday. Nothing definite, and not now. Promise me you'll think about it." He pressed a soft kiss to Josh's temple, squeezing him hard.

Josh swallowed, torn between the safety of what he knew and the exhilaration of discovering uncharted territory with Tyler. "Promise." His breath hitched as he imagined a future away from the community he loved. The very glamor of it felt like a trap. "I still have a battle ahead of me here."

"The book-ban thing. Listen," Tyler continued, tightening his grip around Josh's waist, "we can use my platform to raise awareness, fight back against these bigots in Cinnamar and anywhere else. I truly believe that the NFL can help too. We can protect you, the school, the library. Keep hassles to a minimum."

"They can, you mean."

"Well, I will too, but I can't be there all the time. That's just reality."

As they lay in each other's arms, Josh couldn't help wondering if their feelings could withstand the distance and scrutiny they'd be forced to face. Tyler didn't seem to grasp the risks he was asking Josh to take.

"Joshua." Tyler looked up at him and beamed, seemingly appeased, and nestled into Josh's chest. "How am I ever going to sleep again without holding you like this?" He buried his face in Josh's nape and inhaled deeply. "Thank you," he whispered. "Thank you. Thank you."

Within moments, Tyler's breathing slowed and deepened, as if all his burdens had dropped away. Eventually he slept, his burly frame relaxing into sleep on the big couch with the ease of long practice, the even rise and fall of his ribs under Josh's cheek as steady as a vow.

But Josh lay rigid and awake, his mind racing. Could a long-distance relationship survive? How could he leave Cinnamar? His job, his friends, his family—all here. And what of the media circus that would surely rummage through their private lives?

Josh wrestled with doubt. He envisioned the ambushes, the vile gossip, the savvy bigots who'd take aim at a "proud" couple. Josh might even lose his job, with enough malicious small-town chatter. Tyler insisted he was ready, but Josh worried for them both.

And yet the prospect of being with Tyler, of building something real together.... He wanted those wicked hazel eyes every morning, that dazzling smile every night. A life with Tyler would be as frightening as it was intoxicating.

He craned up to kiss the line of Tyler's jaw.

Josh glanced at the clock. Time was their real enemy. He had always played it safe, avoiding heartbreak through caution and restraint. But Tyler had smashed through those defenses with his megawatt charisma and surprisingly tender heart.

He sighed. Even now, cradled in Tyler's arms, the future was unclear.

Josh closed his eyes and willed his restless mind to stillness as if to slow time itself. They had now, and that would have to be enough. As exhaustion claimed him, Josh surrendered to fitful dreams.

Chapter Eleven

TYLER AWOKE to Josh's arm draped over his chest, their legs tangled beneath the sheets. He cherished these quiet moments together as before the clock forced them out of bed. A week had passed since their first passionate night, yet it felt like a year cocooned in their hometown bubble.

Tyler nuzzled into the curve of Josh's neck, dreading his imminent return to San Diego. The season was already half over, and the owners wanted him to make a show of strength before the Super Bowl stole everyone's thunder. How could he bear leaving this, leaving Josh behind?

His career itself felt precarious. Thirty-three years old on the gridiron felt different than twenty or twenty-five. The injuries hit him worse. He healed slower; he made mistakes. Anyone in the league could tell you why guys got out so young. Head injuries and joint problems did a number on your long-term viability. At its core, the NFL was a business. Cogs in the machine got replaced once they wore out.

Though his cardiologist had cleared Tyler, doubts plagued him. Could his heart handle the rest of the season? Was he making things worse?

Even watching football games now, the violence of the plays bugged him in a way it never had before. Each bone-jarring hit, every player carried off the field left Tyler more conflicted, more unsure.

Yet the outside world would not wait.

Meanwhile, he'd watched Josh wage his own quiet battle to protect the library's "dangerous" books, pushing back against the pressure campaign from parents and even a few uptight faculty members. Tyler didn't want to abandon Josh to these fights alone. Just to buy time, he'd requested another couple weeks, another checkup with Reynolds before doing anything rash. He glanced at the clock.

They had to get up in a few hours so they could get Josh to school in time.

When Tyler held Josh close like this, their bodies snug as two puzzle pieces, everything else faded. The past and future disappeared; only this moment existed. And Tyler knew with sudden clarity he would cling to it, to Joshua, for as long as fate allowed.

Beside him, Josh stirred. "Hi."

"Hey, handsome. Mmmh." Tyler squeezed him and kissed the top of his mussed head. "Five more minutes."

For the past week, they'd fallen into an easy rhythm.

Each morning after a quick breakfast, Tyler drove Josh to work in Josh's truck. They'd run side by side at the track as the mist burned off and then part at the truck before the first bell. Then Josh spent the day at Hamilton coaching and teaching while Tyler went back to Nadia's to work the phones and charmed volunteers for the book-ban battle. On Tuesdays and Thursdays he saw his therapist, which he didn't dread anymore. Then at day's end, Tyler would pick Josh up and squire him home.

Principal Carver had really stepped up with their library campaign. As soon as Tyler had offered himself as a public face for the literacy drive, Carver had given him permission to organize media coverage, a book-club crawl, the story adoption drive, and the library lock-in for next month.

The past couple of days, Tyler had called in favors wrangling signed swag for auctions and videos from friends in the NFL. He'd visited other school libraries in the area to shake hands and meet students. Nadia had built them a snazzy web page. He'd even gotten the Swells to donate thirty grand to improve internet access and fund five years of Overdrive e-book service for the whole valley's school district. Out in the boonies, the web was critical.

For any pro teams, literacy was a perfect cause. For the players, it took an hour tops. For the locals, the lure of big names had made the book bans look twisted and pathetic. The celebs looked civilized and sensitive. And books, above all else, were far more inexpensive than things like surgery or vehicles. Tyler pressed as many NFL players into service as he could. He kept supplying the local media photos of hunky jocks recommending their favorite thrillers, romances, and fantasy series. The press ate it up.

As a result, Tyler hadn't slept in his own bed once this week, which Nadia encouraged shamelessly. She knew Tyler's time in Cinnamar was limited, so he and Josh needed to maximize their remaining days and nights together before reality intervened. The ticking clock made him feel possessive and short-tempered with everyone else.

Today he'd seen his therapist and talked with Dr. Bailey about the future with Josh—which felt great—in between other stuff that wasn't so great. Therapy hadn't turned out anything like he'd imagined. It helped, but it rattled him too, stirring the foul goop at the bottom of his pond.

When he picked up Josh from Hamilton, he was able to confirm another forty-two attendees for the lock-in and a snarky "halftime" video from a trio of Steelers who owed him a solid.

Tonight they cooked together again, this time Tyler chopping olives while Josh sautéed chicken and lemon in a sizzling pan. Lots of laughter and a bottle of cheap pinot. Their mouths met between tastes, savoring every second. After dinner, they lay entwined on the couch pretending to watch a superhero flick, but mostly enjoying being close and quiet.

They fooled around, had another shower, and eventually drifted to bed... not tired but knowing they needed to be up early. They moved slowly around Josh's bedroom, talking and chuckling as they tried to make the time stretch.

Tick-tock.

As he brushed his teeth, Tyler described the sit-down he'd had with the school up in Ocotillo Heights. Same deal: a couple of pissy locals were trying to get books banned if they showed a kiss or took the Lord's name in vain, etcetera. Tense, ugly, and stupid attacks on the library. The principal up there had been painfully grateful for Tyler's visit.

Not long after, Josh climbed into bed. "Well, your day was way more productive than mine. Co-captain drama. Oh, and Elaine Chavez is pregnant. But the big news is the library. After you dropped me off this morning, two weirdos showed up in the parking lot holding a wide 'Save Kids from Porn' banner with a picture of Obama, for some reason. No idea."

Tyler made a face. "That's the problem with staying out here in the sticks. Book bans and bigots. But I don't want to give them a win by walking away. Jesus."

"Didn't go well for them." Josh just shrugged. "The wrestlers spent lunch shouting Bible verses and pretending to jerk off till the weirdos left. So naturally Myra *effing* Waxman came out to make a speech about propriety that only made it worse. And sometime in sixth period, the kids started a TikTok protest."

"You couldn't pay me to go back to high school. It's so different now."

Josh shook his head. "Not as much as you think. I mean, technology is different. Apps and all. Being out and all. But mostly they do all the same stuff anybody ever did. You'd be surprised. What really changes is us. The kids are just the same."

"Probably." Almost absently, Tyler stroked and kneaded Josh's powerful muscles. "Hard evidence. You're stronger than I am now."

Josh's voice was muffled against his chest. "Your fault."

"How's that?"

"If it wasn't for you, I'd still be a thirty-something beanpole who biked past your house twice a day." Josh chuckled and tipped his head up to peer at him. "You realize you're the reason I ever worked out."

"In high school?"

"Oh no!" Josh laughed at that. "Hell no. Up until you graduated I spent two years pining and mooning after you... and then you went off to conquer the world and I spent that summer in a hole. Inconsolable. Full emo. By then, Nadia knew because... obviously."

"Knew what? Hold up." A spike of childish annoyance went through him. "My sister knew you had a crush on me and didn't say anything for *fifteen* years? That little—"

"Angel. *Saint*. She was patient and wonderful. Plus I swore her to secrecy. Dude, I had a crush on her brother and she was a rock. For what it's worth, she kept your secrets too."

Tyler nodded. Josh didn't have any idea what that meant. How could he? Nadia had always kept family business close to the vest. She'd been so young when it all went down.

"Then at the end of that summer, I realized... you'd gone, but one day you'd have to come back. One year, five years... I wanted to be ready just in case. To be visible, worthy. *Ugh*. That sounds awful. But you really were my hero."

Tyler squeezed his hand. He knew what Josh was trying to do by spilling the beans like this. "And so you went to the high school gym."

"Off and on. Or, I tried. The coaches back then were pretty dismissive. The other guys were awful. No, it really happened at college. Freshmen year, I met a cute guy in my anthropology class and joined the swim team."

"No way! Wet Speedos? Hubba-hubba." Tyler squeezed his butt with a leer.

"Terrifying. But I just kept thinking, one day I'll run into Tyler and he'll really see me."

"Oh… I saw you. But back then, I was on a mission."

"Which I didn't know. I thought I was invisible. The guys at Cal State showed me how to lift, how to stretch. And accidentally I discovered that without much effort I could pack on muscle fast. I got shredded by the time spring break rolled around. Shocked the hell out of everyone."

Tyler kneaded his arm, his shoulder. "I bet."

"Then I wasn't just this skinny nerd because I kept getting bigger. Then I won some meets, fooled around some with my buddies. I went on a couple so-so dates. Apparently muscle doesn't solve everything. I started to come out of my shell. Came out to my parents, actually. By junior year, the swim team asked me to be in the calendar, practically naked, I should add."

"I better be getting copies, man."

"You don't need copies. You got the real deal." Josh kissed him. "In the end, I did a whole bunch of calendars. A little physique modeling even. But that was all you too, in a way. Body. Confidence. Calm. I used the idea of you as an anchor and just *reimagined* myself, my body, my friends, my time… so I'd be ready for you when we finally met properly."

"Come on." Tyler squeezed him. "That was all you. I had nothing to do with it. Not really."

"Disagree. I became an athlete to feel seen. Worthy. I became a coach to return the favor. All because you inspired me and the coaches at Hamilton didn't. And now look at me. Full circle." Josh stroked his belly. "Goals make a difference. Approval. Fame. Hope. Anything that kicks your butt, keeps you focused, and greases the wheels is rare and precious. And for me, that would be you, even with a bum ticker and early onset bedhead."

"Hey." Tyler reached up and smushed his springy dark hair down as best he could. "I need a cut pretty soon."

Josh pushed his hands into Tyler's hair till it stood up again. "Crushes are all well and good, but I'd say we're way past high school hormones and lusting after a hot jock in the showers." Josh squeezed him tight. "Although the lusting has only gotten worse."

Tyler actually laughed at that and wiped his nose, wiped his eyes. "Yeah."

Josh dropped his gaze. "I keep thinking of things I need to tell you, but then you already know... somehow."

Tyler's breath caught at the tenderness in his voice. At the realization that he'd held Josh's heart all this time but been blind to it. How many things had he missed by grabbing for the brass ring? Ambition made everything else harder to see.

Tyler shrugged. "Puberty sucks."

"Says *you*. Piss off." Josh swatted him and poked his ribs till he squirmed. "Captain of the football team. High school heartthrob. The whole world loved you. Hey, try being invisible. Or weird." Josh's fingers trailed idly along Tyler's arm as they lay tangled together. "I was such an idiot," he murmured. "Too hung up to even say hello. Pining after the MVP. Pretty lame. You were way out of my league."

"Hardly. It may have looked easier, but it was just as awful." Tyler tensed, a knot forming in his stomach. "I was a big, stupid mess in school. I never stopped feeling like a fraud."

"Are you kidding? You never had to pine. Or fantasize."

"I fantasized too. About other things. Because I was getting into fights, chasing girls, jerking off in the john. Always scrapping and lying to get respect from people I didn't respect at all. Doing what everyone expected me to do so they'd leave me alone."

"Gorgeous, confident, capable. The whole county worshipped you," Josh said. "Untouchable."

Tyler laughed at that, sour inside. "I guess it looked like that. Books and covers." He shook his head, old insecurities rising. "At school, maybe...." He trailed off.

He didn't know how to make Josh understand. High school had taught him plenty, given him a chance to create a useful image that kept him safe, a fancy escape hatch that led anywhere else.

Josh touched his face. "You know you're way more than that, right? Forget football; look at all the things you've accomplished. You're a hero to a lot of people, a lot of kids out in the sticks."

"Maybe now, but big and dumb as I was...." He frowned.

"Hey. Stop beating yourself up." Josh poked him, frowning.

"Football was my only way out. Beating the shit out of meatheads like me over a ball. My mom hated me getting hurt like that. The violence of it." He looked down and shook his head.

"You'll never convince me you weren't amazing."

"I don't think—" His face wouldn't do what he wanted. His therapist had hinted that they would get here eventually, that he'd have to explain to Josh at some point, but suddenly he wasn't sure he was brave enough to do it. He shook his head again in mute pain, terrified of how Josh would see him after tonight. "I'm not."

"Not what?" Josh propped himself up on one elbow, brows furrowing with concern. "What is it?" he asked gently.

"Special. I wasn't special. Or untouchable." He sighed and took the plunge. "I was terrified. I mean… violence is in me. Inside me. She knew. My mom." Tyler pressed a hand against his own chest, over his screwed-up heart. "Ugly. Scary. Bad." He scowled, struggling to make Josh understand but not sure even now if that was such a good idea.

"Not football." Josh got very quiet then, his deep blue eyes confused and a little wary.

"No. Well, later maybe, but not like you're thinking."

Josh just watched him, waiting.

"My father was…." Tyler took a shaky breath. "*Not* a nice person. Ever. He hurt us, a lot. My family. And I couldn't stop anything." Hot tears pricked his eyes.

Josh nodded, his face tense.

"An honest-to-God monster," Tyler whispered. "A drunk. A mean drunk and worse, but we didn't understand that stuff when we were little. Just the hurting and yelling." He glanced up but couldn't fake a smile. "He wasn't home much, and he could be fun, but then some little thing would… set him off. And he'd go after my mom till she screamed." He shook his head like he could dislodge the memory. "They knew us all pretty good at the ER."

"I didn't know."

"Good. Good. I'm glad. Because that means I played the game right." Tyler offered a grim grin that didn't reach his eyes. "High school hero. Big man. What a joke. My therapist said I probably just shut down. Dr. Bailey, I mean."

"You were just a kid, Tyler." Josh pulled him closer, holding him carefully and stroking his hair. "It wasn't your fault," he said firmly.

"I almost killed him. True story. Bare hands and a belt."

Josh didn't react. Maybe he didn't know how to react.

Tyler took a deep, shaky breath. "One night when I was twelve, he was worse than ever. He had Mom cornered, hitting her again and again while he foamed at the mouth. I just... *lost* it. Completely lost control. He raised his arm, I caught the belt he was swinging at my mom, and I took it away. *Zip.* He hadn't noticed how big I'd gotten. I hadn't even noticed, I think, until I caught the strap in my fist and just yanked it out of his hands. He turned, shouting ugly crap, and I started hitting him back, with the buckle end. And I meant it. I beat him and beat him until he fell down with blood running into his eyes, until he begged. Then I threw that evil bastard out into the street. I thought I was protecting us, but...."

The room felt dead silent, as though even the moon had stopped rising. Josh's face was wet too.

Tyler's voice broke. "He left two days later. Emptied the accounts, smashed the house up, and abandoned us. And Mom, she... she was never the same. We don't even know if he's still alive. I assume, but...." He shrugged. "It broke her heart, him walking out. I thought I was saving her, but I just destroyed our family."

"That's not true."

Tyler finally met Josh's calm eyes, tears streaking his cheeks. "I'm like him, you see. You must think I'm a monster too. But I promise, I just—"

"No," Josh said firmly. He cupped Tyler's face in his hands. "You listen. Tyler, look at me. Do you know how *young* twelve is? You were a little kid. What you did was impossible. You stopped him from hurting people you loved. Your father was the monster, not you."

"I never wanted to hurt anyone. I think about that belt all the time." Tyler twisted his fingers together to stop the shaking.

Josh nodded. "Violence. That's what you meant, before. If you could have talked to someone like Dr. Bailey back then, it might have helped you deal with it."

"Sucks." Tyler took a shaky breath, composing himself. "I always figured football would be my ticket out. A chance to do right by my mom and Nadia. A way to prove I wasn't like that son of a bitch, that I could be something good. And it was, for a while. But now...." His face crumpled, and he looked down.

"You're okay."

"It's just slamming people around because I'm so big and nuts. How am I different?" He gestured at his chest, at the heart ticking like a bomb inside him. "It's wrecking me. So when they want me back out there, it's not just my heart holding me back. Here I am: thirty-three, busted up, held together by scars. And I can't help thinking, is this punishment for what I did as a kid? Karma finally catching up."

"It's not a trade. You can't think that way," Josh said. "You were a kid forced into an impossible choice. No one should have to go through that, especially not alone."

"Maybe. But I still wonder if just keeping quiet would have been better. She didn't mind so much. If we'd suffered a little longer, would my father have stayed? Would Mom have been happier?" Tyler's eyes stung.

"Don't do that to yourself." Josh squeezed his hand. "No. You were so young, just defending your family. You can't blame yourself for any of this."

"You make it sound noble. All that blood. They had to sew his face back together. It didn't look noble when I was twelve."

"What you did was impossible. Brave. At twelve years old I was afraid of changing in the locker room, and you fought an ogre."

"Maybe."

How do you lose years of pain and shame?

"You saved them, Tyler. I have never lied to you, and I never will."

Dim as it was, the bedroom felt too bright. Tyler pressed the heels of his shaking hands into his eyes and let out a sob. "I didn't know."

"Don't. You did know. You knew what was right." Josh held him as he wept, murmuring at him. "I'd give anything to take all that back, what he did, but you didn't need me or anyone. You were strong."

Tyler took a shuddery breath. "So sorry. What a mess."

"Listen to me. Tyler? I will never, never think less of you for protecting the people you love." He kissed Tyler carefully, brushing their lips together.

He got so quiet that Tyler finally looked up into his eyes.

"I love you."

Tyler's breath hitched. *No. You can't. You shouldn't.*

"I love you, Tyler Fantana." Josh held his face. "Every second of every day for most of my life, even when we were apart, I loved you. Even before I had a real reason, I knew. You were it for me. My once and forever."

"Don't." Tyler wiped his face. "I'm not worth it."

"Tough. Because I will never stop loving you. Not just the smart bits, the sexy bits, or the nice bits. The ugly bits too. All your pieces.

Everything you got in there." He poked Tyler's chest. "Look at me. And if it takes me the rest of my life to prove it, I'm ready. So help me."

Tyler scowled. "I don't deserve that." He started to shake his head, to explain why that was impossible, but Josh wouldn't let him.

Josh stroked his cheek. "The only thing that matters now is who you've become, no matter what they threw at you. You've got nothing to prove to anyone, least of all me."

Tyler gave a small, grateful smile. "I don't deserve you."

He held Josh close, overwhelmed with gratitude, with relief. Josh still wanted him… all the messy, broken pieces, even knowing the ugliness under the surface. Maybe his father would finally let go of him.

"I know you, Tyler Fantana, every rude, beautiful bit of you. And you know me. That's all. I need you to hear me, because that's the only thing that matters. No games. Just us."

Tyler sniffed, then nodded. "Agree."

Josh pulled him close. "I want all of you. Always."

Tyler tugged Josh down onto his chest, holding him still for a moment, just breathing together, fitting into each other puzzle-piece close, one heart beating in the dark. This was what he wanted. This was the part he couldn't explain away or avoid.

The tender silence that he only ever felt with Josh settled over them.

Josh gave a big, contented sigh. "You and me. Whatever it takes."

Tyler asked, "Josh?"

"Mmmh." Sounded like someone was getting sleepy.

"I love you too." Tyler pulled back to gaze at Josh. "So much. Even if you didn't, I would love you."

Josh smiled. "You don't have to."

"I just wanted you to know." Tyler chuckled at that. "Jeez."

"I don't mean like that. Sorry." Josh pressed lips to his temple. "Hey, I loved you even when you were imaginary. But real Tyler is a million times better than my fake made-up facsimile." His smile turned rueful. "I just wish I'd told you sooner. Can you imagine? We wasted so much time."

"Not wasted," Tyler said. "Maybe we just… needed to grow into this. To be ready for each other. Live some. Grow some. Time isn't always a bad thing."

"Amen. Every minute I get, I get to have with you," Josh whispered.

"I don't know what's going to happen with the Swells. My contract is up soon, but I'm pretty confident they'll renew. What I don't want is any of that crap getting between this. Us." He moved a hand between them. "We talk. We figure it out. We find a way."

Josh blinked. "Okay."

"Nothing wasted." He tilted his head up, meeting Josh's gaze. "Together from now on. Deal? We'll figure it out. Promise me."

Josh kissed him, a sweet and binding silent oath that set the world right. "Deal. Together. Through everything. I promise." He dragged a firm X over his heart. "Hope to die."

Here, in Josh's arms, the past didn't matter. The future was hazy. What he could see was this perfect moment of being understood and accepted completely.

Tyler knew one thing for sure: they would face each challenge side by side. And with Josh beside him, he could overcome anything.

Chapter Twelve

JOSH WIPED the sweat from his brow as he watched Tyler pull away in his truck after their morning run. Alone, he pushed through the locker room doors, his muscles burning and pulse slowly settling. Tyler's imminent departure clouded Josh's mind. The Swells wanted him back in San Diego in the next week or two. No surprise, but they had run out of time.

Inside the empty athletics office, he stripped off his soaked shirt and shorts in the little bathroom and stepped into the coaches' shower. As water cascaded over his sore muscles, he scrubbed sweat off. He hadn't figured out what was supposed to happen after Tyler left.

He turned off the water and toweled off, then tugged on his uniform shirt and shorts before returning to his desk. He still needed to check the softball uniforms Elise had ordered last week.

"Hey, Josh."

Principal Carver was waiting, a folded newspaper in hand and a strange expression on his face.

Josh took his seat, a little unsteady. "Phil. Everything okay?"

"It is. But we have a situation."

Carver passed Josh the paper, his eyes full of concern.

Josh's eyes locked onto a headline: CAPTAIN FANTASTIC GETS DRASTIC.

"Jesus." Josh scanned the page quickly: a snide screed vilifying Tyler's efforts to revitalize the school library. Par for the course, really, but as it went on, the article got weirdly *personal*. The author was anonymous, and they obviously had an ax to grind, but this bordered on libel. "I need a second."

Now Carver looked pissed. "I'm so sorry, Josh. I have my suspicions about who's responsible, but this is beyond anything I anticipated."

"Who do you suspect?" Josh glanced up, bewildered, but Carver didn't elaborate.

How had a literacy campaign become about his relationship with Tyler?

Josh's eyes locked back onto the newspaper, scanning for specifics, anything to give an indication who had done this to him. It came about two-thirds of the way in. Nothing overt, nothing actionable, a few sly hints about the possible "spectacle" of "school showers" and "the faculty bachelor romancing Fantana." The article didn't name him or say anything directly derogatory, just enough to make Josh's blood boil.

Someone in the school had done this.

Josh's mind raced. Nobody knew about the morning runs but people who got to Hamilton at sunup. That meant that one of his coworkers, someone he'd smiled at and covered for over the years, had gone to great lengths to make him seem sleazy and opportunistic in the local rag.

"What the actual hell, Phil? This is in the building. Who would leak this crap to the media?"

Carver sighed. "I wish I knew for sure. But we've had more than a few staff members grumble about the library initiative. And you and Tyler being so… close."

"We jog! I've known the man over fifteen years. Tyler hasn't showered in this building since he graduated. This makes it sound like we're one step from hosting satanic orgies in the Hamilton locker room." Josh knew he was getting too loud. His pulse jerked in his throat.

Carver held up his hands, silently pleading for calm. "I knew you'd be upset. That's why I came here first thing. It's unethical and disgusting. I'm going to deal with it immediately. But you needed to know."

"The kids will see this. Their parents. This evil *crap*." Josh crumpled the paper, livid. "Total garbage. Tyler's just trying to make a difference, to save the library. And these bigots are targeting us. They want to get us killed based on lies."

"I know, I know." Carver swallowed. "We'll figure this out, Josh. If you need to take a day or two…. I just wanted you to hear it from me first before the gossip starts swirling."

"I'm not going anywhere. I wouldn't give these assholes the satisfaction. I don't back down to bullies. Ever." Josh took a deep breath, trying to calm down. But he could already imagine the looks and whispers in the hallways.

"Good man." Carver tried to smile, but the result wasn't comforting.

"Thanks for the heads-up," Josh said finally. "Sorry for losing my cool. I know you've got our backs."

Carver shrugged. "Always."

Josh managed to keep himself in check, but his heart was racing with anger and unease. This changed everything. With Tyler leaving soon, Josh would be alone on the front lines, without his protector and champion. The thought of weathering this storm solo filled him with dread.

Josh trudged through the rest of the day in a fog, barely able to focus on teaching. His thoughts kept drifting to Tyler, wishing he was still here to help Josh face the growing threats. Mrs. Grappo gave him a reassuring pat on the way out of the faculty lounge, and then Stan from the library offered a nervous thumbs-up that made him feel doomed. If the teachers he trusted felt awkward, then things were worse than Carver thought.

To their credit, the students acted totally normal. If they knew, they didn't say a word. If anything, they seemed eager to thank him and not give him any trouble. So maybe they knew and had his back. He didn't trust his instincts at this point. By lunch he realized they were being too nice to seem normal; they absolutely knew. In a town this small, there were no secrets.

He couldn't stop obsessing about it. His job and safety in Cinnamar were in real jeopardy.

During assembly, he called Tyler, desperate for a sensible perspective, but it went straight to voicemail, and then he went completely blank. What should he say? How could he explain without sounding insane or panicking Tyler? He couldn't figure out a reasonable message to leave, so after saying, "Hi," and a weird endless pause, he just punted. He said that something awful had come up, but that he was fine, and he'd explain later.

The last thing he needed right now was Tyler rushing to the school to make a scene and fix everything.

As the day ground forward, Josh's paranoia got worse. Every faculty member he saw could have done this to him. Any student might mouth off for the attention. Tyler's name meant national coverage and worse; anyone in the building might sell them out just for the chance of being on ESPN for ten seconds.

After the last bell, Josh stopped by the front office. Vicky gave him a sympathetic smile. "Hey, handsome. Rough day." It wasn't a question.

Josh just nodded, too exhausted to go into it.

"It's going to all work out. You watch, hon," she said gently. "We've got your back. A whole bunch of people, in fact."

"Thanks, Vicky." Josh managed a tired smile. "I should get going…."

She leaned over the counter and whispered, "She's just jealous."

Josh frowned. "Who is?"

Vicky rolled her eyes and muttered, "The nerve. I remember when that woman was selling lingerie out of her car. And now just because she's bought a vibrator and found Jesus—"

"—to regret this!" A hostile Myra Waxman emerged from the principal's office, red-faced and sputtering.

Josh tensed, realizing she'd just been reprimanded. She was the culprit. "Myra?"

"On leave! On *leave!*" Myra caught sight of Josh and barreled over. "Well, if it isn't Mr. Jockstrap Adonis," she said loudly. "Seems like you and your boyfriend have really stirred things up around here. I'm suspended without pay while you and Fantana corrupt innocent angels. Making eyes at each other. Flaunting yourselves half-naked before the entire community."

Josh clenched his fists and exhaled slowly.

Carver emerged behind her. "Myra, that's more than enough. I don't want to have to call security. And defamation is illegal." He gave Vicky a look, and she started dialing.

"What a joke. I've done my Christian duty." Myra had obviously shown up spoiling for a tacky scene, and Josh had inadvertently stumbled into it.

Carver put his hand on Josh's shoulder. "If you want to wait in my office."

"I don't know what you think you're going to accomplish by tempting students and encouraging defiance," Myra continued. "It's just asking for trouble."

Josh struggled to stay calm. "We teach kids to think. To solve problems. Not blind obedience."

Carver held open his office door. "Josh… please."

Myra scoffed. "Don't pretend you're so high and mighty. Parading around in your little shorts. We all know this is just you forcing your agenda on impressionable young minds."

Josh trembled with anger, but he refused to give her fodder for another scene. Taking a deep breath, he turned and walked toward Carver's open door, leaving Myra shouting insults behind him.

A couple of faces appeared, drawn by the raised voices. A small cluster of students and staff had begun to form in the hall.

The security guard had shown up and was trying to herd her to the exit. "Miss Waxman. Please, Miss Waxman...."

Carver stood between Myra and Josh. "You're not helping yourself, Myra. There will be a review of your behavior, and this kind of—"

"You worthless *faggot*!" she spat behind him.

Vicky gasped. A trio of high school girls stopped in the hall and drifted closer to rubberneck.

Seeing red, Josh turned then. "Say it to my face."

"You heard." Myra stood there looking triumphant yet terrified, like she expected him to hit her but also wanted exactly that. "Corrupting children and glorifying perversion with that trashy reprobate. His father was a drunk. His mother was a maid. From Mexico!"

"Venezuela," Josh muttered, holding it together for the moment.

The crowd was angry now, their faces shocked and souring. Even if they thought those things, no bigot wanted to get caught saying them out loud. Even the assholes knew how dumb and evil it sounded.

"I've been kind to you, Myra. I've helped you." Josh strode toward her, rage roiling through him, but he kept his voice low. "I won't press charges, but I will make certain you never work in a school again. Never."

"Josh." Carver grabbed his arm. "Don't engage. She's not worth it."

Josh shook him off, unable to stop now that the truth had started to trickle out of him. "Bigotry has no place in a school. You don't give a crap about kids or books. That's an excuse. You're angry, Myra. You're jealous. Because of your empty, withered, pathetic life."

Someone else was trying to tug him back, to make him calm, but he shook them all off. His voice slid out of him like a sword, deadly calm and right in Myra's blotchy, blushing face.

"You people," Myra sputtered, breathing fast and trying to backpedal. "This is the work of that godless library."

"Whose god, Myra? I know facts are inconvenient for you, but throughout all of history, the good guys have never banned or burned books. The Nazis did. The Confederacy. Stalin. Slavers and rapists." He looked her up and down. "Well, if the shoe fits."

"How dare you—"

The security guard took Myra's arm and tugged at her, but she braced herself and wouldn't budge.

"An ugly hypocrite and a disgrace," Josh said. "Leering at me and fondling me in the halls for the past six years. I didn't file a complaint because I felt sorry for you."

"I won't stand here and be insulted by the likes of you!" Myra shouted.

"How can I insult you? Your life is an insult to everything decent. Look at you. The full pathetic horror of you." He gestured at himself, at his own face. "This is pity. I'm sorry for you." He shook his head. "You're so jealous of Tyler's success, of him trying to help this school, of our happiness, that you chained yourself to him in print, praying for a Fox News segment and *masturbating* over the misery you made. Desperate. Ugly. Pathetic."

One of the shocked kids in the doorway nodded. "Boom." A father next to her looked genuinely startled but didn't move.

Myra's eyes watered, but she didn't so much as blink.

Carver took a tentative step toward him, but no way was he letting her walk away from this in one piece.

Josh squared his shoulders. "This 'worthless faggot' has met plenty of empty, envious hypocrites like you. You're the kind of hideous fraud that cripples lives, that makes innocent kids run away or kill themselves." He slapped his chest. "I could've been one of those kids, but I got lucky."

He couldn't stop himself, despite Carver's panicked face, despite the security guard's gentle hand on his back. He knew they wanted to help. He knew they couldn't.

The crowd had grown further, watching in horrified fascination as his rage crested. His anger and anxiety flooded out of him in a horrible torrent of undiluted clarity. "You think they don't know what you do in the dark? All these smart people?"

Myra seemed to realize that a large mob now stood watching her abject humiliation, wishing her harm. She turned, peering at them with watery eyes, as if expecting a rescue, but there were no takers.

"Worthless? Faggot?" Josh nodded. His voice got no louder, but he leaned in to make sure she heard every ugly syllable. "Just know this, Myra. You are *loathed*. The kids. The parents. Whether they tell you or not, every person you meet detests you. They wash their hands when you touch them. Everyone standing in this room right now. Look at their faces. You repulse them."

The gathered crowd was silent, eyeing her like they might something runny in a bedpan. She gulped, breathing hard, as though she was trying to make herself hyperventilate.

"Know that every time you step out in public that people you don't even know will cross the street to escape. That random strangers will spit on your shadow until they can piss on your grave." Josh stopped, breathless and exhausted as though he had vomited up something jagged. "A parasite."

Myra quivered before him, her wet lips buckling as she tried to face him and not flinch.

"That's the problem with envy, Myra. You drank poison, wishing everyone else would die. Except nobody's dying to make you happy. No one will ever even care. Because you are"—he whispered, stretching the word to make it last—"*worthless*."

At that she rocked back on her heels and fled.

She moved so fast that she knocked into Mr. Chan and then backed into a junior hall monitor chewing gum, who cackled at her distress until she'd exited the building.

The crowd parted to watch her go and then pressed forward to make positive sounds at him. "You told her, Coach." Josh didn't understand why everyone seemed so pleased... and then he realized it meant they all must have seen the article.

This would only get worse.

Breathing hard, Josh sat down suddenly like his bones had vanished. The rage had left behind a strange, sad numbness. He couldn't quite believe he'd done that, but he refused to regret it for a second.

Carver and the security guard cleared the office of the muttering bystanders and closed the doors.

"Are you okay?" Vicky asked softly and touched his shoulder. Her eyes were red. She offered him a paper cup of water, which he swallowed dutifully. "Can I call someone? Is Tyler home?"

"I know why you did it." Carver pressed his lips into a grim line. "I wish you hadn't."

Josh just nodded. He felt oddly at peace and lighter somehow, as if an ax had been removed from his side, the wound sewn shut. Myra's hateful words still echoed in his mind, but they didn't have the same power over him they had. The horrible slithering numbness spread through him.

Carver mopped his brow with a handkerchief. "I'm so sorry, Josh. I'm going to have to write this up. You understand, right? It's my fault. We should have had her escorted off the property as soon as we knew. This is on me. You need to get home. Let's get you home. I can have someone cover practice for you. Elise should still be here. Vicky?"

Vicky nodded and dialed the phone.

Again Josh shook his foggy head. "I'm fine. Really. I got to go. I should go." His feet moved toward the door.

Josh walked out to the parking lot, the last of the buses pulling away. A few stragglers pointed at him excitedly, probably recounting the story: "He told her." He stood staring up at the brick façade of the high school, the place that had been his second home for almost two decades.

Worthless.

Now he didn't know if he'd ever go back inside. His outburst might well have cost him his job. He leaned back against the bricks, wiping a sleeve over his hot eyes. He hadn't realized his face was wet. He must have been crying in there. "Jesus."

The unfairness of the entire ludicrous situation welled up in a bitter tide. He'd given so much to this place, this town, and for what? To be slandered and threatened for daring to stand up for what was right? The miracle was that he'd stayed calm enough to just *say* things. He'd never felt that kind of absolute rage. His hands still trembled with bottled violence.

He fished his phone from his pocket and dialed Tyler with shaking fingers. He wiped his eyes in frustration.

"Hey, Coach, what's up?" Tyler's voice was warm and comforting.

"Umm…." Josh struggled to find the words, emotion clogging his throat. His mouth felt gummy and raw. "Ty, I…. It's pretty bad. Can you come get me?"

"Joshua. What happened? Are you okay? What's going on?" Tyler's tone sharpened with confusion and concern. "Talk to me."

"Worthless." He didn't know how to start. "Somebody at school made up a bunch of crap about us to the *Gazette*." Josh forced the words out.

"I'm so sorry. You called me, I just saw you tried calling me this morning, and I didn't see it before. Oh man, I'm sorry. I was driving—"

"She didn't accuse us of crimes, but she implied plenty and worse. Myra Waxman, she said a lot of awful things that the entire town has now read, which was the point."

"It doesn't matter, Josh. None of that matters. You're okay. I'm coming right now. Can you find someone to wait with you?"

"There's no one but you."

"Waxman?" Tyler sounded pissed now. His voice went low and hoarse. "Bitch. Is she still there?"

"No. They put her on leave, but as they're dragging her out, she said something really terrible. And I kind of lost it on her in front of, basically, everyone. Oh my God… I couldn't stop. I couldn't stop. I was already so upset because of— Anyways. And I think I might be fired. I think Carver will be forced to fire me. Umm. I'm not doing so great. I don't know what to do. I just want to get home to you."

"Don't move, okay? Stay put. I'm on my way," Tyler said instantly. "Everything's going to be okay. I've got you. Hey. We're fine. You're not getting fired from anything."

The line went dead, and Josh braced against the bricks, his back against the building, and stared unseeing across the empty parking lot. He didn't know how anything could be okay again. But he stayed put.

At least Tyler was coming.

Josh waited, watching the sun sink lower and the shadows creep across the asphalt. His stomach twisted into knots as he thought of facing Principal Carver again, or any of his coworkers. He dreaded looking for a new job and uprooting his whole life. He didn't even know how to move somewhere new, to work somewhere strange. He'd trapped himself in this place out of complacency or cowardice. *Worthless.*

Most of all, he couldn't bear dragging Tyler into this stupidity, not after everything Tyler had survived. For whatever reason, he couldn't stop thinking about Tyler as a little boy swinging that belt. What was he supposed to do?

Overwhelmed, Josh stood frozen in the school parking lot, unable to look at the building he'd staggered out of. Exhaustion and regret swirled inside him as he thought of the danger he'd brought upon Tyler by trying to save the library.

Who cared? Why had he even bothered? Why did anything matter?

Students streamed out of the school, casting curious looks at Josh as he stood in the lot. As a teen he'd felt invisible, and now he felt like a pariah. He didn't regret one word he'd said to Myra, but he knew Carver would file a report with the board. The end.

Alone and adrift, Josh felt stupid for trapping himself here in this small town. The only thing that shone through clearly was his fear of losing Tyler. Maybe he should just abandon his job and follow Tyler to San Diego. Tyler had made the offer more than once the past couple of weeks.

But what if their fledgling relationship couldn't survive the pressure? Tyler didn't need this trouble on top of everything else he'd be facing the next six months.

Josh knew this kind of thinking wasn't safe or rational. Dark thoughts picked at him like crows until he finally turned and walked across the asphalt, all the way across the lot to the gate and then the road. Despair threatened to swallow him whole.

Worthless.

The day's events had shaken his world, leaving him unmoored. He stood alone in the street, heart heavy with turmoil. Josh paced and fretted outside the school gates, struggling to process everything that had happened.

He wrapped his arms around himself, waiting for Tyler, the one certainty in his suddenly precarious world. Even so, Josh realized that depending so much on another person, even Tyler, was childish and risky.

Any day now, Tyler was due to depart. San Diego felt like the other side of the planet.

"Please," he whispered. He walked out into the empty street, staring at the horizon toward home.

When Tyler arrived, he was speeding, and Josh saw the truck from ten blocks away. He just needed to close the distance.

Tyler didn't even bother to park. He screeched to a halt at an angle and clambered out to get to Josh as fast as he could cover the ground. "I got you. I promise. Come here. It's okay. You're okay. I swear."

Josh fell forward against him, and those powerful arms closed around his back to hold him up and keep him close, pressing their hearts together.

Chapter Thirteen

"TYLER?" JOSH called into the house from the doormat, glanced at his watch. No answer, but he could hear noises down the hall.

Josh got back in his truck, the engine still idling, and waited for Tyler to emerge so they could head back to his sister's house. It had been a horrible couple of days, and it was about to get worse.

After Josh's blowup at Myra, Carver had been obliged to officially reprimand him and add the incident to his file. Josh had taken three days of personal leave, and when he came back nobody in the building had the nerve to say jack to him. Mostly everyone tiptoed around him.

In his report, Carver had taken a lot of the blame, for allowing Myra a chance to attack Josh so publicly and worse. One of the bitchier board members had made noises about pursuing the matter and pressing some kind of imaginary charges until Tyler's lawyers rattled sabers and scared them off.

Sometimes it's good to be the king.

Josh didn't want to sue anyone. Something had changed in him. Ultimately that outburst had shaken Josh out of a fifteen-year sleepwalk. Carver's order to take a few days off gave him a chance to think about the bottled rage he had been carrying around. He wasn't proud of saying those things to Myra, but he was sure as hell glad he had. He was relieved there had been witnesses. Truth isn't comfy.

All those years, Myra Waxman had only felt empowered to grope him, smother him, and judge him because he'd allowed it. Playing nice and greasing the wheels were fine, but you had to fight the battles that mattered. If he'd maintained better boundaries or confronted her in real time, he might have defused whatever ugly power she pretended to have.

Never again.

The past few months with Tyler had woken something in him, made him see his choices and actions through clear eyes. Roots are great, but trees grow up and out. Carver's mandatory three-day vacay had also given them extra time together when it mattered most.

Now the moment had finally come when Tyler would return to San Diego. They both knew he had to return to his NFL life, no matter how much they dreaded what came next. He'd been stalling for a couple weeks, but the time had come to face the music.

Josh's fingers tapped an anxious rhythm on the steering wheel as he thought about the looming goodbye. Logically, he understood. It didn't help much. Determined to send Tyler off without making it worse, he plastered a cheerful smile on his face, but it faltered at the sight of Tyler's numb expression as he emerged from the house.

In just a few hours, he would board a private jet to Las Vegas. The San Diego Swells wanted to announce his full recovery at a press conference scheduled for this afternoon before they played the Raiders. The Swells were soldiering through the playoffs as best they could without their MVP.

"Hey, big guy," Josh said, trying to sound cheerful. "All set?" He leaned over and pushed open the passenger door.

Tyler nodded silently and swung onto the seat with a scowl, buckling himself in with fumbling fingers. As they pulled away, his hand found Josh's, clenching tight.

Josh squeezed back reassuringly, but he couldn't ignore the chill in his chest. "You got this."

"Three hours," Tyler muttered, his voice grim. "I hate these dog and pony shows. At least they sent a plane."

"Private jet? Fancy," Josh quipped. "You know what they say—getting there is none of the fun."

Tyler didn't even crack a smile. He only stared out the window, his grip on Josh's hand unrelenting. "They want me in Vegas by five. Big announcement with the coaches." His voice was flat. "Captain Fantastic, back from the dead."

They passed the high school, and Tyler turned to look at it with an odd expression. He shook his head at the familiar buildings, the track peeking out behind the gym. "Sorry. I'm being a pill."

Josh swallowed hard, fighting back the urge to tell Tyler that he didn't have to go or to offer to come with him. Instead, he focused on the road ahead, keeping his thoughts to himself.

They drove in silence through the quiet streets of Cinnamar. Josh wrestled with his anxiety. How would they survive the distance, the tabloids, the relentless pressure of Tyler's career? He knew that Tyler needed to prove something, but at what cost? He snuck a glance at Tyler's grim face. He looked like he was headed to his own execution.

Josh gave his hand a reassuring squeeze. "You'll be back before you know it." Even as he said the words, he wondered if he was trying to convince Tyler or himself.

Tyler just stared straight ahead, his jaw clenched.

"Promise me you'll take care of yourself," Josh murmured, his voice barely audible above the hum of the truck's engine.

"Promise," Tyler replied, low.

They continued the drive in silence, their hands still clasped, no words needed.

They pulled up to Nadia's place, the engine rumbling as Josh put the truck in Park.

Tyler flashed him a tight, false smile. "I should get this over with." He dropped Josh's hand to open the door.

Josh followed him inside, where he hovered near the entrance to the living room.

"I was about to send Mr. Poops with a search party." Nadia walked toward them, cradling the cat. "How we doing, boys?" When Tyler didn't answer, she glanced at Josh.

He shook his head, and she nodded in understanding.

"Tyler, I did laundry last night, and your suitcase is on the bed." She put a gentle hand on his arm. "Why don't you go take a look."

"Right." Tyler nodded. "Thanks." He disappeared toward his bedroom.

Josh followed Nadia into the living room, reminded of how much of Tyler's life had played out in these walls. For one second, he thought of twelve-year-old Tyler grabbing the belt out of Mr. Fantana's hands in this room. Fighting Goliath even though he was terrified.

A wave of intense love and respect washed over him. Tyler was a good man.

Nadia nuzzled the big tabby and put him down. "How's he holding up?"

"Not great." He peered down the hall toward Tyler's boyhood room. "We knew it was coming, but suddenly everything feels like a freaky fast-forward."

Mr. Poops squeaked up at them as if asking a question and then wandered down the hall in Tyler's direction.

Josh just shook his head. "That crazy cat really does love him."
Then, for no rational reason, his eyes welled up and a hot tear snaked
down his face. He wiped it, feeling dumb.

"Oh, hon." She frowned.

"Sorry. Last thing he needs."

Nadia pursed her lips. "You can still talk him out of this. It's too
much, too soon."

"He needs to do this for himself," Josh replied quietly. "I can't
make this decision for him."

"But you're the only one he'll listen to," Nadia insisted, her dark
eyes pleading. "Talk to him, Josh. He's got to know how stupid this is.
Not to mention dangerous."

Josh stayed silent, his jaw tight. Maybe Nadia didn't understand or
didn't want to.

On some level, he could understand Tyler's compulsion. Maybe it
was about the boyhood dream of being a big deal. Maybe it was about
his dad and the fears about violence. Or maybe this really was a macho
fantasy thing—Tyler needed to prove he could still play or he might
never recover from the shame and doubt of his injury. He knew all these
bits were tangled with Tyler and the game itself.

"Maybe you can go with him. You could take some time, right?"

"There's no way." Josh thought about all the drama at the school
right now. "I'm in enough hot water as it is. But even if I could, Tyler
would take it wrong."

She rolled her eyes. "Testosterone. Ugh."

They both looked up as Tyler came back down the hall, an
overstuffed duffel bag slung over his shoulder. "I just crammed a couple
piles in. I don't know what. They'll dress me. Or I'll buy new stuff in
Vegas." He bobbed his head in mock readiness, lugging the lumpy bag
on one shoulder as he headed to the front door.

Nadia stepped into his path, blocking his exit. "Ty, please don't do
this. You're not ready."

Tyler's face clouded. "You don't get it."

Nadia turned to Josh.

He tried to step around her, but Nadia grabbed his arm. "Josh, back
me up here." She gave Josh a desperate look.

Josh hesitated. "More time couldn't hurt."

Tyler's eyes flashed. "Don't. This is hard enough." He shook off Nadia's grip and flashed a bright, false grin. "Vegas, baby. I'm going to be great. Wait and see." He tugged open the door and headed out, refusing to look back at them.

Nadia threw up her hands in frustration. "You two are making me nuts." She grabbed her purse and keys.

"What are you doing?" Josh didn't understand.

"Driving you so you two can actually say goodbye, because he's acting like a macho dumbass."

Josh rolled his eyes. "I can drive a car."

"Hon, it's not like a normal person catching a flight. This has probably leaked on TMZ. You got TV stations, paparazzi. Football is a billion-dollar business."

"Right. Jesus, I hadn't—"

Her brow furrowed. "You need to start, hon. There will be a lot of cameras waiting. Reporters. Maybe fans. It can get physical. Nasty, even." She looked at the door and shook her head. "He's just not thinking."

At that moment, Josh realized how unprepared he was for whatever mess came next. "I'm an idiot."

"A matched set." She smiled kindly at him. "Two idiots, but lovable. You're a rookie, so you get a pass this time. For him, there's no excuse."

Josh took a deep breath and followed her outside, bracing himself for the awful goodbye ahead.

Tyler stood on the little lawn, staring up at the roof or maybe the sky, frowning and shaking his head with the bulgy bag still balanced on his shoulder.

Nadia locked her door and pointed Tyler to her car.

"You're coming?" He gave her a squinty look of confusion.

"Unless you want *Entertainment Tonight* rummaging through your undies at prime time, you guys are going to need some help."

Tyler tossed the duffel in the front passenger seat of Nadia's car, propped up and buckled in like a passenger. "Camouflage," he said. He slid into the back seat, his long legs barely fitting.

Josh climbed in next to him, their thighs pressed together. He was going to miss the closeness most of all.

As Nadia pulled out of the driveway, Tyler laced his fingers through Josh's. "I don't want to go back," he whispered.

Josh squeezed in response. "It's your call. I get it. Proving you can or protecting yourself."

Nadia was not as tactful. "Nuts. What is so important about a game you need to go die for it?" She stared at him in the rearview mirror.

Josh leaned into him. "Just don't let fear make the decision for you."

"I'm not afraid," Tyler said defensively.

Nadia snorted from the front seat. "Please. You're terrified. And you should be. Your heart exploded on live television in front of a billion people." She threw up her hands and smacked the wheel in exasperation. "They got you going on camera tonight in Vegas so they can pretend you're invulnerable."

Tyler scowled at the rearview mirror.

"You do what you need. You're going to make the right choice," Josh added gently. "Closure is worth it."

"Maybe." Tyler tucked his chin over Josh's head and sighed. "I wish you could come with me."

"Me too." Josh took a deep breath of his shirt, trying to memorize the scent of him. "But we'll figure this out, okay? It's only for a little while."

Nadia glanced back at them, then again in the mirror, her expression softening. "Distance sucks, but you deal."

"Deal." Tyler chuckled and nodded above Josh. "Agree." She didn't know that *deal* had become a kind of code word between them. She wasn't wrong.

"And for God's sake, don't get all macho and stupid. And that goes for both of you." Nadia glanced to the side and changed lanes. "Just listen. Set expectations. Tell the truth. Don't let stuff fester. Make time."

Josh nodded, trying to take her advice to heart. But his own fears still gnawed at him.

The drive turned out longer and shorter than he'd expected. Tyler got confirmation of his Vegas car service on the other end, and he showed the screen to Josh as if proving he was taken care of, that everything would be okay. As Josh watched, another chime as someone named "SwellsJim" texted the name and number of the assistant the team had assigned to get him situated upon arrival.

Tyler turned to him. "I gave them your info just in case. Emergency contact. I hope that's okay. They had Nadia, but they need to be able to reach you."

"Of course." He nodded. "Thanks." In some office, an NFL secretary had typed in his number and done a Google search to file his basic details under "boyfriend."

Some weak and sneaky part of Josh wanted to make a scene or beg him to stay. As off balance as Tyler seemed, all it would take was a nudge.

Except ultimatums could backfire.

Another chime on Tyler's phone announced a dinner reservation had been made for him at a steakhouse and a new suit would be delivered especially for the press thing.

"Easy on the red meat." Josh squeezed his big knee. "At least they're trying to take care of you."

Nadia was less impressed. "They better. As much money as you make them."

Tyler stared out the window, still holding Josh close. "It's just a press thing and some stills. Then I'll go sit in the box with the owners. Dinner with the wives. Easy. The worst part is having to watch the game without getting on the field."

Eventually, Nadia exited the freeway and followed the feeder onto a grid of streets that looked like an industrial park. Overhead, the dull roar of a plane confirmed they weren't far now.

A sign indicated they should shift to the left two lanes. The airport loomed ahead, and dread pooled in Josh's stomach. He wasn't ready to let Tyler go.

As they took the long, banked curve toward the terminal, Josh gave up on stupid what-ifs and just tried to memorize each detail of Tyler pressed beside him for later. The cars started to bunch up as they approached the terminal, but Nadia kept to the outside lanes, peering ahead as she navigated the traffic.

Even from a couple hundred yards away, Josh could see the swarm of people near the terminal doors.

From up front, Nadia grunted. "Told you."

"Sorry, gang." Tyler craned to see. "One of the Swells press reps must have leaked it for the bump. I'm not even flying commercial."

Sure enough, the drop-off lane was deadlocked, an ugly crush of legitimate passengers trying to get past news vans and the scrum of reporters and their crews.

"Holy crap." Josh's pulse quickened.

Nadia scanned the crowd but kept on moving. "Everybody wants to get their hands on America's Tightest End."

On the curb, paparazzi and a couple of reporters jostled for position, cameras at the ready. Passengers shoved past them, but the TV crews shoved back.

Beside Josh, Tyler's whole body tensed. "Here we go," he muttered.

Josh gave his big hand one last squeeze. It was time to say goodbye. The next time they were this close, everything would be different.

"I don't believe it. You see?" Tyler tapped on the window and leaned toward the front seat. He pointed at a bright red head among the crush of press waiting to ambush them. "Cilla Miller."

Nadia nodded. "The better to eat you, my dear."

Josh craned to see. "It sure is. Isn't this out of her way?"

"Absolutely. From San Diego? An hour at least." He glowered. "She's an associate. She doesn't even have a producer yet. How did she get herself here?"

"Ambition." Josh shrugged. "She drove."

"But someone must have tipped her off." Tyler wiped his face and sat back. "She's nobody."

"Everybody is nobody." Josh gave him a rueful look. "Until they're not."

The driver behind them leaned impatiently on the horn, and Nadia yanked the wheel left, changing lanes with no warning. Other horns joined in.

Tyler's stoic mask cracked as he scanned the chaotic scene. "I can't do this. Not like this."

Nadia kept driving, peering ahead for an opening in the press scrum. "You do if you plan to get on that plane, bro."

"Nadia's right," Josh said gently. "We'll figure it out."

Tyler dragged a hand over his face. For a second, real panic flashed in his eyes, the same raw dread consuming Josh.

Nadia craned her neck, searching for a way through. "I could loop around. Maybe there's an access road."

"Could be." Josh nodded. "Worth a shot."

Again, Nadia swung the wheel hard, and they looped back around toward the cell phone waiting lot. Other passengers honked and shouted as she cut them off.

"Sorry, folks, emergency!" Nadia called out the window. "My brother's having a baby."

Tyler barked a harsh laugh and fiercely gripped Josh's hand. "Who is better than you two?"

The U-turn took them back past the long-term parking. Nadia drove slowly through the waiting lot, squinting toward the gates. "Don't see another way in."

"At least not one that doesn't throw you to the sharks." Josh racked his brain. Maybe they could get him onto some kind of airport tram? If Tyler showed in the front now, it would be a total circus.

Tyler turned to them both. "I'm open to ideas."

"We disguise you," Nadia suggested. "Hat, glasses. Maintenance uniform."

"I'm six foot five, 257 pounds at present." Tyler gave her a skeptical squint.

"And gorgeous. He's one of the most famous faces in America," Josh agreed. "They'd be able to see you from orbit."

"Plus good luck finding a uniform." Nadia glanced out the window. "Just a thought."

Josh said, "Too bad we can't smuggle you aboard. Like Dracula."

"In a coffin?" Nadia giggled at that. "Can you imagine? What an entrance."

"Wait." Tyler grinned then. An actual real smile spread across his face, and he shook his head as though he'd woken up from a crazy nightmare. "Buckingham."

Josh gestured at him to continue. "What?"

"Trust me." Laughing, he squeezed Josh's hand and kissed their laced knuckles. "How does D'Artagnan reach Buckingham?"

"Tyler," Nadia demanded.

"I got it." Tyler smirked, some of his old swagger flickering in his eyes. "I got to do… what I do."

Nadia sounded unconvinced. "I don't get it."

Tyler turned to Josh, eyes glinting. "You two need to dump me at the nearest loading dock. I'll take it from there."

"Buckle up, boys." Without any further discussion. Nadia started driving against the traffic, barreling into areas marked Private and swerving left where the arrows pointed right.

She nosed around corners and raced past offices until they pulled into a loading area on the far side of the terminal. She swung the car into an empty spot marked Employees Only, hiding them behind a couple of cargo vans.

She turned the engine off and they sat, catching their breath while the engine ticked in protest. "Well, that was entertaining. Have you missed your flight yet?" She sounded hopeful.

Tyler frowned. "Stop it. No. Private jets wait."

Josh said, "You're not going to miss the flight."

"I'm going to miss this." Tyler considered him a moment and blinked softly.

Nadia groaned and hauled herself out of the car.

Tyler climbed out himself, peering around the corner of a cargo van.

A scruffy young man in a reflective vest drove their way on a big luggage cart, almost like an ATV, with six wheels and a separate open-topped trailer, which was stacked with even more luggage.

Tyler turned to Josh and Nadia. "Stay put for a second. I got this."

The handler guy pulled to a stop at the dock and climbed out, shuffling around to the trailer without any hurry.

Before Josh could protest, Tyler slid out of hiding and strode over with a superstar grin. "Hey, brother. Mind giving me a hand with something?"

Warily, the luggage handler looked up.

Tyler flashed his most disarming smile. "I'm in kind of a jam." He started to say something in a low voice until the scruffy man's eyes went wide and his face blanched.

The baggage handler fell back a step in surprise. "No way, you're… Tyler Fantana? Number eighty-six. My grandpa loves you! I love you. My whole family loves you. Not in like a weird way, but— Wow. I can't believe…."

"That's very kind, Dale." Tyler squinted at the name tag on the guy's chest. "Your name is Dale?"

"You know my name. Oh, wow. My girlfriend ain't going to believe this."

Tyler pointed at the tag, but Dale wasn't making a lot of sense.

The kid grinned, awestruck. "I swear, this is the greatest day."

Tyler held out his hand and shook Dale's firmly. "I'm really happy to meet you, Dale. And I could use your help with a small problem." Then Tyler's voice got quiet again as he leaned in and muttered.

Josh started to step out toward them, but Nadia touched his arm and shook her head. "Give him a second."

"Is this something he does?"

"Not exactly, but he's got this *way* with people." She tilted her head, watching.

Josh sighed and smiled at Tyler working his magic over there. "He does."

From the body language and the luggage handler's expression, whatever Tyler had said had made the guy nervous.

Dale glanced around with wide eyes before he spoke up. "I don't know, man. If my union found out, I could get in all kinds of trouble."

"I would never let that happen. You'd be saving my ass," Tyler promised. "Tell you what. If you can help me out, I'll make sure you get an autographed football and a jersey."

Dale's face lit up. "Yeah?"

"Are you kidding?" Tyler clapped his shoulder. "I owe you."

"You don't owe me nothing." Dale nodded, hustling back to the driver's seat of the large luggage cart. "Tyler flippin' Fantana, man."

Tyler beckoned surreptitiously to Josh and Nadia. "All set."

Josh's throat tightened. This was really happening. He hadn't expected to feel this terrified.

"Dale, this is my sister, and this is my boyfriend."

Josh and Nadia raised their hands, and Dale waved back. "So cool, huh? This is so cool. You're so effing cool! I got to call my granddad."

"I need to get—" Tyler looked at his sister. "Back in a sec."

He turned to Josh, clasping his hand tightly. "Walk with me?"

Josh did. Tyler led them back to the car.

They moved slowly toward the cargo vans and Nadia's hidden car, the rumble of planes in the distance underscoring each step. Josh tried to memorize the exact shape of Tyler's grip, the slight brush of his shoulder, the sweet crinkle of his eyes.

Tyler popped open the door, pulled out his big duffel, and plopped it on the roof before he stopped and looked at Josh. He gave a big sigh.

Josh steeled himself and stepped even closer.

"I don't uh… I'm not sure I'm going to be able to say what I need to, so I need you to just assume that I said all the things I should have."

Josh nodded, not trusting his own voice.

"I love you, Joshua Ayres." His voice broke then. He blinked, bent, and kissed Josh firmly on the mouth, holding their lips together for a long breath. "Every bone in my body, every beat of my heart is just me loving you."

Josh wiped his eyes. "Me too."

"I still don't know just how you did it, but you put my busted ass back together. You got my heart beating right for once. I can do this. I promise."

"I know you can." He pressed a hand to Tyler's chest.

"We can. You're not allowed to worry about me, okay? I'm a cinder block. I'm a boot. These dummies can't even chip my paint."

"I'm not going anywhere." Josh nodded. "And if you need me there, you better say. I just don't want to get in your way."

"We'll make this work." Tyler drew back, eyes shining. "I promise."

Josh kissed him then, a slow, soft brushing of their mouths that lasted as long as he could make it. He savored the scratch of Tyler's cheek and the adamant solidity of his body. "Awful."

Tyler nodded. "Worse."

He looked up. "I don't care what it takes. I don't care what it costs, you come back the second you can. You call me the minute you want. Day or night. Anything, anywhere. I can get anyplace you need me to be."

"Trust me—" He held up his big index finger and dragged a cross over his heart. "—X marks the spot."

Josh nodded.

"Okay, then." With another tight squeeze, Tyler walked back to Nadia and Dale and his cart. He raised his voice to them. "All set?"

Dale beamed at him. He lifted Tyler's bag onto the edge of the trailer but didn't slide it into place. "We're golden, Mr. Fantana."

"Tyler." He shook the guy's hand with firm gratitude. "Anyone who saves my life and protects my family calls me Tyler." He winked and walked to the back of the trailer.

"Thanks"—Dale blushed and climbed back into the driver's seat—"uhh, Tyler."

"Don't get stupid." Nadia looked up at her brother and nodded. He nodded back. "If you let them hurt you again, I'm going to drag my butt to San Diego and do something nasty to those pricks. I mean really gross. I'll make Josh help, and we'll both end up in real jail."

Tyler hugged her and kissed the top of her head. "Take care, huh? And tell Poops I'm sorry I ran off like this."

Nadia's face got tight, but she didn't cry.

Tyler gave her a tentative boyish smile, then turned to Josh. "I'm sorry."

"No. Don't be." Stepping to the back of the cart, Josh pulled Tyler into a fierce embrace. "Just remember," he murmured. "Promise me."

Tyler held him, rocking slightly, and kissed his forehead. "No choice. Best thing in my life."

Overwhelmed, Josh could only nod. They leaned together for one last searing kiss, a silent vow passing between them.

"I'll call tonight. After." Tyler hopped up onto the trailer, climbed past the piled luggage, and sat down in the empty center space. He propped up the duffel to hide himself from any prying eyes. The cart and trailer just looked like a heap of luggage bound for no place in particular. From underneath it all, Tyler's muffled voice said, "All set, Dale."

"You guys take care." Dale waved, and just like that, the trailer lurched forward and sped off, smuggling Tyler to his plane, hidden by suitcases.

Josh watched until they disappeared, a hollow ache in his chest.

Nadia touched his arm. "Let's get you home."

Numb, Josh let her guide him back to the car. The road ahead seemed so much longer without Tyler beside him. But he knew they'd take it one step at a time.

Josh climbed into the passenger seat, feeling unmoored and adrift as Nadia started the engine.

"He'll be okay," she said, her voice firm despite the sheen in her eyes. "We'll make sure of it. You run each morning and sleep every night like he's there. And keep telling him the truth."

Josh just nodded, staring out at the acres of concrete and the tarmac beyond the fence. In his mind, he could still see Tyler's jaunty smile surrounded by heaped luggage, could still feel the press of Tyler's lips.

"I speak from experience. You cannot protect Tyler," Nadia continued as she pulled out of the airport. "He always figures it out for himself. Solves the thing. Proves the point. Needs to know if he can do it. Otherwise he'll always wonder until it drives him crazy."

Like taking his father's belt away. He'd fight the whole world to make things right.

"I know." Josh looked at his lap. Tyler had seemed so hopeful and determined when they first arrived at the airport. Now Josh wasn't sure if Tyler had been trying to convince himself or Josh. "Thank you for driving. I wouldn't have been able—"

"Of course."

They drove in silence for a few minutes before Nadia spoke again. "You're coming over for dinner tonight. I could use the company, and you could use the practice. Tyler says you can almost boil an egg."

Josh managed a small smile. "Yeah. That'd be nice." He reached over and squeezed her hand.

As they turned onto the feeder leading back to the freeway, Josh stared ahead.

He couldn't shake the sense of foreboding that had settled over him.

What if it was too much, too soon? What if Tyler got hurt again? What if the distance and scrutiny tore them apart?

Josh glanced over at Nadia. Her jaw was set, eyes fixed on the road. She was probably more worried than he was.

He thought back to their childhood, their father and the abuse that had shaped so much of Tyler's anger. Josh imagined that's where Nadia's protective streak came from. She'd spent so many years anxious for her fearless big brother.

Josh felt a swell of gratitude for her. She'd always been a wonderful friend, but knowing her better made him admire her in a different way. She was like wild roses, prickly if you messed with her and growing where she wanted. However blunt her manner, he knew she cared fiercely for Tyler, just as he did. He gave her hand another squeeze. "Thanks."

She looked up at the rearview and abruptly changed lanes. "I still don't understand who Buckingham is."

He chuckled. "We'll get through this," he said softly.

"Don't doubt that." Nadia's eyes flickered to his, and she held his gaze for a moment before returning to the long concrete arc before them. "Only thing I ever learned about football. Best defense is offense."

The sky dimmed and purpled as they took the exit for Cinnamar, making the turns toward the Fantana house. Streetlights flickered on, casting a ghosty glow.

"You good with white wine?" Nadia put on her blinker. "I'm thinking stir-fry. Or maybe mac and cheese. Plus I've got cupcakes and gin. We could watch something dumb."

"Perfect." Josh took a deep breath, swamped by gratitude. He didn't know what lay ahead, but tonight, at least, he wouldn't be alone with his thoughts.

Chapter Fourteen

TYLER BLINKED against the glare of the studio lights as the photographer snapped away. "That's great, Tyler, eyes right. Lift the chin and… grin. Little more. Little bit more. That's the deal. Eyes here," the photographer said.

Three weeks after his triumphant return to the San Diego Swells, the media blitz was in full swing. Since the Vegas press avail, Tyler had emerged as the NFL's darling, the comeback king, his resurrection from a career-ending cardiac injury fueling countless human-interest stories. The Swells were milking it for all it was worth.

"All right, Tyler, relax your mouth, eyes left. Shoulders relaxed. No… really relaxed," the photographer called out as Tyler stood under the bright lights of the studio. The camera never stopped clicking. The photographer's name was Pedro, and Tyler had shot several promo campaigns with him.

This morning's photo shoot for *Sports Illustrated* was Tyler's eleventh since returning to the Swells. He felt like a show pony trotting around, but he couldn't deny the thrill of being back in the spotlight.

"Anna, can you get the shine on the arm?" Pedro's wife did simple hair and makeup, which kept shoots faster and friendlier.

Anna patted Tyler's arm with something and then smoothed his eyebrows with a quick thumb.

"That's the one." Pedro signaled to him. "Twist to me. A little further. Think of something good. Exhale! And… got it."

This was his third photo shoot since Monday. He'd done Wheaties on Wednesday and some kind of sexy "jocks and socks" social media campaign for the San Diego Zoo, which involved lounging around outdoors wearing nothing but those two items—socks and a jock—with his bare ass toasting on a flat rock that overlooked a trio of bored giraffes.

At least today he got to keep his clothes on.

This kind of publicity stuff was glamorous and whatever, but to be honest Tyler would have paid ten thousand bucks to be running around the track at Hamilton Hugh right now, his arm bumping against the only person he needed.

As the camera clicked away, Tyler couldn't help but think about Josh. He missed his calm presence, that reassuring voice in his ear. It was a stark contrast to the constant whirlwind of empty activity and attention he now faced daily.

For another forty minutes, Pedro kept him hopping and then let him go earlier than expected. "I think we got more than we need, actually. At least three options if they decide to give you the cover. But more than enough for insert and inset. You can get dressed whenever."

Tyler exhaled and shook out the tension. Standing immobile for long stretches of time only made him conscious of the aches and twinges. "Thanks for today, man."

He started walking toward the bathroom to change and noticed the big wall of battered books next to the kitchenette. "Pedro." An idea struck him. "Weird question?"

"Might get a weird answer." Pedro looked up from the screen on the camera. "Shoot."

Tyler pushed his hands into his pockets and unleashed the smile that had kept him from ever paying a traffic ticket. "You read a lot."

Pedro laughed and glanced at the packed shelves. "Guilty. My wife makes me store all my paperbacks here instead of home."

"I'm working on a pro-literacy thing. Anti-censorship. You know. In my hometown." He nodded.

"For the miracle man? Anything." Pedro winked. "You're the toast of the town."

"Would you be up for doing some shots of me for my boyfriend's charity?"

"Sounds serious. Congrats."

Tyler blinked gratefully. "Amen. I'm trying to keep him out of the grinder as much as I can."

"What kind of charity?"

Tyler grinned. "He's trying to save the high school library in our hometown from a bunch of blowhards."

"Anything." Pedro snapped a picture of him and stared at the screen to check it. "I mean, you're here. I don't have anyone else till noon." He snapped again, capturing Tyler against the wall of books. He glanced up and looked at the shelves. "This okay?"

"Perfect."

Pedro spent another ten to twenty minutes getting shots. Tyler swapped his clothes out a couple times just for variety, but in the end they got a bunch of useful images. Even if Josh couldn't use them, Tyler could have the press team send them to the media with info about the campaign.

As he left for good this time, Tyler turned to slap and shake Pedro's hand. "You're the man."

"My pleasure, Fantana. Hey, if you're interested…," Pedro said behind him.

Tyler turned in the doorway with a question on his face.

"I'm doing a couple covers for Condé Nast this month. Everybody needs good grease, right? I could hit up some other celebs." He shrugged. "See if they'd be interested in helping out."

Tyler shook his hand again. "That'd be amazing. I really appreciate it. I'll send you the details." After a wink and a salute, he jogged down the staircase to the street, feeling excellent about surprising Josh with some outside celebrity muscle.

"Breathe. Find the path before trying to run," Tyler whispered to himself. Josh kept reminding him. No matter the pressures from the team, the media, even the fans. Because deep down, all he wanted was to protect his heart, in every sense, and find his way back to the man who had captured it so completely.

Tyler headed for practice that morning feeling a little better.

Right after the Qualcomm Stadium had been rebuilt as the Snapdragon, Boris had spent $190 million to build the Swells a fancy compound. He'd bought eleven acres southwest of I-8 and erected a mirrored office tower, a state-of-the-art gym, and a full training facility near Mission Valley East, all just ten minutes from the new stadium.

Practice was… fine. He participated in about half the drills. The coaches gave him enough grief that he started to believe they actually still wanted him on the team.

To their credit, all the coaches seemed to be keeping a close eye on him through the agility drills and dummy tackles routines. McBride and Janowitz made him sit out the strenuous bits, just to be safe. All of them offered encouragement that felt sincere, even when Tyler wondered just how irreplaceable he was.

A couple of hours later, the Swells offense wrapped up for the day. Tyler wandered back toward the locker room, muscles pleasantly sore and loose from the morning workout. As his cleats clicked across the tiles, he traded friendly insults and shoulder checks with some of the guys from his practice squad.

"Hey, gramps, hope we didn't bust your catheter," jeered Odell, a cocky second-year quarterback with dreads and braces. He'd transferred in from Detroit and had golden hands. "You still hit plenty hard."

"Sorry if I knocked the tit out of your mouth, junior," Tyler fired back with a grin. They jabbed at each other and chuckled.

As always, the camaraderie with his younger teammates energized Tyler. Their competitiveness made him feel like part of the team again, not just some battered charity case.

After Tyler rinsed off and returned to his locker, some of the veterans came over to check in.

"How's the ticker holding up, pa?" asked Calvin, a starting linebacker.

"Still ticking," Tyler replied. "We'll see if it stays that way whenever I go full contact."

"Don't push it too fast, Fantana." Calvin lowered his voice. "You listen. Ain't no shame in taking your time, no matter what they tell you. We need you at a hundred and one percent, not the glue factory. You'd best pay attention to that heart."

Tyler nodded, appreciating the candor. The coaches wanted to fast-track his return, but his teammates seemed to understand the risks. Their concern meant everything right now.

After toweling off and pulling on dry shorts, Tyler headed to the training room for his biweekly PT session. Maureen, his physical therapist, put him through a gauntlet of exercises, massage, and soaks to continue rebuilding his strength and mobility.

"Damn, take it easy on me, lady!" Tyler joked after a brutal set of squats with resistance bands. These exercises started out like nothing, but the ache snuck up on you.

"Got to get you back in shape if you want to survive out there." She poked his side.

He nodded. Humor and honesty—with so much pressure coming from all directions, they helped him remember what mattered.

"I can't believe they dragged you back so fast." Her expression turned serious. "Take your time. You know your limits better than anyone."

"You sound like Josh." Tyler nodded. "I'm trying to listen to my body. Just hard to say no when they all think I'm ready to rock."

Rolling his legs to one side and then the other, Maureen adjusted his hips expertly and then quickly cracked his back three times for good measure.

"God, that feels good. You got to teach me how to do that."

"Once you're back to a hundred percent. I mean it. Keep trusting yourself. Only you really know what you can handle."

She popped a towel over his shoulder and gave him a thumbs-up. "Tuesday. Hot tub for thirty minutes. I've set it hotter, but you can adjust if you need."

He nodded. He skinned out of his shorts and briefs and slid into the scalding bubbles. Maureen was a proponent of old-fashioned Epsom salts, and over the years he'd come to associate the smell with practice days. Tyler leaned back in the hot tub, letting the heat penetrate his sore muscles.

As the water pummeled him with delicious pressure, Tyler sighed and sank deeper, wishing Josh was here with him.

He ended up soaking for an hour and a half because he knew it was helping his muscles, and when he finally hauled his big butt out of the tub, his entire body was steaming and wrinkled. By the time he reached his condo and got upstairs, the sky was dark over the Pacific Ocean.

Tyler was so exhausted he ended up crashing on the balcony watching the glitter of the waves before he could take off his shoes.

Ringing jolted Tyler awake. The moon was up now. How long had he been asleep?

Fumbling for his phone, he saw it was Josh video-calling. Tyler's heart leaped as he answered, Josh's handsome face filling the screen.

"Hey, Coach."

"God, it's good hear your voice. I was starting to get worried." Josh's smiling face filled the screen, the familiar backdrop of his kitchen behind him. Even the sight of it made Tyler feel calmer.

He shook his head. "Passed out. What a day."

Josh hesitated, considering the screen for a moment. "You're not overdoing it already, are you?"

Tyler chuckled and rubbed sleep from his eyes. "Of course I am. What kind of a candy-ass do you take me for?"

When he'd first returned to San Diego, Tyler had really struggled with the fakeness of all the technology they had to use to keep in contact… never touching him and having to fill the air with stilted chitchat because talking was what people did on phones. Just because they weren't together didn't mean they needed to act differently with each other.

One of the best parts of his time with Josh had been the easy silences. But for now, this was what they had to work with. At least now it felt less stiff and artificial.

As Tyler made himself a salad, Josh shared an amusing story about his students attempting to build a model trebuchet out of paper clips.

Tyler laughed, the tension in his shoulders easing. "Life skills."

"Yeah, if they want to fight the Gauls. But I can hardly fault them. Oh, and the auction wrapped up yesterday. Twenty-three thousand dollars and another sixty-one families on the petition. Carver said to tell you thank you for the extra jerseys. The library is extremely pleased."

Even though it was so late, Tyler lived for these calls, the lifeline keeping him tethered amidst the mania.

"Everything okay there? How was the *Sports Illustrated* thing? That was this morning, right?"

"Fine. Well, better than the zoo deal at a minimum. At least they let me wear more than tube socks and my jockstrap."

Josh laughed. "I bet the tigers loved you in your jockstrap. I, for one, am a big fan of you in nothing but your jockstrap and tube socks."

"Are you now?"

"Okay, embarrassing. I guess that one hasn't come up yet." Josh squirmed and looked flustered. "Yeah. Big-time." He closed his eyes and exhaled slowly.

"Noted." Tyler leaned closer to his phone. "Joshua, are you having impure thoughts about me in my work clothes?"

Josh frowned. "That is completely unfair. Your work clothes are a widely acknowledged sexual fetish in most civilized countries and all porn sites."

"Well…." Tyler wiped his mouth and said, "I've got a surprise for you."

"You do?"

"Not that. Although I'm going to save that one for later when you need some special convincing." As he rinsed his plate, he explained about Pedro donating shots, as well as his offer to recruit some extra celebrity support. Josh was even more thrilled than he'd hoped. Just seeing him so happy and energized steadied Tyler's heart.

Over the past few weeks, Josh had questioned Tyler's nonstop schedule. He seemed anxious about Tyler pushing too hard too fast. Josh always told him the truth.

"I know you want to prove yourself, but don't do it at the cost of your health," Josh said. "A smart athlete finds the path before trying to run."

"I will. I'm not going to let any of these clowns bully me," Tyler assured him. "The coaches keep telling me how strong I look, but looks aren't what I'm worried about. I'm still exhausted a lot of the time."

"Why?" Josh smiled at him.

"I can't even sleep right without you in my arms. I miss you so much."

"Tell me about it. You just listen to your body," Josh advised. "Slow. Steady. Strong. No rushing. No risky moves."

"Duh." Tyler rolled his eyes. "Thanks."

"Hey... I prefer you in one big glorious piece." Josh sat back into the cushions of his couch and reached for the remote. "You still have time watch a show?"

During the night calls, they had gotten into a habit of watching cartoons and movies together, mostly on the weekends or when Tyler could sneak out of an event early.

The first week, Josh had suggested they work their way through *The Powerpuff Girls* and *Dexter's Laboratory*. They hit Play in tandem and enjoyed them like they were lounging on the same couch. The shows were short and silly enough to give them an excuse to sit quietly doing something together without having to voice all the worries preying on them.

Tyler shook his head. "I don't think so. You look seriously beat. I'll make it up to you."

"Deal. If you'll wear your jockstrap and socks next time." Josh grinned.

"Give me two minutes and I will blow your mind."

Josh's brow creased. "Next time. I'm worried about you, big guy."

"'Kay. Sorry." Tyler started nodding off on the couch. "I shouldn't be so exhausted."

"Get some rest," Josh whispered. "I'll talk to you tomorrow." Then he ended the call.

Tyler frowned at the dark phone in his hand. The distance between them felt immense, even though he knew Josh was just a drive away.

Maybe he was asking too much, trying to maintain a relationship under the glare. He longed for the day he could return to Cinnamar and find out if what they had was built to last.

Maybe Josh deserved someone simpler, someone who could offer a quiet life back home. But the thought of losing Josh after finally having a chance with him made Tyler's chest ache in a way that had nothing to do with his injury.

He didn't even try for the bedroom, just curled onto his side and zonked out without bothering to turn off the lights.

Chapter Fifteen

JOSH PULLED into the empty high school parking lot, gravel crunching under his tires as he parked next to Principal Carver's sedan. The cold night air rushed in when he opened the door, making him shiver. He hurried across the asphalt toward the dark gym entrance, unease tugging at his gut.

What had Carver called him here for at 2:00 a.m.? He'd said something about an arrest. Did burglars target schools? Had one of the kids done something crazy? January was way too soon for the seniors to start acting out.

He slipped through the propped-open door into the equipment room, the baked-in pong of sweat and disinfectant familiar and oddly comforting. Shrill voices echoed down the hallway, rising and falling in agitation… two women bickering, it sounded like.

As Josh stepped into the athletics office, he froze.

Principal Carver stood with his arms crossed, wearing jeans and sneakers. Sneakers? Josh could not remember him wearing anything less casual than a blazer in ten years. *Never.* Carver must have been hauled out of bed too.

Carver was leaning over a teary Elise Tattersall, Josh's fellow coach and fake-flirting buddy. Elise was mumbling rapidly and gulping air while she tried to get words out. She was cradling her arm in a gym towel soaked with red.

Josh cleared his throat. "Elise? What happened?"

Everyone turned, relief washing over Carver's face.

Elise stood and hugged him tightly with one arm. The other seemed to be wrapped in the stained towel. "Oh, Josh, it was horrible. She's a lunatic." She gripped Josh's shoulder like a life raft. "An animal."

Over her shoulder, Carver stared at him, eyes wide, shaking his head. He looked exhausted, brow furrowed. "Josh, thank God you're here."

And then a sharp, sneering, all-too-familiar voice. "What you are going to do is unhand me." Cilla Miller sat in a black sweatsuit, blocked by two annoyed-looking police officers.

"Cilla." Josh sighed and steadied himself. "Why am I surprised?"

She whirled to face him, her ginger helmet unmoving around her panicked, swollen face. Her eyes were bloodshot and oozing a steady stream of tears. Her wrists were handcuffed in front of her. "I am a deeply respected member of the press."

"Respected! Hmmph." Elise spun and glared at Cilla. "In a dog park, respected. Deep in a gutter, maybe."

"Miss Tattersall." Carver spoke up and took Elise's arm to guide her to the other side of the room. "Officers, if you'll just give us a moment to explain."

The cops seemed as baffled as Josh felt, one of them the parent of a Hamilton sophomore. Vasquez was her name, and Josh knew the family. The other was an Officer Hurley, based on his badge, and he seemed equally freaked out by these odd circumstances.

"We're going to…." After some muttered discussion, the two officers opted to stand with their backs to the door, barring any sudden escapes.

Had Cilla already tried to make some kind of break for it? Why was she cuffed? Why was there blood? Why were Josh's papers and clothes all over the floor?

Josh asked, "What exactly has been happening in here?"

Carver spoke calmly and slowly. "We have what you might call a *situation*."

"No kidding." Josh's gaze careened between Cilla and the cops. "Care to explain why we're standing here at two in the morning?"

"My job. My job is what." Cilla grinned and bounced, words clattering out like coins from a jackpot. "I swung by briefly, shooting a little B-roll for my producers, when this fat maniac attacked me. She assaulted me out of the clear blue."

"ZZZZZZT. Try again, Little Orphan Anorexia." Elise scowled, her good arm crossed over her athletic department sweatshirt. Was she actively bleeding? Why was she bleeding?

"To be clear," Carver tried to interject, "Miss Miller has offered four or five different explanations so far—"

Elise jabbed a finger toward her. "None of which are anywhere close to what happened. Because it happened to me, you bitter bitch. Because the entire school has actual cameras and your bony ass is going to jail. *Real* jail." She held up the red-soaked towel around her arm and pointed at it. "On camera."

"Then what did happen?" Josh asked. His bafflement had started to tip over into dismay. If Cilla Miller had been prowling around campus in the wee hours, whatever had gone down tonight meant nothing good for him and Tyler.

"So...." Elise took a deep breath and launched into a reenactment with melodramatic gusto. "I finished painting the yoga studio kind of late, and I realize my laptop isn't in my bag. Because I'd taken it out to do the raffle posters. Anyways, I came back here to grab it around midnight or maybe half past. Lot was dark. Building, dark. Sure enough, my laptop was on my desk." She pointed at it. "But then as I'm leaving, I hear a... scrape or something from the locker room. I stepped out into the hall to listen. I figured it was kids. Scuffling or rummaging, stuff getting knocked over. And then that basket rattle, like someone's trying to get into one of the wire bins. I'm no wimp, so I called 9-1-1 for backup and went to go check it out with my flashlight."

Cilla bristled. "That is a lie." She raised her cuffed hands to wipe her face.

Elise gestured angrily at her. "Lo and behold, before I even turn on my light, I spot Princess Dye Job of Bony Butt here on her way out of the locker hunched over. Creeping along like a rat. Trespassing. Theft. Maybe something grosser." She hissed at Cilla. "You're disgusting."

Cilla stared straight ahead. Her swollen eyes looked raw and painful.

Carver frowned in impatience. "Miss Tattersall...."

"Sorry. So I follow her. I had a pretty good idea.... Sure enough, she bends down, rattle-rattle-rattle. Our office door opens. Breaking and entering too. I think, 'This is getting good.' In she goes."

"It was a perfectly innocent—"

Elise huffed in disdain. "Innocent my ass. She comes into our office here and starts rifling through our desks. Files. IDs. Pulling out drawers, tossing papers around, taking pictures of whatever. She had a big stack of files and folders already piled up on your desk. Then she gets to your

locker and starts going through your… well, your stuff. Your shorts."
She lowered her eyes.

"My what?" That stopped Josh cold. "Do you mean underwear?"

"Jockstrap, actually."

Cilla sniffed. "Lie. You planted that on me."

"How could I?" Elise shook her head. "You had this man's actual
jockstrap in your blouse with his papers on your way out the damn door.
And then she jumped me."

"You jumped me."

Elise sighed. "Like a meth-lab den-mom. Not surprising, I mean,
look at her. Trash. Lady, they're going to love you in prison."

"Miss Tattersall." Carver was getting exasperated again.

"I have no idea what she's talking about." Cilla scoffed and
wheezed. "I was just taking some B-roll footage of the school trophies
when this lunatic attacked me."

Carver squinted. "In the middle of the night. Your crew can
verify this."

"Well… no. With my phone. I was having dinner nearby and
thought I'd kill—"

"—everyone's appetite with your snooping and sniffing of people's
privates," Elise interrupted, indignant. "I caught her red-handed stealing
private documents and student records. She was shoving your jockstrap
in her bra."

Worse than he'd expected.

Josh turned slowly. "Miss Miller…. Let me understand this." His
anger started to unfold and spread inside him like a terrible black bird,
but since the incident with Myra, he'd learned to take a breath. "You
went through my personal belongings? By accident."

Cilla laughed nervously. "I've absolutely no clue why she's lying.
Your underpants? Ew, no. I'm a journalist."

"Ask them." Elise pointed to the cops.

Officer Vasquez held up a plastic evidence bag containing Josh's
jockstrap. His brand, his size, his initials on the waistband.

Made no sense. Why had she wanted a jock? *His* jock. What had
she planned to do with it?

Elise smirked. "Stuffed in her blouse, along with a folder of
medical records, employee reviews, and coaching files. She picked this
place clean."

"I resent the insinuation. I would never stoop so low."

"You don't need to stoop... because you're a *snake*. And I'm not insinuating anything. I am an expert eyewitness. You're on camera, bone-bag." Elise pointed up at the ceiling. "The only reason we don't have a camera inside this office is because there's a shower. I'm going to come visit you in prison just so we can compare bite marks once you start your own collection." She held up her bleeding arm.

"What is it with reporters?" Josh widened his eyes at Cilla. "You people are psychotic." He shook his head, disgusted that some pushy stranger would violate his school and his privacy like this. Gross. He needed to stop her, but he couldn't risk stirring up the media hornet's nest. *Tricky.*

Cilla gave a sad sniff. "You're holding me here against my will. This is kidnapping." She raised her cuffed wrists.

"No." Principal Carver scrutinized Cilla Miller with disbelief. "Those are police officers who just restrained you for your own safety, ma'am." The fluorescent lights buzzed overhead. "You've already committed several crimes here tonight. Felonies."

"Says her. She almost killed me."

"Trust me. Not difficult if I wanted to." Elise snorted and rolled her eyes.

"Do you have any idea—? There is something wrong with you, Ms. Miller." Carver folded his arms across his chest. "The officers have already downloaded the recordings. Trespassing, stalking, breaking and entering, burglary, harassment, assault, faculty belongings, *children's* belongings."

Cilla opened her mouth to protest, but Elise cut her off. "Don't even think it, missy." With pursed lips, the coach lifted her forearm to reveal a bloody oval of teeth marks. "Perfect set."

Josh goggled. "Jesus, Elise."

"I can't wait to call your dentist. Better than a fingerprint right here." Elise pointed at her bloody arm. "And if I have to amputate a limb 'cause you have some tabloid sex disease, I'm going to sue your whole crappy channel into the poorhouse."

Cilla started to look a lot less sure of herself. One of her knees bounced rapidly.

"I tried to stop her from running off, and she bit me with her fake Chiclet teeth!" Elise said. "Broke the skin and everything. Blood all over.

Probably infected. Soon as they book her, I'm going to the hospital to get rabies shots. And penicillin."

"You grabbed me," Cilla cried, her voice echoing shrilly off the hard walls. "I was just… surprised is all."

Josh couldn't believe the gall. "With my jockstrap in your bra. And my records." The creepiness of this was off the charts. He wanted to tell Tyler, and at the same time he was deeply grateful that Tyler was in San Diego, blissfully ignorant of this stupidity.

Cilla's face flushed nearly as red as her hair. Her lips moved as she sputtered for a response, but none came.

Carver raised an eyebrow. "When you sneak into private property to steal items and assault people, you get arrested."

"Says who?"

Elise got in her face now. "The law. The law says. And I, for one, cannot wait to testify, skin-tag. I think I have a new hobby. Making your life miserable."

Cilla stared at each of them in turn, imploring them, her face a baleful mask. "I am almost *completely* innocent."

Josh felt a swell of gratitude for Carver and Elise having his back. His friends. The one thing fame hadn't stolen from him. Josh breathed a little easier knowing they were on his side against the Cillas of the world. No matter how far he and Tyler came, these media parasites would intrude and try to dredge up dirt.

Josh turned to Elise. "She grabbed you in the dark?"

"Yeah. When I caught her arm, she elbowed me hard in the gut, but I dropped her with a sweep. Next thing I know we're rolling around in the dark, she's yanking out my hair." Elise grinned. "But I am no dummy. I got my pepper spray, and I gave her a good long spritz."

Cilla shook her head with indignation, but her hair didn't move. "For which I will sue."

"Try. Try and sue me, hairspray."

"Ms. Tattersall, please. This isn't helping." Carver was starting to lose his patience.

Josh held up his arms and stood between them.

"Didn't see that coming, did she?" Elise huffed. "I sprayed her like a roach and then sat on her fake tits till the cavalry arrived." She extended a grateful arm to Hurley and Vasquez by the door.

Josh couldn't help but crack a small smile. Trust Elise to go toe-to-toe with an unhinged reporter. Under different and less grueling circumstances, the image of Elise sitting on top of Cilla, Josh's jockstrap and a can of pepper spray in hand, would have been hilarious.

"Soon as we showed up, Ms. Tattersall demanded a lawyer and a rabies test," Officer Vasquez added dryly. "She had completely incapacitated the suspect."

"Rabies test?" Josh asked, raising an eyebrow.

"Indeed." Carver's lips twitched ever so slightly.

Elise gestured impatiently at Cilla. "Look at her. I can only imagine where that mouth has been."

"Gotcha," Josh muttered, trying to maintain a serious demeanor. But he couldn't shake off the nagging sense that all this would reach Tyler somehow, that pressing actual charges wouldn't help anyone but the sleazy media. "Thanks for having my back, Elise."

"Always, hot stuff," she replied.

Absurd. But then everything seemed absurd. This is what happens when you date out of your league. *Literally*. In Tyler's world, the Swells could just bribe someone or hire a crisis management team to make things disappear. But Josh was just a high school coach who still lived eleven miles from the house where he was born.

This entire farce—Cilla's relentless pursuit of a scandal, the catfight with Elise, the cops looming on the sidelines—weighed heavily on Josh. It was up to him to decide how things would proceed from here. What would be best for Tyler? For himself? And, ultimately, for their relationship?

"Josh, are you okay?" Carver asked, concern etched on his face.

Josh realized he'd been lost in thought, staring into the empty hallway. "No. Yeah. This could get really ugly."

Carver nodded at Elise, Cilla, the cops getting impatient by the door. "You see my dilemma."

"Y-yeah," he breathed out, forcing a smile. "Thank you for calling me before anything official happened."

Tall and composed, Carver ran a head over his bald head before looking up from the floor. His deep voice resonated in the otherwise silent office. "Josh, as the principal, I need to report Ms. Miller's break-in, theft, and assault of a staff member… *officially*. The county should know. The school board should know. This is a serious criminal matter."

Cilla, her red hair gleaming under the harsh lights, screwed up her face. "Sure, sure. You want this whole misunderstanding all over the media. I don't think Mr. Ayres is equipped for that. Relationships are fair game." She stared at him, the threat direct. "Look, Tyler Fantana is a public figure, and so you are a public figure. Clickbait."

Josh clenched his fists and took a deep breath to calm himself. The scent of floor cleaner and stale air filled his nostrils.

Cilla huffed and scowled at them all in turn. "None of this is real. 'America's Tightest End' is a character. A product. Quid pro quo. Grow up. Captain Fantastic? It's a trade." She exhaled in a puff of indignation. "I am doing my job here."

She just wanted the headlines. He had to do *something*. Myra Waxman had taught him a powerful lesson about letting assholes slide. He glanced at Elise, who stood by his side, her eyes narrowed and lips pressed into a thin line.

Carver shook his head. "It has to be your call. The officers understand."

Officer Vasquez nodded. "What you did for my kid? I can never repay you, Coach. So we can book her or we can call it in as a false alarm. Miss Tattersall and Principal Carver just have to press charges."

"Or not." Carver watched him. "And that's why we called you here. We will have to report a break-in, but identifying a culprit is a whole other deal."

"Josh," Elise said, "you know what I want. But this is your life. Your boyfriend. Your privacy. Your *jockstrap*." She glared at Cilla. "You decide. Whatever you want, I want. Press charges, file a complaint, let her off with a warning, strip her naked and dump her out in the desert to crawl home over hot sand?"

Swallowing hard, Josh turned his gaze to Cilla. Even with the puffy, smeary eyes, her faux victimhood only fueled his frustration. Myra had pulled the same crap: *boo-hoo, poor me*. "I need an explanation, Cilla. A believable one…. I'm waiting."

Cilla's runny eyes flicked to the bitemark, the jockstrap, the cops, the desk, her cuffed wrists. "I don't think I should say anything else, actually."

"Wow." Josh frowned. "Nothing…. You can't even manage a lie. So you 'accidentally' entered a locked school, 'mistakenly' searched a locker room full of kids' gear, and 'inadvertently' picked that lock before my used jockstrap and private files 'happened' to fall *upwards* into your brassiere? Seriously? That's your play."

"Stranger things…." Cilla shrugged.

"I told you." Elise rocked her weight from foot to foot.

"Look, Mr. Ayres, we're just trying to do right by you." Officer Hurley said. "Paperwork's done. This list of charges, she won't make bail. She went through kids' underwear too. We know just where to stick her."

Cilla crossed her arms. "This is disgraceful. I'm going to call my lawyer."

Elise stood. "Do it, honey. Please."

"Indeed," Carver said, "but if you do that, it'll be from holding downtown."

Cilla didn't like that one bit. "I'm not a criminal."

Josh shook his head, unable to hide his incredulity. "You're worse. Criminals do it for money. You vultures live off misery."

"The public wants the juicy details. Closeted players. A potential porn star swap ring. Fantana is no angel." Cilla's eyes narrowed, but she plastered on a smile. "I got a job to do."

"You mean this, all this, is what people want: Robbing people. Biting them. Jockstraps." Josh stepped closer, crowding into her space.

Cilla's cheeks flushed an ugly red. "This is so unfair." She blinked in self-pity.

"This is a school, young lady." Carver spoke to the redheaded reporter the way he'd address a toxic thirteen-year-old. "Do you understand? The nice police officers there"—the cops waved—"have taken over seventy-five pictures: of you, the bite, the locks, muddy footprints, multiple crime scenes. Those bracelets are called *handcuffs*. We have you on video from six cameras committing multiple felonies on school grounds." He pointed up at the ceiling. "Your car is outside, clamped. The only person on God's earth that can save your—" He turned to Elise.

Elise smiled. "Bony ass."

"Yes, that, is this nice gentleman who you've been stalking and harassing inside my school. The officers have your ID, your employers, your fingerprints, your bite mark, your social security number, and several DNA samples. Elise here"—Elise waved—"is headed to a hospital to document her injuries. So maybe you want to dial it down before someone sensible loses their temper."

Elise cackled. "Any bets, McRibs? You better pray he's nicer than me."

Cilla swallowed.

Josh tensed, starting to spiral. He couldn't give her a pass, but he didn't want to make an even bigger mess in the press. "I don't trust her. Anything she says is a lie. The way she sits and smiles is a lie." His hands curled into fists at his sides. "God, this is so gross. You people are so gross."

Cilla's plastic smile melted into a genuine scowl.

"I'm not even a person to you. The way I figure…." Josh peered at her. "Only someone truly repulsive would invade a school to exploit someone's private life in front of kids for a buck." He cocked his head. "Not you, though. You care about sports. Or are you disgusting? Let's find out."

Elise grabbed Josh's arm, her grip firm and grounding. "It doesn't matter. Let the cops handle her. Some bony mooch with a Botox addiction. Just kill her job and let the courts have her carcass."

"Or let it go, Josh." Carver spoke low, looking him straight in the eye. "Consider the long game. How can you keep all of this foolishness contained? What will help you? What protects Tyler? You might win the battle and lose the war with this one."

Cilla nodded slowly at the principal. "Smart man."

"Hardly. I've seen a hundred of you, young lady. A thousand. This is a high school. Envious bullies aren't anything special." Carver glanced at her with something like pity, then back to Josh. "It's the middle of the night. She has no family. Her producers don't care about her. Nobody does. They'll boot her butt by midday tomorrow and a smarter, nastier one will take her spot. Hundreds of these hungry ticks trying to suck their way up the ladder."

Josh realized what he was suggesting. "You think I should let her walk."

"I think this is a long game, here. I think you should play the field with what you've got."

Josh nodded. In a perfect world, he'd call Tyler and the Swells would send a PR team to make all this vanish. Or someone would lean on Channel Twenty-four and kill whatever fake story she had planned.

But Carver was right. Cilla Miller was one in a long line of leeches. As long as he stood anywhere near Tyler, these vermin would scuttle out of the cracks to steal and falsify whatever they could.

Officer Hurley said, "Mr. Ayres?"

Josh shook his head and turned. "Sorry, Elise." He needed to let her walk, for Tyler, for himself. Carver looked relieved and sad.

Elise blinked in confusion. "Sorry why? Oh. Okay." She glanced at Cilla, who was now sitting very still. "Are you sure? She won't let up. She's never going to stop."

"She will. Cilla won't say one goddamned word about me or Tyler." Josh leaned over to her. "Got it? You say a single negative word about either of us in public to anyone, and I'll bankrupt myself putting you in jail and keeping you there."

Cilla stood. "If you aren't going to charge me, then I haven't done anything wrong."

"Wrong, sweet cheeks," Elise hissed at her. "It looks like I just forgot who did all this... for the moment. But any minute my memory might come back with all this handy evidence, and officers will drag you downtown before you can get to a phone. They will be stamping out license plates with your bony ass for the next ten years. I bet the prisoners will love you."

Carver crossed his arms. "Your lucky night, Ms. Miller."

Josh smirked. "You get one warning. But we're not clickbait. If you ever set foot in this school again, if you continue to harass me and the students or try to drag Tyler and me through your slime, I will drop you into the grinder faster than you can say 'prison food.'" He exhaled slowly.

"She doesn't deserve it." Elise sniffed ruefully.

"What about her phone?" Hurley held up a bagged iPhone with a baby blue cover.

"Oh no! Not a chance." Cilla stood, raising her hands in the cuffs, but Vasquez kept her where she was.

"Excellent." Josh plucked the baggie out of Hurley's hands. "We'll hang on to that."

Cilla's eyes bulged. "You will do no such—"

"You're right. I won't." Josh tossed the phone, and Elise caught it with genuine pleasure. "She will. It's her blood, after all. She's a witness and an assault victim who's having trouble remembering. We wouldn't want you getting any more bright ideas."

Elise held up the baggie. "You give me one reason, one excuse, and I forward the contents to every station in southern California."

Cilla's smug expression faltered. She glanced at the police officers and Principal Carver, who were all eyeing her with distaste. "Crystal clear," she said through gritted teeth.

Josh turned back to Carver and the police. "Please escort Ms. Miller from the premises. And formally warn her that if there are any further incidents, the school will prosecute her to the full extent of the law. You've been warned. Now get out of my sight."

Hurley and Vasquez each took a pale arm and walked her out.

Josh watched Cilla's retreating figure until the doors slammed behind her. He sighed and ran a hand through his hair, suddenly exhausted. Somehow it was three in the morning, and he didn't know how he would ever get to sleep again.

"I'm so sorry, Josh," Principal Carver said. "Elise."

"You two saved my bacon tonight. And Tyler's," Josh said. "I can't even explain how grateful I am."

Elise hugged him. "Oh, hon. What wouldn't I do for my guy?"

"You did the right thing." Carver nodded. "Call me if anything else comes up. I'll be in my office making some notes while everything is fresh. Elise?"

She nodded. "Good idea. And I'm headed to a hospital. You going to be able to get home okay?"

Carver gave Josh's shoulder a comforting squeeze. "Try to get some rest."

Josh managed a tired smile. "I will. Good night."

"Night, Coach."

Josh stood alone under the dim lights of the hallway for a long moment. His racing thoughts slowed, but a weight had settled on his chest.

Cilla's threats echoed in his mind, but he pushed them away. She was grasping at straws, and he wouldn't give her lies any power over him. Still, he couldn't ignore the worry that had taken root since Tyler went back to his real life. He knew that trust was fragile, that every detail of their relationship would unfold under a microscope, twisted by sleazoids who preferred scandal to truth.

He sighed and headed outside, the damp night air cool on his neck.

The old track stretched before him, a familiar comfort. How many times had he run that loop with Tyler? He swallowed hard, an ache forming in his throat as he wondered if they'd ever find their way back to that easy stillness again.

For now, Tyler was asleep seventy miles away, blissfully unaware of this ugliness. Josh hoped he'd done the right thing by not pressing charges. As much as he wanted to call and fill Tyler in, he knew he couldn't ever.

The others wouldn't mention tonight's events, would they? He should have warned everyone to keep this quiet. Tyler didn't need another thing to worry about. They'd understand. He'd make a point of touching base with both of them tomorrow.

Josh peered up at the moon, high in the inky sky. Tonight's bizarre ruckus had finally started to fade away to the point he could almost believe he'd imagined the whole stupid mess. But no, the bloody oval bite on Elise's arm, his jockstrap in the baggie, Cilla's raw swollen eyes glaring at everyone like a trapped rat… he'd never forget those as long as he lived.

He shook his head and took a deep breath of the night air. Tyler mattered more. They'd weathered crises before. This was just one more obstacle in their path, and they'd both faced worse and won. He sighed. All this craziness felt overwhelming because he was still getting used to it. Tyler was a pro. They'd find a way. He'd learn.

He headed for his car, heart lighter than before. The game ahead would not be easy, but he was playing to win.

Chapter Sixteen

TYLER RUSHED into the team conference room, late to the meeting with Boris Jarlson and the San Diego Swells coaching staff.

"Aaaand… Captain Fantastic." said one of the marketing reps, eyeing Tyler skeptically.

Boris and the coaches regarded him with a mix of thinly veiled irritation and feigned good humor.

"Sorry I'm late," he said, slightly out of breath. He felt embarrassed by his disheveled appearance. He was unshaven, his clothes were wrinkled, and he probably smelled of stale sweat. The soreness in his muscles from yesterday's workout made his movements stiff.

"No problem, kid, we're just glad you could make it," Boris said with an exaggerated smile and scratched his gray-blond comb-over.

Tyler took a seat, trying to shake off the fogginess of a poor night's sleep. This meeting was about his future with the team, and he needed to have his wits about him.

"You see my point I'm making here." Boris launched right into business, extending a hand toward Tyler but looking around the table at his coaches and staff. "We're making TV dinners. I came from nothing. But a little sauce, a little sizzle, and enough pressure you can crack anything."

Coach Fawcett, who headed up defense, leaned forward. "And we appreciate what you're saying, but Tyler's still breathless too soon. He's 21 percent slower than just last season." He nodded at the monitors, which were running clips of Tyler's yardage over the past year. "We're worried about meat, not sauce." He glanced back down the table at Tyler. "Sorry, Fantana. You know what I'm saying."

Tyler said, "I do."

"Listen," McBride chimed in, "your performance has been solid, but you're not a hundred percent yet."

"Given. We all agree." Boris took the reins again. "But who's a hundred percent? Right? You serve what they buy. Frozen meatloaf is a *meal*."

"Sorry." Tyler shook his head. "What is the meatloaf here? You mean me?"

"Nah. The game. Packaging. Shelf space. Customers. These I know." Boris spread his arms like a magnanimous patriarch. "Kid, you been busting your butt the past few weeks. Hell, the past three months. Right?"

Tyler nodded. The coaches around the table nodded.

Boris shrugged and smiled. "What we got is a *story*."

Tyler held up a finger. "But—"

As if heading him off at the pass, Boris lifted stapled pages. That had to be Maureen's PT report highlighting his progress. "Mo says you're doing way better than a normal guy would. Off the charts."

"All due respect, that doesn't mean I'm ready, sir. That just means I'm healing faster than Joe Average."

Tyler knew Boris was ignoring the caveats, that he still had a long road ahead, but Maureen had sprinkled her assessment with plenty of vague positives to document how hard he'd been working. Nice thing to do, but not a clean bill of health by any stretch.

Boris seemed confused, his optimism almost delusional. "She says so right here."

Tyler didn't know how to counter that level of denial. "I'm still struggling to keep up, sir." He crossed his arms and sat up. "I'm not a quitter, but if you think I can head back out—"

"No. No way. You're too valuable. I want to send a clear message of strength. You're hurting but you're strong. Right, Zack?"

The head publicist and his flacks nodded.

Tyler wasn't about to exaggerate his progress for anyone. "My speed, my reflexes, none of it. The pain and exhaustion is pretty rough, sir. I'm not using any painkillers, but it's touch and go some nights."

"That's only natural after such a long break, son," Coach McBride reassured him. "You'll get back into it soon enough."

"You say so." Tyler forced a smile, grateful for the encouragement even if it seemed nuts. He knew he needed more time to heal and build up his strength before he could compete at the level he was used to. He thought back to Josh's advice, warning him not to rush, to pay attention.

This all felt bizarre. Nobody was asking him anything. It seemed to him that this meeting wasn't a conversation but marching orders. Apparently they'd decided his fate without any input from him.

Boris tapped another stapled report that had pink highlights and some yellow tabs stuck to it, flagging specific pages. "This is the last one from that Reynolds broad. Look at these numbers… EKG. Reflex times. Oxygen uptake. Range of motion. Heart rate. You're feeling great, seems to me."

"No." Tyler uncrossed his arms and sat up. "Not great. Not even good, if you want the God's honest truth. I'm stronger, Mr. Jarlson, but that doesn't mean I'm ready for a couple thousand pounds of meat thrown at me tomorrow."

Coach Fawcett raised a hand and tried to interrupt the owner's flow. He closed his lips, and his mustache moved as he tried to put something into words. "Boris, I think Tyler is trying to keep our expectations reasonable."

"Reasonable. Who's reasonable? A billion-dollar game chasing a pointed ball isn't reasonable." Boris held out his hand toward Tyler. "He's a godsend is what he is. Have you seen the press numbers?"

Jarlson's assistant slid a folder to him. "You have those right here, sir."

Tyler felt isolated and numb. Somehow he'd walked into this room off balance and determined to be cautious, and now they were rushing him right into the most dangerous of all the options. He wanted a time-out, a break to regroup and reset his dislocated brain.

Around him the flacks and staff murmured excitedly, already floating promos and hashtags. Tyler felt his stomach twist into knots.

Just then Zack, the team's head publicist, piped up. "Tyler, my team and I just want to thank you. Your interviews last week generated tremendous buzz. And the library campaign angle did wonders for our brand image too. A lot of goodwill aimed your way. Definitely keep that book crap up."

"Uhh. Great. It's really important to me." Tyler managed a weak smile. "I wouldn't call it crap, exactly."

"No. Oh! Right… absolutely." He made an awkward face and continued. "Books are great."

A gushy blond at Zack's elbow nodded and raised a finger. She said, "Hi. Image management here. Don't underestimate the body stuff. All these shoots you've done the last couple weeks." She spread her fingers wide, just shy of jazz hands. "Golden! Any stills of you showing some skin are extra useful. Especially featuring that beautiful butt. I guarantee the TMZ piece and *Sports Illustrated* will have you trending on porn sites for a month at least."

"I— That doesn't— Why?" Tyler started to feel like he was short-circuiting. "Porn? You want pornography?"

Her eyelashes fluttered as though he'd paid her a compliment. "Not porn of you, but porn *searches* for you. Amazing. Swimsuit shots. Locker room. You know."

"No, I don't."

She spread her fingers close to jazz hands again. "PG stills and freeze-frames. Gifs of grabs, ass taps, you getting tackled. We're seeing a lot of high-value facial expressions too. And that's going to stir up serious fanfic, of course, which is excellent for your numbers."

"Fan what?" Tyler blinked and turned to face her fully, which seemed to make her blush.

"Fiction. Fic. Stories people write." She beamed at him like she'd won a prize. "About you and... Josh? I think his name is. Mr. Ayres. A few sites dug up a few photos of him on some swim team, and I got to say, the stories are bonkers. Really hot." She fanned herself and tipped her head conspiratorially, eyes wide with glee.

"About Josh." Tyler swallowed, his heart rate so high he started to feel faint. "Fans are writing about Josh and me?"

"Totally tracks." She nodded. "You're, like, magical now. Because of the heart attack. I mean, just this morning we got offers on you from producers pitching *Jock of Love* and one of the Kardashians who needs a hot boyfriend for a show. But love triangles score poorly in most markets."

Tyler blinked at her. He felt like a rumbling volcano of bewilderment and anger. Any second now, he'd blow. Had they called him in here to trigger a psychotic break?

She misinterpreted his silence. "We said no. They weren't willing to pay half our ask."

Zack, obviously sensing imminent disaster, weighed in again to shut down the blond and shift gears. "With you headed back out on the field, people have practically forgotten about last season's, ahem, *unpleasantness* from some of your teammates. That time-share scam with Timmons, Ira's coke scare in St. Louis, everything else has dropped to the second page of searches. You're pure gold."

Tyler chewed his lip. Is that all he was to them? Soft soap to wash off the dirt? A hot ass? They were even pimping out Josh. The team, the fans… they expected a performance. And Tyler didn't know if his heart could take it.

He thought back to Josh's advice about finding his path first. *You get where you're going one step at a time.* But what if there wasn't a path to find? How could he find anything when he felt so lost?

Tyler fidgeted in his seat. *Think like a musketeer.* He should have brought his agent, his lawyer. The Swells brass had ambushed him, and he was only just now waking up.

Coach Ojibwe tried to slow things down. "Tyler, we don't want to rush you. We're just laying out a few options. A couple different contingencies depending on how things play out."

"Based on this report, we think you're ready to start playing in some scrimmages," Boris declared, gesturing toward the rest of the table. "Fantana, we know you got the spirit. We just want to see how you perform against some real competition before making any big decisions."

Tyler's heart raced at the thought of finally getting back on the field. But he also felt a twinge of anxiety at the risks involved. He knew they were right—he was an experienced player and had proven himself time and again on the field—but he still couldn't shake his fear of his heart giving out on him during a game.

"When?" he asked, torn between worry and excitement.

"We got a scrimmage scheduled for next week. If all goes well, Jerry and Mike want to give you a crack at that," Boris stated, looking around at the coaches for confirmation.

Mike nodded in agreement, but Jerry didn't seem too enthusiastic.

A general chatter from the coaches let him know that everyone didn't actually think this was a fantastic idea. If anything, they seemed to think Tyler wanted to do it, more than they wanted to force him to do it. Exactly what Josh had warned him about.

Boris snapped his fingers, remembering something. "And uhh… one other thing. Zack and his people are telling me this literacy library thing has been a big positive. More of that. Books. Swag. Anything you need," he said. "Getting other celebrities on board was a real coup. We could almost keep you on the sidelines the rest of the season for more PR events."

Tyler forced a smile. "Right. Maybe you can prop my corpse up on the sidelines so the fans don't forget who owns Captain Fantastic's contract."

"Good one!" Boris let out a booming laugh. "But seriously, when do you think you'll be ready for the field again?"

Tyler's stomach dropped. Any second now Zack and his team would try to stuff Josh into a "Ty One On!" thong for Mom-stagram. He glanced at the coaches, who were all mute and obedient.

"Soon," Tyler said carefully. "I'm not a quitter, but I am scared. With good reason."

"You guys kill me," Boris bellowed. "Our players get knocked around every game and they're out partying till sunup. You just need to get back on that horse."

Tyler clenched his fists under the table, digging his nails into his palms. He had to fight to keep his voice steady. "I just need a little more time. All due respect, a bruised rib is a little different than a catastrophic heart attack."

Every single person at the table besides Boris seemed to realize just how close he was to snapping. The coaches shifted in their seats. They were well acquainted with his temper.

"Fantana, our insurance adjuster has given the okay for you to play." Boris smiled like a kindly patriarch offering charity. "These guys never lose. They wouldn't risk having to pay squat. He's seen all the data, watched your tapes the past three weeks. They're willing to let you play against a guarantee of six million dollars."

To his credit, McBride winced.

Tyler blinked at the shameless arrogance of it. "Mr. Jarlson." He sighed heavily and looked at Boris straight in the eyes. Josh had told him to keep chill, so he made his voice low and slick as black ice. "I'm not an idiot. I understand the economics. I get that you want me to return as soon as possible."

"That sounds bad. Look—"

"You look." Tyler interrupted the man without raising his voice. His banked anger swirled inside him like a hurricane. "You asked me here to talk. I have serious concerns about the risks even *if* some insurance jackhole is willing to gamble"—he counted out the obvious risks on his fingers—"my spine"—he tugged one finger—"my brain"—another finger—"my heart"—and another—"my life, to squeeze a hefty premium out of you." He scowled and made a fist, which he lowered to the table with exaggerated patience. *Keep it together.*

Janowitz swallowed audibly. The other coaches said nothing, but for some dumb reason Zack the flack decided to chime in, "Tyler, we know how hard this is for you, but the Swells believe in you. If something hurts you, it hurts all of us."

For some reason that last little squirt of BS double-talk got under his skin. "All due respect, Zack? No, it doesn't. You didn't flatline in front of the whole world. Your family didn't watch you have a seizure and croak on TV. When my heart stops, the guys sitting around this table don't fall down dead." He slapped the wood surface with his hand.

The image-management blond flinched at the bang. Real fear. All the grinning yes-men around the table fell quiet, and the last half-assed smiles melted. Everybody knew 262 pounds of anger could do serious damage. In his mind, he heard Josh saying, *Calm, buddy.* He needed to stay calm.

"We don't." Coach McBride looked him straight in the eye. "We won't put you in harm's way, Tyler. I promise you. If you say you can't do something, you don't even have to give a reason."

Boris frowned, but around the table Fawcett, Ojibwe, Delawn, Janowitz, and all the other coaches and flunkies mumbled agreement.

Tyler sighed again. So Boris had told them about the insurance and the ROI before he'd even gotten here. They knew, and they were just as trapped as he was. He could see it in their eyes.

"Fine." Tyler took a deep breath and forced a smile that made him think of Cilla Miller's shark teeth. "You're right, in principle. I just need to get back out there. When the time is right. One hundred percent. I'm going to get out there as soon as I'm ready."

"That's the spirit!" Boris beamed, clearly satisfied with Tyler's apparent capitulation. "Couple weeks, tops. You're almost there. Right? Everybody says."

"Mr. Jarlson, I'm thirty-three. I died on camera a couple months ago. My heart stopped beating and I was stone-cold dead until they ran lightning through me in the middle of a football field." He let out a shaky breath. "I want to play again more than anything, but I need to be smart about my recovery." Already he was squeezing the arms of the chair so tight he'd bent one of them permanently. "Sir."

Boris waved his hand. "You watch. You'll be great. Once you're in the action again, smashing all those big strong guys like you do, the nerves will fade. Muscle memory and all."

Tyler blinked. This rich idiot refused to listen. The team was a toy to him. Making a scene wouldn't fix anything. For now, Tyler had to bide his time and prove he was ready when the moment came.

Boris didn't seem to notice. "Look, Tyler." He nodded. "I get your concerns. I do. But you got to trust we'll do right by your talent. I didn't get this far by playing safe or being stupid. We wouldn't push for a comeback so soon if we didn't think you could deliver."

"Again, all due respect, you act like it's nothing, but not one person in this room could go out there and survive. Not a single one. Everything else is a whole bunch of 'who shot John?' None of you want to end up in a coma or a coffin no matter how much money someone throws at you. So it's all for one and none for me."

The room got super quiet all of a sudden. Janowitz put a reassuring hand on his arm. "It's okay, Fantana."

"We know. You're right. I just get excited." Boris nodded with a contrite expression. "We got your backside, kid. We just want to show 'em number eighty-six ain't been eighty-sixed." He held up his hands as if to reassure Tyler. "Couple minutes, tops. Just so the fans can see."

Taking a deep breath to steel his resolve, Tyler finally spoke up. "Okay," he said quietly. "I'm willing to risk it, but I'm going to need help staying alive. Even one minute out there is one dangerous goddamned minute."

Everyone around the table nodded in agreement.

Boris grinned widely at Tyler before cocking his finger like a gun and firing it. "You got it! Whatever safety pads or special whatever you need. No matter what happens out there, we got you covered."

Tyler hoped he meant well, but the way Boris said it, *covered* sounded less like safety or insurance and more like extra cameras to make sure they got the footage.

Boris knocked on the table, jolting him from his thoughts. "Don't look so glum! Comebacks are instant classics. Everyone wants their hero back from the dead."

Hero. Dead. The words echoed in his mind. He just wanted to get back to Josh and feel whole again.

"Right. We all want that." Tyler nodded, though he still felt doomed. He knew the team's motivations were about the bottom line. But he wanted to prove himself, and they wanted to help him do it. That was something, at least.

And with that, the train started leaving the station.

Boris clapped his hands together loudly. "All right, sounds like we all agree. Tyler keeps training and flexing for the cameras whenever he can." He pointed down the table to each person as he named them. "Mike, you're going to run him in that scrimmage. Zack, see about the cover of the *Union-Tribune* and the *Valley News*, maybe twenty or thirty billboards around town showing off his assets."

Tyler sat numbly as Boris and his people put the periods on the meeting, their canned enthusiasm grating on him. All roads led to what they wanted: they had blithely decided he would play for a few minutes in the game against the Cowboys next week, just to prove he still could.

"Didi, Roger, you two leak some teasers to the press with some muscle shots. Nothing definite but get 'em juicy. Maybe some more library stuff if they'll fluff a little. Human-interest crap. And if we roll sevens, then we can announce Captain Fantastic's big return game in Dallas. That's just over a week out."

Tyler nodded mutely, not trusting his voice. He knew they wouldn't listen to reason. Josh's calm voice echoed inside his skull: *don't let fear or anger make the decision.* No matter how much he wished he could walk away, the field called to him. He just prayed his heart would be ready to answer.

"Now, one last thing before you scram. I understand you've been seeing a new person recently? Some muscle guy. They showed me a picture."

Tyler stiffened. What picture? How much did Boris plan to interfere with Josh? He specifically hadn't told anyone on the team yet, wanting to keep their relationship private for as long as possible.

"I, uh…," Tyler stammered, flushing. "Yeah."

Boris waved a hand. "No need to be a princess! He's a looker too. Between us, I think it's great, two hot guys for the red carpet. You poke whoever you want. The ladies love it. We got an NFL badass dating a hometown hero who reads books. It's a PR dream!"

The gushy blond girl nodded enthusiastically. "Crisis response confirms that Joshua Ayres is already gaining nice buzz from the paparazzi photos. Clean-cut, masculine, ideal 'boy next door' beefcake." She offered a chef's kiss. "Gossip sites are eating it up."

Tyler's face burned with anger and embarrassment. Privacy didn't mean squat. They were going to exploit the only person who mattered to him? He wanted to tell Boris exactly where they could shove their PR dream, but he bit his tongue. He could feel the worst of his dad inside him, the rage wanting to loose itself on the room, the blind strength coiled like a razor snake at the base of his spine.

No way in hell was he going to let Josh get mauled by the media to sell season tickets.

"I appreciate your support," Tyler said through gritted teeth. *Violence*. It coursed through his limbs, begging to be let out. His hands, his arms, his back could feel how easy it would be to lift the entire table and flip it over on top of them all. Instead, he exhaled. "But my personal life is off-limits. Josh is a private person. I don't want him exploited or hassled in any way."

Boris frowned, clearly displeased, but nodded. "I think that's shortsighted, but if you don't like it, we don't like it. All we care about is you feeling comfortable. Of course, maybe *he* might like it. Who doesn't want to be a star?"

Tyler needed to leave. His fingertips were numb, and his heart beat so hard that his vision had started to blur at the edges. He let go of the wrecked chair arms. Coach McBride looked sad, and Fawcett wouldn't even meet his eyes.

The owner shrugged. "The offer stands if you change his mind. Ask him. Your... friend. Who knows? A lot of reality shows are booking the wives these days. As filler, you know." He nodded, and the blond fanfic PR woman nodded back.

"Overkill." Zack looked at Tyler with genuine fear. He must have done some quick math about how long they'd have to scrape remains off the ceiling if anyone messed with Josh. "Let's table that, I think." He nodded at Boris. "Tyler has given us plenty to work with."

Before anyone could add any more fuel to the bonfire, Tyler stood up, knocking the chair back a little too hard, eager to escape before he threw someone out a window. "Thank you all for understanding. If there's nothing else, I should head home." Rather than wait to listen to another word, he turned and left.

"Of course," Boris called after him from the other end of the room. "Ezra and Robin will be in touch about leaking your miraculous recovery schedule. Let's get cracking, people."

Tyler barreled out of the room, pulling out his phone as the elevator doors closed behind him. He scrolled through his contacts until he found the one he needed.

As he strode to the elevator, he left a terse voicemail for his agent. "Fantana. Call me back. Now."

More than anything, he yearned to call Josh. To hear that calm, steady voice grounding him. But for the moment, Tyler didn't trust himself to keep it together on the phone. Josh would sense his distress and know if he held anything back. Tyler refused to lay this burden on him.

Josh would tell him to refuse, to walk away rather than risk his life to salvage his career. But Tyler couldn't bear to slink offstage, leaving a legacy as a weakling and a failure. On some horrible level, he wouldn't give his father, wherever he was holed up, the satisfaction.

And just maybe, deep down, he was worried Josh still held on to that high school fantasy, Tyler as the big, sexy superstar. Not the broken man he had become. He wanted to deserve Josh. He'd finish out his contract, and everything would work out, maybe.

Downstairs, the security goons gave him a high five. Tyler slid into the sleek black sedan the team had sent to collect him this morning.

As the car glided through the streets of downtown San Diego, his thoughts spiraled darker. He imagined himself dying midgame, for real this time, his life snuffed out on national TV as the world watched. If he wanted to prove himself, he would have to do it alone. And he knew the NFL wouldn't do a damn thing to protect him.

All he wanted was to get back to Josh in Cinnamar.

Tyler had to see this through. Had to find a way to protect himself, body and soul. But he ached at the thought of how his choices might impact everything left ahead of them both.

Tyler squeezed his eyes shut, cutting off the thought. He had nine days if he got lucky. Or he would die.

Chapter Seventeen

As Josh arrived for the lock-in Saturday morning, the charged atmosphere at Hamilton High School hit him like a wave. Cars filled the parking lot, while demonstrators and concerned citizens mingled, their voices blending into a cacophonous chorus. News vans from San Diego stations idled nearby, cameras rolling as reporters documented the tense scene. In the distance, Principal Carver and the librarians engaged in animated conversation with one of the TV reporters, their expressions determined.

Josh's heart chugged. Last thing he needed during the next twenty-odd hours. Press was good, but they needed to focus on the library and the kids' access to books. He just wanted to stay out of the public eye.

Rather than risk a run-in with any vultures, he parked his truck behind the gym and slipped through the dim locker room to enter the school. As he walked down the hallway, the faint echoes of the crowd outside filtered in, reminding him of the stakes.

He couldn't help but glance at his phone again, the screen stubbornly devoid of any messages or calls from Tyler. His chest tightened. It'd only been a day and a half, but the ominous silence worried the hell out of him. Something must have happened.

Stepping out of the gymnasium, he froze.

A light was on in the athletics office. He could see a hot sliver under the door. Just what he needed: ESPN going through his dirty socks.

He inched forward, praying that the tabloids hadn't gotten that crazy.

When he opened it, Elise popped up from behind her desk, looking guilty. "Hey, Josh!" she called out, her eyes twinkling. She was wearing duck-themed footie pajamas. "Ready for the lock-in?" She bent again, shifting something back there.

He exhaled in relief. For one second he'd thought the press had found another way inside. He circled her desk.

She was busy loading one of the team manager's red plastic wagons with chips, bottled water, and home-baked brownies. The lock-in was scheduled to take just over twenty hours, so the cafeteria had prepped sandwiches, wraps, and water, but snacks were another way to raise funds. "I'm on the fence. Gatorade or no?"

"I say skip it. You're good," he replied, forcing a smile. "I just need to change into something more lock-in friendly."

She waggled her brows. "Well, if you need a hand, sailor...."

Josh ducked into the little bathroom and quickly changed into sweatpants, socks, and a threadbare Hamilton Class of '08 T-shirt. Tyler couldn't be here, but this was a dumb way to make him feel closer.

When he emerged, Elise had finished piling the wagon and slung her purse over her shoulder, her jittery excitement palpable.

"Looking good, Coach," she said with a wink. She gave him an approving once-over. "Nice!" She pointed at the T-shirt and at herself. "Oh-eight. I see what you did there." Then she froze and clutched his arm. "He's not coming, is he?"

Josh shook his head. This might turn out to be a long night. "Who?"

"Fantana." She peered at his shirt again. "I mean... he graduated in 2008. Is he, like, a midnight surprise or something? Pop out of a cake waving his big sword?"

"He's on the road right now. They're playing the Cowboys next week."

"Right. Sure. NFL stuff." She chewed her lip thoughtfully. "I just thought he might surprise you. That'd be super romantic."

"No." He trudged forward. Elise didn't understand what she was doing. He just needed to survive the night.

Elise clutched his arm again. "I'm so psyched for tonight. I get to read chapter forty-five... you know, the *conjugal* one." She made it sound salacious.

Josh squinted at that. "Well, it's not as racy as it sounds. It was written in the nineteenth century and printed in the newspaper."

"Oh, I read it to practice. Just so I didn't mess up." She grinned mischievously. "But *conjugal* makes it sound dirty, so Meredith wanted a teacher to take it. Got to make sure none of the jackasses try and sex it up too much."

Josh chuckled as he took the wagon handle from her. "I'm sure you'll keep them in line." He held out an arm to escort her back to the library. "Shall we, milady?"

They headed out into the empty hallway, the squeaky wheels echoing off the lockers.

"So," Elise began, glancing sidelong at Josh. "You and Captain Asstastic, huh? How's that going?"

Josh tensed. Elise meant well, but her hinting and probing felt unpleasant, like being investigated by a cow's tongue. "It's… going," he said carefully. He glanced at her with vague concern.

She was just dazzled by the fantasy. Surely Elise would never say anything to the press. He hated thinking it but hated the serious possibility almost as much. His students always talked about being famous. If this was being famous, it sucked big-time.

Josh maintained a calm exterior as Elise prodded him about the salacious stories and pictures of him and Tyler online, but internally he was churning. He worried that the world saw their relationship as a joke, just a famous jock slumming it with a small-town dweeb. Even worse, Tyler's feelings might turn out to be a fleeting fling in the heat of his recovery—not the deep bond Josh had felt.

"Long distance is tough, but we're making it work."

"I bet," Elise said, nudging him. "Dating a celebrity. America's Tightest End, huh? You must get swarmed with paparazzi everywhere you go."

"Elise." Josh frowned. He hated feeling so exposed, like his private life was public property. "It's not like that. And it's nobody's business but ours."

Elise put her hands up, looking contrite. "You're right, I'm sorry. I just think it's exciting, is all."

"Not even a little." Josh frowned at the floor. "It's not what everyone thinks. The attention. It's not fun or even interesting. It's like having strangers stick their fingers in you on a dark bus."

Elise stopped walking and clutched his forearm. "Oh, honey. Oh, Josh, that's awful."

They walked in silence for a moment. Josh's thoughts drifted to Tyler. He wished he could talk to him right now.

The crowd at the library doors was obviously getting big. He saw parents and kids with sleeping bags and pillows making their way inside. Everyone had planned for the long haul.

"I have a right!" Up ahead, a familiar skinny redhead brayed at the security guard who held her upper arm tightly. "Let go of me."

Elise stiffened. "No way."

"Ma'am, we've warned you. You understand the consequences. You've made several kids uncomfortable already." Principal Carver was forcibly ejecting a pajama-clad Cilla Miller and scruffy crew out of the library's front entrance toward the school doors and the parking lot.

Elise growled beside him. "You have got to be kidding."

Cilla spat and twisted as she tried to get loose. "This is outrageous. This is assault."

"You're on school property and you're making a nuisance of yourself. You cornered a fourteen-year-old—"

Elise stepped in front of Josh, blocking Cilla's view. She raised her bandaged arm. "Bad mistake."

"Coach Ayres!" The reporter's voice cracked like a whip, and she struggled in Josh's direction with little success. "Cilla Miller, Channel Twenty-four." She waved at him. "I've talked to concerned locals right here in Cinnamar about the pornography this library gives children. Which you came here tonight to defend. You got a woman fired, Josh. Why are you so eager to corrupt—"

The kids and parents around her recoiled. Nobody wanted to take a side, but a couple of them raised phones to film her tirade.

Obviously whatever contrition and fear Cilla had felt a couple of nights ago had evaporated. She looked frantic and desperate.

Elise looked Josh in the eye and muttered, "First thing Monday morning I'm calling Channel Twenty-four. She has no clue what's coming."

He shrugged. "Doesn't matter."

Cilla wasn't giving up; she ducked under the security guard's arm with her mic held out toward him. "Hey, Coach! Any comment on those naked photos of Tyler in Miami? Josh, is Tyler depressed? Did you dump him?" She showed her teeth like a piranha. "You can't silence the truth."

"Ma'am." Carver blocked her advance, shielding Josh from the onslaught. "This is a school event. I'm going to file a formal complaint with your station. You know there will be consequences."

"Josh, is it over? Have Tyler's injuries caused erectile issues?" Cilla kept craning around Carver and Elise while the guards held her flailing arms from behind. "Is he back to partying again? Joshua, the people have a right—"

Cilla's voice vanished as the doors closed.

A couple of families turned to look at him to see his reaction. Embarrassed? Disgusted? Afraid? All of the above?

Josh stood silent. With everyone's eyes on him, he felt like a freak. Worse than high school.

Elise glowered at Cilla. "Jeez. What a piece of work." She turned and saw his face. "Oh. Oh, honey."

He shook his head, cheeks burning, and exhaled. "Exciting enough?"

"I forgot." Elise touched his arm gently. "I didn't even think. I wasn't thinking."

"It's okay," Josh said. "You didn't mean any harm."

Elise smiled. "You're safe. We got musketeers and brownies. What can go wrong?"

They'd reached the entrance, where Meredith was checking folks in. Around them, kids and parents milled about, swapping snacks, cradling pillows and blankets for later.

Elise touched Josh's arm. "Really, I'm sorry," she said softly. "Your life is yours. I'd never say anything, do anything. I hope you know that. Josh?"

He nodded, exhaling slowly, wishing he did know that. Not trusting anyone really taxed the heck out of his goodwill. "I know. Let's just focus on the books tonight." He ducked inside the library.

Josh allowed himself to be steered back toward the front entrance, where Carver, ever the politician, was greeting parents. Overall the library looked great. The atmosphere was cozy and communal, cushioned nooks clustered with chatting friends and families. This was what Tyler had meant: interactivity. Remind people the library is alive.

If only Tyler were with him too. But Josh's boyfriend was far away tonight, making this separation sting even more.

Shoving down his longing, Josh focused on the kids' anticipation. He would make this a wonderful night for them no matter his own mess. Saving the library meant something real. The tale of the musketeers, loyal friends fighting for honor, was just what he needed right now.

The room felt buzzy and ready to rock. All the drama of a curtain time and a live audience, without any rehearsal. Parents and local do-gooders stood like friendly sentinels around the perimeter, scanning the crowd and helping folks get situated. After the Cilla Miller scrum,

Principal Carver seemed to have taken it upon himself to guard the entrance like a Doberman.

Stan and Meredith stood and gave Josh a thumbs-up. That meant most of the names on the list were checked off. Meredith would man the door for the duration.

Stan started to move toward the microphone to kick things off.

"Josh... thanks for organizing this whole deal," Meredith said. "We'll never be able to thank you properly. Or Tyler. You guys have been like guardian angels for this place."

"This library means a lot to me," Josh replied. As Stan made his way through them, families hunkered down and lowered their voices, sharing bags of popcorn and sipping from cups of soda.

Meredith fussed over the potential mess. "Cleanup is going to be something."

"You don't worry 'bout that none," drawled Otis from his post by the shelves. "I got three kids with detention who will be happy to work it off straightening things up in here."

Josh nodded in approval before turning his attention to the main event. Nadia had snuck in at some point and was chatting with her old drama teacher.

For the next twenty-odd hours, students and faculty would be reading *The Three Musketeers* aloud, each participant taking a chapter. They'd start at ten and would probably finish around sunup Sunday morning. Meredith and Stan had set a comfortable schedule, with a couple of breaks and backup readers in case anyone bailed or balked. It wasn't every day that a whole community came together to share a story.

Kids got practice speaking in public, the library seemed full and fun, and this particular story by Dumas was a humdinger.

As Tyler had pointed out, that was another benefit. Sitting down and reading a "classic" scared some people, but sharing a book like this took the sting away. If a kid got confused, someone could explain. If parents had never bothered, they had a chance to brush up on a great work in a safe space. Everybody won.

The excitement in the room was palpable. Teachers in casual clothes gossiped and compared notes. Students whispered excitedly about which chapter they'd been assigned and how they planned to make it fun for the audience.

At the doors, Carver and Meredith were letting the last few stragglers in, pointing them toward possible seats.

"All right, folks!" Stan called out, rallying the crowd. "We're going to kick off! Remember, we have sixty-eight chapters, no duds in the bunch. Snacks for sale along the wall and simple meal options courtesy of the cafeteria. Bathrooms down on the left." He pointed toward them. "I just want to thank everyone who helped put this together, but especially Josh Ayres and Tyler Fantana, who proposed this whole deal, spread the word, found us sponsors, and so much more." He nodded at Josh, who stepped over and claimed the microphone from him.

"Thanks, everyone. Put your hands together for the librarians, who keep this library alive and healthy for our whole community."

They did.

Carver nodded and made a show of locking the doors.

"All of you are now prisoners for a day and a night." A couple of kids cheered, and the whole room applauded. Meredith and Elise gave him a thumbs-up. "We are locked in with some of the most powerful creatures in the world. Right on those shelves, magical beasts. Back before Christmas, our very own Tyler Fantana reminded me that libraries are alive. It's easy to forget because the books can only move us and change the world when we pay attention to them."

"Hear! Hear!" Mrs. Grappo and her husband applauded, along with one of the new English teachers.

Josh nodded at them in gratitude. "Before we unlock those doors in the morning and turn you loose again, we're reading every single word of *The Three Musketeers* by Alexandre Dumas." He grinned.

What he wouldn't give for Tyler to be here.

"Dumas. Note the pronunciation. I don't speak French, but it's pronounced 'doom-ah' not 'dumb ass.' If anybody wants a dumbass, you'll have to go back outside, because all the dumbasses are out there trying to stop you from reading the books on these shelves." He winked.

The crowd laughed and clapped again. Josh relaxed. He'd been worried someone would get offended, but obviously people who read books didn't mind a little off-color humor. Doreen blushed, but Nadia laughed loud and winked back at him.

He smiled. "Now Monsieur Dumas had a phenomenal life. His father was born into slavery and then freed. His mother was a society heiress. Dumas was born when Thomas Jefferson was president, and grew up mixed-race in France. He became famous as a playwright, a party monster with forty mistresses, the most generous man of his era. He's remembered as one of the most successful authors of all time, with a string of swashbucklers he wove out of his own life and forgotten bits of history. But what he knew better than anyone was *fun*."

Josh couldn't help but think of Tyler: their sunrise runs, the Renaissance Faire they'd visited together, the quiet secrets that had forged an unbreakable bond between them. He missed him more than ever, but this event was too important to wallow.

"Before we start, I want to say this. Books matter. Words matter." He smiled and put the pages of the first chapter on the podium. "All for one, one for all."

And so he began.

"On the first Monday of the month of April, 1625...."

Rather than a stiff or "correct" reading, Josh did his best to bring the story to life, using different voices for the narrator and dialogue, adding dramatic pauses and comedic sounds, melodramatic looks, even making the sounds of horses galloping and swords clashing. The audience got into it right away, gasping at zingers as they munched their snacks.

As he read, Josh's thoughts turned to Tyler again. More than anything, he wished his boyfriend could be here to see how it had all come together. At the Renaissance Faire, Tyler had reminded him, "The books are static, just sitting there. Bring them to life."

He hoped he was doing that, transporting the crowd to seventeenth-century France. In a way, this felt like reading a bedtime story to an entire room full of eager, rowdy children. Everyone, young and old, gave their full attention, nodding at the best bits, riveted by the characters.

More subtly, Josh saw the other readers dotting the edges of the room, clutching their pages. He tried to show them how to have fun, to cut loose, to make silly faces if it would help the story along. By leaning into the words, Josh didn't have to work all that hard. Dumas's sentences did most of the work. All he had to do was keep his voice animated and listen to the story as it unspooled.

Tyler had said something about that too. That back when books were luxuries and not many people could read, every story had been written to be read aloud. The keen listening faces proved him right.

Josh neared the end of his chapter faster than he'd expected. The crowd sat perched, edge of their seats. He looked up to see Vicky standing to his side, waiting in the wings with cheeks pink and a twinkle in her eye. Holding her rolled pages, she looked excited to keep the ball in the air. He nodded at her, and she nodded back.

We got this.

He felt a swell of pride. This reading was bringing the community together and showing how vital books and stories were. Josh knew Tyler would be proud too. Now he just had to make it through the rest of the book missing the man he loved.

The room applauded as Josh stepped aside to let Vicky take over. As she enthusiastically dove into the story, adopting silly voices for the characters, Josh glanced around at the rapt faces in the crowd. Kids and adults alike looked invested already.

During a brief lull as Vicky paused to take a sip of water, Josh did a quick head count. Nearly everyone who had signed up had shown. Mr. Chan had promised to stick around at least through chapter fourteen, which he was reading. Mrs. Grappo had come with her husband, and both of them were taking chapters. It was amazing to see the town collaborate like this, united by a shared love of books. If this evening succeeded, they had a real resource moving forward.

His gaze landed on Carver, hovering by the doors. Josh caught his eye and gave a little wave and an encouraging smile. All safe, no more press foolishness.

Josh tuned back into the story just in time to hear Vicky finish the chapter with a dramatic flourish. The whole audience crowed at the cliffhanger and erupted into applause. As the next reader headed up to the mic, Josh made his way around the room, checking on the food set up by the drama kids, chatting with parents, and making sure the students were still engaged.

Mostly, though, his mind kept drifting to Tyler. He wondered what he was doing right now. Josh pictured him in a hotel room somewhere, hopefully getting some good sleep after a punishing practice. Or maybe he was back in San Diego already. He wasn't sure.

As the day advanced and the chapters whizzed by, Josh caught himself just listening along at several points. This hundred-and-eighty-year-old story really had everything: romance, betrayal, slapstick, swordfights, disguises, seductions. It kept people nailed to their chairs. Dumas was no dummy.

Even during the breaks when people scurried to use the toilets, grab a sandwich, or top up their snacks, they talked about the story, the characters, the living history that made up the background.

"Had you read this?" One mom turned to a friend and mumbled, "I had no idea. This is better than *Real Housewives*."

The friend pooched her lips. "Honey, this is better than dating *The Bachelor*."

Josh chuckled and drifted away. Mission accomplished.

Up front, parents and their kids had drifted over to make requests of the librarians. Meredith started to keep a list of requested titles, everything from *The Wizard of Oz* to *Beowulf* to *Don Quixote*. It made sense. When you love a book, you want to share it with people you care about.

Around six that night, during the dinner break, Josh checked his phone. Still nothing from Tyler. By now all the attendees had changed into sweats and pajamas. The French teacher got swamped with questions about titles and traditions. A trio of Josh's tenth graders asked about the actual musketeers, and he told them he'd recommend some history titles after class tomorrow if they wanted to stick around.

What the book did was make the room *curious*. The kids and the parents. Even the faculty in some cases. The more Josh thought about it, the more potential he saw. The entire Hamilton staff seemed to agree.

Sometime around four in the morning, after the poisoning at the convent, Carver came up to him looking very serious. "Coach... I hope you realize what you've done."

Josh shook his head. "I don't think so."

"I got kids trying to sign up for classes next year. Teachers who want to propose electives and after-school programs. Sanjay's family wants to sponsor a lock-in next month. The theater department wants to teach fencing." Carver shook his hand with a warm smile. "I wish Mr. Fantana was here to see what he started. This is way beyond those book-ban jerks."

"Good. I'm really glad, sir. Tyler predicted this. But this is only the start." Josh tipped his head.

Carver squinted. "It is?"

He leaned in conspiratorially. "Think about it. Let's say you got a couple teachers wanting to cover a complicated era or a thorny topic— we can set them up for success. Get kids interested beforehand. Plant the seeds here. Help parents help them with the homework. Everybody tuned in, coming together."

Carver nodded. "All for one, one for all. Cooperation."

"Exactly. They work together to do the right thing because the right thing is hard. A community solving a problem with honor." Josh looked around this old room. How many hours of his life had he spent hiding in here, growing in here? How many books had his name written on the checkout cards in their back covers? "That's what a library wants to be."

"Josh... I'm overwhelmed. I'm... I'm so grateful." Carver's voice dropped. "I wish Tyler was here so I could thank him too, but this is unbelievable. You have to tell him. Please let him know from the entire school. What you two have done is going to change lives."

"I'm so glad, Phil." He sighed.

All because Tyler had put on a pair of tights and kidnapped him. Josh hoped he was staying safe, wherever he was.

Josh was pulled from his reverie as Stan tapped him on the shoulder.

"We're almost to the epilogue." He gestured to the front, where, with ghoulish glee, the Hernandez twins had just finished acting out Milady's execution in chapter sixty-six.

Josh nodded, a bittersweet feeling washing over him. On the one hand, he was excited to wrap up such a successful event. But ending the book also meant the lock-in was nearly over. Outside, the sun was coming up.

Next came Nadia, who got a massive round of applause as she came forward to claim the mic for chapter sixty-seven as only she could, and then Josh headed to the front to tackle the bittersweet finale.

Eighty-something pairs of sleepy but attentive eyes turned to him as he began to read.

Dumas's wrap-up was characteristically satisfying, and Josh animated it with gusto. When he reached the last sentence, he paused to look over the crowd and delivered it with a slow and satisfied smile:

"...the opinion of those who seemed to be best informed was that he was fed and lodged in some royal castle, at the expense of his generous Eminence."

As he read the final words, a cheer went up from the crowd.

"Thank you, everyone. And remember...." Josh capped the whole event with his favorite quote from the book: "Never fear quarrels, but seek adventures."

As everyone packed up, Josh said his goodbyes, exchanging thanks and handshakes with the parents. Kids gave him high fives, their faces lit with excitement as they chattered about the story and asked about next month's lock-in, which didn't exist yet.

"We'll see. We'll see." Josh knew it would happen but wasn't sure if he'd be as involved. Everything depended on what happened with Tyler.

Parents hugged sleepy children as the attendees stood smiling and gathered their things to head home. Blankets got folded, hampers closed. Grateful families carried some of the dozing younger siblings who had conked out.

With a sigh, Josh turned to help Carver, Meredith, Otis, and the others clean up, which took much less time than anyone expected. Several of the football players had volunteered to clear up trash and sort recyclables. A few enthusiastic parents lingered and pitched in to move the furniture back where it belonged.

After the last few stragglers had left, Josh stood looking out at the empty library, filled with a sense of accomplishment tinged with melancholy. They had done it. He was beyond exhausted, but grateful. Now all that was left was to find out what had happened to Tyler yesterday.

"Hey-hey." Stan slowly ambled over to him and gave him a big bear hug. "Six grand in one night. Parents gave us six thousand dollars for new titles and programs. Meredith cried when she counted it. Thank you so much, Josh."

Josh cracked his back and his neck and started stacking chairs outside in the hallway. Through the big doors, he could see the new day outside, a peachy glow creeping up the hall. A couple of weeks ago he would have been stretching on the track, waiting for Tyler. He glanced down the hall toward the athletic office. Before he headed home, he'd zip in and take a hot shower.

His phone rang in his pocket. His heart sped as he fished it out. Sure enough—

"Tyler? Hey! I can't believe you're up. Hi."

"Hi, baby. It's been… uhh. It's been something is what." On the end of the line, Tyler sounded hoarse and weary. "Sorry."

"Don't apologize. It's so good to hear your voice. Oh my God. We just finished. Hi." He was smiling so hard it hurt.

"How did it go?" Tyler asked.

"What go?"

Tyler laughed. "*Three Musketeers.* The lock-in. C'mon, you're killing me."

"Oh! Amazing. I can't even explain." Josh paced down the hall to get a little privacy. "Way better than we hoped. Better than anything you could have expected."

Tyler's voice got low and sexy, which was even better. "Well now. I was expecting a whole lot, Coach."

"Well, whatever it was, we topped it. Whatever you had in mind, we beat it by miles." Josh reached the athletics office and unlocked the door. "Carver said thank you. The parents, the students, everyone sends massive thanks to you personally. We missed you."

"Sorry. I tried to get there. I wanted to surprise you so bad. I would have given just about anything, but the coaches threw a fit."

"Don't worry about it. You were here all the same." Josh skinned out of his shirt and sweats.

"Good." Tyler exhaled, sounding happy and exhausted himself. "God, I miss you."

"You don't even know." Josh sat down at his desk and tugged off his socks. He wiggled his toes. "As it happens, I was just about to shower."

Tyler groaned. "Are you trying to kill me, Coach?"

"Long hot shower. Here I am, all alone in briefs, and I'm feeling pretty dirty. But that's all you need to know, big guy."

"Evil."

Josh twisted to stretch and grunted.

"Come on!" Tyler made an impatient sound. "I can hear that."

"Hear what?" Josh lowered his voice. "Tyler Fantana, I am not having phone sex sitting in school." He stretched again, his bones creaking. "Mmmph. I'm just stopping to rinse off, and then I'm about to go home and sleep for a month."

Tyler sighed in his ear. "Yes, please."

"You're welcome to join me. Open invite. You know the way. I'll be naked and leave the door open."

"I wish."

Josh nodded. "You okay? You sound funny."

"I… I think so." Tyler didn't elaborate, and the pause started to feel awkward.

Something had to be seriously wrong. "Tyler?"

"Yeah. No. They… uh… called me up to the office this morning. Well, yesterday now. I overslept and they sent the car. I met with Boris and the coaches to hear their dire predictions and stupid ideas."

"Sorry."

"It's nothing. Dummies being dummies. My agent will take care of it. I don't want you to worry." Tyler sighed. "Congratulations, huh? I'll call tonight. Or better, you call me whenever you wake up. Enjoy that big, lonely shower." He chuckled. "Good luck getting clean without me." Tyler hung up.

Josh looked at the phone in his hand a moment. Something way off there. He turned on the shower and tested the temperature with his hand, making sure it got hot enough to wake him up for the drive home.

The spray pelting his face and muscles felt incredible, but he kept replaying the last several seconds of the phone call as he scrubbed and rinsed. Something had gone wrong. Tyler would tell him the next time they talked.

Chapter Eighteen

TYLER KNEW he should have come clean to Josh, tried to explain at least, but he'd spent the past week carefully bluffing and dodging the topic every time they spoke. And then for the past two days, they hadn't spoken more than a few minutes.

Now he stood on the field at the AT&T Stadium in Dallas, his eyes narrowing as he took in the taunts from the opposing team. The Dallas Cowboys were a force to be reckoned with, and they made sure Tyler knew it.

"Better watch that heart, Fantana!" one of the Cowboys jeered, smirking as he passed by. "Wouldn't want you to keel over on us."

"Seriously," another chimed in, "you got life insurance?"

Tyler clenched his jaw but kept silent, focusing on surviving today's game. During the warmup, McBride only let him participate in about half of the position drills, conserving his energy for the real battle ahead. The rest of the time, Tyler got sent to sign jerseys and snap selfies with the fans. At about thirty minutes out, the guys were limbered up and the slow sizzle of aggression had taken root all around him. Kickers practiced their moves while small clusters of Swells and Cowboys players drifted to the sides to sign autographs.

Tyler glanced up at the boxes. Somewhere up there Boris and the other VIPs were going to be watching his every move. What happened today would determine if he stayed or got traded. Keeping up a long-distance relationship between San Diego and Cinnamar was bad enough, but cross-country might be more than even Josh could bear.

I hope he isn't flipping out, Tyler thought. Josh might not even be indoors today. They'd chatted briefly this morning, a stilted, strained conversation that left him uneasy. As they'd ended the call, he had made a point of saying, "I love you."

Just in case.

A sharp pang of missing Josh made his knees buckle for a moment. Part of him wished Josh was up there in the box with Boris and the team families, but another part prayed that Josh wasn't watching at all—that he was mowing the yard, vegging out on cartoons, or taking Nadia for tamales.

No chance. Josh would watch. He had been determined to come in person, but Tyler had asked him to wait. He didn't know if that was better or worse. He should have told Josh a bunch of stuff, but by then it had been too late to say anything.

How did Dumas put it? "Love is the most selfish of all the passions."

He pushed away the pang of guilt and the petty thirst for approval. None of that crap was useful to him right now. He needed to focus on the game; if he made it out the other end in one piece, he'd have plenty of time afterward to explain it all to Josh.

Tyler's hands were shaking again, so he took a swig of Gatorade and almost gagged at the sweetness. He took another run through the bad pass drills.

"Stop it," he muttered to himself. He hadn't told Josh about the risks he was taking or the decisions before him. They had enough trouble without him piling on his own ego. He twisted to stretch his back, using his breath to expand the fascia gently, the way Josh had taught him.

Raised voices drew his attention, so he straightened and turned.

Near the fifty, one of the Swells linemen had gotten into a chummy scrap with a Cowboys rookie with an exaggerated Spartan beard and a tribal scalp tattoo. Both of them looked young and sprung until coaches from both teams stepped in to defuse the drama. "Save it for the gridiron, boys."

Fifteen minutes out and the air crackled with a wild charge. Smack talk flew between the two teams as they crossed paths, each attempting to rattle the other. It was all part of the game, but for Tyler, the stakes felt deadly.

The hostility of the Cowboy fans drifted over the field like a low storm cloud, and Tyler felt the weight of the other team's disgruntlement. Even warming up, the Cowboys seemed grumpy in general, even sour, which was out of character. Then again, Tyler had gotten a lot of glowing puff pieces in the national press the past month, so maybe the Cowboys offense planned to make him pay dearly for the tacky charm offensive.

Ten minutes before kickoff, the referees and the chain gang took their positions on the sidelines. Cheerleaders began pumping up the crowd, and news crews captured final thoughts from the players. As the teams left the warm-up, Tyler flashed a big thumbs-up to the cameras, knowing Nadia would be watching with Josh back home in Cinnamar—worrying about him, no doubt. As the noise of the crowd swelled around him, Tyler steeled himself for the game, stretching properly just in case Josh was keeping tabs.

"Head in the game, Fantana," he muttered to himself, remembering Josh's steady voice in his ear, urging him forward. Like a musketeer surrounded by his fellow fighters: "He who chases the eagle takes no heed of the sparrow."

He missed Josh. He missed his sister. He needed to be home but wanted to be here. Conflicting fears dueled inside his mind, but he refused to let them show—or slow him down. Today, he would prove himself on this field once more, even if it killed him.

McBride and the other coaches signaled them back into the locker room to suit up. Tyler gripped the turf beneath him, then pressed himself to his feet, feeling the weight of the moment and the challenge ahead. The Cowboys were formidable opponents, but Tyler loved the fight. With every jeer and taunt, he steeled himself further, determined to rise above it all and emerge victorious—for himself, for his team, and for Josh, who'd known him before America's Tightest End even existed.

"Let's do this."

In the locker room, Tyler's teammates buzzed with excitement and anticipation as they began to gear up for the game. Surrounded by the Swells players, he too focused on getting dressed and ready. Nervousness and determination surged within him as he prepared to step onto the field for his first NFL game since... everything.

On their home turf, the Cowboys always wore their white jerseys, so the Swells had to wear their home uniforms too: teal up top and white pants. Tyler had always nursed a secret superstition that their teal jerseys made defense harder because it drew the other team's eyes. Still, they were visiting, and one more crappy bit of news wasn't going to change much.

As he pulled on his socks, snapped in his cup, and strapped on his pads, Tyler couldn't help but flash back to his earliest games. The first time he'd put on pads, he felt invincible. Nothing could hurt him like this. He'd started playing football out of desperation—first to placate his abusive father, and then to avoid his rages, and later to escape the mess he'd left behind. Those old wounds still ached under the scar tissue, yet they also reminded Tyler of how far he'd come and just what he was fighting for today.

"Hey, Fantana," Calvin called out, breaking into his thoughts. "You look like you seen a ghost. Nerves at eleven?" The others laughed, but Tyler could see the concern hidden behind the affectionate smack talk. They knew, as he did, that this game would be a test of their bonds, as well as his own questionable fitness.

"If you really want to know, I was thinking about the barbecue we got last time we played here. Hutchin's? Something like that. There's an old smokehouse out in Plano that does the best ribs in Texas," Tyler replied with a grin, trying to hide his own fears. "We win today, I say we go buy everything they got in the smoker and haul it back to the suites. My treat."

"In! I am in, my friend." Calvin high-fived him and the other players who crowed at the idea of wrecking their diets. "Who's in?"

Tyler nodded to himself as he snapped on his pads. Ribs sounded great, but he doubted he'd get anywhere close. Today was survival, and his odds were crap.

In truth, he suspected that he might die today if just one thing went wrong on the field. And from the looks exchanged between his fellow Swells, it seemed most of them thought what he was doing was crazy and dangerous… even with imaginary barbecue as camouflage.

But Tyler refused to let them down—or himself. He carefully taped up his wrists and pulled on his uniform, trying to summon every ounce of courage and resolve within him. Today he would face the Cowboys and emerge stronger, no matter the cost. For his team, for his family, and for Josh.

Last night he'd been rereading the Dumas again, wanting to call Josh but knowing it would make things worse. A quote in the book had leaped out at him: "The merit of all things lies in their difficulty."

"Remember who you are," he whispered to himself, feeling the sweat start to bead on his forehead. He cracked his neck slowly and deliberately, enjoying the staggered crunch of it. Again he heard Josh whispering inside his helmet: "All for one, and you for me."

Tyler took a deep breath as Coach McBride gathered the team. At the end of his speech, he addressed the elephant in the room.

"Listen up, men," McBride bellowed. "Cowboys are going to be gunning for Fantana out there every second he's in play. To try and kill him."

The players murmured angrily at this. Tyler shifted his weight, unsure where this was going.

McBride pointed at him. "I guarantee they see his bum heart as a weakness to exploit. Now you fellows know, Fantana knows, I know, that's a load of BS."

"Sir," Tyler barked in agreement, mostly for the public chest-thumping. Still, he appreciated the pep talk and the reminder to the other players that he'd be a constant target.

"Well I say, to hell with that!" McBride shouted. Janowitz and the assistant coaches clapped and nodded in assent. "In his hospital gown, Fantana can run circles around those pantywaists. Five minutes is all we're giving them to try."

The Swells growled and thumped their chests back at McBride. Fawcett shouted something and raised his fist at his squad.

McBride scowled at the whole team, his mustache bristling as he found his words. "Let me be clear, gentlemen. Your primary job during those five minutes is to protect him with everything you got, even if it gets ugly. You have my full permission do whatever it takes to keep Tyler safe out there. Anything."

Fawcett said, "Hear! Hear!" and nodded in agreement. He glanced at Tyler and gave him a direct thumbs-up.

"You all know what that means, what that takes." McBride sounded adamant. "You are his shield. I want you running interference, blocking tackles, keeping them off balance and out of range, doing whatever you got to keep this man's heart beating for those five minutes." He thumped Tyler's shoulder pads with affectionate violence. "Until we can get Ass-tastic off the field safely."

Tyler nodded at the head coach in gratitude. The team roared their assent.

McBride muttered something positive, but Tyler couldn't hear it above the rest of the shouting. He felt a surge of gratitude for his fellow Swells. The coaches and the players wanted him to know they had his back. Someone must have said something, expressed concern about the management's cockamamie idea to gamble Tyler's safety as clickbait.

Tyler's gratitude overwhelmed him. Still crappy odds, but better than fifty-fifty, at least.

"Out in three," McBride dismissed the huddle, and Tyler headed to his locker. He tugged his jersey on, number eighty-six, and for once it felt unlucky as hell.

Odell ambled over, squinting at him. The young quarterback looked almost sheepish. Today he'd be starting for the first time, so the pressure had to be messing with him too.

Tyler bobbed his head. "S'up?"

"Got a sec?" Odell said quietly. "We on you. You need to know I got something special for you ready to go. A Hail Mary if anything goes south." He stared into Tyler's eyes a moment, unblinking. "Screw them. I don't give a damn what they making you do, but if we need it, if you want it... I got it." He gave Tyler a hard, scared stare.

Tyler's eyes widened; finally he leaned closer. "Hail Mary? You serious?"

Odell nodded, and a couple of rookies nearby did as well. So a few guys were in on it. "Kids don't want to watch our Great White Gramps humping around the shallows waiting to go boom like a movie shark."

"Me neither." Tyler chuckled and leaned in, thumping Odell on the back and muttering in his ear, "Thanks, man."

Odell got somber, real concern in his eyes. "Things get rough, you look my way."

"Let's hope it doesn't get that crazy." Tyler realized what he meant, what he was saying. *Loud and clear.* They shook hands firmly.

"Same. But it does, no matter what, you look sharp." Odell nodded and walked backward away from him. "Inshallah, brother."

Tyler felt calmer at least. The team had begun to drift to the door and the lineup.

It was time to take the field.

Tyler took a deep breath as the team lined up to head out of the tunnel and onto the field. The roar of the crowd was deafening, even from inside. The thrum of energy vibrated through the concrete walls.

His heart was pounding, and adrenaline chased through his veins. Time to step back into the spotlight.

The players in front of him started jogging onto the field. Tyler hesitated, doubts creeping in along with a brash urge to work up the crowd the way he normally would. Captain Fantastic, right? They wanted a show. He couldn't back down now. With another deep breath, Tyler followed his teammates out.

The explosive din slammed into him, thousands of Cowboys fans booing and jeering as the Swells took the field under the blazing lights. Tyler scanned the sea of jerseys, the flashing cameras, the commentators pontificating from their booth. Over the loudspeaker, the announcer introduced the team.

"…and retaking the field after his dramatic heart attack last season, tight end Tyler Faaaan-tanaaa!"

A mixed chorus of cheers and boos greeted Tyler's name. He raised one hand to the crowd, faking a cocky smirk for the cameras even though his stomach was churning.

Out of the corner of his eye, Tyler spotted the Swells' kicker and punter warming up on the sidelines. Pretty solid odds that the next couple of hours might be his last. The team had prepared for it, putting precautions in place, but nothing was guaranteed.

Violence. He thought of Josh's sad eyes the night they'd talked about his dad and the belt. He felt wobbly and weird as he jogged to the sidelines.

What if this went wrong? He should have told Nadia and Josh to be here. He could have flown them out, at least. What was he doing? This was insane. He'd been an idiot, thinking he could step back into the NFL after everything. Tyler blinked hard, trying to focus through the fear threatening to swallow him whole.

All for one, he told himself. One play at a time.

Tyler paced in the sidelines, glaring across at the massive Cowboys linemen currently sizing him up like meat for their grills.

"Park it, Fantana." Coach McBride grabbed Tyler's arm as he passed and pulled him aside. "You're benched until we're up by at least fourteen."

Tyler shook his head. "Coach, come on. I'm ready." The sidelines sucked.

"For some first-quarter yardage? No chance. Not even Jarlson is that stupid." McBride's frown etched deeper lines into his weathered face till his mustached drooped.

Tyler ground his teeth but nodded.

His teammates offered slaps on the back and words of encouragement as they took the field.

"Hang tight." Duchesne shrugged as he backed onto the field. "Going to clean the kitchen before we let you start cooking."

Tyler smiled and nodded, pride warring with frustration. As the team headed out for the kickoff, Tyler settled. Once the game started, he analyzed the plays, watching for any weaknesses in the Cowboys' line he could exploit.

After a couple of messy possessions, the Swells intercepted a pass and started driving downfield. Bit by bit, they ground out the yards until Calvin pounded into the endzone for six.

The Cowboys responded in kind, evening the score, but the Swells' offense was clicking now. Two more touchdowns put them up 21-7 at the half.

The cheer squad took the field to do their thing, and the Swells trotted back into the locker room feeling pretty frisky.

Grudgingly, Tyler realized the coaches had played it smart. By tucking Tyler off to the side, the coaches had hijacked everyone's assumptions. The Cowboys had forgotten all about his triumphant return, focused instead on containing the Swells' other offensive weapons. His moment was coming. All he had to do now was prove he deserved it.

After the second time-out of the third quarter, McBride pulled the trigger, nodding at Tyler to take the field. "Fantana, you're up."

Tyler stood and went to him. The Swells had the ball. Maybe he could survive this.

"Five minutes, tops." The coach eyed him for a second. "Make 'em count."

"Yes, sir."

Miratto was already shuffling their way to be replaced. He gave Tyler a sympathetic grimace and thumbs-up.

"Tyler, you don't have anything to prove. You know that, right? And for Christ's sake, let them boys keep you safe out there."

As Tyler stepped onto the field, the fans realized what was happening and a tidal wave of energy swept through the stadium. Even the Cowboys stopped to watch. The crowd went berserk, standing and stomping, bellowing their approval.

He wasn't even their player, but he held a piece of them.

His heart pounded against his ribs—whether from nerves or excitement, he couldn't tell—as the deafening roar of the crowd surrounded him, rattling his bones. Stepping onto the familiar field bathed in blinding lights, cameras flashing, felt so foreign after everything he'd been through. *Violence.* The terrible burden of their expectations bore down on him.

What would Josh say to him if they were jogging together?

Let all the craziness out of you. Take a breath. He felt the tension drizzle off him like sweat.

He jogged across the grass. For all the shouting, Tyler felt quiet, almost still… as though time had slipped. As though it were just before dawn and he was running beside the person who mattered most. *For you, Joshua.*

"'Bout time." Odell grinned up at him and then over his shoulder at the stands. "Let's give 'em a second to change their panties."

Tyler took his position in the huddle, adrenaline coursing through his veins. He just needed to do his thing for five minutes while the cameras rolled.

Bracing himself as the first play was called and the ball snapped, he saw the Cowboys' defense barreling toward him. Dodging a tackle, spinning away from a hit, he started to recall what had made him a star way back when. But he no longer cared about fame or glory. He only wanted to prove he still had the wins in him. *Like a musketeer.*

The sheer physicality of the game engulfed Tyler as he dodged malicious hits and dueled as nimbly as possible with the Cowboys' defense. Sweat coated his brow, muscles straining with each canny play. He had forgotten what it felt like to play at this level, surrounded by pros who shared his passion for the game. And still he felt that odd stillness he associated with running with Josh. Time seemed to blur, melting past him in tackles and feints that kept him untouched. *Panache.*

In a heartbeat, Tyler saw a chance to take possession of the ball. Instead of pressing his advantage, he faked out the Cowboys by turning back the way he'd come and handed the ball off to Duchesne, who picked up nine crucial yards.

Now the Cowboys were grumpy.

The hits kept coming, each one more vicious than the last. Tyler's teammates tried to run interference, often taking brutal falls on his behalf. He wanted to tell them not to sacrifice themselves for him, but there was no time. The clock ticked mercilessly on.

On the next play, he saw a massive fullback hurtling toward his flank. In that split second, Josh's voice echoed in his mind: *Brace yourself. Be strong.* Planting his feet, he summoned all his strength and reversed the hit just before impact, sending the player reeling. *En garde, Athos.*

The Cowboys were out for blood now. The same three linemen swarmed him every play, but by some miracle, Tyler's defense kept picking them off so he could slip past their grasp. The ref called penalties, but it did little good. The Swells offense was outmatched, and he was out of time.

On the next play, Tyler opted to block a linebacker coming at Odell from the outside.

That odd predawn stillness from the school track seemed to buffer him and focus him. He flashed on a memory of grabbing his father's belt midswing, the smack of the leather as it hit his hand when he made a fist around it and pulled it free. At the last second, he braced and reversed again, almost flipping the player, who hit the ground with a nasty thud.

As the minutes passed, he kept hearing Josh in his head, believing in him more than he did himself.

The ferocity and danger of the attacks intensified as the Cowboys targeted Tyler with calculated brutality. A couple of the Swells ran interference, taking ugly falls for him, their bodies colliding with the turf in bone-jarring impacts that left them skidding across the grass. The clock seemed to slow further.

Boris had insisted he stay in play for five minutes, but this felt closer to seven.

His chest was agony now and his breath ragged. He'd almost bitten through his mouth guard.

He worried that if the Cowboys actually managed to bring him down, his chest would simply burst like a piñata and the medics would have to collect all his bits for the funeral. Whatever happened next, he needed to get off this field, stat.

He glanced at McBride and across to the receivers. *En garde.*

By now the Cowboys knew what he could and couldn't do. His body was at its limit. A few more plays and they'd have him completely boxed in. Play by play, they'd gauged his stamina and range of motion. The Dallas coaches had probably assigned defense players to hit him at exactly the right heights to kneecap him permanently.

Game over.

Tyler signaled to Odell, who ducked his head in understanding and crossed himself. *Hail Mary.*

Odell turned as though about to cut left and hand the ball off, but at the last minute he froze, defying all the coaches' orders to play it safe.

The crowd got quiet, waiting to see. Calvin and Duchesne trotted forward, then split suddenly and tore off in opposite directions.

My turn.

Twisting free of the grasping Cowboys, Tyler swung toward the startled box man at the line of scrimmage before looping back toward the goalpost. Big as Tyler was, they hadn't expected a full sprint from a dead stop. *I can run now.* His arms pumped as he hauled ass, covering ten, twenty, thirty yards faster than he could remember moving since he was a kid. His legs burned, churning under him.

Thank God Josh had taught him how to run properly. All those miles, all those mornings… those dark blue eyes crinkled with a smile first thing. *Hey, buddy.* He ran like Josh was waiting on the other side of that line, arms wide for him. *I love you. I love you.*

His chest throbbed and stuttered, but he tore across the grass without looking back or doubting himself, focusing only on the end zone ahead. His whole being bent toward the line with his feet racing to catch up. His heart was a scorching fist behind his sternum. *Closer, nearly, almost.*

Tyler hoped the pounding he heard was just his straining pulse, not the footsteps of some massive Dallas defender bearing down on him. Almost there. When he was a couple of yards away, within striking distance, he glanced back as Odell wound up and let loose a long, arching, perfect pass right into the cradle of his arms, if he could get them there in time.

The crowd stood frozen in the stands.

Finally the Cowboys on the twenty-yard line realized what was up and took off, cutting diagonally toward him. *Come home.* The ball sailed through the air as Tyler closed the gap to where the ball would be, angling toward everything.

At the last possible moment, Tyler twisted to see two Cowboys barreling at him just as Odell's Hail Mary pass started its descent. Summoning his last inch of strength, Tyler leaped upward, reaching-straining-stretching for the ball….

The crowd jumped up and down, the lights flashed, and the ball spun through the air directly into Tyler's outstretched hands. He tucked that beautiful little nugget against his chest and rolled just before the two Cowboys could slam into his legs, a second too late. He hit the ground on his front, stunned but steady. The ball cradled against his chest had saved him. "Hey, buddy."

Finally, pressed against the ground in the perfect silence, he began to hear his breath and his heart, which seemed to still be beating. Three-three-three. His fingers still worked, and his feet. His face too. He smiled, and then the smile got bigger. *I love you, Joshua.*

The deafening applause and cheers shook the stadium as Tyler pulled himself up and got his legs under him. He had done it—scored his last touchdown for the Swells. His shouting teammates sprinted toward him, leaning forward, mouths wide, while the Cowboys could only look on in mute defeat. Even if the Swells lost the game in the last quarter, he hadn't.

Tyler shook his head in joyful disbelief. "And won for all."

All over the field, his exuberant teammates were jumping and celebrating the impossible play. On the sidelines, McBride stood smiling and shaking his head. Odell saluted and bowed to him. The crowd was hugging and snapping pictures.

"FAN-TAN-A! FAN-TAN-A!" Their raw chanting shook the stadium. He could feel the rumbling coming up through his cleats.

The glare of the stadium thrown up at the clouds overhead made it look like sunrise. So still. So bright. He closed his eyes, and his heart was so full it hurt to breathe. Standing in the end zone, overwhelmed by the roar of the crowd, Tyler felt a swell of gratitude and love for Josh.

Tyler almost thought, *He should be here*, but then he shook his head. "I should be there," he whispered.

He looked down at the ball in his hands, then back up at the sky, bright as dawn, wide as heaven.

He lifted the ball over his head and then slowly, deliberately knelt to set it down on the ground. He stood up with his arms raised... and walked away.

Tyler headed off the field, shedding his jersey and pads as he went, along with "America's Tightest End," "Captain Fantastic," and all the other dumb crap. It was time to just be Tyler again and go home.

When he reached the tunnel, his cleats clicking on the tiles, he turned and waved one last time—to the boisterous crowd, to the cameras and blazing lights—and disappeared into his own future.

Chapter Nineteen

WINTER IN southern California meant rain… or at least most of the rain they got during the year. In Cinnamar, they got showers from the mountains and the runoff kept the lawns green.

Truth was, Josh didn't like driving in crappy weather, and already that morning he'd had to dodge a couple of news vans and a cluster of sleep-deprived jerks who had camped outside his driveway all night.

He'd watched Tyler's insane game last night, the epic fake out and that perfect, miraculous pass. Truth be told, he'd gotten nervous that Tyler had stayed on the field longer than his five minutes, but then he'd made that beautiful touchdown and exited stage right in one piece. Tyler had called him from the locker room right after, breathless and triumphant, but he hadn't made much sense in the moment. His mood ranged from manic to mellow to pissed to proud.

All that mattered: Tyler was alive and negotiations with the Swells were ongoing, even if he didn't seem to know when his next game was or what came next.

Josh knew the sports press hoo-ha would die down and they'd lose interest eventually, but the constant sense of anxious anticipation sucked, especially when they got up in his face. By now he'd gotten the hang of it; getting to school just meant moving fast and treating them like ugly scenery.

Fun? No. But manageable.

The wet streets hissed under his tires as he threaded through the early morning streets. Soccer season was upon them, and that wasn't his turf. A little breathing room and spare time sounded pretty sweet.

He might even get a couple of weekends off so he could finally get to San Diego.

Tyler had ended their call last night in a funny mood, almost dazed but super affectionate. Whatever was bugging him about negotiations with the Swells was starting to intrude on every conversation they had. Were they trading him after all? Something worse? Josh didn't want to push him, but he also knew that Tyler didn't like overthinking any of this.

Instead of dealing with whatever the trouble was, Tyler had wanted another full blow-by-blow of the *Musketeers* reading and again asked when Josh might have a couple of days they could escape somewhere.

What the hell?

As Josh pulled through the Hamilton gates, tacky TV madness had taken over the school.

Instead of the empty lot, there were eight vans, about forty people, and a set of police barriers blocking the high school entrance. Lights and flags lined the sidewalk. Kids and parents were pushing and shoving themselves in front of cameras while cops waved the jostling news crews back toward the parking spaces. A mess.

Fortunately everyone was too busy acting stupid to notice Josh's approach, so he steered well clear, hugging the outside lane and hooking around toward the back and the loading zone where deliveries reached the cafeteria.

After parking his truck, he pulled his hood up and tucked his chin, sticking close to the wall. He popped open one of the emergency exits with his keys. More noise at the main doors and around the high school office, but he didn't see Principal Carver.

A cold knot settled in his stomach. Was this more library blowback? Or had Cilla finally blabbed? Had someone caught wind of her fake jockstrap story? Was all this why Tyler had been so cagey on the phone? A weird blend of fear and rage chilled him as he navigated the dim halls to his office.

As Josh arrived at the Hamilton Athletics office, he was surprised to see Elise coming out the door with her purse and a cardboard box of personal items.

"What's up?"

Elise shivered like a puppy. "I'm taking the day off. And then some." She looked down at the box. "Driving to San Diego. Well, to be totally honest, I just handed in my notice to Carver, and I could pee." She bobbed in excitement. "I should have said that first. So not the day, I guess I'm taking the rest of my life off. Eee!" She actually squealed.

Josh gawped at her. "Elise. Why would you do that? Are you okay?"

"So get this," Elise announced. "I've been offered a TV show by station KSDF."

"What now?" Josh faltered, not certain he'd heard that right.

"After some vigorous conversations"—Elise flashed her eyes excitedly—"station KSDF, Channel Twenty-four, wants to produce and broadcast *Yoga for Oldies* for thirteen weeks to start. And they're even paying for cosmetic surgery to fix the bite mark on my arm."

He cocked his head. "You sent the evidence."

She smirked and arched an eyebrow. "So much evidence. A mountain *range* of evidence."

"Because of Cilla flipping out before *Three Musketeers*."

"Well, that and everything else. You warned her. We gave her plenty of chances to save herself. But nope. Her phone was chock full of landmines. Gracious!" Elise seemed to relish the redheaded reporter's comeuppance. "Let me say, her former producers have been incredibly accommodating. The station lawyers couldn't kiss my butt fast enough." She nodded, a smug smile spreading across her face. "We made a deal to settle any claims against them. Originally they even offered me some weather girl position, but it's California! I was like, 'What weather?' so I negotiated for my own yoga program instead."

Josh stood awkwardly in the doorway. How would her departure or Cilla's arrest impact his own situation? Or Tyler's, for that matter?

"I'm really sorry, Elise."

"Sorry! For getting me a television show? Boo-hoo." Heartbroken she wasn't.

"The chaos. All of… this." He gestured at the parking lot outside, filled with cameras. "Just a bummer. But I'm really happy for you."

"No bummer. I'm going to be in San Diego, where Captain Fantastic has been known to brown his buns. Maybe whenever you two are around, we can double date. 'Cause I plan to be dating finally. Plenty of fish there. Better than Cinnamar, for sure."

He nodded. "When do you leave?"

"Right now, actually. My bags are in the car. I have a meeting at ten thirty with the Channel Twenty-four lawyers to finalize the settlement," Elise replied. "I just came by to give you and Carver the news, had no idea the press would be swarming outside so soon."

Josh twisted to try and see, but the scrum seemed to be focused on the front doors across from the office. "Is that because of Cilla? I figured she must have run her porn thing or my jockstrap. Some gross story that got the vultures circling."

Elise gave him a funny look then. Her brow furrowed, her eyes flicking to the right. Was she telling him everything?

"What?"

She shook her head with a worried frown. "I think.... Uhh. So he hasn't called you."

"Carver? No!" Why was she eyeing him like that? "Elise, you're killing me."

"It kind of sounded like Carver's already trying to find a replacement. You know... just until things calm down. Everything has been nuts. Plus the board terminated Myra, and so they need a college counselor too, so I think he's trying to kill two birds with one stone. He got on the horn immediately."

Josh felt a spike of anxiety, wondering if he was next on the chopping block due to all the stupid melodrama of the past three months. Hell, the past week.

"But don't worry, hon. Nobody terrible. In fact, he wanted to talk to you the second you got in," Elise added with a crisp grin, embracing Josh tightly. "I'll stay in touch, I promise. And San Diego."

Josh shook his head, confused. "San Diego?"

"Tyler. Double date?"

"Right." He felt numb.

"I'm going to try and sneak past them out the back." She blew him a kiss. "Talk soon." And she vanished through the locker room.

As Elise exited, Josh was left with an icy knot in his gut. He called Tyler but only reached voicemail. Feeling off balance and panicked, he headed for Carver's office, dreading the conversation ahead.

Josh walked down the empty hallway, his anxiety mounting with each step. He passed Otis carrying two empty trash cans and nodded hello. A few teachers stood outside their empty classrooms looking equally perplexed and unsure of what was happening. "Boy, it's crazy out there today, huh?"

Mr. Chan shook his head and shrugged as he passed. Nobody knew yet.

What if he was being fired over all the drama with Tyler and the reporters? What if Tyler got traded or lost interest or moved on? Or what if Cilla's gross jockstrap plan had gotten leaked somehow?

Josh kept his face turned from the doors as he got closer, angling his back to the mob as much as he could.

When he reached the receptionist desk, Vicky gave him a strange, evasive look. "Oh, Josh. Phil was... uhh... just asking after you."

Before he could respond, the door to the inner office swung wide. "Vicky, please give Coach Ayres a call down in athletics right away. Otis says he just saw—" Carver stopped short when he saw Josh already standing there. For a long, awkward beat their eyes shifted uncomfortably.

"Sorry about the circus outside. I've called the police again to clear them out," Carver said with an exhausted sigh. "Between the sports nuts, that Miller woman, and the book burners, it's been a hell of a morning already... and the kids haven't even made it inside yet."

Josh shifted nervously. Was this it? Was he being let go?

"Josh...." Carver paused, sizing him up, as if assessing him or worried about him. "I know it's been a chaotic couple of weeks around here. But I wanted you to know— Well, I'm not sure how to put this. Elise has—"

"I just saw her." Josh cut him off with a curt nod. "Yep. Good for her."

"Bad for us, though. Or not. See, I'm interviewing an amazing candidate for a new coaching position right now."

Josh's heart sank. So he really was being replaced.

Carver must have read the distress on his face. "Now, Josh, I know the timing is bad, but just come in and hear me out."

Josh glanced at Vicky, but now she wouldn't even meet his eyes. How had everything gotten so screwed up?

"Come in, come in." Carver ushered Josh inside. He closed the door behind them.

Josh stared at his feet, feeling like an abject failure.

The applicant sitting in the chair before Carver's desk looked pretty big... and then he stood and Josh looked up.

"Hey." It was Tyler, looking tired but gorgeous and absolutely elated to see him. Without hesitating, he stepped forward and wrapped his arms around Josh, lifting him into the air and squeezing the breath out of him.

"Oh my God. Tyler? What are you doing here? Why didn't you tell me?" His heart beat so hard it hurt.

"It's okay. We're okay."

Carver sighed. "He swore us to secrecy."

"Sorry about the cameras. It's kind of a long story. But I wanted to make everything official before anyone tried to spin it wrong."

Carver shook his head. "No worries there. Elise kicked that reporter's butt so hard all the stations will be playing nice for a while."

"Tyler?" Josh gasped. "*You're* the new coach?"

"Well, assistant. I hear the head coach is a real hardass." Tyler grinned sheepishly. "If he'll have me."

Josh laughed in disbelief. After everything, Tyler had come back. The tangle of doubt unfurled in his chest like a flag.

Tyler was home, and that was all that mattered.

Josh settled into the chair across from Principal Carver, his palms sweaty. Tyler reached over and took his hand, lacing their fingers together.

"Everything happened so fast," Carver began.

Tyler chimed in, "And by accident, in a way."

"In a lot of ways." The principal steepled his fingers. "After Cilla showed at the lock-in, Elise made good, but good. Yikes."

Josh jerked his thumb back toward the gym. "She just told me."

"So now Elise is headed off to be a fitness instructor on some daytime talk show in San Diego. That leaves us short an assistant coach for you this year."

Tyler's hazel eyes twinkled at him. "I quit."

Josh nodded, his throat tight. Had Tyler just come to break the news that he wouldn't be coming back after all? "You just got hired." He wasn't following, obviously.

Tyler squeezed his hand. "The Swells. I quit the NFL."

"On live TV, I might add. We all saw him do it, but he didn't tell anyone." Carver shook his head. "Craziest thing I've seen in a playoff game in twenty years. He just quit in the middle of a game."

"You did what? But you won. That was you quitting? I thought you just did your five and split. We talked right after. You didn't say anything. Nobody said anything."

"The team didn't know. This just happened yesterday. I didn't know it was happening until it did. And then I just knew."

Josh's eyes widened in surprise. "Off the field and out the door." Now he understood the camera bloodbath outside.

"Beautiful." Carver beamed.

"You okay?" He squinted at Tyler.

"Are you kidding, I'm fantastic. Everybody knows that."

"Shut up." He chuckled. "I can't believe you didn't tell me you were quitting."

"I had to get back here from Dallas so I could tell you right now, in person. But I had to protect you. And me. Which meant I called your principal last night from the plane." Tyler looked extraordinarily pleased with himself.

Carver rocked back in the chair. "Which shocked the absolute hell out of my wife, for the record. America's Tightest End calls me from a private jet and says he wants to apply for any job in the building. For anything. This joker says he'll mop floors."

"Are you serious?" Josh laughed wetly. He punched Tyler's shoulder. "Jerk."

Tyler shook his head apologetically. "I told him I'd quit the team and needed a job. My degree is sports medicine anyways."

Phil leaned forward, elbows on the desk. "I still think you should consider taking over as college counselor. But that's a separate discussion. Getting you cleared will be no trouble. Credentialing for someone with your record? Gimme a break."

Tyler jumped in, squeezing Josh's hand. "I'm sorry I worried you. After I did what I had to, I couldn't stay one more second." His hazel eyes were earnest. "I was at the airport within the hour. All I could think about was getting back here to you."

Josh exhaled in relief, tears pricking his eyes. "I thought… when you acted so cagey, that you'd gotten traded or changed your mind about me or worse."

Carver smiled. "Quite the opposite. Tyler wants to come work here as your assistant coach, if you'll have him. I guarantee we can get a certification waiver until next year."

Tyler leaned closer. "You see? Boris almost killed me, and the team saved my life. I had to get back before anyone tried to talk me out of it. The fans were berserk. The press was camped outside my place laying siege." He squeezed Josh's fingers. "And I didn't want you to try and convince me to be reasonable."

Josh nodded. "Fair."

"Because I didn't feel reasonable. I don't now. I'm tired of pretending to be reasonable with these maniacs. I knew the vultures would descend. I knew the Swells would flip out. So I met Phil here this morning."

Carver grinned. "But what he *didn't* know about was Cilla's break-in."

"Which, I might add, you didn't bother to tell me either." Tyler raised his eyebrows.

Oh. Right. "About that…." Josh grimaced. "You had enough to worry about."

"Hi? Pot, kettle, black." Tyler glared at him. "Nice try, Coach."

Josh rolled his eyes. "Nothing happened. Not really."

"Nothing." Tyler scoffed. "Well, aside from several crimes, a bloody assault, Cilla Miller arrested, an apology from three TV stations, the Swells publicist falling on his sword, and a fat settlement from Boris Jarlson, who orchestrated all this ugliness with KSDF to get me back out on the field so he could make me go smash a second time."

"Wait... Cilla?" Josh looked up at him in horror. "Clickbait. Jesus." He squeezed Tyler's hand and kissed the knuckles. "You put me through hell this week, you know that? Get ready, because I plan to make you pay in spades for messing with my head."

Tyler grinned sheepishly. "I know, I'm sorry. But I'm here now. For good." His voice softened. "If you'll give me a shot."

Laughing and crying at the same time, Josh just shook his head in wonder. "Of course I will, you big idiot." He pulled Tyler into a tight hug, beyond grateful to have him home at last.

"I'm so sorry. I should have told you everything instead of trying to handle it solo."

Josh sighed, breathing in Tyler's familiar scent. "We've both got some making up to do."

Carver cleared his throat, a smile on his face. "We do have one or two other bits of business to discuss."

"Sorry."

"So as I've explained to Tyler, the lock-in did more than just raise money. Demand for round two is through the roof. We've gotten more requests for a follow-up than questions about prom." Carver spread his hand wide. "As of Sunday at 11:00 a.m., the town council has funded our library fully and put protections in place to combat censorship. Thanks to you two."

Tyler squeezed his hand. "But that's not my big news."

"Ditching the NFL isn't news?"

"No. It is, but it's not why I waited to say anything." He nodded at Carver.

"Mr. Fantana has asked, and the district has agreed, to host a pilot program."

"It's a lot of money, Josh, from Jarlson. A whole lot." Tyler grinned like a naughty kid ready for a tear. "We're going to launch a charity focused on abused and at-risk kids." His eyes were wet.

"Oh, Tyler."

"An athletics camp with visiting pro players, free academic tutoring, and long-term counseling for the families." Tyler wiped his eyes. "I'm going to name it after my mom. Nadia will run the internals. She gets a big fat salary. I get to do something that matters."

Carver said, "And I'm honored to say that Hamilton High will be the pilot program."

Tyler squeezed his hand tight again. "All the communities in a fifty-mile radius. And then we expand to cover families across the entire country. If it's okay with you."

Josh nodded, crying for real now and wiping his face. "Sorry."

"Don't be sorry."

He gazed at Tyler, who was practically vibrating with excitement discussing the details. After everything they'd endured, they were finally able to work together to help others. And Tyler was here to stay.

Carver stood up. "Now I suspect you have details to discuss. Maybe in your office." He smiled then.

Josh rose and embraced Tyler, unable to contain his joy, his pride. "Thank you," he said to Carver. "For everything. We couldn't have gotten this far without your support."

Carver waved him off. "You two have worked harder than anyone. I'm just happy to play a small part. Go get cracking. You've set a high bar."

"Yes, sir," Tyler said, giving a mock salute.

"Congratulations, gentlemen." Carver extended a hand and shook both of theirs. "All for one."

"One for all," they said. Tyler opened the door to go.

Outside the office, Vicky reached out to squeeze both of their hands, her face aglow. Outside the school, the police had cleared a path for the students, who for their part seemed downright amused by the pushy press. If anything could drive the buzzards off, it would be a steady stream of ripe adolescent ridicule.

Nearly eight o'clock now. A group of kids hunched over textbooks raised their hands in greeting. "Hey, Coach." When they noticed Tyler, their eyes got wide, but they tried to play it cool.

Good job, Josh thought.

Mrs. Grappo waved hello from the door of her classroom.

As Josh and Tyler walked toward the athletics office, there was a crackle between them, a sense of relief and possibility after the tumultuous events of the past weeks.

"You did it," Josh said, glancing over at Tyler as they walked. "Nobody else could have."

Tyler smiled, his eyes crinkling at the corners. "*We* did it. We make a pretty fantastic team, Coach."

He reached out and took Josh's hand, intertwining their fingers. The simple touch made the tiny hairs on Josh's neck stand up. After being apart for so long, that brush of connection meant everything.

"I'm so proud of you," Josh said. "Walking away couldn't have been easy."

Tyler nodded, his expression growing serious. "The hardest thing I've ever done. And the smartest. I felt so alone. But I knew if I stayed, I'd never make it back where I belonged."

Josh squeezed his hand tightly.

"I swear I wanted to call you or say something," Tyler continued. "But it was such a mess. I couldn't drag into it more than I already had. I needed to sort everything out on my own first, but it kept getting bigger and stickier." He shook his head. "Maybe I'm done leaping without looking. You taught me to take a look, weigh the options."

"Well, a little looking and a little leaping make a good combo," Josh replied with a smile. "From what I can tell."

Tyler chuckled. "Mixed properly."

They reached the office then, and Josh unlocked the door, ushering Tyler inside with a hand on the curve of his lower back.

As soon as the door closed, Josh couldn't wait another moment. He pushed Tyler up against the desk and claimed his mouth without apology, kissing him hard and lifting him up to sit on the scatter of pages.

"Mmf. Hi." Tyler grunted in pleasure and kissed him back. "Golly, Coach. This is so sudden. I haven't even started working under you and you're already sexually harassing me. Please continue."

"I missed you. I don't ever want to miss you like that again." Josh licked his lips and ground against him, savoring the heat and strength of the big body.

"Me either." Tyler dropped his head back, giving Josh access. "I think I might have a serious injury. Some kind of big swelling."

Josh took a handful of the thick erection between them. "Tell me about it, jerk. Do you know how much I've whacked off the past month?"

"Is that so?" Tyler nipped at his lips. "What if you go blind, Coach?"

"I'll learn to use my hands." He reached inside Tyler's waistband and took a juicy handful of Tyler's slick stiffness.

"I don't think you need practice there. Oh. Oh God." Tyler hissed and pulled his hips back. "Easy. You're going to make me make a gooey mess all over your nice office."

"Promises, promises." The heat and hardness were not helping Josh's self-control any.

Tyler rose up to kiss him hungrily, his hazel eyes glimmering with heat. He spread his thighs and tugged Josh closer to the desk. He wrapped his legs around Josh's hips and pulled him close. "You taste so goddamned good."

Josh drove himself against the hunk of meat stretching Tyler's sweats, rutting and pushing the swell behind his nut sack. He grunted, wondering how it would feel to split Tyler open and take him entirely. He groaned in frank appetite, unwilling to let Tyler get any farther away from him than this.

Tyler responded in kind, sliding his hands down to grip Josh's waist as their erections jousted through the bunched fabric. Tyler whimpered and shook under him, against him. He reached back to cup Josh's flexing butt and drove their hips together, riding the full hard length of Josh's erection like he wanted it inside him, like he could take as good as he gave.

Josh held himself in check, barely. As much as he wanted to, he didn't yank Tyler's sweats down. He didn't rip open his shorts. His full balls ached and shifted inside his briefs.

Tyler kissed the corner of his mouth, then his jaw, making Josh quake and shiver against his massive body.

Josh felt himself starting to crest, falling over the edge. "Wait. Hold on. Jesus. Give me a second. I'm sorry about that. Stupid. Whew! Okey-dokey now."

When they finally broke apart, panting, Tyler pressed his damp forehead to Josh's. He chuckled, and his body relaxed gradually as his breath slowed and steadied. "I missed you so damn much." He licked Josh's jaw.

"Me too," Josh laughed, the sound shaky with emotion. He took a handful of the soft cotton of Tyler's T-shirt, holding on. "Sorry about that. I'm not usually that impatient."

"I'm not going anywhere." Tyler nuzzled his neck, his ear, and whispered, "Hey. Josh. It's okay. There's no rush. Save it for home. I want to take our time together. We have all the time you want. I swear."

Josh chuckled. "You're right. I just missed you pretty terribly, Mr. Fantana."

"Why don't you give me the full tour?" Tyler smirked shamelessly.

"I think you've seen every square inch of it."

"As a player, but now I'm assisting you in all ways. I need to know every nook and cranny."

"Home sweet home," Josh said, opening his arms to the familiar space. "My desk. Your desk. Our lockers. Private shower."

"Yes, please." Tyler stepped behind him, his hard cock tucked into the small of Josh's back.

"Don't start something you don't plan to finish."

Tyler took a small step back. "I always figured the coach's shower felt way better than the locker room's."

"You don't even know. So much better." Josh turned in Tyler's arms and kissed him, soft at first and then deeper.

Tyler grinned and kissed him again, slow and strong. "I'd forgotten how good you smell. How right this is." He ran his big hands over the planes of Josh's chest and back and hips.

The words sent a wave of warmth through Josh's chest. He pressed his mouth against Tyler's again, harder this time, desire welling up sweet and sharp inside him. It had been so long, and he didn't know if he could last until they got home.

Tyler seemed to sense the shift, kissing back just as fiercely, his hands roaming over Josh's body, kneading and pulling him closer, crushing his body close.

Josh slid his hands under Tyler's shirt, reveling in the feel of smooth skin and hard sinew.

When Tyler started undoing the buttons of Josh's shirt, Josh forced himself to pull back. "We should stop." His voice came out rough. "I've got a gym class in an hour. And apparently, so do you."

"Oof. Harsh." Tyler groaned. "You're killing me, Coach." But he took a step back, running a hand through his hair. His cheeks were flushed, his eyes dark. "I see how it is."

"Payback. Plus I think we need to keep it cool here, for obvious reasons. Just as a rule."

"Same. Besides, I'm a selfish bastard. You get too loud, and I don't like to share."

"*I* get too loud." Josh swatted him, laughing.

"But you're right, as much as I hate to admit it."

"Patience." Josh grinned and did up the buttons of his shirt again. "We've got all the time in the world."

Tyler blinked at him. "That a promise?"

"Absolutely." Josh straightened his collar and smoothed his shirt front. Having Tyler here, in the flesh and larger than life, felt better than any dumb high school fantasy.

Tyler tipped his head, just gazing at him with a goofy expression. "Look at you. I see a lot of cold showers in my future." He reached down and shifted his enormous boner to make it less obvious. "Just a heads-up, I'm still going to sneak a feel and steal a kiss now and again... so long as the door is locked and we don't get frisky."

"Deal." Josh laughed. "I know it's not exactly an NFL locker room—"

"It's perfect." Tyler turned to Josh, his expression open and earnest. "You know glitz doesn't matter to me. I just want to do work I love, with folks who care about something besides clickbait."

"You will. It's a pretty great gig, this place. And that charity is going to save so many kids."

Tyler shrugged and scrunched his lips together as though he felt abashed. "I hope so."

"I don't need to hope. I know."

Tyler came up behind him and wrapped his arms around Josh's shoulders. "You okay?"

"I'm fantastic." Josh leaned back into him, covering Tyler's hands with his own. "I'm so glad you're here," he whispered.

"So glad I'm home." Tyler hugged him tightly. In that moment, standing together in their office, the future felt bright with promise.

After a moment, Tyler blew out a breath and scrubbed a hand over his face. "Right. I should go check in at Nadia's, anyway." He gave Josh a rueful smile. "She only knows I quit. I need to let her know I got hired."

"And Poops." Josh was smiling too. "Take my keys. I'll make it up to you."

Tyler took them and pulled him in for one more searing kiss, then stepped back. He opened the door, checked the hall, winked, and sauntered out whistling. "Practice makes perfect."

Chapter Twenty

TYLER WOKE up to Josh's chest rumbling beneath him, his husky breathing sending a shiver through Tyler as he nuzzled into the warmth of Josh's torso. His strong arms were draped over Tyler's back, their bodies slotted together, and Tyler had never felt so protected, so cherished. His muscles still had a delicious ache, and his mouth felt sore and swollen with kisses.

The exhaustion from the previous night's superhero binge faded as his cock twitched against Josh's thigh in a sweet reminder of how rough and how tender Josh could be. Tyler smiled. Things kept evolving between them, and over the past six months, they had taken their trust to a whole new level—naked, sweaty, passionate, exhilarating.

In the best possible way, Tyler could no longer hide from Josh; he had confessed his desire to explore what was possible between them, to finally be with someone who understood him. Tyler had never loved anyone the way he loved Josh.

Tyler pressed his lips to the secret notch behind Josh's ear, a weak spot he'd discovered and exploited as often as possible. He could get Josh from limp to leaking just by licking him there for a couple of minutes.

Josh murmured sleepily, "Mmmm...." and shifted to tug Tyler in tighter, hunching his hips absently.

The scent of sex and sweat mingled with Josh's rich musk filled the room.

Josh's powerful arm was warm and heavy on Tyler's back, his muscular frame softened by sleep. Tyler's morning wood pressed against Josh's hip, hard and drooling. They were still connected, always connected. Josh's naked perfection, the sweeping lines of his abdomen and broad shoulders, made Tyler's mouth wet. He wanted to keep Josh pinned under him in these sheets forever.

Tyler grinned to himself. Still early yet. They didn't have to be up for another half hour. He lifted one hand and grazed Josh's chest until his nipples pebbled and peaked. Then brushed over his dick with the faintest of touches, till it stood stiff.

"Hmmh." Josh shifted under him, opening his legs again, as if swimming toward consciousness.

The lazy, horny comfort of Josh's surrender made Tyler's dick flex. He couldn't help it. He'd pounded Josh so hard last night they'd almost broken the couch. And then again in the shower before they made it to the bed. What was he supposed to do with Josh squirming and begging for him to go deeper, go harder, go rougher.

He'd lost track of time, burying himself as far as he could. They fallen asleep like that, his cock inside soaking in his own juice while Josh crooned at him. Just thinking about it, he got hard again.

The truth was, some nights he wanted Josh to hump him stupid, so hard he couldn't think straight. Josh knew exactly where all his buttons were and had screwed him into a happy stupor more than once.

But then sometimes, like last night, he needed to claim Josh, possess him. Mark him with his mouth and his seed.

Josh's dick pulsed, and a drip fell toward his perfect navel.

Tyler would have caught it with his mouth or licked it up, but he didn't want to move too much.

Instead, he shifted himself, filling his hand with a squirt of oil and reaching down between Josh's splayed thighs. The crease between Josh's cheeks was still slick and his hole hot to the touch.

"Wuh." Josh sighed under him.

Carefully, Tyler tickled and pressed, tickled and pressed, slowly pushing against the pink ring of muscle.

"Ohhhh. Yeah." Josh pushed back, awake now and feeling the itch. "Ty. So good."

"You're still wet there. Can you feel? Beautiful."

Josh nodded and flexed against him. His hole clamped down, squeezing Tyler's knuckles, but not enough to stop him driving all the way home. "I lost count." He turned and kissed Tyler's brow. "I loved it."

"Not as much as I did. Nnnf." He sighed.

Josh grinned, his eyes still closed. "Debatable. There it is. Oh my Jesus." His blue eyes snapped open and his cock jumped. "Are you—?"

Tyler leaned in and kissed him, soft and unhurried. The kiss deepened naturally, their bodies pressing closer. Hands roamed over bare skin as their lips moved together languidly, still heavy with sleep.

Tyler rolled Josh onto his back, leaning over him. The pale morning light illuminated Josh's physique.

Tyler's eyes drank him in hungrily even as his hands explored Josh's body with reverence. "I'm not going to last."

"Me neither." Josh's muscular legs spread and splayed as Tyler clambered between them. "Do it. Put it in me, big guy. Make me feel it."

Tyler sank into the slippery heat and moved slowly, in and out.

Josh tangled his fingers in Tyler's dark hair, guiding his lips back to his own. The sloppy, urgent kisses made him feel stupid with lust.

"See how hard you make me." Tyler stroked his torso possessively, driving into him with relentless steady force.

"Oh! You feel—" Josh wrapped his legs around him and squeezed him closer, his dark blue eyes wide and shimmering with need.

"You too, baby." Tyler kissed him, nuzzled him with his nose. "I'm not going to be able to hold it."

"I don't want you to."

"I love you. I love you, I love you." Tyler chanted whispers into the nape of his neck, into his hair. "Josh... Josh. I love you. I'm going to—"

"Uh-huh." He pulled Tyler into him, his arms and his legs, his lips searching as his cock burst against Tyler's belly. "Give it to me. Jesus. I love you so much."

Tyler drove forward to the hilt, kissing Josh hard as he spilled inside.

When they finally lay spent and satisfied, Tyler pulled Josh over onto his chest.

Josh sighed contentedly, fingertips tracing idle patterns on Tyler's skin. No words needed.

Tyler licked the brine from his lips and smiled. He had made Josh squirt that high.

Gradually, Josh relaxed, his legs falling wide and open. He wore a drunken satisfied smile. "Well, good morning," he murmured. His voice was gravelly with sleep.

"Hey, you," Tyler whispered back. He trailed his fingers down Josh's side. He slid out slowly. "Hottest thing in the world."

"No arguments here, superstar." Josh stretched, his muscles bunching and extending like a living statue. "That's what we call a high-protein diet." He blinked slowly and exhaled with genuine contentment, his hot eyes meeting Tyler's.

"Want me to get you breakfast?" Tyler whispered, reaching down to give Josh's swollen dick a soft squeeze. The action made Josh moan softly.

Josh nuzzled Tyler's neck and sighed contently. "Yeah... scrambled?"

"Anything milord desires." Tyler kissed the corner of his mouth and chuckled as he slid out from under Josh's arm, feeling his body's reaction to the cool air.

He stood up and stretched, enjoying the flex of his heavy muscles. He ran a lazy hand over the spray of dark hair on his chest and realized something. "You covered me in jizz, man. I'm spackled."

From the bed, Josh chuckled low. "No regrets, no apologies, no worries."

As soon as Tyler stepped into the kitchen, a plaintive "mrreoow" made him smile. They'd only adopted Mrs. Scoops four months ago, but already she had taken control of the house. She was a marmalade tabby as well, with shorter hair, but also lankier and much more talkative than Poops.

Tyler tipped his head at the sight of Mrs. Scoops sitting on her favorite armchair in the sunny parlor, one yellow eye opening to regard him lazily. As if in answer, she stretched out one paw and yawned wide.

"Morning, trouble." He scooped kibble into her bowl. Mrs. Scoops came alive at once, purring as she butted against his shins and chatted with him in squeaks and rumbles. He gave her an affectionate scratch between her ears. She turned her chin up so he could also stroke her throat.

The coffee machine gurgled, the aroma intensifying. Tyler poured two mugs and doctored them with almond milk.

When he returned upstairs, Josh was in the shower. Tyler sat on the edge of the bed, sipping his coffee and listening to the sound of running water and Josh gargle-singing.

A few minutes later, Josh emerged in a cloud of steam, a towel slung low on his narrow hips. Tyler openly admired the lean, defined muscle of Josh's torso, the dusting of dirty blond tapering to his navel.

"Your coffee, milord." Tyler held out the mug.

"Overkill is what we call this, Fantana." Josh took the mug and sank down beside Tyler, kissing his bare shoulder. "Screw me silly, snuggle me into mush, and then pour fresh caffeine into me. Who says chivalry is dead?" He gave Tyler a peck.

"Just trying to keep my man happy. Big day." Tyler showered and dressed before returning to Josh in the kitchen.

They finished their coffee in companionable silence. By the time they headed back to the living room, Mrs. Scoops was dozing in a patch of sunlight by the back door, her belly full and her paws twitching in some feline dream of happy hunting.

"First day of school. Brand-new year." Josh asked, "Ready?"

"As I'll ever be."

Josh smiled, his eyes crinkling at the corners. "Well, I did spackle you. I suppose you need to go sweat it out."

"Sweaty with you? Count me in." Tyler grinned and stole a quick kiss.

They headed out to Josh's pickup, climbing in with their duffel of gear in tow. The drive to Hamilton High was a short one, the roads quiet before sunup.

When they pulled into the parking lot and around back to "their" spot, Tyler took a deep breath.

Josh reached over to squeeze his knee. "All good."

At this hour, the Hamilton campus still looked like a peaceful postcard even for the first-day madness, with its sprawling brick buildings and the clusters of coyote mint and beardtongue in bloom. In an hour or so, butterflies would arrive to hover around the tubular blossoms. This early in September, the pepper trees produced pinkish berries and the feathery leaves started to fade to a dull red.

They exited Josh's truck in sync, closing doors simultaneously with a single loud clunk.

Tyler chuckled. They'd never discussed it, but more and more, he noticed an odd telepathy.

Ever since Tyler had moved back, they had unconsciously started to do things in tandem—matching strides, silent jokes, sometimes wordlessly anticipating a move the other would make. Josh finishing Tyler's sentences, Tyler catching what Josh dropped. It had seemed freaky at first, but Tyler was continually delighted by the goofy magic of it.

Hell, NFL teams spent ages trying to cultivate that kind of instinctive cooperation, but somehow Tyler and Josh had stumbled into a mind meld.

Over the summer he'd taken Josh to Rome and then backpacking through Tuscany—the best three weeks he'd ever spent. They'd already started planning next summer's trip: a month in Venezuela and Brazil. They traveled together even better than they lived together, which was some kind of miracle.

They dropped their duffels in the athletics office and went back outside for their run. After stretching together on the track, they started jogging side by side, energy sparking between them the way it did.

Tyler glanced over at Josh, whose toned body glistened with sweat, and caught Josh doing the same. They both laughed. *Busted.*

Because it was the first day of school and Tyler still had some residual nerves, they only did a mile. "To get the blood flowing" was how Josh sold it last night. They both had a lot of new names to learn, new classes to test... and a whole football team to cobble together that afternoon.

As ever, that perfect quiet settled over and between them in the silvery predawn light, as though the world was listening to them, steadying Tyler's nerves and anchoring him for the day. He still worried about his blood pressure, but Reynolds kept telling him he'd never been stronger.

They pushed each other, hearts pounding, lungs burning. Tyler loved their playful competition, when Josh challenged him to sprint the straightaway or Tyler jogged backward to watch Josh react to a story as he told it.

After their workout, they slowed to a walk, their bodies glistening with sweat and their faces flushed with exertion. Tyler snuck glances at Josh's flushed face as they caught their breath together.

As they stretched, Josh caught him staring and they winked at each other. Funny all the things they knew now without saying a word. Funny the way they never ran out of things to say.

In the distance, the early bell rang. *On your mark, get set....*

A couple of minutes later, they sauntered into the school building together via the locker room, where Otis was loading a paper towel dispenser. "All right, guys?" he said.

"All right." They smiled back.

They stopped in the athletics office for a quick rinse and to change into real adult clothing appropriate for the first day of school. They'd already made the discovery that the little shower in here was too cramped for both of them. Tyler had been disappointed at first, but all things considered, the size was a good thing.

At Carver's insistence, Tyler had agreed to take a whack at college counseling under something called Eminence Credentials, or as Josh put it: *NFLOLOL, suckers*. So in addition to helping with gym classes and afternoon athletics, Tyler would be meeting with juniors and seniors to get them ready for prime time. After all, he had been speaking to students all over the country for the better part of a decade. Jury was out for now, but signs were good.

While Tyler was letting the water wash away the last suds, Josh called to him, "What period is your first batch of juniors?"

"I've got two today. One third period and one second to last. Is that fifth?" Tyler climbed out and started to towel off.

"Sixth. That's a pretty nice block because the kids are more chill. Vicky hooked you up." Josh pushed into his knit shirt, every inch the dreamboat teacher.

"Wow. I got to catch up." Tyler jerked on briefs and socks, then the pink button-down so he'd look like a real teacher. Josh had made fun of that one. "What time is your AP history?"

"Second, I think. I have to check at the office. 'McCarthy and the Red Scare.' You were right about that shirt. Unf."

"I'm always right." Tyler stepped into his khakis and zipped. "Big group?"

Josh ducked his head, cheeks flushed. "Carver said they had to cap the class. First time I've ever had a waiting list. Thank the musketeers."

"Well, Coach, you're doing something right."

Josh winked and tossed him an apple. Tyler caught it as he pulled open the door. "Maybe we just make a good team."

"The best," Tyler whispered before they left the athletics office and headed down toward the main entrance.

Technically saying hi to the students like this wasn't necessary, but Josh always tried to make his athletes feel welcome when they kicked off a year, and Tyler was happy to make that happen.

As they walked, teachers greeted them. Already he felt like part of this building.

To his relief, a lot of the awkward celebrity stuff had died down. Not completely, but enough that it didn't waste a chunk of every day. Now that Tyler was a small-town human-interest story, the media simply moved on. By the end of last year, most of the kids just called him Coach Fantana. He still got the odd stare and the occasional gushy parental comment, but overall he had become part of the scenery.

"Well, hello, sailors." Vicky gave them a flirty wave from the desk in the main office. "Fresh hot schedules!"

"First-day jitters." Josh tipped his head at Tyler.

"You were here last semester." She scoffed and passed them each a green folder. "You both look so nice."

"I'm totally faking." Tyler grinned at her. "'Cause I'm the naughty one."

Josh jabbed his ribs at a ticklish place. "No doubt."

As they approached, Vicky lowered her voice. "I heard the camp wowed everyone. We've been getting calls for a month."

"So great. Twenty-six kids. And all of them want to sign up for the next one. We got commitments from another eleven schools for next year."

Vicky checked her perimeter and leaned over farther to mutter, "Well, a little principal told me that two other schools called him last week to see how they can participate. Your sister is in there now."

"Nadia is?" Tyler asked. "Are you sure?"

Vicky nodded. "They found a big donor willing to match funds."

"Seriously!" Josh said "Oh, Vick. Thank you." He squeezed Tyler's arm. "Congratulations, Mr. Fantana."

Tyler shook his head in wonder. His eyes got hot. "You're amazing. That's... amazing."

Vicky's eyes twinkled. "If I'm going to spy for you, I better get seduced a little. Cocktails and kisses accepted." She pointed at her cheek.

Tyler bent to kiss her cheek, and Josh kissed the other.

They straightened and started to go when Vicky waved her hand at them. "Oh! And Channel Twenty-four just renewed Elise's yoga show. Lots of bendy grannies in San Diego."

"Vicky! Really. That's—"

"—good for her." Josh nodded happily. "She—

"—totally deserves it." Tyler finished the thought.

Vicky blinked. "You two...."

They laughed and left, flipping through their schedules as the first students cautiously made their way in the doors. Josh and Tyler were on separate schedules until the afternoon, but they had a half hour to greet students before the madness began.

So Tyler confirmed his second batch of anxious juniors was sixth. He'd have plenty of time to unwind and be ready to run football tryouts today. If everything went as planned, college counseling should leave him time for coaching and the new charity. Going forward, he'd take over the team.

After running the charity camp in July, he had no anxiety. After the second week with those kids, Josh had insisted Tyler take over Hamilton's football team come fall. At first Tyler had balked, until Josh offered to be *his* assistant coach in the afternoons.

"Revenge!" Tyler had shouted.

Coaching the team felt like a gift; plus it gave Josh more freedom to teach a history elective when he felt like it.

Actually, Tyler's whole first day at Hamilton as a full-time staff member turned out better than he could have hoped. Presentations cool, kids cool, even crisscrossing Josh's path as the day passed felt wonderful.

Now, as they ambled out to the field after school, he peeked at Josh. "I think we're early, Coach."

"Showing up early is on time."

Tyler pretended to be outraged. "Did you just try to Yoda me?"

"There is no try…."

Tyler shoved him playfully and chased after him. "I hope you realize I'm going to be really hard on you."

"Unnecessary roughness?" Josh didn't look sorry at all. "I can take it. Between you and me…." He knocked their shoulders together and lowered his voice. "I can't wait."

Tyler was probably even more excited than the players coming to try out this afternoon.

The bell hadn't rung yet, but Tyler felt a surge of the fizzy, busy energy that always pumped through him when he had a good game ahead of him. But for all that, his heart beat steady and strong.

"Fifteen? No." Tyler glanced at his watch. "Twenty minutes, probably, because they have to change."

He looked up and caught Josh watching him with a soft, silly smile hovering on his lips. "What?"

Josh shook his head. "Nothing."

"What are you doing?"

"Pining?" Josh gave an apologetic little grimace.

Tyler's brow creased. "But I'm right here."

"So? Just because you're right here doesn't mean I don't still fantasize like a lovesick teenager." Josh crossed his arms, and the blush creeping up his face made his eyes even bluer. "I still pine after you all the time, only now I get to do my pining up close and personal."

Tyler laughed out loud at that. "I swear...."

"What?"

"Nothing. Everything. You." He shook his head and smiled at the ground before raising his eyes to Josh's. "I'll never get tired of hearing that, Coach. Long as I live."

"I'm not too sure about that."

"I am." Tyler kissed Josh and held him close. He dragged a finger across his chest twice, without looking away from that smile, that face, those eyes. "Cross my heart."

Keep reading for an excerpt from
The Inside Edge
by Ashlyn Kane

NATE TIPPED his driver extra; the guy had made it from O'Hare in record time. He sidestepped around the office workers in the plaza like they were opposing defenders and entered the enormous revolving door as the big lobby clock struck the hour. It almost felt like beating the buzzer—he was going to just barely make it in time for makeup and a brief rundown, but barely was good enough and far better than he'd hoped, after spending an hour waiting for a gate at the airport. The stress of being late—Nate hated tardiness in himself as much as in others—was only eclipsed by the situation at the network.

"Don't worry about it; it's handled," Jess had told him in their too-brief call before the flight took off. That didn't make him feel better. The few subsequent messages they exchanged during the flight hadn't helped, especially as it felt like he was also getting texts from everyone he'd ever met—all variations of the theme: So what the hell is up with John Plum? Not that he'd answered. Nate had already gotten a very firm, if unnecessary, voicemail form his agent that he should not, under penalty of torture, say anything but "no comment" about the situation.

What would he even say? *Sorry my cohost is a xenophobic misogynist douchebag with no control over his basest impulses?* Silence was the better part of valor.

"You're late," Gina the PA told him, falling into step next to him as he beelined for Makeup. "I sent a rundown of tonight's show to your phone. You have time to look at it?"

Nate shook his head. "It died halfway through the flight. Too much Candy Crush. Forgot the charging cord in my hotel room." He glanced around as they walked. "Is Jess around? She told me not to worry, but—"

"Yeah, on second thought, maybe I better let her tell you in person. I think she's with—uh." Gina pasted on a smile. Good thing her work was mostly behind the camera, because she didn't convince Nate. "You know what? I'll just go tell her to find you."

That didn't inspire confidence, but Nate didn't have a lot of time to argue. He had a call in... well, basically now. "All right," he agreed, but Gina was already scampering down the hallway, talking on her headset.

Jess didn't come in while he was in Makeup, and the usual chatter was suspiciously free of office gossip and sports talk, focusing exclusively on the relative merits of different varieties of Girl Scout cookies. Nate happily shared his opinion (Samoas best, the peanut butter ones disappointing), but he found it weird that no one was even referring to the elephant that was no longer in the room, and that made him feel wrong-footed. Someone had passed him a portable charger for his phone, so he was able to read through the rundown he was now expected to do by himself. It might be a little flat with just one body behind the desk, but they were going to cut away to the game in Brampton, and Kelly was always good. Maybe they'd use this as an excuse to give a little extra time to the women's game. John would hate that. Nate couldn't resist smiling at the image of him fuming about it.

"You're done." Samira batted him on the shoulder as she finished. "Now get out of my chair and y'all have a great show."

Y'all. Plural. Was that significant? Nate turned to ask, but Samira had already scooted out of the room.

Something strange was definitely going on.

"Nate Overton to the set." The voice over the PA made it clear he didn't have any more time to wonder. In fact, he barely had time to change—he unbuttoned his shirt on the way to Wardrobe, where Tony was already waiting to help him into its replacement.

"Little behind today?" he asked, turning to grab the jacket and tie—helpfully already tied—while Nate buttoned up.

"O'Hare," Nate said grimly.

"Say no more." Tony held the jacket for him. "Not going to miss your old cohost's wardrobe peculiarities, you know?"

Nate figured Tony wouldn't miss him, period. "Maybe his replacement will be easier on the eyes."

Tony opened his mouth to say something, but Nate didn't have time. He took the tie to go, waving his thanks over his shoulder.

"Cutting it a little close," their primary camera operator commented as Nate stepped onto the soundstage.

Jeez. You get twitchy about people being late a few times and you'd never get any slack. "Yeah, yeah," Nate said. "Point taken." He took another three steps—

And stopped.

Someone was sitting in his chair.

A handsome—very handsome—dark-haired man had his elbows propped on the desk as he leaned forward, grinning at something Carl the camera operator was saying. Carl gestured with his hands, and the handsome brunet laughed, tossed his head back, and turned a million-watt smile on Carl. If Nate didn't know better, he'd think the guy was flirting with their straight, married, sixtysomething grandfather of three. Whatever. The guy was in Nate's chair, and Nate needed to politely inform him of the fact and give him the opportunity to move… and maybe to introduce himself, since no one else was going to tell Nate who he was. Where did they get him from? Nate squinted as he approached. The guy looked vaguely familiar. Local news? A weatherman maybe?

"Nate!" Carl intercepted him before he could make his case to the usurping newcomer. "Glad you made it! I thought I was going to have to join Aubrey up in front of the cameras tonight," he joked.

"Uh, yeah." Nate pasted on a smile, more confused than ever. He tamped down on a surge of change-induced panic. "You kn—"

"And Emmy would've loved that," Carl continued, still chuckling.

"Well, I'll make sure she gets that autographed picture," the guy—Aubrey—said. "Always happy to hear about a fan. Give her my love, Carl."

There was more batting of eyelashes until Carl ambled back to his station.

"Hi."

And now the guy was making eyes at Nate. Nate, who'd just spent twelve hours in travel with a dead phone. Nate, who hadn't been able to wrangle a straight answer out of his producer all day. Nate, who had no fucking idea what was going on and needed to be on the air in minutes.

Right now Nate didn't care if Aubrey was the only other gay man on the planet. He wasn't going to flirt with him. Definitely not at work, and especially not while he was sitting in Nate's chair. "You're in my seat," Nate said.

The eyelashes stopped fluttering and instead narrowed around clear gray eyes. "My apologies," he said smoothly, and all the warmth of his initial greeting faded. "Ms. Chapel told me to sit here."

Why would she do that? Nate knew ratings had suffered with John. Had Jess decided to go in a totally different direction? Would she call him to set just to fire him?

The guy in Nate's chair leaned back, eyes still narrowed in assessment. The movement drew Nate's eye to his suit—cut very close, expensive too, and Nate knew expensive suits. This one had a silver line of stitching around the lapels. Flashy, but with class. John would've hated it.

"I'm Aubrey Chase, by the way," the guy said, holding out a hand, and oh. That was why Nate recognized him.

"The figure skater." It came out sounding a little more cringeworthy than Nate intended. He had nothing against figure skaters. He knew what kind of tremendous athleticism the sport demanded. But this was a hockey show. "Uh, nice to meet you," he offered belatedly and shook the guy's hand. "Nate Overton."

"My pleasure." Aubrey's smile was polite, if not warm, as if he could read Nate's thoughts. "You're the senior now, so I guess that's why you get John's old spot. Kind of surprised it looks just like a normal chair, you know? It's not like it's velvet or ermine-lined or anything."

Nate adjusted his earpiece since he couldn't manage to adjust the nagging sensation of disorientation.

"Two minutes," Gina's voice said in his ear.

Nate glanced over the paper in front of him. To his right he noticed Aubrey smoothing his own sheet and shrugging and shaking out his shoulders a bit as if he were about to step into a spotlight on the ice. He was getting ready for his audience, obviously. Just Nate's luck that after all the times he'd dreamed of getting rid of an overbearing bigoted buffoon like John, the replacement would be a different sort of diva.

"I see we're hashing out Kazakov's new contract."

"That's what it says," Nate replied. He hated that he felt he'd gotten off on the wrong foot, but somehow blaming Aubrey for his own lack of grace made him feel better.

"Five and a half by five. That's going to be a squeeze with Dallas's cap issues," Aubrey offered.

"Well, it's not like top-four defensemen grow on trees, and Popov's not getting any younger." Nate probably sounded more definite than he felt about the issue, but it had been a long day.

"Dallas wouldn't know if they did grow on trees, unless they were trees in Russia. They can't seem to draft one from anywhere else." Aubrey clicked his pen for emphasis.

Nate swiveled on his chair to glare at the handsome but misinformed face. "They traded for Svensson at the last deadline!"

"Trading for a thirty-four-year-old isn't the same as developing or draft—" Aubrey insisted, but Gina's voice interrupted.

"Forty-five seconds."

Nate felt like his nose was going to hit the desk in forty-five seconds. He should have chugged an energy drink or three, and now a figure skater was trying to debate him on the finer points of building a blueline.

Worse, he wasn't entirely off base. At the very least he was competent, which was better than John, and unlikely to spout some of the more offensive bile that seemed to fall like flowers from John's mouth. Nate needed to focus on that and on staying awake and alert, and then he could apologize to his new cohost and try to start over.

"I really need a coffee," he grumbled, and Gina piped in over his earpiece.

"I'll get you one for commercial break."

"Thank you," Nate said fervently. He made a mental note to buy her something really nice for Christmas this year.

"Thirty seconds."

He took a deep breath. He'd be fine. He could talk about hockey in his sleep. He had, in fact, done so on enough occasions that he'd chased Marty out of bed to the guest room, which probably hadn't helped when everything went to hell. And wow, he needed to think about something else. Anything else.

"Are you okay?" Aubrey asked, one eyebrow raised. "You look a little… gray."

Despite himself, Nate prickled. Now Aubrey was calling him old. Great. As if he needed a reminder that he'd just stepped into the senior role. Nothing like feeling your age. "I'm fine," he snapped. "Let's just get this over with."

"Live in ten!"

"I love your enthusiasm," Aubrey deadpanned. But then Gina held her hand up for the countdown, and Nate could see the moment he switched into broadcast mode. He sat straighter, corrected his posture, and his features relaxed into something open and friendly instead of just openly hostile. He brushed a hand through his hair and somehow avoided messing it up. Instead it looked like he'd just paid a hairdresser a hundred dollars to do it. Nate would have sworn his skin even looked nicer, which was patently ridiculous.

Of course. On top of being a charming, shmoozing flirt, his new cohost was hot. Fuck Nate's life.

The red broadcast-indicator light came on and Gina gave them the signal—they were live.

"Good evening and welcome to *Off the Ice*. I'm Nate Overton and this is Aubrey Chase. Tonight, the Chicago Snap take on the Toronto Furies. We'll have that game for you live, as well as news updates, scores, and highlights from around the leagues. The puck drops in ten. For now we're going to our women's correspondent, Kelly Ng, live with Snap Captain Dominique Ryan. Kelly?"

Scan the QR code below to order

Quietly weird M/M author DARCY ARCHER loves Hallmark mysteries, amateur dramatics, and old sword-and-sandal movies—the bulgier the better. After a friendly divorce and a long overdue job change, she moved back to the woods of northern California to get away from the grind. She cohabitates with a couple of bossy, opinionated rescue cats who now supervise her writing career.

A proud stage craft junkie with a theater degree from UC Santa Cruz, Darcy participates backstage in local community theaters as a stage manager and occasional director, which means she consumes way more coffee than salad. She watches football for the butt-cams and K-dramas for the sighs. Other obsessions include mushrooming, vintage bodice rippers, and positive activism, including nine years volunteering with PFLAG and the Trevor Project.

Somehow Darcy's two grown sons managed to reach their twenties safely and headed off to conquer the world, quadrupling her writing time. She works remotely in customer support, surrounded by nature and a mellow community, which keeps her cats happy, her garden green, and her characters steamy. When not writing, she can usually be found binge reading, running a rehearsal, or out back growing way too many tomatoes.

Darcy is a social media skeptic, but you can find her on Goodreads, Bookbub, and Amazon.

www.ingramcontent.com/pod-product-compliance
Lightning Source LLC
Chambersburg PA
CBHW051146030726
47504CB00004B/1069